WITHDRAWN FROM
COLLECTION

Circle
of Jinn

Lori Goldstein

Feiwel and Friends
New York

To all of my families, the "Montsteingos,"
for their love and support.

A FEIWEL AND FRIENDS Book
An Imprint of Macmillan

Our books may be purchased in bulk for promotional, educational, or business use.
Please contact your local bookseller or the Macmillan Corporate and Premium
Sales Department at (800) 221-7945 ext. 5442 or by e-mail at
MacmillanSpecialMarkets@macmillan.com.

Library of Congress Cataloging-in-Publication Data
Names: Goldstein, Lori (Lori A.) author.
Title: Circle of Jinn / by Lori Goldstein.
Description: First edition. | New York : Feiwel and Friends, 2016. | Sequel to:
Becoming Jinn. | Summary: As she embraces her powers as a genie, sixteen-year-old
Azra fights to help her fellow Jinns become free of a tyrannical leader.
Identifiers: LCCN 2015031058 | ISBN 9781250055408 (hardback) |
ISBN 9781250086846 (ebook)
Subjects: | CYAC: Genies—Fiction. | Magic—Fiction. | Wishes—Fiction. | BISAC:
JUVENILE FICTION / Fantasy & Magic. | JUVENILE FICTION /
Legends, Myths, Fables / General.
Classification: LCC PZ7.1.G652 Ci 2016 | DDC [Fic]—dc23
LC record available at http://lccn.loc.gov/2015031058

Book design by Ashley Halsey and Liz Dresner

Feiwel and Friends logo designed by Filomena Tuosto

First Edition—2016

1 3 5 7 9 10 8 6 4 2

Zar Sisterhoods

Mothers

Nadia	Raina	Kalyssa	Samara	Jada	Isa
↓	↓	↓	↓	↓	↓
Hana	Yasmin	Azra	Laila	Mina	Farrah

Daughters

1

I'M SIXTEEN YEARS OLD, AND I LIVE WITH MY BOYFRIEND.

At least I think I do. I mean, I know where I live. I know I'm living with Nathan Reese. What I don't know is if Nathan Reese is my boyfriend.

Or if I want him to be.

Who said wishes don't come with tricks?

Oh, right, that was me. But what do I know? I've been a genie for less than two months. I've granted the sum total of six wishes, two of which I botched, one of which I would have botched had my mother not been there, and the last of which I'm currently in the process of botching. Not to mention I'm fresh off probation.

If one could be fired from becoming Jinn, I'd be rocking a pink slip right about now instead of this silver bangle. This intricately carved silver bangle doled out by the Afrit, the council—I mean *family*—that rules over our Jinn world. The family that I've just learned is my father's family. Which means it's my family.

The all-powerful, arguably sadistic Jinn who govern with not just a stick but a two-by-four are my "peeps."

A chunk of my long, dark hair falls across my eyes as a late-summer breeze wafts through the kitchen window. It's not even September and the hints of fall are already trespassing, igniting a row of goose bumps across my bare shoulders.

I gather my hair into a loose bun, using a strand to keep it in place. Of all the things I learned from my mother, this has turned out to be the simplest.

A stronger gust rattles the wood blinds inside and creaks the thick metal chains hanging from the swing set outside. The green plastic seat sways, and I'm back there, sitting on it, the day Nate said good-bye to his father and hello to a new life, a life he never wished for. At least, what with me being a genie and all, the life he did wish for—the one where he can take care of his little sister—I was able to give him. More or less.

I trace circles along the granite countertop as I stare out the window that frames the backyard swing set like a canvas painting. Except the picture I see, the one I see whether my eyes are open or closed, is from the day of Nate's father's funeral, almost two weeks ago.

Me on one seat and him on the other. Him planting his feet on the ground, seizing the chains above my head with one hand, spinning me, turning my body to face him, drawing me closer. His knees bumping against mine, his finger drying the wet tears on my cheeks, his breath warming my neck, his lips brushing my forehead, and then, before I could stop him, before I could think what it meant, what it might mean, his lips pressing on my lips.

Soft and then hard. Like the beating of my heart. Then and now.

"Something's burning," Goldie says, rounding the corner into the kitchen.

Something's burning all right.

"Oh, the cookies," I say. "Damn." I look at Megan. "I mean, darn. I mean, oops."

Megan pauses the hunt for split ends in her shoulder-length dark hair. "I'm twelve, not two. I've heard worse. Hell, I've said worse."

"Not in this house, Meg," Goldie says.

My gaze returns to the groaning swings as the harbingers of autumn make my sun-darkened olive skin shiver again. *Right, Azra, it's the wind. And what are you going to blame when the windows are sealed up tight?*

A chocolate chip ricochets off my ear.

"Earth to Azra," Megan says, popping a semisweet morsel into her mouth. "Did you even set a timer?" The perfect roll of her eyes that answers my head shake makes me think she's spent all twelve years of her life perfecting the move. "The batch in the oven's going to burn."

Goldie sniffs the air. "*Again,*" she says, sidling up next to me. "The batch in the oven's going to burn again." She moistens her thumb with her tongue and wipes a stripe of war paint made of flour off my cheek.

I do my best imitation of Megan's eye roll, and Goldie winks at me. The warmth in more than the crinkles around her eyes screams "Grandma," the name she refuses to be called.

I'm sixteen years old, and I live with my boyfriend. And his sister. And his grandmother.

A deep voice floats in through the screen door. "I'd take a gander at those puppies if I were you."

And his grandfather. I live with the entire Reese family.

It's the first time I've ever had to share a bathroom.

For the past sixteen years, my mother's had hers and I've had mine. Though we may live in the human world, the Jinn world—my world—is mothers and daughters. Not that there aren't brothers, fathers, and grandfathers, there just aren't brothers, fathers, and grandfathers *here*.

All male Jinn live in the Afrit's underground world of Janna. Including Xavier Afrit. My father.

We've never met.

Because my job, my sole purpose for living here—for living *period*—is to grant wishes for the humans assigned to me by the Afrit council, a group unseen but plenty heard. Giving and taking away our magic, our freedom, our loved ones for infringements against their dictatorship-like rules. Rules I've just learned my father's been covertly working to change.

My mother's job is to teach me to use and control my powers, the magic that lives inside me, passed down from the generations of Jinn who've come before us. Her gold bangle symbolizes her retirement, allowing her to practice all magic save for the granting of wishes.

Granting wishes is for the young. For those of us with silver bangles. Bangles spelled to release our powers. Spelled so the Afrit can monitor us. Spelled so only the Afrit can remove them.

The upside is that I can conjure mint chocolate chip ice cream, levitate my sugary iced coffee from table to lips, and travel via Jinn teleportation, apporting myself from blizzard to beach in an instant.

The downside? It's not exactly a shackle or handcuff, though it might as well be. We grant wishes, nature allows us to keep our magic. We grant the wishes the Afrit order us to grant, we keep our lives. As fishy as it smells, the wishes the Afrit have ordered me to grant include ones for Nate and now Megan, my current assignment.

Though it feels like a long summer of learning to use my powers, of learning to grant wishes, my bangle's a relatively new accessory. Two months ago, the day of my birthday, the bangle silently locked around my wrist. I was sixteen. I was a genie. I was no longer free.

Or so I thought. I thought so much then. That like all other Jinn I needed this silver bangle in order to do magic. That the circle of Jinn daughters I was to be bonded with in the tradition of the Zar would never live up to the name we give one another— sister. That the Afrit's harsh punishments for refusing to grant wishes, for screwing up, for exposing our Jinn world to humans weren't real. That my mother never loved my father. That I'd never fall in love. That I'd never again have a best friend. That I'd never want to become Jinn.

I was wrong.

I half smile, half wince as I slip the red oven mitt embroidered with the words "Hot Mama" on one hand and open the oven door with the other. I also thought human families were more stable than Jinn ones.

Again, I was wrong.

The car accident that tore Nate's family apart has proven that. With Nate's father gone and his mother still in the hospital, I live with what now constitutes the entire Reese family.

I set the metal tray on the cooling rack. This is the third batch of cookies that's come out of the oven like charcoal briquettes. If only I could use my magic, I could fix them. But I can't use my magic in front of humans. And lately, here, in the Reese home, I'm always with humans, one human in particular: Megan.

"Let me guess," Megan says, hopping off the center island and scraping the top of a blackened cookie with a fingernail I helped to paint blue. "You work the register, not the fryer at the snack bar at the beach."

Her voice chokes on the final *ch* sound. Immediately, Goldie spreads her arms wide, and the fabric hanging from her dolman-sleeved sweater shrouds Megan. She closes her own eyes against the tears forming.

Megan may have lost her father in the car crash on the road to the beach, but Goldie lost her son-in-law, almost lost her daughter.

I hang back, trying not to make a sound, but it's not easy for me to swallow past the golf ball wedged in my throat. Once again, I'm intruding on a private family moment. By now, it should feel less awkward.

It doesn't. Because I can't shake the suspicion that, one way or another, this is all my fault. Either the Afrit assigning Nate as my wish candidate on the night Mr. and Mrs. Reese's car went off the side of the road was a total coincidence, or I should have started the wish-granting ritual with Nate sooner. Early enough to save his father.

So what if Jinn can't heal humans? There has to be something I could have done. Because why else would I have been tapped to grant Nate a wish that day? I'm not buying the coincidence thing. Which leaves only one other alternative: that the Afrit somehow knew or maybe even caused the accident that killed Nate and Megan's father and seriously injured their mother.

I can't breathe if I think about that for too long. Because that would mean not only is this all my fault, but that I could have prevented it. It would mean that my selfish need to have Nate in my life cost someone theirs. The Afrit warn against getting too close to humans. Even with all I've recently discovered about my father's family, I still have a hard time believing something this cruel could be their punishment.

Call it a perverse loyalty to the family, to the father I used to think I'd give anything to meet.

Goldie releases Megan, whose sun-freckled nose is red and runny. I hand her a napkin, but instead of taking it, she takes me. Grabs me with the force of someone twice her size and burrows into my neck.

The pained but grateful smile on Goldie's face twists my stomach into a pretzel. How much I'm to blame for Mr. Reese's death may be a question I'll never know the answer to, but this, right here, Megan's anguish, that's something I'm 100 percent responsible for. Because that I can end.

That is something my powers can do. If only I could figure out how.

2

The hockey pucks land on top of the first two batches of burned cookies in the kitchen trash. I wedge the dirty cookie sheet in one side of the double sink and run the hot water until steam puffs, hoping to dislodge the charred remains.

Megan exaggerates a sigh and scoops out a handful of chocolate chips that she drops in my palm before nabbing the entire bag on her way into the living room.

"Where are you going?" Goldie and I say at the same time.

We both want to make sure she's okay, but I have another reason for asking. I need to know where Megan is going because when I don't, it hurts—a lot. It's like my internal organs are hitched to a semi barreling down the highway at top speed.

It's a curse in every sense of the word.

One that started on the day of the funeral when the Afrit left me their calling card with Megan's name on it. She was to become my next assignment. I could have—*I should have*—waited.

But after the funeral, I was overcome by emotion, both Megan's and mine, and rushed into conducting the wish-granting ritual for her right upstairs in Nate's bedroom. The wish she made, to no longer see the pain in Nate's eyes, is not an easy one. Short of going the literal and gruesome eye-gouging route, mind control is the only way to achieve it. Though this power is beyond the reach of most Jinn, it seems to be an inherent Afrit perk. I've used it once, though I have no idea how. Even if I did, I'd still be cautious. Because mind control is dangerous, bringing with it the very real risk of permanent brain damage.

Which is why I still haven't taken any steps to grant Megan's wish. With the twenty-four-hour grace period to get the wish-granting ball rolling long since past, I'm now bound by the circulus curse, magically compelled to stay within one hundred and fifty feet of Megan until I complete her wish. As curses go, it's not so bad. At least mine binds me to Megan. And, as a side effect, to Nate.

But, see, this is why it's tough to be on board with the coincidence theory. Megan being my wish candidate on the heels of Nate is too much coinky dink for me.

"We still on to go to Mrs. Pucher's later?" I call to Megan, who's nestled into the corner of the couch with the mermaid book I loaned her and the bag of chocolate chips. So she's on the Azra diet of mainlining sugar. At least she's eating again.

She gives a thumbs-up and pulls the afghan hanging off the back of the couch over her bare feet. The afghan knit by her mother. More evidence of what's been lost and what's been left behind. It doesn't take an experienced tracker to follow the trail of Mr. and Mrs. Reese that fills this home.

Goldie nudges me aside with her pleasantly plump hip. Her Rubenesque figure, round face, and naturally jet-black hair make her look more like a 1940s pinup girl than a grandmother. She's right to stick with "Goldie."

"I've got this," she says, jamming her pudgy hands into a pair of too-tight hot-pink dishwashing gloves. "You take Meg." She yanks the cuffs up to her elbows. "Although I've been trying, it's you and your magic that's finally gotten her off her tush and out of her own head. One step closer to walking through those hospital doors and visiting her mom, which they both need. You might not be able to bake 'em, but you're as smart as one, Azra Nadira."

I turn my flinching at her casual use of the word "magic" into a dismissive shrug. "Mrs. Pucher's the smart one, not me."

Goldie flings a soap bubble at my head. "Nonsense. Meg and Nate . . . Oh, let's be honest, Georgie and I wouldn't have half as many reasons to smile without you. Why do you think we're having you stay here?"

Because my mom used a spell to make you think it was a brilliant idea.

Goldie pushes her pink-gloved fingers through her barrel-curled bangs. "We'd be lost without you, love."

A blustering whoosh sends prickles down my spine. Not trusting the strength in my voice, I simply nod to Goldie. I then reach around her to close the window above the sink, pausing when I notice the blinds inside are still. The swings hover outside, motionless.

But, again, a tingling like pins and needles trails across my shoulders.

I focus on the window, and though Goldie's kind words make it feel like a betrayal, I let myself revisit the scene once more. The green plastic seats, the twisting metal chains, the pair of friends, best friends, entwined in a way that best friends usually aren't.

Which is why I need to see him. Henry, my best friend, my *human* best friend, the only human to know I'm a Jinn.

I shut the window and close the blinds.

Enough.

I know every stroke of the painting I call *Henry's Kiss.* A discussion with the artist is long overdue.

⁂

"Hey hey, where's the fire?"

At the top of the stairs, Nate cups my shoulders and pries me off his chest. His chest that can't be touched, seen, or thought about without the word "chiseled" coming along for the ride. All three of which I know from firsthand experience.

"Sorry," I say, unusually quick to remove my fingertips from his biceps, getting harder by the day from his amped-up lacrosse training. If Megan went inward to cope, Nate went outward, mostly to the gym. "I wasn't looking."

"Well, that's better than the alternative." Nate extends his neck toward the stairs and breathes in deeply. "I was afraid you were running from an out-of-control kitchen fire."

"Nope, perfectly contained in the oven." I start to inch toward the bedrooms. We've been avoiding each other all day. At least I assume he's been avoiding me, but since I've been avoiding him, I guess I can't be sure.

"So," he says, "no need to call the fire department, but I'm assuming this also means no cookies?"

Like me, Nate has a sweet tooth. All the Reeses do.

"Maybe I can pick some up on the way home," I say. "I mean,

back." A mutual love of sugar is one of the many things making it easier and easier to think of this place as my home. "I'm taking Megan to Mrs. Pucher's again."

"Third day in a row? You're . . . That's really sweet, Azra. You've been so good to her. And to me." His eyes find his feet, which are shuffling against the white carpet that blankets the second floor. "Which is exactly why I should . . . What I mean is, why I need to . . . About last night—"

"Don't," I say, pressing my hand against his forearm. In response to my touch, his eyes flicker to mine before lowering again, this time settling on my neck, on the *A* pendant I wear because I know how much he likes it.

Talking to my exposed collarbone, Nate says, "I've made things weird between us."

Things are already weird between us for so many reasons: me being Jinn, my ability to read human minds including his, the wish I granted for him to be able to take care of Megan that leaves me connected to a piece of his soul—*his soul*. Oh, yeah, and let's not forget my little lip-lock with Henry.

Fortunately, Nate doesn't know any of this. Unfortunately, that does little to ease my guilt.

I stroke his cheek before lifting his chin, forcing his chocolate ganache eyes to meet my gold ones. We hold each other's gaze, which, despite all that's between us, including what happened last night, turns out not to be weird at all.

It was long after dark when a shaking woke me. I had expected it to be my roommate, Megan, who, since the night I arrived, has started each night in her own twin bed but finished it in mine. Goldie knows, and I think it's this, even more than the spell my mother used, that ultimately convinced her to let me stay. But last night, for the first time, Megan was curled up in her own bed. I knew before I flipped onto my side that it was Nate.

Tears had finally broken through the brave front he's been pushing himself to maintain. Words, even if I knew the right ones, didn't seem necessary. I simply pulled his head to mine and we lay there, squished together side by side, until his tremors no longer rocked the bed.

When I woke up this morning, he was gone.

I took my cue from him, not tracking him down, worried that he might be embarrassed even though he shouldn't be.

I slide my hand down his arm and lace my fingers between his.

If anything, I feel even closer to him. And as I can tell from reading his mind, he feels it too. Spending the night in the same bed will do that to you, which I should know since it's happened before. Except it was me, upon having just discovered my Afrit heritage, in need of comfort, and Henry was the one giving it, not Nate.

And you're surprised by the kiss?

I was . . . and I am. With two strides, Nate presses me into the wall, nearly knocking the wind out of me. He hears my gasp and pulls away, but I clutch his other hand and pull him right back. He starts at my necklace, at my collarbone, a whisper of a touch so light it could be a breeze. But when his lips travel the length of my neck and his teeth graze the tip of my earlobe, the only breeze this could be is a tornado.

It feels both right and wrong for this kiss to be every bit as intense as the one on the beach the night of our second date, the night his father was killed.

Lost in Nate, it's only when my fingertips hit warm skin that I realize I inadvertently unbuttoned his shirt with my magic. I skim my hands up and down his torso, rumpling and twisting the fabric, to cover for what I've done. Not trusting myself or my powers, I playfully break away and roll down the wall into Megan's seafoam-green bedroom, leaning with my hands behind me against the hand-painted emerald vine that winds its way across this side of the room.

Nate follows but hangs back, his fingers toying with one of the paper flowers attached to the vine that gives the whole mural a killer 3-D effect. Mrs. Reese was—is—Mrs. Reese *is* something of an artist.

"Was that not okay?" Nate asks, self-consciously raking his hand through his cropped black hair.

I allow myself a nod, but my breath is too short for verbal communication. And my mind is too jumbled, juxtaposing *this* kiss with *that* kiss, for me to trust what may spill from my lips anyway.

Then, for the third time this morning, a tingling floods me like head-to-toe pins and needles, but the only part of me that's numb are my lips.

Nate's an extraordinary kisser, but this is more like walking out into a nor'easter. No, that's not quite right. It's more like the sensation we Jinn get when another member of our species is about to apport in. But this doesn't feel like any Jinn I know—not the five lifelong friends who make up my mother's Zar sisterhood and not their sixteen-year-old daughters who now make up mine.

From the sting of a wasp (my Zar sister Yasmin) to a stereo vibration (my Zar sister Hana) to the tickle of a feather (my mother's best friend and Zar sister Samara), apporting Jinn have their own signature. Funny, I've never asked anyone what mine is.

With my back to Nate, I toss sweaters for myself and Megan into a backpack and tap into my abundance of adrenaline to strengthen my magic. I don't sense another Jinn in the house. As nonchalantly as I can, I move to the windows and survey the backyard.

When my mother stops by to check up on me, she comes by car. She knows better than to magically teleport herself here. Besides, if she did decide to apport, she'd be more careful than this. Apporting Jinn can detect the presence of humans, and my mother wouldn't risk apping in with people this close. Neither would any of my Zar sisters, especially Laila, Samara's daughter and my former best Jinn friend. Since she's the only one whose apporting signature I have yet to feel, this could be hers. But I know it's not. As much as I want to see her, she's not ready to see me. I'm up to three texts a day and still not a peep from her. Not even an angry-faced emoticon. There's no way she'd app here.

I turn around to find Nate buttoning his shirt. The sensation of my fingers on his abs lingers. I shake out my arms as I fling the backpack onto one shoulder. I'm being paranoid. There's no reason for me to be tingling.

Nodding to my bag, Nate starts walking backward out of his sister's bedroom. "Now you really are running from something too hot to handle."

He winks and there's ample reason for me to be tingling.

3

A BOWLING BALL–SIZED WATERMELON SOMEHOW HIDDEN UNDER the leaves of her squash plants has Mrs. Pucher gushing the moment we arrive.

My next-door neighbor deserves the credit for drawing Megan out of the cocoon she's been in since the accident. As much as I understand Megan's need to cloister herself, the circulus curse means I'm cooped up right alongside her. Three days ago, the combination of stir-craziness and wanting to see Henry led to me feigning a severe case of homesickness. Even so, Megan only agreed to come when I sweetened the pot by telling her she could raid my bookshelves.

Henry's house across the street was empty save for a living room full of Carwyn moving boxes, but the trip proved more than worth it thanks to Mrs. Pucher, my neighbor, my childhood babysitter, and my very first wish candidate. In order to practice before we receive our official assignments, the Afrit allow us to grant a wish for three candidates of our own choosing. Though I was initially peeved that my mother chose Mrs. Pucher for me, granting her wish to reconcile with her sister was the first time I realized (admitted) that being Jinn can actually help people.

And someone as kind as Mrs. Pucher definitely deserves to be helped. Three days ago, as Megan and I were waving good-bye to my mother, Mrs. Pucher pushed herself up from her gardening kneeler and waddled over to us. She shoved a cherry tomato into Megan's mouth and a pair of clippers into her hand.

Like much of our small coastal town, Mrs. Pucher knew about the accident. And, somehow, she also knew that by occupying Megan's hands, she'd occupy her mind. In pruning the dead roses that first day, the pink in Megan's own cheeks came back, just a little. In planting the line of arugula seeds yesterday, a bit more of her pain was buried. Whatever task Mrs. Pucher has planned for today will tend Megan more than the garden.

"Do you think it's ripe?" Megan asks as Mrs. Pucher squats in front of her camouflaged watermelon. "We could maybe make that sorbet I was telling you my mom makes, you know, the one with the mini chocolate chips for the seeds?"

My lungs deflate as she says this, but the usual crack in her voice is missing. Mrs. Pucher doesn't skip a beat and simply rattles off the ingredients she suspects we need. As Megan whips out her phone to search for the recipe, Mrs. Pucher picks up the watermelon. The watermelon with the sticker from the grocery store still attached. She scrapes it off and gives me a wink.

"Heavens, dear," Mrs. Pucher says to Megan, "those contraptions aren't meant for the eyes of someone with this much gray in her hair." She takes Megan by the hand and the two go inside to look up the recipe on the Jumbotron-sized iMac Mrs. Pucher's sister recently gave her.

And just like that, I'm alone. I sink into the Adirondack chair on the stone patio and toss my head back, soaking up the late-August sun. Between my magical attachment to Megan, my magical-of-another-kind attachment to Nate, and George and Goldie's attachment to us all, I've had little opportunity to be alone. Which translates to having little opportunity to use my magic.

Not that I've minded. If a thirst for power and control runs in my Afrit bloodline, maybe being careful in my use of magic will stall my own conversion to the dark side.

I stretch out my legs and breathe in, relishing the familiar scent of the lilacs my mother's magic keeps in perpetual bloom that mixes with the briny notes from the nearby beach. My second home, a place I miss even more than my first. A place I haven't been to since the accident.

I should use this time to check in with my mother next door or Henry across the street or even to leave yet another voice mail for Laila that she'll probably delete without listening to.

The breeze rustles my hair, but the rest of me is still, savoring this bouquet custom-made for me.

Until a wet mop rams itself into my stomach.

Pom-Pom. Mrs. Pucher's Pomeranian, whose usually fluffy fur is plastered to his body and dripping muddy water all over my white shorts. Apparently the sprinklers are on.

Serves me right, since what I really should be doing is practicing. Despite all my trying over the past two days, I haven't gotten Mrs. Pucher's beloved Pom-Pom to do so much as fetch a tennis ball. Aren't dogs supposed to *want* to do that?

If I don't figure out how to get the mangy thing to follow one of my telepathic commands soon, I'll be cramming my lanky sixteen-year-old body behind a seventh-grade desk next to Megan instead of an eleventh-grade one.

It's not like I want to fry any furry creatures' brains (not even Pom-Pom's), but practicing mind control on animals is better than hot-wiring a human's brain without having any clue what I'm doing. And so I practice with squirrels, birds, and Pom-Pom. More accurately, I fail with squirrels, birds, and Pom-Pom. And no, I'm not even sure this power works on nonhuman critters.

I sigh and haul myself out of the Adirondack. I force myself to try to get Pom-Pom to stop gnawing on the hose for five minutes before I give up and walk across the street to Henry's house. Well, halfway across the street. Because that's as far as I can go without my spleen being sucked through my belly button.

Standing in the middle of the road, I hear a thunk and see Henry dragging a round lump of a black garbage bag to the curb.

We haven't seen each other since the day of the funeral. He looks up and our eyes meet. My muscles pull taut like a rubber band, but the tension releases as soon as his dimples appear. He drops the bag and rushes to the middle of the street, where the hug that appears imminent dies abruptly.

"I'm here for you, Azra, always."

That's what Henry said after I finished telling him how I was going to have to use mind control on Nate and Megan and risk hurting them, maybe even hurting myself. He dug the heels of the dress shoes I had magically shined into the patch of dirt under the swing to come to a complete stop.

"You know that, don't you?"

That's what he said after he grasped the metal chains above my head with one hand. He turned me toward him and tugged, gently closing the gap between us. The plastic seats met with a soft tap.

"I need for you to know that."

That's what he said as his light green eyes bored into mine, chilling me like a gust of wind in a snowstorm, but then his thumb was on my cheek, his breath was on my neck, his lips were on my forehead, and I was whisked inside to a crackling fire, and that's what I felt, warm and safe and home, and that's what I was thinking and that's where I wanted to be in that moment, home, my home, away from all the pain and hurt and tears and wishes to be granted and then . . . all of that was gone.

Because he was kissing me. I no longer knew where I was, let alone where I wanted to be.

Henry pushes his glasses up the bridge of his nose, and I shove my hands into my back pockets, casually shifting my weight from one foot to the other to hide my nerves.

"Megan at Mrs. Pucher's?" he asks.

I nod, pushing past the memory to match his nonchalant tone. "So you do read my texts. You just don't reply."

"I replied."

"Three times. In ten days."

He flicks the top of his head toward his house. "Things have been busy with the move. Back and forth. We're doing it ourselves."

Because they couldn't afford movers, which is why they're defecting to New Hampshire to live with Henry's grandparents in the first place. After more than six months of being unemployed, his father finally found a job near where Mrs. Carwyn's mother and father live. So even though it's Henry's last year of high school—he and Nate are both a year older and incoming seniors—he's . . . leaving.

"So," he says. "How is . . . ? How are . . . ? You okay?"

This is not my Henry. He's being so distant. He's been distant since the day of the funeral. Why? Oh, I don't know, choose one:

We went to a funeral. We kissed. I told him I'm the spawn of Jinn Satan. We kissed. I'm living with Nate. We kissed.

Staring through the lenses of his glasses and into his eyes, I'm about to read his mind, which he's explicitly asked me not to do. Unlike most Jinn, but very much like the Afrit side of my family, I can read human minds outside the confines of the wish-granting ritual.

I've gotten a better handle on dipping in at will. Living with my maybe-boyfriend Nate and his grieving family provided excellent incentive to rein in the involuntary nature of my mind-reading skills. But here, in the middle of the street, where Henry and I stood not long ago, with him basically saying he thought I was so pretty he didn't have a shot with me, temptation tugs at me.

Reading his thoughts would be simpler, and less mortifying, than having to actually *ask* him what that little swing-set rendez-vous meant . . . not to mention having to hear him answer . . . and hear me answer.

No, I can't. He has a right to privacy.

To distract myself, I say, "What's up with the glasses?"

He adjusts the arms that are tucked behind his ears. "I ran out of contacts."

"You should have told me, I'd have conjured you more." I gesture toward his messy hair, back to its normal sandy color without all the goop he's been adding lately. "Run out of gel too? Not sure I can conjure that."

I can, I just don't want to.

He raises his palms. "I don't want you getting into trouble on account of me."

I snort. "Contacts and styling products are not on the Afrit's radar."

He crosses his arms in front of his chest. "Which you know for a fact? Because you know everything there is to know about the Afrit? Because your mom's been so forthcoming?"

She hasn't. He knows she hasn't.

Henry knows as much about being Jinn as I do. I smile, remembering the string of questions that followed the shocked, then mesmerized look on his face when he caught me in the act of granting a wish at the start of the summer. I had no choice but to tell him I was a Jinn.

That's not true. I did have a choice, but I made the selfish one. I chose to break the Afrit's biggest rule and out the Jinn world to a human because I wanted to. Granted, when I made that decision I wasn't in possession of all the facts about becoming Jinn.

Since then, Henry's become my confidant, my best friend, and the one I trust most in this world. Just like his sister Jenny. My best friend for the first nine years of my life. Before she fell from the swing in my backyard. That was the day I learned magic has its limits. It can't heal humans, and it can't bring someone back from the dead.

Though, in a way, it has. It's magic, it's becoming Jinn, that brought Henry and me together this summer. Before my sixteenth birthday, I didn't have friends. I thought it was a side effect of being

Jinn, of having to hide who we are. But it wasn't a side effect of being Jinn. It was a side effect of being me.

"Azra," Henry says with frustration in his voice, "you found out about your father from your mom's *diary*. A diary that she hid from you. Haven't you stopped to think what else you don't know?"

What else I don't know has been all I've been thinking about for the past two weeks. Because, as it turns out, my mother's been keeping secrets from me about the Afrit my entire life. Not just that I was one of them, but that threats and coercion are how they keep us Jinn in line. Tortura cavea, a jail, literally of our worst nightmares, awaits not just me, but my mother, her Zar sisters, and my own if I screw up, and maybe even that or worse for Henry. Because if the Afrit find out I told Henry about our world, they'll use mind control to make him forget. And this power I'm struggling to learn is tricky even for them. Done improperly, it can leave humans as amnesiacs or in a vegetative state or even . . . even dead. Maybe by accident. And maybe not.

Still, despite all the secrets, something about Henry's attitude and that family loyalty thing makes me push back my shoulders and defend my mother.

"She's only trying to protect me. And besides, Lalla Samara wouldn't lie to me."

I purposely use the "lalla," a term of love and respect similar to the "aunt" and "uncle" that humans use for close family friends unrelated by blood.

Henry tosses his head back and laughs. "Your mother's best friend? Believe me, she's in on whatever your mom's got cooking."

It's like flares have been lit inside my cheeks. My chest tightens, and all I'm thinking is where my Henry went. Why he's being so . . .

mean. Especially after our lips did their little meet and greet. I pivot to return to Mrs. Pucher's. If he wants to move away like this, then fine, don't let the Massachusetts border hit him on the way out.

Henry seizes my elbow and draws me to him. His sweaty shirt sticks to my bare arm.

"I won't let you risk it," he says. "Not for me. I won't let you risk so much as magically swatting a fly away. Not with what's at stake. Not after everything else you've done for me and my family."

He's talking about granting his sister Lisa's wish—my third and final practice one—to be rid of her stutter. And more. More that I have to . . . need to ask him about.

Beepity beep beep!

And just like the last time we were standing in the middle of the street, Chelsea appears.

A gleaming Fiat convertible weaves around us and pulls into the Carwyn driveway. Chelsea the cheerleader, Chelsea the bikini-clad lifeguard who used to make fun of little girls who stutter and ignore me closes the door of her brand-new car. Red. The same color of the lip gloss she always wears at the beach and in the Reese kitchen. True to her word, Chelsea has been helping me with Nate, coming by several times to help cook food and even clean the house for Goldie, which is why my teeth shouldn't be grinding the way they are right now.

"Hey, guys!" Chelsea says, skipping toward us and popping up on tiptoes to peck Henry on the cheek.

Right. Chelsea the maybe-girlfriend of Henry.

A summer in the sun (and perhaps a visit to the salon) has added shimmery gold highlights to her buttery blond hair. She's practically glowing.

"You here to help us paint, Azra?" she says.

"No," I say. Henry didn't ask me to help paint. Even if he doesn't want me using my magic, which could paint the entire house in seconds, I do know how to use a paintbrush. Well, not *know* know, but how hard can it be?

"I've got extra brushes." Chelsea rests her fancy yoga bag on the ground and bends over. "Let me find you one. With three of us, we'll get it ready for those lucky renters in no time."

She may be in downward dog, but Henry's the one on the leash. My teeth grate against one another. If I don't leave right now, I won't have any enamel left.

❧✦❧

Stupid bike. I don't have a car, or a license, so I'm riding behind Megan, who happens to be as good at biking as she is at sailing, not that Nate can get her to the beach and out on the ocean. I had to quit my job at the snack bar early because Megan refuses to even pass by the road to the beach where the car accident occurred.

I used to like biking—when I could go at my own pace. But by the time we roll into the Reeses' driveway, I'm wheezing and Megan's barely broken a sweat.

I miss apping.

She hops off, unhooks her helmet, and is texting before the wheels on her bike stop rotating. The "Thanks, Azra" and teary embrace that followed our last outings are replaced with a backward wave. The running to Nate or Goldie after inching past her mother's sedan is exchanged for a diet soda and a flop on the couch.

The sadness in her eyes? That's still there.

Even so, it's progress. Unfortunately, no one else is home to see it. Dropping my backpack with the container of Mrs. Pucher's homemade fudge on the counter, I pick up the note from Nate. He's at the gym, naturally, and George and Goldie are out for a walk. It doesn't say "at the beach," but I know that's where they go when they need to escape. They're drawn to it as much as Megan is repelled by it.

The screech of two squirrels heralds their arrival in the backyard. Prime test subjects. Which, considering my dismal performance with Pom-Pom, I can't exactly turn away from.

One check on Megan confirms she's engrossed in her phone and her book at the same time. When I tell her I'm going outside, she grunts instead of looking up. Definitely progress.

I trudge through the kitchen and slide the glass door open. I'd like to be able to sit in the sun and read. I'd like to be able to walk on the beach and swim in the ocean before the New England cold takes it away for another year. I'd like to be able to apport to see my Zar sisters, especially Laila, whose constant presence in my life I feel most acutely only now in its absence.

But I can't do any of those things. Not until I grant Megan's wish. And, considering last night, not seeing the pain in Nate's eyes anymore ranks pretty high on my wish list too.

Slipping out of my flip-flops, I dig my toes into the dirt beneath the grass and focus. Nothing. Again. How am I supposed to delve into Nate's mind and ease his pain when I can't even get this squirrel to jump from one tree limb to the other?

Concentrate, Azra. Nate's wish was an intricate, complicated one, and yet you managed to successfully grant that just two weeks ago.

Legally, financially, if anything impedes his mother's recovery, all the paperwork's in place for Nate to be able to take care of Megan when he turns eighteen in a few weeks. But I went further. As big and strong as Nate is, even without his renewed dedication to pumping iron, he lacks confidence. The spell I did to boost it seems to be working. I've seen the results of my handiwork in person these past few days. And felt it this morning. I liked feeling it this morning.

Which makes the lingering memory of Henry's kiss that much harder to reconcile. Though it's a bit easier after seeing him with Chelsea.

"Jump, you stupid rodent!" I shout.

And it does. It jumps! But not to the maple tree I intended. To the swing set. It's running along the top as if mocking me.

I kick the cedar frame. I should use my powers to burn this thing to the ground and the memory of Henry's kiss right along with it.

A kiss that was probing, searching, just like Henry himself.

Suddenly, a twitch starts in my big toe. Then full on, the pins and needles are back. My body is wracked with an electric charge.

I'm not being paranoid; someone's coming.

I whirl around to see a silhouette materialize out of thin air amid the trees lining the edge of the backyard. My heart beats like a tribal drum when my eyes see what they cannot possibly be seeing.

The telltale signs are all there: tall, thin, thick, shiny hair, and, of course, gold eyes. The gold eyes of the Jinn. But this isn't just any Jinn.

This is a male Jinn.

A male Jinn. Disbelief keeps me frozen in place. Male Jinn live in Janna. With the Afrit. Not here in the human world. With us.

The figure, wearing a tan leather waistcoat over a long white tunic and what looks like 1980s baggy parachute pants, ducks under a branch and emerges from the trees.

He—it's most definitely a he—squints as the sun hits his face. The bulk of his costumey getup can't hide his muscular form underneath. He glides gracefully across the yard until he's standing directly in front of me.

The color of his eyes steals my breath. Gold, with a touch of red. Copper. Around his neck is a chain made of elongated, barrel-shaped silver beads engraved with the same design that's etched into the silver bangle around my wrist.

He's definitely a Jinn.

He touches his right hand to his heart and says, "Hello, Azra."

My name from his lips snaps me awake like a shot of adrenaline to my heart. Goldie, George, Megan, Nate—*Nate*—could come out any second. See him. See me with him. See him do whatever it is he's going to do to me.

I grab his wrist, but before my fingers curl all the way around, a mixture of Pop Rocks and Coke explodes in my veins and I drop his hand like it's a grenade.

Ping, ping, ping. Not a sound in my ears, but a feeling under my skin. Rebounding off the walls of my veins, the ricochets echo the strange sensations I've had all day. Only stronger. *Ping.* And more painful.

A car door shuts with a slam that echoes all the way out here. Which means it's close. Too close. Goldie? Nate? Doesn't matter. We can't be seen.

I seize the hem of the male Jinn's tunic—soft, so unworldly . . . unearthly . . . soft—and drag him back into the woods, as far as I can go without the circulus curse stopping me.

Rubbing my forearms and trying to calm the eruption under my skin, a million questions—a million fears—hurl themselves against the walls of my heart and head, but the one that comes out first is the simple, "What were you thinking?"

His smooth brow creases, his copper eyes grow quizzical, his small smile turns . . . sheepish. *Sheepish?*

"I thought I was greeting you," he says. "Is that not how you do it here?"

"No, I mean, yes, well, sort of." *Social graces? That's his most pressing concern?* "That was fine. You did fine." I wave. "Hi." *And mine, apparently?*

The bubbling spreads through my every limb like it's my

heart's job to manufacture Pop Rocks and Coke. I broaden my shoulders and lengthen my torso to eke out as much height as possible. He's still got at least three inches on me.

I steady myself. "What I mean is, how could you risk apporting here? What are you doing here? *How* are you here? And who . . . who are you?"

"Here?" There's a mischievous glint in his copper eyes.

I cock my head. "Here? Where?" I flex my fingers, trying to push through the pings. "I mean, what?"

"Here. You ended every other question with a 'here,' I was simply finishing for you."

Ping.

What a cheeky, cocky ass—

"Apologies," he says. "I'm afraid this isn't going quite as planned. Shall we start over?" He places his hand over his heart again. "*Hala.* My name is Zakaria Anemissary."

"Anemissary? What kind of last name is that?"

"It's not."

"Not what?"

"A last name."

Did a male Jinn apport all the way here just to bicker with me? The flaring of my nostrils I feel, he sees.

He laughs. There's something eerily familiar in it.

"Third time's the charm, isn't that what you say?" He claps his feet together and bows. "Greetings. My name is Zakaria. I am an emissary sent to investigate the unusually lengthy delay between the invocation of the circulus incantation with a Ms. Megan Reese and the completion of the wish she expressed."

My face is one big empty slate.

He rolls his eyes. "No wonder you haven't granted the damn wish yet." He flings his head back toward the sky, sending the espresso-colored hair parted over his right eye bouncing against his forehead. "Look, I'm Zak. I'm here to light a fire under your little Jinn butt to grant the freakin' wish before—instead of me—it's the Afrit coming for you."

My stomach flips at his words. Too close to ones I will never forget.

"They'll come for her, you know they will."

Words said to my mother by a speaker I heard but didn't see, though a feeling in my blood—my Afrit blood—makes me 99.9 percent certain the voice belonged to another male Jinn. To my father, who somehow, though I have no proof, must have been visiting my mother in secret for who knows how long. My mother and not me.

"It's time, Kal. If not now, when? How much longer does she have, really? They'll come for her, you know they will."

And have they? Is this a trick? Am I in danger? My mother? Megan?

I inch backward, away from Zak, and a rock scrapes the bottom of my bare foot, giving me an idea. With my hands behind my back, I do something I haven't done in days: use my magic. The icy tingle that accompanies conjuring snakes up my spine as I conjure a rock. A big, heavy one. So big and heavy it's a struggle to hold on to it while keeping my hands hidden from view.

I turn the mammoth beast end over end, trying to get a better grasp, but it's so smooth I can't get any traction, and it's now pinning my thumb to my spine and . . . *Whump!* It slips to the ground.

I retreat faster and faster but I lose my footing, and with a harsh smack, I land on the ground right alongside it.

Zak rushes forward, dropping to one knee beside me. "Are you hurt?"

Like a reflex, his hand reaches out to touch my forehead. And all of a sudden the ricocheting in my veins stops. Replaced by . . . nothing. But a good—a welcome—nothing. When our eyes meet, he quickly retracts his hand, picking up my conjured rock instead.

He runs his fingers along it. "It's so shiny. And dense. What is this made of? Lead?"

I rub my lower back and mutter, "Could be anything. Guess I should have paid more attention in geology class."

Oops, I just admitted I conjured a weapon. But that's not the part that surprises Zak.

"You can conjure?" he says.

"Of course." I wiggle my wrist and point to his matching necklace. "Can't you?"

A rosy undertone blossoms under his olive skin.

"But your necklace," I say. "Don't you have your powers? Of course, you must if you apped here."

He says slowly, "We have the powers the Afrit allow us to have."

The bitterness in his tone ignites a kinship between us.

I let him help me to my feet and magically brush the dirt from the backs of my legs.

"Where were we?" he says.

"I'm not really sure." That's an understatement. My head is telling me to conjure a machete this time, while my heart wants to take him in like a stray puppy.

He leans against a large pine tree. "We don't have these," he says.

"Pine trees?"

"Trees."

"Why not?"

He shrugs. "Because that's the way the Afrit want it. Which, if I had a mescouta cookie for every time that's the answer to a question in Janna, I'd be a fat Jinn."

I laugh despite not knowing what a mescouta cookie is. "Sounds about the same here. But we don't have any fat Jinn."

"Neither do we." There's an impish look in his widening eyes. "Aha, common ground."

The smile comes too easily to my face. *This is a male Jinn. From Janna.* Here to check up on me.

I begin to picture a baseball bat.

"I'm not here to hurt you," he says softly.

My belief, from a place deep inside, swells. I feel it so strongly in my Afrit blood. That I can trust him. Then again, anything having to do with the Afrit can't be trusted.

Even me.

With a deep inhale, I summon my jaded side, well honed from years of not wanting to become a Jinn. "Why should I believe you?"

His shoulders inch down and he clasps his hands in front of his stomach. "Because I swear on my life. I swear on my family's . . . on my father's life."

I study his copper eyes. "For all I know you two are bitter enemies."

"He has enemies, but I am not one of them."

Sadness and fear darken his eyes.

"Azra," he says. "I know how hard it must be, but I hope you can give me a chance to earn your trust. I'm here on behalf of someone who has your best interests at heart."

My father. It has to be. My mother used the exact same words the last time I was in a wish-granting mess and someone she refused to name helped bail me out.

Like a tidal wave, my million questions rise back up, flooding my brain. Is he part of the potential uprising I read about in my mother's diary? Is that why he's here? What about Raina, Yasmin's mother? The Afrit took her from this world just a few weeks ago. Is she okay? Will she ever come back? Does he know who I am? Does he know who my father is? Does he *know* my father?

Fighting against asking, fighting against trusting him to ask him, forces a battle between my heart and my head. But my head wins. It knows the facts. This is a male Jinn, from Janna, who apported here. The only question to ask is why.

I clear my throat. "So you're like, what, the advance team?"

"In a way."

"Sent by the Afrit?"

"In a way."

"Are you going to tell me exactly in what ways?"

"That's not really important."

"And what is?"

"The reason you haven't granted your candidate's wish."

"Megan."

"A little girl."

My hackles rise. "That doesn't mean her wish isn't important."

"I didn't say it wasn't." He closes his eyes and shakes his head. "You don't make it easy, do you?"

"What?"

"Helping you."

"Who says I need help?"

He tugs me forward, out of range of Megan, and I yelp.

"Fine," I grumble, "but it's not something you can help me with."

"How do you know if you don't ask?"

My head's spinning from the pain of having my kidneys wrenched, not to mention from this entire conversation, and I almost blurt out what I need, because I do need help. Help my Zar sisters can't give because none of them are part Afrit; none of them have the ability to do mind control. And me telling them that I can, that I'm an Afrit, will reveal a secret my mother's been keeping my entire life—a secret that, though it's about me, doesn't quite feel like mine to share.

I can't ask my mother for help because she'll say the risk is too great and shut me down, force me to find some other way. But there is no other way. I need to ease Nate's and Megan's pain. And their need comes before mine.

But what are the odds of Zak actually being able to help me with this?

If he can, wouldn't that mean—since this is something only Afrit can do—that he's one of them?

If he's not, and I ask for help with this—something only Afrit can do—won't I be revealing something that might put me in danger?

Then again, if he's telling the truth, I'm already in danger. I have to give him a chance, but asking Zak for help isn't the same as trusting Zak. Not by a long shot.

My voice trembles despite my opposite intentions as I say, "Mind control. That's what I need help with."

He doesn't flinch and simply taps his baby-smooth, hairless chin. "Aha, dragooning."

"Dragons? I need to conjure a dragon to use mind control?"

Zak laughs that familiar laugh. "You Jinn girls really do lead sheltered lives, don't you?"

His know-it-all tone irks me, and I conjure a miniature cage. "Not so sheltered that we can't do this. And don't doubt that I can make one big enough for you. Bummer that you won't even be able to conjure the key . . ."

More amused than unnerved, he says, "Dragooning is the technique you refer to as mind control."

Technique? As in there's a method I can learn?

"You can do it?" I ask.

His face tells me he can't, and the hope I didn't realize had built up inside me deflates like one of Samara's conjured soufflés. At least this means he's not an Afrit.

"But," he says, "that doesn't mean I can't teach you. All I need from you is one thing."

"What's that?" I ask tentatively.

"Jeans," he says, plucking the fabric of his baggy pants. "I've felt like an idiot in these things all day."

Not again. My little Jinn butt's getting a massage worthy of a luxury spa.

Though they apparently don't have smartphones in Janna, Zak's a quick learner. He's particularly fond of texting. All. The. Time.

"Seriously?" I raise an eyebrow at Chelsea and the pink crocheted sweater she's holding up. "Let's try baby steps, okay?"

When Chelsea stopped by this morning with a basket of homemade apple-cinnamon muffins, it took less than three minutes of her and Megan being alone for them to concoct a plan to force me to come here, to the mall.

I now understand why my mother opted to conjure my back-to-school clothes instead of taking me shopping. The clomping of too-high wedge sandals against the marble floor, the double-digit lines (fitting and restroom), and the three tussles over the last size in a skirt or short or skort we've witnessed so far have me cursing out my circulus curse.

Megan shoves a mint-green cowboy hat on my head. "You

could get away with wearing . . ." She scans my long-legged, curve-less, A/B-cup body and scoffs at the shapeless black tee and white shorts I've put on it. "Well, that, and still have all the boys drool-ing, but aren't you sick of the black and white?"

"You're like a checkerboard," Chelsea says, bouncing her head in agreement. She's traded in her summer ponytail for a sleek reverse bob that better suits her petite face. "A hot one, but still."

I tug on the end of the messy side braid Megan wound my hair in this morning and resist the urge to magically fling the cowboy hat in their direction. "I don't want all the boys drooling." Snorts from both of them. "I mean, any of the boys drooling."

Chelsea reapplies her cherry-red lip gloss using the store mirror. "Except for Nate. And he already does."

Megan wrinkles her freckled nose. "Gross, that's my brother."

Her brother, who asked Mrs. Pucher for her recipe and then made me the most lumpy, gritty, even-too-sweet-for-me batch of chocolate–peanut butter fudge that if I didn't know better I'd say was laced with truth serum. Because once I managed to unstick it from the roof of my mouth, all I wanted to do was confess to what happened with Henry. Not to mention stop lying to him about what I've been doing for the past three nights. I stifle a yawn.

From the very first day that Zak arrived, the urgency with which he insists I master mind control has worked as well as caf-feine to keep me and my magic burning the very real and magi-cally, unnaturally bright candle.

Practicing mind control *with a male Jinn from Janna,* a place I wasn't even sure actually existed for most of my life, has taken a backseat to the fact that I'm *practicing mind control.* There's only so much one's brain can take in without exploding. Zak being so . . . normal makes it easy to accept the former while I adjust to the latter.

My mouth grows wide in another yawn. Megan shoves her finger in between my lips, making me gag. I shoot her the eye roll I've perfected by watching her.

Not that I can blame her, but it is technically her fault that the only time I have to practice *dragooning* undisturbed is after dark, when everyone else is asleep. When I should be asleep.

The few moments Zak and I have been able to steal during the day are, surprisingly, thanks to Chelsea. Though Megan still refuses to step even a pinky toe inside the hospital, she's come around to Chelsea's idea of writing letters to her mom. This way, when Mrs. Reese returns home, she'll feel less like she missed out on weeks or months (hopefully just weeks) of Nate's and Megan's lives. Lately, Nate's lacrosse practice consumes him, and George and Goldie spend their days at the hospital and their evenings walking the beach.

Still, it's only at night, when Megan is asleep, that I'm fully free (well, as free as one hundred and fifty feet allows me to be) to slip into the woods and practice with Zak.

Zak, who reminds me of myself when he marvels at the abundance of ice cream flavors in the local shop. Zak, who makes me feel guilty when he tells me he's never had a crush let alone a girlfriend. Zak, who has somehow managed to acquire a menagerie of animals to serve as my test subjects.

I didn't question the rabbit. I didn't want to go near let alone question the snake. But the pig? Apparently since this power *should* work on nonhumans—save for fellow Jinn—Zak's hoping size may be the key.

If it is, I'm still turning it the wrong way. I've never been good with locks.

In exchange for him helping me with mind control, I've been teaching him to conjure. Turns out, it's not that he can't—it's that he can't in Janna. Like me, he's a natural. Unlike me, he's a clotheshorse. I keep catching him fabricating new pieces. Ones not even in his size. When he returns to Janna, he's going to go into conjuring withdrawal.

The ricocheting in my veins at the thought of Zak leaving doesn't surprise me. Even though it's only been three days, the rhythm Zak and I have fallen into has been almost effortless. Easier than anything I've had since Jenny.

Unfortunately, Zak's not exactly a fountain of information about the Afrit's underground world. It seems if the Afrit do *come for me*, he'd be punished for revealing secrets about Janna. So I haven't pushed him—much. I know Jinn there live with their family members much like we do here. Except for the Jinn locked away in tortura cavea for some infringement against the Afrit, but he won't talk about that.

What he won't stop talking about are the smartphones, apps, music, movies, and TV shows we have here. They occupy him during the day while I'm tied to Megan. His phone's going to meld into his hand by the time he leaves.

I've dropped hints about the uprising, but he hasn't picked up a single one. I have yet to figure out if he truly knows nothing or he's just as good at pretending as the rest of us Jinn.

"I'm so not ready for fall," Chelsea says, turning her nose up at a stack of turtleneck sweaters. "You know what that means, chickies. Clearance rack!"

Just as Chelsea slides her hand into mine to drag me to the back corner of the store, I spy someone who looks like Laila walking out of the frozen yogurt shop. But it can't be, because Laila doesn't live anywhere near here. Neither does Yasmin . . . but there she is too.

Which means, that someone doesn't just look like Laila. *It is Laila.* Laila, after her sixteenth birthday—the day she became a Jinn, received her own silver bangle, and magically reached the full maturity that amps us up to *va-va-vooms-ville.* The day I missed because I was still on probation, unable to apport to her. The day I missed because I broke her heart.

She disappears down another spoke in the mall, and I fight the ache that's causing tears to pool in my eyes. I can't go to her. She's too far away. Even if I could, what would I say besides, "I miss you. I'm sorry. And you're every bit as gorgeous as I knew you would be."

Standing beside Chelsea, I reach for a pair of aviator sunglasses stacked on the clearance table in front of us and hide my eyes behind them. Which only serves to elicit more moisture, for they're the same style of sunglasses that Laila wears.

Stealing her locket was wrong. I knew it when the gold chain coiled itself against the seam inside my pocket. But when I took it all those months ago, I was bitter, well, more bitter, about being Jinn. Being Jinn meant a life defined not by me but by the Afrit, and the picture of Laila's Jinn father inside the locket represented everything I wanted but couldn't have.

Back then, I didn't know how much my mother loved my father, that the Afrit ripping Jinn families apart as punishment for the last failed uprising scarred her as much, if not more, as it did me.

I didn't know the lengths my mother—and father—had gone to in order to protect me. I closed myself off from love, from life, all the while blaming magic, blaming being Jinn, for what I didn't have. Maybe it played a role. But I played a bigger one.

The irony is, I was just starting to figure all this out when Laila found the locket tucked away in my nightstand. It was the night of our official Zar initiation, just a single day before the Reeses' car accident.

The six of us—Laila, Yasmin, Hana, Mina, Farrah, and I—grew up thinking the Zar our mothers were in was nothing more than a declaration of lifelong friendship. We knew it was tradition for female Jinn to belong to a Zar.

We also knew their friendship was to become ours—whether we, which was mostly me, wanted it to or not. As Hana's red hair deepened, so did her obsession with Coco Chanel and Diane von Furstenberg and Tim Gunn. Take every fashion trend Hana studied like a scholar, sub in "teen heartthrob," and you have Mina's academic—theoretical and real-world—pursuits. Her delicate features, mahogany hair, and soft pink lips are a front, camouflaging the inner party girl she was born to be. Lately, Farrah's caramel-colored bangs, sticking out of the headband she uses to hold back the rest of her pin-straight hair, flirt with her eyelashes as she bounces to the music she's constantly listening to, thinking about listening to, or talking about listening to when what she should be doing is practicing her magic. She's the least magically gifted of my Zar sisters. The opposite of Yasmin.

I used to think Yasmin and I were simply oil and water—actually, more gasoline and a lighter; one false move and we'd explode. She was bold, I was reserved. She was aggressive, I was indifferent. She hated humans, my best friend for nine years was a human. Psychotherapy moment: I now know that's the root of our problems. For her, magic is everything. That it never was for me made me the target of her bold aggression.

Through it all, Laila stood (heads shorter) by my side.

For all their differences, they've always shared one thing: They've always wanted to become Jinn. The thing that unites them is what separates me. But not anymore.

Over the course of the sixteen years we've known one another, we've been close, not so close, and then, maybe, on the way to being close again. The Zar initiation was to cement our bond, but not in the way we thought.

That night, to our surprise, the six of us became magically linked, able to draw on one another to bolster our powers, able to feel one another's emotions, able to live and work as one if we so choose. But because of me, because of the locket I stole all those months ago, our Zar merged and then fractured within minutes of each other.

I've been trying to tap into each of my sisters since with no luck. I don't know if they're choosing sides between me and Laila. If they are, of course they'll choose Laila. I would.

As much as I don't want to feel Laila's emotions, I need to feel them. I need to know if I've finally succeeded in doing what my moody, mopey, egocentric self had been trying to do for years: push sweet, kind, loyal Laila away. And I need to find out if I have any shot at pulling her back.

"Ooh," Chelsea shrieks. "This."

I spin around to see her holding up a see-through lacy black shirt with a push-up bra sewn inside.

Groaning, I snatch it out of her hand and stick the hanger back on the rack. "You said no more black."

She frowns and scoops it back up again. "Not for you. For me."

The concrete's barely set on this newly paved road of friendship Chelsea and I seem to be on, so I don't know if telling her she needs to stop acting—and dressing—like someone I'm slowly discovering she's not will cause a sinkhole.

With a click of metal against metal, Chelsea puts the shirt back. "Not your size?" I ask.

"It is," she says. "I'm just not sure it's really me."

Wait, what? That's close—almost bull's-eye close—to what I was thinking. I squish down my involuntarily rising eyebrows. *Was that . . . did I . . . can I . . .* Let's try it again.

Selecting a floral cardigan with a lace collar that somehow seems to match Chelsea's muffin-baking personality, I hold it up, and like Zak's been saying, I stop thinking and start doing.

Instead of simply thinking of words in my mind that I want Chelsea to say or do, I picture her saying or doing those things. I picture *her* picturing her saying and doing them. I feel how she'd feel while saying and doing those things. The patterns in her brain that tie into thought and speech and muscle movement all require energy. I need to make that energy work for me, to draw on nature and connect with her. To tune myself to the tiny electrical signals that race along the neurons in her brain and power them myself. We need to move in sync, like award-winning tango dancers.

At first nothing happens. And then it does.

Chelsea stands in front of me, reaching out to touch the cardigan, fingering the lace, pausing, and studying. "Do you mind?"

She takes the hanger out of my hand. "I kinda think this might be more me."

It worked. Fireworks rock my insides and I'm about to explode.

Suddenly Chelsea starts jumping up and down.

Oops, we're still connected. My deep breath works to extinguish the sparklers alit inside me. One final hop and Chelsea's feet remain on the ground while I concentrate on breaking our link.

Back under her own control, she covers her mouth with her hand and squeaks out an embarrassed giggle. "I guess I love this even more than I thought."

Zak's going to flip when I tell him.

Zak? That's my first thought? Not the wish I can finally grant and the curse I can finally end?

Chelsea leads us toward the now even longer line for the dressing room. My buzzing butt makes me crash into the redheaded girl in front of us. The fifteen hangers she had been so perfectly balancing fly from her grip and skid across the floor.

"Clumsy much?" she says with a scowl.

Before I can open my mouth, Chelsea flings herself between us, standing on top of the pile of strewn clothes. This gives her an extra half an inch, maybe. The other girl looms over her, but that doesn't stop Chelsea's flaming red lips.

"Rude much?" Chelsea rustles the pile of clothes with her platform sandal and snickers. "We're actually doing you a favor. You might as well scoot right out of line, honey, because you . . ." She raises one eyebrow. "You can't pull off any of this. *Any* of this."

She sweeps the whole lot aside, grabs me with one hand and Megan with the other, and moves us all up in line.

"Damn," Megan says.

I can't reprimand her. That's the only word that fits.

"Skank," Chelsea hisses at the redhead.

"Chelsea!" Her I have to reprimand.

She rounds her shoulders and clutches her floral cardigan to her chest. "Sorry."

Megan and I devolve into giggles when my butt vibrates again. *Seriously, Zak?* Except now that I have actual news to report, I'm equally as anxious to connect with him. Since snails move faster than this line, he'll have to come to me. I pull out my phone and text Zak with the name of the store we're in, telling him I'm heading for the door.

I'm about to make an excuse (that has more than a nugget of truth in it) about needing some non-hairsprayed air so I can wait for Zak by the entrance when Laila comes up beside me.

I forget all about breathing.

Once only blond, her soft waves cascade past her shoulders in a hue that's a delicate mix of butterscotch, honey, and apricot. Her eyes shine the traditional Jinn gold but tiny speckles of her original powder blue remain. She's no longer the tiny Laila, always shorter than the rest of us, but she's not nearly as tall as Yasmin and I. My eyes float down to her bursting cleavage. I can't help but smile, remembering how eager she was to inherit the ample bustline that runs in her family. She must be thrilled.

Out of my mouth spills, "I miss you. I'm sorry. And you're every bit as gorgeous as I knew you would be."

I clasp a hand over my mouth and feel everyone's eyes on me: Chelsea, Megan, Laila, and Yasmin. Yasmin, whose uncharacteristically pale skin against her raven-black hair makes her look like she's aged years since the last time I saw her on the night of our

Zar initiation. I know from both Megan and Nate that losing a parent will do that to you.

And then, in strides Zak. In his conjured designer jeans, tight black T-shirt, and slightly crooked sunglasses (guess he's still having trouble conjuring metals). Like Henry, he's also discovered gel.

He approaches from the other side, coming to a halt when his eyes focus on Laila.

Speech eludes all of us. Except, of course, Chelsea. "Talk about every bit as—"

"Gorgeous," Laila finishes in a whisper.

Zak?

I spin my head around and see he's about to remove his lopsided sunglasses. But he can't. His eyes. Yasmin and Laila would see. Laila's preoccupation with his sprayed-on tee suggests the meaning might not register for her. But Yasmin, she'd know with one look at Zak's copper eyes that he's a Jinn.

And I can't have that. Too many questions whose answers put them in too much danger.

"Come on, Zak," I say, grabbing the hem of his so-soft-I-don't-know-how-he-could-have-possibly-conjured-it T-shirt.

"Not so fast." Yasmin flips my sunglasses to the top of my head and peers into my eyes. "Aren't you going to introduce us, Azra?"

My tongue goes limp.

Zak places his hand over his heart.

Oh, no, he better not do that weird speechy thing he did to me when we first met.

"I'm Zakaria, Azra's cousin."

Yasmin's almond-shaped eyes grow wide. "Really?" She pulls Laila toward her. "Because so are we."

Again, all eyes on Azra. To avoid confusion, in the outside world, my Zar sisters and I have always called one another "cousin." Though Zak couldn't have known this, why didn't he just say "friend"?

With a shrug, I say, "Different sides of the family."

The ticking of this time bomb is way too loud. And so even though it's the last thing I want to do now that I'm finally face-to-face with Laila, I take Zak's hand and walk away.

"What were you thinking coming inside?" I move to a bench opposite the store window, staring at a mannequin dressed in a sequined skirt, silk zebra-stripe tank, and camouflage backpack. Perfect first day of school outfit. School for what, I don't want to know. "Didn't we talk about low profile?"

Bent almost in two to get a last glimpse of Laila through the mannequin's plastic legs, Zak forces himself to straighten and turn toward me. "I thought you were in trouble."

"Trouble? What would make you think that?" I ask this instead of "what kind" because we both know what kind he'd be afraid of.

"What would make me—" He throws his hands in the air. "*Rahmah!* Mercy, Azra. I don't know, maybe the fact that you didn't answer any of my messages all day and then when you do, it's to tell me you're heading for doom? Doom? That wasn't supposed to light my lantern?"

More bizarre colloquialisms. I refrain from my usual teasing because my heart stings at being so close to Laila and yet remaining so far from fixing things between us.

Instead, I shake my head. "What do you mean, 'doom'?"

"Doom. Your text." He fishes his phone out of his jeans. Which takes a while since they're so tight. When he manages to extract it, he flips to the texts and holds the phone in front of my face.

Heading for doom.

Door. It was supposed to say "door."

The door that Laila and Yasmin are strolling through right now. The constant din of the mall—music spilling out of stores, toddlers shrieking, elevators dinging, kiosk hucksters huckstering—seems to hush as my two stunning Zar sisters glide toward the ladies' room.

Perfect spot to apport home from. How many sets of eyes will be fixated on the dingy metal door, waiting for them to return? And for how long?

How long would Zak wait?

We're not the first female Jinn he's seen, but we may be the first female Jinn he's seen within twenty years of his own age. Females transition into Janna after their job—raising us genie daughters—is complete. Which means Janna is filled with teenage male Jinn and cougars. Guess I can't blame him for looking. Though he's never looked at me the way he's looking at Laila and Yasmin. No, not "and." Just Laila.

His back is to me again. He can't see me. He can't see the heavily made-up woman in stilettos either. She's aiming the bottle of perfume she's selling at shoppers, who all duck, bob, and weave to avoid a squirt.

If I tell Zak about my use of mind control—dragooning—that'd probably get his attention. But why tell when you can show?

And that is how Zak winds up smelling like passion fruit.

I don't want to go. But I no longer have a reason to stay.

Nate and Megan and George and Goldie. Yes, George and Goldie too. When on a mind-control roll, it's difficult to put on the brakes.

After successfully getting the perfume lady to douse Zak with eau de fruity drinks and then talking with her for an interminable ten minutes about oils and essence and her Chia Pet collection (don't ask), I knew I had accomplished dragooning without inflicting brain damage (despite the deviation into Chia Pet territory; it made sense at the time).

Wearing her newly purchased, multicolored chandelier earrings, Chelsea drove me and Megan home. Zak soon followed. I bought myself some alone time by suggesting (not via dragooning ... at least I'm pretty sure it wasn't via dragooning) that Goldie make one of her specialties for dinner: handmade corn tortilla tacos. Knowing my lack of kitchen skills would exempt me, I ventured into the woods while Megan helped Goldie roll out the masa dough. Zak was waiting for me, having set up an obstacle course worthy of a military exercise. Rabbit, snake, and pig wound their way through on the first try at my command.

Zak insisted I was ready. I was and I wasn't. I wanted to ease Nate's and Megan's pain, but I was still terrified of hurting them.

My risk with the perfume lady paid off, but what I needed to do with Nate and Megan was much more complex than shooting liquid at Zak's neck. I wanted more test subjects. More human test subjects. But what were we going to do? Nab someone off the street? It wouldn't be right. It wouldn't be fair to them.

Part of me didn't care. Hurt Megan and Nate or a complete stranger? Easy choice. Well, not easy, but the only one I could ever make. Just like my mother, who would always put those she loves—especially me—first.

The way she did the day Jenny fell from the swing in our backyard. She used her powers to try to save my nine-year-old best friend's life. But she was seen. Mrs. Seyfreth, our other next-door neighbor, witnessed my mother using magic. I now know all the horrible things that could have happened if the Afrit had found out. Which is why my mother did what she did. To protect us, she made Mrs. Seyfreth forget.

Since my mother's not of the Afrit bloodline, she can't do mind control the way the Afrit—the way *we*—can. But her magical talent allows her to come close using spells. Unfortunately, my mother's spell wound up hurting Mrs. Seyfreth, damaging her brain and accelerating the dementia that was just beginning to show. My mother has never forgiven herself. She insists what she did was wrong and that she wouldn't do it again. I don't believe her. I know she'd do whatever she had to in order to protect me.

Which is why, fair or not, when I returned to the woods after a break to check in on Megan and thought I saw Zak talking to someone, I was relieved. I thought he really had found a random stranger for me to practice on one last time.

He hadn't. It was just a neighbor whose dog had freed itself from its leash. There would be no more practicing. It was time.

And so, one after the next, I made their memories of Mr. Reese heavier on the sweet than the bitter. I made their fears about Mrs. Reese's recovery less than their hopes. I made their hurt less. I didn't take it all away. Even if I could, it wouldn't be right. It wouldn't be the best way to honor Mr. Reese's memory.

The weight that comes when remembering someone who's gone gives that someone weight. It makes them real. It makes them—their past and their future absence—a part of who we are and who we will become. And that's not something anyone—even me—should be messing with, no matter how good the intentions.

Pain never completely goes away, but I know from firsthand experience that the grief that constricts our minds, our hearts, our lungs loosens with each day, month, and year that we manage to fight through.

Like a gentle fast-forward, I nudged the Reeses through the passage of time, redistributing the weight of their memories so that the pain might fade and allow their happiness to, not all of the time but simply more of the time, outweigh their sadness.

When I was finished, the family sat down for their first dinner since the accident without a side of melancholy. They also sat down for their first dinner without me.

Because by the time I was done, exhaustion had invaded every inch of my body. It was like walking with suction cups attached to my feet.

With an excuse about promising to have dinner with my mother, I made it to the garage and onto my bike seat. Zak did the rest, apping us both to the beach, which is where we sit now.

The circulus curse is broken. My life can return to normal.

But it can't. Not even Jinn normal. Because what I've just done is not Jinn at all. It's Afrit. I am an Afrit, and I just acted like one.

I'm curled into a ball with my chin to my knees on the fluffy blanket Zak conjured when we arrived. It's the first time I've been at the beach since the night of the car accident. We're in the same spot where Nate and I had our date but everything's different. Yes, my push-up bra is and will remain unseen, but it's not just that. The black rocks seem sharper, the surf is louder, the sand is coarser. Tangible drops of mist cling to the air as if mocking the end of summer.

My shivering makes Zak conjure a second blanket, softer than a newborn kitten's fur, that he wraps around my shoulders.

"Why didn't you tell me it was like connecting with the human's anima?" I ask.

"Their what?"

"Their anima. Their psyche. What we connect to after we recite the circulus incantation."

Zak's face displays no signs of recognition.

"During the wish-granting ritual? So we can discover their true wish? So we can link to the human's soul?"

Still no recognition. Simply fascination.

"You enter their soul?" he says.

"Sorta." Of course Zak doesn't know any of this. Males haven't granted wishes for eons. "Temporarily. It's not as creepy as it sounds."

The connection with Megan is fresh and raw, as full of lightness as it is darkness, just as my mother said the aftereffects of granting a wish can be. The link with Nate's there too. A piece stays with us for each wish we grant until, eventually, we have no more room. One day I'll recite the circulus incantation and my powers won't be enough to reach the human's anima. I'll be retired from granting wishes like my mother and all the Jinn in her Zar. I'll have to start raising the next generation of Jinn. The circle of Jinn is never-ending, thanks to the Afrit.

Zak smoothes out the sand in front of us. "Doesn't sound creepy. It sounds . . . like a privilege."

"It is, actually." Something I didn't believe until I felt it for the first time with Nate. Maybe that's what the Afrit were trying to teach me. Maybe assigning Nate as my candidate wasn't for some sinister reason. My mother said granting wishes for those you care about can be messy. It's hard to distance yourself from what you might want to give them versus what it is they truly want. But maybe I needed to be invested in someone to become invested in being Jinn.

I watch as Zak gathers a collection of rocks from the edge of the marshy estuary. He places them in a ring along with some small pieces of driftwood.

The fire, I light.

"You really are the master," he says. "Conjuring, fire—"

"Dragooning." I shudder as I say this.

Zak tosses another piece of wood on top of the flames. "What's wrong? You should be proud of yourself. Jinn would kill to be able to do what you just did."

"And they have, right? At least the Afrit Jinn."

"Just because you can do what they can do doesn't mean you're one of them."

No, my Afrit father is why I'm one of them.

I change the subject. "Funny word, 'dragooning.' Sounds too silly for what it is."

Zak conjures a stick that he uses to poke the fire. "Oh, that's just what we call it. 'Dragoon' is an old military term for an infantryman. Even if permanent damage isn't done, mind control works by assaulting the cells in the brain. The official term is 'hadi.' I believe the translation is something akin to 'guiding to the truth.'"

I slap Zak's arm.

"*Rahmah!*" he cries. "What did I do to deserve such abuse?"

"It's what you didn't do. You should have told me that was the term for it from the start. Because that's it. That's the key."

He massages his arm. "Since we're not all masters of mind control, a little more explanation, *min fadlik*. Please."

"Believing, that's the key." I turn to face him. "It's why it worked with Chelsea, but I didn't understand it then. I think for mind control to work, the one doing it has to truly believe in what they are making the person do. If I don't believe it's right, I can't make *them* believe it."

Zak rubs the back of his neck and then smells his hand. "So you really believed I should smell like a cocktail?"

I laugh. "I guess I did."

He smiles and then starts bobbing his head. "That follows logically. The essence of all our magic comes down to belief, in some fashion. Belief in our abilities, in nature, in the avenues open to us to manipulate the environment. Stands to reason that the use of hadi would work on the same principle."

I jump as if an invisible hand is sliding an ice cube down my spine.

"What is it?" Zak's tone is filled with concern. "Are you okay?"

Drawing the blanket tighter around my shoulders, I hesitate before nodding slightly. "If we're right, do you realize what that means? It means when the Afrit use it—"

"They believe what they are doing is right."

When the Afrit use mind control to keep Jinn in line, the pain they inflict, the loved ones they tear apart, the humans they hurt, the Afrit must believe it is right. Just.

Being bullies, even sadistic bullies, is one thing. But sociopaths? Tortura cavea is a jail where the inhabitant is locked away with their greatest fear.

I have just found mine. My family.

"There's no reasoning with someone like that," I say.

Zak hurls his conjured stick into the fire. "Which is why they must be overthrown."

7

I'M STILL REELING FROM ZAK'S BOMBSHELL.

The shock on his face right before he apped me back to the Reeses' woods and then disappeared means that was an unintentional slip.

Too bad my hadi powers don't work on fellow Jinn. When I see him tomorrow, he's in for one hell of an interrogation.

I will see him tomorrow, won't I? What if where he disappeared to was Janna? Megan's wish is granted. The Afrit don't have a reason to *come for me*. Maybe Zak had to leave? No, he's still here. He wouldn't leave without saying good-bye.

Though I know how tempting it is.

My bags are packed and sitting on the floor beside my bed in Megan's room. When I returned, I told everyone that my mother wanted me home since school was starting soon. They all understood, though I swear I saw tears in George's brown eyes when he drizzled extra sweet butter on my popcorn.

It's my last night living with Nate. We spend it as a family with his grandparents and his sister. Everyone seems less wounded. Not quite happy, but not unhappy either. They're all lighter, except for me. But that's the way things go. Jinn work for the greater good. Not for their own good.

But that doesn't mean the good can't come to those who wait. Nate.

In the doorway of Megan's bedroom. Sliding my bags aside with his bare, tanned foot. Pulling back my covers, eyes lingering on the hem of the not-quite-long-enough tee I sleep in, finger pressing to his lips to prevent me from making a sound, hand grabbing mine, body guiding me across the hall. To his bedroom.

This is why sixteen-year-old girls should not be allowed to live with their maybe-boyfriends.

"We're going to miss you, doll," Goldie says, squeezing me like an orange she's juicing for her Sunday brunch mimosa. "I want to see you at our dinner table at least a couple of times a week."

I lift my head from her bosom and suck down air. "Sure, I'll bring dessert."

"Nonsense." Goldie plasters on a smile. "We wouldn't want to put you out. Don't you cook for us." She pushes me back by my shoulders. "Seriously, don't."

George comes up behind her and pats the top of my head. "There's a nice little Italian bakery in town center. Wouldn't say no to a chocolate-covered cannoli."

"Georgie!" Goldie nudges me aside and plucks George's suspenders, letting them snap against his chest.

Across from us, in the far corner of the living room, is Megan.

Stacked next to her are the books she's borrowed from me. I slip past Nate, unable to look him in the eye, and sit beside her. I rest my hand on the top book, a cyberthriller that I devoured in a day.

"I hadn't realized you'd gotten to this one," I say.

Megan's eyes flit to mine for only a second before returning to her blue thumbnail. She scrapes at the edge, prying off a jagged chip. "I haven't. But it's yours. And you're leaving, so . . ."

"So you keep it, and I'll trade you for the sequel when it comes out."

"There's a sequel?"

"Course. When something's that good, we always come back for more." I hold her hands in mine, pretending to survey her nails until I see her frown transition into a weak smile. "I'm not going to paint these for you again if you keep gnawing the polish like it's part of the food pyramid."

The edges of her lips rise a bit higher. As much as I want to see a full-on smile, I know she's not quite there yet. That will come in time. She—all the Reeses—need to continue to mourn in order to heal, which is why accelerating, and not eliminating, their grieving process was the right way to grant Megan's wish.

I drop her hands and am an inch off the sofa cushion when her torso collides with my side, her fingers entwining themselves in the hair that hangs loose around my neck and shoulders.

"Just come back, okay?" she says.

My heart swells. "So much that you'll be sick of me." No one's ever needed me this much.

Nate extends a hand. "Let her go, Meglet. I'm dropping her off before practice."

Except maybe Nate. Though the way we needed each other last

night is way different. Both feel good. Both make my face as hot as a habanero.

I follow Nate to the front door, stockpiling images of the Reese house: the model sailboat on the dining room buffet, the hand-knitted afghan, the artist's easel tucked into the corner of the kitchen, the briefcase wedged under the entryway bench. Mr. Reese's briefcase. It took me sixteen years to realize the good being Jinn can do. Is it possible it's taken just one wish to discover the same about being Afrit?

My bike is impressively wedged in the back of Nate's hybrid. I convinced him to let me ride to the high school with him. I'm not ready to go home yet. Going home means confronting my mother about all the secrets she's been keeping from me, finding a way to make it up to Laila, and saying good-bye to Henry.

I'll do all those things. Just not yet. Because, right now, Nate's driving with one hand on the steering wheel and the other on my knee. He used to be my escape from everything Jinn, the one thing that made me feel normal. And he still does, but now, because of Nate, normal has taken on a new meaning. It's no longer a choice between being Jinn and being me. With Nate, I don't think, I just act, and react. And I like it. I like him.

Green plastic seat. Metal chains. Lips on lips. Guilt, guilt, guilt.

No, that's not fair. *Henry* kissed *me*, not the other way around. So this guilt needs to strap on some boots and go for a very long hike.

Nate lets go of my knee and returns his hand to the wheel as he makes the turn into the school parking lot. The still and silence of my phone means I haven't gotten any texts, but I can't stop myself from double-checking. Nope, nothing from Laila and nothing from Zak. By now the first is expected, but the second . . . I'm starting to worry.

As Nate parks along the athletic field fence, a couple of his lifeguard buddies wave—at him *and* me. Last year, the beautiful bods, of which Nate is the king, didn't do much waving, or much of anything else, with me. What a difference a summer can make.

"Everything okay?" Nate asks. "Your vibe today has been different."

My vibe? Is he sensing my Henry guilt? Or something else I thought was in the past? Part of the reason my high school experience has resembled solitary confinement is apparently because of some I'm-too-good-for-you-so-don't-even-think-about-messing-with-me mojo I unconsciously emitted like stink off a pissed-off skunk.

Nate tucks his chin to his chest and says gently, "Did things go too far last night? If so, I'm sorry and what can I—"

"No," I say quickly. Things went further last night than they did on the beach but not *that* far. I don't think either of us is ready for them to go *that* far. "It's just weird to be going back to real life." I mean that for so many reasons, but right now I mean it mostly because it's weird to be going back to a real life that includes Nate.

Nate's knuckles tighten around the wheel. "I know. At first I wasn't sure I could go back to school. But now . . . I feel like my dad would want me to. He'd want me to go to school, still gun for that lacrosse scholarship, hell, maybe even give a run at going premed next year."

I'm sure he would, and Nate's sure too, subconsciously at least. When I found those thoughts in his mind, I simply nudged them to the surface.

"But," Nate says, "people are going to treat me differently. They already have been. I know these are just clinics, but the guys let me win every face-off."

I'm stuck between a nod and a head shake, having no idea what a clinic or face-off are.

He turns to me. "Have you ever seen a lacrosse game?"

I give a noncommittal shrug.

"That we have to fix." He wraps his hand around mine. "How can I have a girlfriend who's never seen a lacrosse game?"

"Girlfriend?" I blurt out.

Nate retracts his hand and sinks into his seat. "Oh, did you not want . . . Are we not . . ."

Last night, when Nate and I weren't going *that* far, Henry was the furthest thing from my mind. So I say, "I want. We are."

And I believe them both. That is, until Henry knocks on my passenger-side window.

8

Though the sun shines, the metal bleachers are giving me a chill. Or maybe that's Henry.

"Nostalgic last loop around the halls?" I ask him.

He holds up his backpack. "Stuff I left in the computer lab."

I nod.

He swirls his head around. "No Megan. Wish granted, I presume?"

"Minds controlled."

Henry smiles so wide his dimples carve craters into his face. "No freaking way."

And we're back. Dragooning, Zak, the rabbit, the snake, the pig, the Chia Pet lady. I fill Henry in as I have so many times before.

I've missed this. Talking with Henry like this. Nate's a great listener, but he's also okay with me keeping things to myself. If it had been Nate who found me granting my coworker Zoe's wish to be tall, he'd have probably rushed off, closed the door to the snack bar, and apologized for invading my privacy. He wouldn't have grilled me about being a witch and part of a seaside coven.

He wouldn't have asked me to use my third and final practice wish to grant his sister—and not himself—the thing she most wanted.

Okay, so that part isn't true. Of all the ways Nate and Henry are alike, that's the strongest.

Don't forget about their feelings for you.

Shut up, Azra.

Henry opens then closes his mouth. He's taken it all in—well, all but one thing. And so he says for the fourth time, "But a male Jinn? How do you know you can trust him?"

Same way I knew I could trust you.

To my unhelpful shrug, he says, "Just be careful, Azra."

"When am I not careful?"

"Yeah, I don't think we have enough time before the sun sets to cover that."

Down on the field, Nate catches a ball with something that looks like an old mop and raises his head to make sure I'm watching. I am, and so is Henry. I cringe, not wanting Henry to move away with things weird between us. When he told me New Hampshire was happening, he said maybe it was a good thing—maybe it'd be easier for me to be there for Nate without having to worry about him.

Am I horrible for starting to think he was right?

"One of your texts said something happened with Laila?" Henry says.

"Not something. Me."

And the answer is: yes. I am horrible for contemplating for even a second that Henry was right. Because when I tell Henry how I stole Laila's locket, vowed for weeks to return it to her, and then, simply, for no real reason other than cowardliness, laziness, and a preoccupation with other things, didn't, which led to her finding it all on her own and realizing how I'd lied to her, Henry does what a best friend is supposed to do.

"She'll forgive you," he says. "She'll want you in her life in whatever way she can."

It's not just the Laila sin Henry's absolving me of.

"I'm going to miss you," I say.

"You better."

But why should I have to? Why can't I help him stay? My mind control opens a whole world of ways I could help him and his family stay.

I drum my long fingernails against the cold bleachers. He's going to say no like he has before. I know it. But I still have to try one last time.

"I'm not on probation anymore." I wiggle my wrist to draw his attention to the silver bangle he knows I'm wearing. He was there when my probation was lifted and the bronze bangle meant to restrict my use of magic save for the granting of wishes was replaced with this one. He's well aware of my ability to use magic to help his family. And I'm well aware of him refusing to let me.

"I could whip out the help wanteds," I say. "See what I can do about getting your dad a job somewhere that doesn't require you to wear hiking boots and plaid all the time."

"Massachusetts snob."

"Is that a yes?"

"How does that sound like a yes?"

"The lack of an *n* and an *o*."

Henry points to his face and his overexaggerated "N-O."

I want to fight him on this, but I know he's right. I can't pretend there aren't consequences for defying the Afrit anymore. And doing magic for a human, especially with that human's knowledge, is the biggest defiance there is.

"It's too late anyway," he says, running his hand through his haphazard hair, longer than it used to be and getting even longer. "Renters are moving in this week."

I sigh a long, hard sigh. "That's it, then."

"It's not like I'm moving to Guam. Which wouldn't matter anyway since you can blink your eyes and magically appear anywhere you want."

"That's not how we do it, you know."

"The point is, we'll see each other."

"As much as we've been texting?"

His gaze zeroes in on the metal bleachers his foot now taps against.

We're finally getting to it. The reason he hasn't been texting back, the reason why things have been weird. He's the one responsible, but apparently that responsibility doesn't translate to being the one to initiate talking about it.

"So," I start, "the funeral was—"

"Sad."

"Strange." I pause, waiting for him to take the lead.

"Brought up a lot of emotions about . . . stuff that's . . . complicated because of other . . . stuff."

"Eloquent."

"I try."

I'm really going to miss him. But talking about this further will only make things between us even weirder. So I drop it. "I'll visit whenever I can, and you'll be better at texting?"

"Is that what you want?"

"Of course. Who wouldn't want their best friend to text them back?"

"Is that what I am?" He stares at me, his Granny Smith–green eyes unblinking.

"Always."

He smiles and winces at the same time. He sminces.

And I feel like a guilty, ungrateful liar and phony all at the same time.

On the run, Nate catches a ball from his teammate and flings it into the goal from halfway down the field. I don't have to know anything about lacrosse to know he's on his way to that scholarship.

"That confirms it," I say. "My dragooning seems to have left Nate unscathed."

Henry's lips thin. "Technically. But I think it's cheating not to feel the hurt."

He's thinking of Jenny. Of leaving the house where Jenny last lived. Maybe even of leaving me? Would that change if he knew the one secret I'm still keeping from him is all about Jenny?

Once the Afrit forced their way to power, many of the rules surrounding the Jinn and wish granting were changed, including where males and females are allowed to live, which humans are eligible to have a wish granted, and how we access our powers. They came up with a way to block our inherent magic and release it on their terms. The bangles we female Jinn wear and the necklaces the males—apparently, as I've learned from Zak—wear unlock our powers.

That's the rule.

I'm the exception.

Turns out, maybe because of my Afrit ancestry, I don't need a bangle to do magic.

Knowledge I have that part of me wishes I didn't. Because it means Jenny, Henry's sister, my best friend from birth to age nine, didn't just fall from the swings in our backyard. It means she fell because of me. My mother thought she'd found a way around my anomaly. This *A* necklace I wear that Nate loves so much? It's a fake.

The real one, the one that belonged to the grandmother I'm named after, is spelled to inhibit my magic. My mother made sure I wore it every day of my life until the day I turned sixteen, when she stealthily swapped it out for this one I'm currently wearing. One of the few times the spelled *A* left my neck was the day Jenny died.

That day, with my necklace off, my nine-year-old self unconsciously tapped into my powers to push us higher on the swings. To push us to the sky. I never intended for Jenny to fall to the ground.

My mother's magic couldn't fix what my magic had done.

I know I should tell Henry the truth. But I can't. I can't bear to see him look at me the way I now have to look at myself.

It may be cheating not to feel the hurt, but right now, I'd give anything to be a cheat.

BEEPITY BEEP BEEP!

As Henry and I near the parking lot, "other stuff" rolls right in.

"Hey, Chelsea," I say as she waves through the open roof of her convertible.

She unsnaps her seat belt and springs up, kneeling on the driver's seat. She thrusts her boobs at us. "Whaddya think?"

The daisies on her breasts look lovely. She's wearing the floral cardigan from the mall.

"You were right, Azra," Chelsea says, bouncing in her seat. I don't know how much of a leader she is, but she's got the cheer part down. "And since I trusted you, it's your turn to trust me. I've been thinking about your first-day outfit. Because, now that you actually talk to people, it'll be kind of like your very own cotillion."

Henry stifles a laugh. I turn to glare at him when I see Zak out of the corner of my eye. He's on the far side of the lot next to the high school. He's facing the brick wall, so I can't see his face, but if the motion of his hands is any indication, he's one unhappy Jinn.

Chelsea's still outlining her strategy for my fall wardrobe and so I shuffle back for a better angle. Henry shuffles right along with me.

Covering with a fake cough, I say, "Zak."

"And?" Henry's shock makes him slip and use his normal voice.

"Glad you asked!" Chelsea says. "Layering's a must. I'm impressed, Hen-Hen."

Hen-Hen?

I can't go there right now because Henry's "and" actually refers to the individual I now see leaning against the redbrick wall in front of Zak.

Though his hair is a bit longer and shaggier, his height and the way he's dressed make him look like Zak's twin.

"Oh," Chelsea cries. "Henry, we must vacate. Mom's expecting us."

There's only so much teasing I can leave on the table. I nudge Henry's foot with my own and whisper, "Mom?"

He grunts and kicks me right back.

Chelsea drops down into the driver's seat and drapes her hand over the side of the door. "Azra, want a ride?"

"Yeah, why don't you come with us?" Henry says, tipping his head toward Zak. "It's not safe to leave you in an empty parking lot alone. Who knows what sorts of species may be lurking."

Chelsea giggles but I know Henry's covertly referring to Zak and whoever he's with, since Jinn are technically a separate species from humans.

"I'm all set." I point to my bike, secured to the fence with the new black-and-yellow U-shaped crossbar that Nate insisted I needed. Two weeks of using this fancy bike lock that matches his own, and I still can't open it on the first try. "Besides, I should say good-bye to Nate first."

Henry reluctantly walks around the car and opens the passenger-side door. "Pop in later?"

"If I can. Might be hard with it being my first night home."

Chelsea frowns. "How sad! Probably got used to having someone to share your bed—"

I jolt like I've been stung by a nasty greenhead fly.

"—room," Chelsea finishes. "Well, see you later, Ra-Ra!"

Ra-Ra?

Henry laughs. He then mouths "Get home" right before his lips meet Chelsea's cheek.

Good. Great. Happy for him—them.

Or at least I'm trying to be.

I take a deep breath and focus my attention on Zak and mystery boy, who are still in a heated discussion. *What's going on?*

I slip my phone out of my pocket and send Zak a text:

Leaving Nate at practice. On my way home. Can we talk?

While I'm waiting, I resist the urge to stash myself in the trunk of Nate's hybrid as a stowaway and instead text my mother that I'll be home tonight.

She replies:

Kiddo, that's wonderful! Mrs. Reese is being released, then? I'm so relieved and can't wait to have you home and hear all the details. I'm at Sam's. Be home in a while. *Make* us dinner, if you want.

Yeah, so, I didn't exactly tell my mother the truth about why it was taking so long to grant Megan's wish. She thought Megan wished for her mother to come home, which, considering we can't heal humans, isn't something I could easily do. The only options were to wait it out and hope Mrs. Reese would be sent home soon or to come up with a genie trick. She wasn't keen on me going the literal route, and so she agreed to let me stall on the wish granting. Of course, that means each time we talked, I had to stick to this story.

Thankfully, being Jinn's made me really good at lying.

"Greetings!" Zak appears directly in front of me and I almost drop my phone. He's sweating, which is odd. All Jinn love the heat, and it's not even that hot today.

He wipes his forehead with the back of his hand. "Want to hear something crazy? Remember that guy who lost his dog at Nate's? He was running on the school's track, and the beast got away again. He really needs to invest in a more secure leashing system. Can you believe I ran into him here?"

Not really. I wonder if being Jinn has made Zak as good at lying as it's made me.

Zak hovers in the doorway. It's strange to see him here among all our things: my mother's Russian nesting doll collection, her pumpkin-colored armchair, our array of Moroccan lanterns. It's even stranger how well he seems to fit.

I wanted to probe him further about the guy who needs a dog

leash and his "overthrown" slipup in private. But he only agreed to come home with me when I told him my mother wouldn't be back for a while. Still, I can't get him to venture deeper into the house.

"Wine?" I finally ask.

Zak zooms in with the speed of a cheetah. "Where do you keep it?"

Sucker. Stereotypical Jinn. Fill a glass with booze, line the rim with sugar, and set it outside on a ninety-degree day and Jinn will descend like pigeons on a bag of cheese doodles at the beach. I unearth my mother's favorite bottle of red and pour some for each of us. He sits on the couch only after draining his glass.

Sipping mine slowly, I struggle to find the best way to ask him about the uprising against the Afrit. I was ready to tell him all I'd learned from my mother's diary (*not much*) and grill him about what's going on in Janna. But Henry's fears coupled with Zak's less-than-believable Mr.-I-Can't-Hold-on-to-My-Mutt story have made me question everything he's told me. I know he's been keeping things from me. I thought he was doing so to protect me, but suddenly I'm not so sure.

Zak's pouring his second glass when the feel of a breeze rustling a pile of fallen leaves overcomes us both. He jumps to his feet and sprints toward the front door just as my mother appears in front of it.

"Azra, I brought ice cream ca—"

The familiar white box holding my favorite dessert from the shop near Samara and Laila's plummets toward the wood floor.

I catch it with my powers and float it into my hands.

My mother's usually olive skin pales, making the espresso-colored hair we both share seem darker.

The espresso-colored hair we all share.

My mother grips the molding around the door as Zak places his hand over his heart and says formally, "*Hala*, Kalyssa."

She stiffens slightly. "The least you could do is call me Mom."

The cake box wobbles.

"Hi . . ." Zak stuffs his hands into his constricting pockets. ". . . Mom."

A smile consumes her face. "Now that's more like it."

Her bangle, identical to mine save for its gold color, slides down her wrist as she throws her arms around Zak and clutches him to her chest.

And ice cream cake hits the floor with a squishy splat.

10

I HAVE A BROTHER.

"But how?" my mother says, not bothering to wipe away the vertical stripes of tears lining her high cheekbones. She holds Zak at arm's length. Her eyes drink in his smooth dark hair, the hint of a heart shape in his chin, the slight upturn of his nose. The traits I now see we all share like clones.

A new stripe paints itself down her face. "He gave me images of you over the years. I knew they weren't enough, but I didn't know how not enough until now."

Zak's face, solid as stone, melts into putty as my mother brings his forehead to her own.

I have a brother who lied to me.

"But you're an Afrit," I say without thinking, without remembering my mother has no idea that I could possibly know this.

Zak steps back and faces me. "I'm as much an Afrit as you are."

My mother sucks in a sharp breath.

She lied to me too. Like mother, like son.

"I trusted you," I say, the bitter taste on the tip of my tongue fueling my words. I'm looking at both of them, and I mean this for each of them, but for now, I home in on Big Bro. "I trusted you with Megan and Nate. I could have hurt them! Or is that what you were trying to make me do? No wonder you knew so much about hadi—"

"Hadi?" My mother's hand flies to her temple. "Azra! You used mind control?" Her hand lowers, covering her mouth. "On Megan and Nate? To grant a wish?" Her palm slides down and rests over her heart. "You . . . *you* lied to *me?*"

My pent-up anger at my mother unleashes like lava from an active volcano. "No way. You don't get to do that. You don't get to make me feel guilty. Especially since lying is clearly the Nadira go-to. And I learned from the best."

Her voice quivers. "That's not fair."

"Not fair? *I'm* not being fair?"

Zak moves between us. His face is longer and narrower than mine and my mother's. He must get that from his father . . . his father, which is my father. Xavier is *our* father.

"Azra," he says, "we'd all be better served if you simply calmed down and allowed us to talk this out."

I give a harsh laugh. "Really, Zakaria Anemissary? You think you have a chance in tortura cavea of stepping in and filling the role of family peacemaker? You try being calm after being lied to for sixteen years."

My mother, usually as graceful as a gazelle, stumbles as her kitten heel snags on the edge of our antique Turkish prayer rug. She recovers and extends her arms toward me. "Azra, just let me explain."

"Explain? Which part, Mom? How my father—how *I'm*—a

member of the Afrit the entire Jinn world fears and hates in equal measure? How my Afrit father has been sneaking into our world, our home, to snuggle up with you but to not even wag his tail in my direction? How my whole life all I ever wanted was a family. Turns out, I had one. But you decided to keep it from me."

Along with the truth about my ability to do magic. Along with the truth about my role in Jenny's death.

I'm perched on a spinning top, fumbling for an edge to cling to, but the only thing I can actually hold on to, the only thing that can stop me from soaring out of control, is across the street.

Facing the front window, I see a light go on in Henry's bedroom. The blinds fall, concealing him behind them.

I turn away from the hurt gleaming in my mother's gold eyes and the desperation filling Zak's. I don't mention Jenny. I don't mention how I know I can do magic without this silver bangle. Everything Zak's told me might be a lie. I have no idea why he's really here or what the Afrit know or don't know or what might happen to me if my *family* learns the truth. Me being unlike all other Jinn may have been my mother's secret, but I'm taking ownership. And there's no way I'm revealing it now. Certainly not to him.

Hot tears prick the corners of my eyes, but I can't let them fall. I can't admit how much they've both hurt me. I steady my breathing and picture the model AT-AT that sits on Henry's bookshelf, though by now it might be packed in a box on the floor of his bedroom or set up on a shelf in New Hampshire or even lumped into that garbage bag he tossed to the curb. Instead I picture Henry. Just Henry. I ground my feet into the floor and begin to feel the searing heat that comes with apporting when a hand clamps around my elbow and yanks me back.

"Get off me!" I shout, pushing Zak away.

But he doesn't. He wraps his thick arms around me and propels me into his hard chest. I struggle to free myself when thoughts and feelings and memories charge at me like stampeding bulls.

We're at the beach, a younger me and Zak and Mom and... *Dad?* Zak adding a rounded column to an ornate sand castle while my mom, tanned and smiling, faces me and Xavier... me and my father in the ocean. My father, floating me with his hands under my belly as I kick and plunge my arms into the water, trying to swim, trying to learn how to swim. We're on the swings in my backyard—our backyard—with Mom behind me and Xavier behind Zak, pushing us, laughing with us, conjuring fake clouds for us to burst with our tiny fingers each time we ride higher. We're in my bedroom, Zak's arms, skinnier but nearly as strong, around me like a shield, telling me it'll be okay, that we'll see each other again, that this won't be the last time, but somehow, some way, we both know it will be. They're leaving. Zak and my father are leaving for good.

"You... you were here." My words come out muffled, and Zak eases me off his chest. "Both of you. You were here, over and over again."

My mother rushes to us and spins me toward her. "Azra, how do you know that?"

I'm struggling to figure that out, but she won't stop.

"Azra, answer me, how do you know that?"

"No," I cry. "I can't... can't..." It's like my lungs are inhaling smoke and my legs refuse to support my weight and my eyes lose focus and... and Zak swoops in again, holding me, grounding me, forging a path through the dark cloud and filling me with oxygen.

It's like it was the night Nate's father died. When I was at the hospital and Henry held me, made me feel like the world wasn't ending, and a memory buried in the furthest reaches of my mind sprang forth, retreating before I could grasp it. It was this: my memories of my brother and father.

The memories my father erased.

"I'm so proud of you, kiddo." My mother's hand shakes as she twirls her hair into a messy bun. The strand she winds around barely keeps it in place. "You must have truly opened yourself to all that your magic can do if these memories have returned to you on their own."

My brother and my father were a part of my life, and I never knew it.

"But you understand now, don't you?" she says.

She's just finished explaining that my father had no choice but to make me forget him and Zak because the Afrit's abilities allow them to mind-read and mind-control both humans and Jinn. But not one another, which is how my father's deception hasn't been discovered.

My mother squeezes Zak's forearm like she's afraid he'll disappear if she lets go. "If your father let you remember and the Afrit ever had reason to come here, to come to us, they could discover he'd been here. He'd be . . ."

He *wouldn't* be is more like it. So yes, I understand. But it doesn't make it hurt any less.

Still, now that I have the tiniest glimpse into what their abilities can do, it makes me realize something.

"Wait," I say, wiggling to the edge of the sofa cushion, "if the Afrit can use mind control on Jinn, why don't they implant whatever they want in our heads? Why do they need any other way to control us or punish us?"

Scratch that, it makes me realize two somethings. Because if, like the Afrit, I can use mind control on humans, does that also mean I can use it on Jinn? For a second, I try. I try to make my mother's fingers release Zak. I try to make him lift his arm. Neither budges. Guess my half-Afrit status only gives me half their abilities.

Zak turns to me, addressing both of my somethings. "Unlike with humans, using mind control on Jinn requires an additional incantation that is only known to members of the council. Even then, mastery of such a complex skill isn't guaranteed."

"Plus, they tried," my mother says. "Early on, when the Afrit first came to power and realized their abilities, they tried to control us that way. But not only is it difficult magic even for them, turns out, it also drains their powers at an exponential rate."

"Drains?" I say. "As in uses up? Like the circulus?"

My mother nods. "But even worse. When the circulus no longer works for us to grant wishes, we still have our powers. Too many uses of the hadi incantation completely eradicates an Afrit's magic. Especially when the subject resists. The greater the resistance, the more damage it inflicts—on both sides. It's not a long-term solution, which the Afrit quickly realized. They only use it on Jinn now in the most extreme cases." She snickers. "In truth? They're selfish cowards. Not willing to sacrifice their own well-being even in support of their cause. While it does take longer to inflict permanent damage on Jinn than humans, it can cause the same things. Amnesia, dementia, insanity—"

"Death," I finish. "And dead Jinn can't grant wishes. We're of no use to them. Enter tortura cavea, Jinnies and Jents."

"Azra, this isn't funny," my mother says.

But Zak laughs his familiar, for a reason I now know, laugh. My mother can't help but smile, at least weakly. She then conjures a glass—slightly misshapen—and with a shaky hand attempts to pour herself wine.

Zak holds the bottle still for her. "Father thinks hadi not working on Afrit is a combination of our strength . . ."

Our.

"And keeping the bloodline pure."

"Pure?" I snort. "Isn't that just a fancy term for inbreeding? No wonder they're insane."

Zak's jaw tenses. "They're our family, Azra."

Is he serious?

"They're not all bad. You don't know them. Some of them, a lot of them, want what our father wants."

"And what's that?"

"To change things. To change everything."

Just like my mother's diary said he was going to do.

"He's taking his sweet time" spills from my lips before I realize how harsh it sounds.

Zak pops up from the couch. "Are you actually that self-centered? Do you have any idea what he's done for us?"

I jump up to be more equal in height. "Haven't you been paying attention? Of course I don't know. No one's let me know. Unlike you. Why did he let you remember? If it's so dangerous, why do both of you know he's come here and I don't?"

Darkness flits in and out of my mother's eyes. "It's not just you, Azra. He used to make me forget too. For a time, he was allowed to come and visit, even to bring Zak to us." She clasps her hands in her lap and her red fingernails dig grooves into her skin. "But then the council tightened the apporting shield even further. Only Afrit could pass through, and only those Afrit of the highest strength, those like your father who could—"

"Shape-shift," I say.

"So you did see him." She latches onto my arm and pulls me back onto the couch next to her. "He thought so." Her smile contrasts with the longing in her eyes. "He's a beautiful canine, isn't he?"

Shiny chestnut fur, thick, strong legs, my father's animal form would win him the first-place ribbon in any dog show. I've only seen him once, from a distance, on the night Nate's father died, the night I—correctly—thought I heard him tell my mother the Afrit would "come for me."

My mother strokes my arm. "He was glad you saw him. You can't know how hard this has been on him."

My instinct is to bristle at this, but the warmth of my mother's soft hand against my skin stops me. From this very room's two fireplaces to the wool sweaters in my dresser to the chocolate cakes on my plate to the hugs around my often-resistant body, my mother has kept me warm—inside and out. Safe and protected my entire life. While my father's been playing double agent. Of course this must be hard—harder—on him than it is on me. Even I'm not selfish enough to deny that.

My mother reaches for Zak's arm and settles him back on her other side. "The restriction meant I couldn't see Zakaria anymore.

At least not in person. Thankfully, your father's abilities allowed him to play images in my mind."

"Play?" If I were a fuse, I'd have blown by now.

"Truly amazing." She presses her shoulder against Zak's. "I was able to see you make your marks. I watched you receive your silver necklace. I even saw you use your powers for the first time."

"You mean you saw me apport myself directly into a pool of quicksand?" Zak's cheeks flush. "You saw that? Why would you want to see that?"

"I'm your mother, I want to see everything."

Apporting right away? Impressive. "Apping was the first magic you used?" I ask.

"It's the first magic we all use. Janna is quite large. And we lack automobiles. Why, what was yours?"

"Conjuring."

"Tools," my mother adds. "She conjured tools to get her bangle off."

I clink my bracelet against hers. "Didn't work."

"But why would you want it to?" Zak says.

"You aren't asking me that with a straight face, are you?"

Zak's voice lowers. "For us, it's an honor. We have to earn our powers. We don't all just get them."

My Zar sisters and I always wondered if the boys in Janna received the same injection at birth that we do, the one that blocks our magic. Why would they? As little girls, we might unwittingly reveal our magic to humans, but there aren't any humans for the boys in Janna to out themselves to. It didn't seem to make sense. But I'm learning the Afrit don't care about making sense.

They care about control. They dole out powers to the males

like they're a reward. I sure hope I don't have to start deprogramming Zak from a bad case of Stockholm syndrome. Especially since I can't do so via hadi.

My mother sips her wine and looks over the uneven rim of the wineglass at me. "You know what's interesting? Me thinking I distinctly asked you never to use mind control again—"

"What's this?" Zak interrupts. "I thought you didn't know how to dragoon?"

"I didn't. I only used it once by mistake. Led to my probation. And Mom and Samara scared me so much, there was no way I was going to dip a toe in again and risk hurting anyone. Especially Megan and Nate."

"But you didn't, right?" my mother says warily. "You said you used it to grant Megan's wish, but they're all okay?"

"Perfect. Better."

"And you're okay?"

"As far as I know."

A small bit of pride creeps onto her face. "You inherited your father's abilities to use it on humans, then." She looks at Zak. "But you haven't?"

He shakes his head.

"Good." She wipes the pride away and turns serious. "No matter how careful you are, it's still dangerous. Azra, you know you can't—"

"Can't use it. I know. Even though Xavier used it on all of us."

"Your *father*," she says with emphasis, "used it with great care. And only when absolutely necessary. Which happens to include him loving you so much that he couldn't stand never seeing you again."

"And you," I say.

The warmth in her gold eyes echoes the way she looked in the two pictures I found of her and "X"—the initial, along with her "K," that was marked on the back of one of the photos. I should have known then that was a look reserved for those she loves.

She gives me that look now. "After it was forbidden for him to visit, I initially wanted him to stop sneaking back in. I was worried about his safety as much as ours if someone came around. Making us forget was the compromise. But each time your father returned, he had to unlock my mind. And every single time my memories flooded back to me, I'd go through the pain of losing him again. I couldn't take it anymore. Either Xavier had to let me keep my memories or that was it. I told him not to come again." She takes a long sip of wine. "We tried. He didn't come for an entire year. Even though I didn't remember he had been visiting in the years since the Afrit ordered him not to, it was like a part of me knew he had. Something felt off. I was restless."

"I remember," I say. "That's when you left me with Lalla Samara for the whole summer?"

She nods. "I was trying to figure out what was wrong. I was in Morocco, walking through the crowds at a souk in Marrakesh. It's where I found our tagine." She gestures to the glazed red conical dish perched on top of the cabinets in the kitchen that she uses to make my favorite meal, chicken tagine with tomatoes and sweet caramelized onions. "I was placing the money in the merchant's hand when I felt your father apport in. I bought him a dog bone, and he followed me back to the riad I was staying in. He never made me forget again."

Lost in her memories, she plays with the crooked stem of her wineglass. Finally she sets it on the table, where it wobbles but remains upright. "It was dangerous and risky. We both knew that. But we couldn't survive otherwise."

I want to be mad at her, and a part of me is, but a bigger part of me understands. I *am* selfish enough to understand wanting something you aren't supposed to have, even if it means that someone—or someone else—might get hurt.

"But what about him?" I jut my thumb at Zak. "Why did he get to remember?"

"Him?" Zak says. "I'm a 'him'? After everything, I'm relegated to just a 'him'?"

I conjure another lead rock. Zak laughs as he takes it from my hand and places it on the far side of the coffee table. "*Him* only had his memories unlocked right before Father sent me here."

"He did send you, then?" my mother says. "I wasn't sure if—"

"If I'd learned to shape-shift? No, that's still for one hundred percent Afrit, same as using hadi. Except for Azra, it would appear. Father tried to teach me dragooning, for my protection, but I could never accomplish it on the creatures he had me try on."

My heart beats faster as I realize what this means. Zak's my brother. But he can't do what I can do. "So you really can't? That wasn't a lie?"

"I have never lied to you."

I cock my head.

"Did I ever say I wasn't your brother?"

"You never said you were."

"Not the same thing."

The delicate creases around my mother's gold eyes deepen as she smiles at our entirely normal sibling bickering. Entirely normal *sibling* bickering. Who would have thought?

Zak glances at her from under his long eyelashes and I can just see the little boy he used to be, desperate to please his mother. He refocuses on me. "I wonder if it's not opening yourself up to magic but you learning how to employ hadi that allowed your memories to return to you all on your own. Father had to use a spell to make mine return to me."

But I had traces before I learned to use mind control.

"You never felt anything before?" I ask. "No thoughts or weird feelings?"

Zak shakes his head. "Did you?"

I pause, and my mother draws in a breath. "Azra, why didn't you tell me?"

"Because I didn't know *what* I was feeling. It only started recently. After my birthday."

"It must be the release of your powers that triggered it, then," Zak says. "That permitted the memories to begin to return to you."

My powers that I've actually always had. This is the one thing that remains unsaid. My mother doesn't bring it up and neither do I.

My father's mind control left my mother feeling like something was off; it went a step further and left me with ghosts of my past. I hope it has something to do with my unfettered ability to do magic or even my Afrit heritage. Because I'd hate for this to happen to Nate or Megan or George or Goldie. For them to be left with perpetual déjà vu because of me.

Did I always know, deep down, that something was missing? Is that why I pushed so hard against everything Jinn, including my Zar sisters? The lies my mother told me made me who I am. What if I had known? Would I still be me?

Like cars on a Ferris wheel, my emotions go round and round. Hurt, anger, shock, joy, longing, fear. Just when I think one car has settled on the ground and off-loaded its passengers, it finds its way back to the tippy top. Right now, feeling left out is riding high.

I face my mother. "Did you ever want to tell me the truth?"

"Every morning, every afternoon, and every night," she says.

"We could have shared it," I say.

Zak pours himself more wine. "She shared everything else with you, Azra. She shared herself, which she didn't have to do."

"What do you mean?" I say. Zak's lips flatten into a thin line. I ask my mother. "What does he mean?"

She ignores me and kneels in front of Zak. "Your father told you?"

Zak takes a swig of wine and nods.

"I'm sorry," she says softly. "It . . . it was an impossible choice."

I bend down and cram my face so close to my mother's that our noses touch. "What choice? What are you talking about?"

My mother swats me away. "The only thing I couldn't bring myself to put in writing. And don't think we won't talk about you using spells and reading my diary, Azra." Then, with a deep breath, she begins to speak slowly, unable to look directly at me or Zak. "Your father being an Afrit came with some advantages. He and Zak did have to leave here. There was no way around that. But . . ."

"But what?" I prod.

"She could have left too," Zak says briskly. "She could have left here and lived in Janna with our father and—"

"You," I say.

"Or remain in this world with—"

"Me." Suddenly I feel like I'm two inches tall.

My mother chose me. Over my brother. Over my father. She chose me. Every time I lashed out at her, blamed her, made her hurt, made her angry, made her cry, did she regret it?

Though he speaks to me, Zak's eyes are focused on the glass he has just placed on the table. "Her choice came with lying to you in order to keep you safe. You can't resent her for that any more than I can resent you for being what made her stay."

My mother takes his hands. "But you resent me, don't you? At least a little?"

Zak shrugs, but it's clearly a "yes" shrug. "But I understand. That's the way it was. That's the way it still is. And that's what Father is trying to fix."

He then begins to tell my mother—our mother—how Xavier sent him here without the Afrit's knowledge, let alone consent. Because in just a few more days, my delay in granting Megan's wish would have been discovered. Zak was the only one Xavier trusted to see what was taking me so long.

But Zak wasn't supposed to risk getting into contact with our mother or revealing himself to me. He confirms what little my mother has told me: that a growing number of Jinn do want to challenge the Afrit. Xavier—it might take time to call him "Dad"—has been working to prevent a true revolt of this faction in Janna, hoping to change things diplomatically instead. He's deep into his plans to win over the council, to convince them to reverse all of the restrictions the Afrit have put in place over the years.

Zak doesn't seem to know more. I can't tell whether my mother knows more and isn't telling or there isn't more to know. All her diary said is that she's been under pressure from both Raina and

Samara to admit that things couldn't go on as they have been and that it was time to do something about it. She's been too afraid to risk it, writing in her diary that she's lost too much already. I now know that "too much" means Zak.

Though I want to know more about all of this, my mother wants to know more about Zak. While she asks him about his favorite food (cookies, especially ones made with mescouta, which I learn are dates), I head into the kitchen to put together a plate of snacks. Clearing the skeletons out of the closet has made us all hungry.

And Zak is quite an old skeleton. Nineteen years old, to be exact. They all lived together as a family before I was born. I never got the chance to be a part of the full Nadira clan—the full Afrit-Nadira clan. Zak left with our father shortly after I was born, when the Afrit commanded all males to return to Janna.

Their time together was short, but it's more than I've ever had. Even if you add up all the times they visited, it doesn't equal three years. Still, my mother chose me. I can't be bitter about what could have been, especially when what *could have been* could have been a hell of a lot worse.

The wish I've made on every birthday, on every shooting star, on every eyelash since I can remember, the wish I thought could never come true, has. I have the family I've always wanted.

But the holes—left by my father, left by Jenny, left by the Afrit who forced us to lose so much of our lives together—are still there.

The difference is, I'm ready to fill them.

I load on the pita chips and plop an extra scoop of hummus on the mosaic-tiled plate because we are now three.

11

When I wake up, it's like nothing has changed. The lilac bush under my window fills my room with the same sweet, floral scent. My wardrobe spills from my closet in the same boring black, white, and gray color scheme. The framed picture of Jenny and me kneeling on the grass with the tiny Laila standing on our backs sits in the same spot on my nightstand.

My entire world has changed, but nothing in this room shows it.

With the tingle of pins and needles down my spine, Zak apps into my bedroom.

There, that's better.

He rests on the end of my bed. He's wearing the same clothes he arrived in that first day.

"Mom doing your laundry?" I ask.

When I went to bed last night, the two of them were still on the couch. I've had days alone with Zak. My mother deserved some private time with him—and he with her. I heard them talking, softly, until I fell asleep. In a house that's normally silent once I burrow under my down comforter, it was strange. And nice.

Zak fiddles with the silver beads around his neck. "Considering I'm not supposed to be here, I can't exactly return in human garb."

"Return?" I say in an innocent voice. "You're not staying here? There's plenty of bedrooms. Mom and I can butch one up for you if they're too girly." I give a nervous laugh. "Which reminds me, where have you been staying, anyway?"

"Azra." Zak inches closer to me. "Sister. It's time. I have to go home."

I draw my white comforter up around my shoulders. "But this is your home."

"It was my home. Maybe it will be again. But at the moment, this is not my home."

"But don't you want to get to know Mom?"

Don't you want to get to know me?

Zak sighs. "More than anything. I don't want to leave either of you, but I must. Father and I have no way of communicating while I am here. He had to lower the shield that blocks apporting between the worlds save for those who can shape-shift so I could come through, but he couldn't leave it down. Someone would find out. We agreed on a single day that he would lower it again."

"Today."

"Neither of us believed my mission here would take this long. He padded my time so I could get to know you, even if it wasn't supposed to be as your brother." He gives me a devilish smile. "It is a good thing he tacked on the extra, is it not?"

I punch him in the arm.

"*Rahmah!*" he cries.

My heart swims all the way up to my throat. This is how my mother must have felt every time my father returned. This must be how it was every time she faced him, waiting for him to make her forget again.

"But we just got you back," I say.

Zak finds the outline of my fingers under the comforter and presses his hand on top of my own. "I will always come back, Sister. This will be for now, but not forever."

He pushes up the sleeve of his tunic. An intricate tattoo of curled lines and shapes marks his upper arm. I study it further. It's not lines and shapes. I tilt my head. It's a collection of letters. Letters that form words. Tattooed onto Zak's arm are the words "Always. But not forever."

They are the words our father said to our mother before he left for Janna—before both he and Zak left for Janna. I read them in my mother's diary.

"*Always. I'll love you both always.*" He said this to my mother while I was still cocooned in her belly. "*This will be for now, but not forever.*"

I lean in and trace the letters with one finger. As I inch back, Zak traps my finger, then my hand, and then me, drawing me into his arms.

"I told you it wouldn't be the last time we saw each other," Zak says. "And neither will this."

We spent the day at the beach as a family. Me, Zak, and my mother. With our picnic basket, our red-and-white-checked blanket, our

Frisbee throwing, and our kite flying, I'm pretty sure the waves were crashing to the beat of "Kumbaya." It makes me glad it was Nate's day off.

Now, as Zak and I sit on the front steps, the sun hangs low in the sky. My mother's upstairs in her bedroom writing a letter for Zak to bring to our father. She asked me to do the same. But I don't want to waste a single moment Zak and I have left together.

Suddenly, Zak stands. "There's something I have to do before I go. It won't take long."

Apparently my brother doesn't feel the same as I do.

"What?" I say. "I'll come with you."

"I can't tell you, and you can't come with me."

I start to protest when he puts up his hand.

"For the love of Janna, please don't," he says. "Just trust me. Father's going to stuff me like a leg of lamb when he finds out I told you as much as I did. Can you please not add more balsam to my pyre?"

I nod reluctantly.

"Now that's a good little Jinn," he says as he enters the house.

"Don't you mean Afrit?"

"We're all the same, Sister." And with a wink, he disappears.

My brother's more forgiving than I, just like Henry. And my brother's leaving, just like Henry.

At least I'll have another couple of days before Henry's gone, which is good. Dropping the A-bomb that is Zak shouldn't be done via text.

Neither should the embarrassing silly-faced emoticon I'm currently sending to Nate, but I can't help myself. I've never lived with anyone other than my mom. It's only been a day, but already I miss Goldie's Nutella-laced oatmeal, George's cursing at the Red Sox, and Megan's breathing beside me at night. And Nate. I miss Nate. The way he'd sit at the end of the couch, tickling my feet while I read, the way he'd lean in when I checked my phone for a reply from Laila, and the way he'd wrap his hand around mine and we'd both know we weren't alone.

For a fleeting second, I thought Zak would help fill the hole left by the Reeses and the Carwyns. But once again, the Afrit's desires come before mine.

Across the street, the front door of the Carwyns' home opens and out comes Chelsea. Her car was parked in the driveway this morning and doesn't appear to have moved all day. Since both of Henry's parents already started their new jobs, he's been finishing the move solo. With Chelsea's continuing help, it seems. So more like solo-ish.

She waves but barely meets my eyes as she scurries to her car. She leaves the top up as she backs out and drives away. I don't get a beep, let alone a beepity beep beep.

I tuck my phone in my pocket and walk across the street. I knock before I let myself in.

"Henry?" I call as I enter the living room. The empty living room. There's an ache in my chest as I survey the Carwyns' home, the place I knew every inch of when Jenny was alive.

But now the crack in the wall where Henry shot a plastic arrow at Jenny's head when we were seven is gone, covered by spackle and a new coat of mocha paint. I wonder who chose the shade, Chelsea or Henry?

The carpet on the stairs still flaunts its age, though my hand skims over a fresh layer of glossy white on the railing. I pause before the second-to-last step, afraid it won't creak in the center. I put my foot down.

It does.

I breathe a sigh of relief as Henry pokes his head out of his bedroom door, one down from the room that used to be Jenny's, then Lisa's, and will now belong to a complete stranger.

"Hey," Henry says.

I follow him into his bedroom. Gone are the guitar he hasn't gotten around to learning how to play, the map of the world, the model AT-AT. No desk, no red footlocker at the end of his bed. The only thing in the room is a mattress on the floor. Home to a pile of crumpled sheets.

"Weird, isn't it?" Henry says, running his hand through his gelled hair. "Seeing the place like this? I'm not sure what's worse. This or the storage unit jammed with everything that's supposed to be here. My mom wanted to leave it all. Let the renters trash it and every bad memory she associates with this place."

"And your dad wanted to take it all." Henry's dad being unable to leave the house he believes is his last connection to Jenny is why the Carwyns are moving. His dad refused to relocate to New York and lost his job.

Henry nods. "Even the blinds. So now it all sits in limbo—nowhere."

Like us?

I sigh. "Life is compromise, after all."

Henry grins. He knows as well as I do that this is my mother's favorite saying.

As he gestures for me to sit on the bed, he notices the mess of sheets and flings the top one up toward the pillows. Is this where he and Chelsea spent the entire day? What could they have possibly been doing in this room where there's not even a chair to—

Oh. No. Really? *Oh . . .*

I levitate a pillow and sit cross-legged on it a good distance away from the bed.

Henry drops onto the mattress across from me.

Neither of us says a word.

I shift on the pillow and use my powers to snag another. The instant it floats up from the mattress, something falls down.

Henry reaches for it, but my magic's faster and it's in my hand in an instant. I open my palm to find an earring. Pale blue, pink, green, and yellow stones dangle from the silver chandelier earring. One half of the pair Chelsea bought at the mall.

We spring up at the exact same moment.

"Azra, wait," Henry says. "I can explain."

"We were in the same health class, Henry. I think I've got a pretty good handle on all this." I race for the door but a whirlwind of sensations overwhelms me and I plant my hand on the doorjamb to steady myself. "They're . . . they're all coming," I stammer out.

"All? Who all?"

"Yasmin and Samara and . . . and I think Laila."

Samara's deep sexy laugh echoes through the empty house for a split second before it zaps out and we hear it through the open window of Henry's bedroom.

They must have been about to apport into the house when they sensed Henry's human presence and rerouted to the front door. But why would they app here? They couldn't have all misjudged so much that they'd arrive here instead of our house across the street.

The doorbell rings.

"Were you expecting someone?" I ask.

Henry's puzzled face becomes even more confused. "No. And what just happened?"

A triple rap on the door downstairs precedes Samara's "Hello? Mr. and Mrs. Carwyn?"

My "What the—" and Henry's "Is that—" collide the same way our bodies do as we hurl ourselves out of his room and to the staircase landing.

Standing below us, outlined against the coffee walls, are Lalla Samara, Yasmin, and Laila. And more suitcases than I can count.

"Well, isn't this a lovely surprise," Samara says, giving me a wink.

12

"WHAT ARE YOU DOING HERE?" I ASK, GLUED TO THE LANDING upon seeing Laila again. After running into each other at the mall, she's finally started responding to my texts. Though mostly fishing for information about Zak.

Yasmin places her hands on her curvy hips. "Nice to see you too, Azra."

Her lips parted, Laila seems incapable of making the decision to speak. Samara's mouth moves at its usual warp speed, commenting on everything from the large picture window to the dated but functional kitchen to the screened-in porch behind it.

"Charming, simply charming." Samara glides back across the small living room. "This will do nicely." She pauses to peer into the wood-burning fireplace. "Perfect for our purposes."

Henry brushes past me down the stairs. "You're Mrs. Nelson?"

"*Mizz*, darling. Ms. Malak," Samara replies. "Or better yet, simply Sam, dear Henry, since the cat's out of the bag. So much for my nom de plume."

"That's for books," I say.

"Really?" Sam asks skeptically.

"Pretty sure."

"Well, now that's a shame. It's got such flair." Her golden waves float down her back as she shrugs and faces Henry. "Hope you don't mind us dropping by. We wanted to take some measurements."

"Measurements?" I ask, following Henry to the first floor. "For what?"

Samara surveys the room. "Well, now that I'm here, I'm thinking a cozy love seat over there and a fluffy armchair somewhere over here and, oh, maybe even a pouf or two. What do you think, Laila?"

Laila crosses her arms in front of her D-cup chest. "Oh, now I get a say?"

I move deeper into the room. The apricot aroma that has accompanied Samara as long as I can remember greets me as I stand in front of her. "You're moving in? Here?" I turn toward Henry. "But the renters—"

Yasmin huffs. "We *are* the renters. All that time in the sun around your hunky lifeguard fry one too many brain cells, Azra?"

"Way to stereotype, Yasmin. My hunky life—I mean, my lifeguard—I mean, Nate isn't dumb."

Laila realizes she's smiling and sucks in her cheeks to stop.

With a rumbling laugh, Samara circles around to Henry and drapes an arm around his shoulder. Like my mother, but unlike my Zar sisters, Sam knows that Henry's in on our Jinn secret. "This will always be your home, Henry, dear. We're honored to keep"—she twists him to face me—"*all* that you leave behind safe while you're away." She looks from him to me and back again before guiding him toward the stairs. "But in the meantime, would you be a love and show me and Yasmin upstairs so we can choose our bedrooms?"

"Perfect." Laila snorts. "Because why should I get a choice in anything?"

She pushes her long blond hair off her neck, and I notice she's not wearing her infinity necklace. I clutch my *A*. Neither am I, though if I had known there was even a chance of seeing her, I would be. On my sixteenth birthday, Laila gave me and the rest of our Zar sisters matching silver chains, each bearing a pendant in the shape of a figure eight on its side—the symbol for "never ending."

And I thanked her for her generosity by not fessing up about stealing the locket with the photograph of her father inside.

Samara shoves Henry and Yasmin up the stairs. "You have plenty of choices, Laila, dear. Let's start hoping you make the right ones. Both of you."

I catch Laila glancing my way, and when our eyes meet, she turns away, conjures a square pink pouf, and flops down on it. "Subtle as brain freeze from an ice cream cone."

She crosses her newly longer legs, and I can't stop staring. She's still the Laila I grew up with. But she's different too. She's finally the genie she always wanted to be. She's been the one distancing herself from me instead of the other way around. And while she's my oldest friend, she's no longer my only friend. But that doesn't mean I don't need her—desperately.

I conjure a matching though intentionally subpar lumpy pink pouf and sit across from her. "You're actually moving in here? Across the street?"

"Apparently." Her hand travels the length of her body. "*This* means I can no longer attend my school."

Does that mean she's going to be coming to mine? My heart flutters for an instant before it sinks. Because my happiness is at the expense of hers, which I vowed to never let be the case again.

"I'm sorry, Laila. I know how much you didn't want that to happen. I also know from personal experience how much your friends are going to miss you."

Her eyes meet mine, lingering longer this time. Gold replaced their former blue and being Jinn replaced their innocence. With the most minimal of movements, she nods to me and her face softens.

This new Laila seems a lot more like me. We'd get along well. No, we *will* get along well. It's just too bad I can't read Jinn minds like my Afrit family can. If I could, then maybe I'd know the right thing to say to Laila. I tread slowly, starting with the simple, "How has it been, living with Yasmin?"

"Sad." Laila adds fringe to the side of her pouf, and my heart balloons with pride at her skill. "She's Yasmin, so she's not exactly open to many heart-to-hearts. But I know she's hurting."

An understatement, but the right words to describe what Yasmin must be feeling don't seem to exist. Her mother, Raina, was removed from our world and thrown, presumably, in tortura cavea for having a role in the burgeoning uprising against the Afrit.

While both my mother and I were hoping Zak would know more about Raina, it seems to be just me who was hoping he'd know more about the uprising and just how burgeoning it is. Unfortunately, he's out of the loop on both counts.

As much as there might be to gain from a successful coup against the Afrit, there's a lot we can all lose. Especially us active Jinn. Because unlike with retired Jinn, the Afrit don't just punish the perpetrator of the crime against them. They punish what the perpetrator loves. If I screw up again, the path that leads to my cozy jail cell with my greatest fear for a roommate won't be a straight line like Raina's.

The Afrit need Jinn to continue granting wishes for humans. It is this act of using our magic for the "greater good" that maintains our side of the bargain with the natural world and allows us to keep our magic. Since the Afrit can't afford to lose me and my wish-granting skills, they'll punish me by hurting the ones I love— my mother, her Zar sisters, and the humans I've grown close to. Henry and Nate and who knows who else. I always knew attachments to humans were discouraged, but I didn't know why.

It's one thing to make a personal sacrifice, like Raina did (though one look at Yasmin would challenge the definition of "personal"), but it's another to put the innocent at risk. The Afrit have us by our *couilles* (though Henry and I both take French with Mrs. Olsen, I learned that's the word for "balls" from him).

"Wonderful idea your mother had, isn't it?" Samara's bubbly voice floats down the stairs a moment before her voluptuous self follows. "Our house is being fumed, this lovely home was in need of bodies, so here we are!"

This was my mother's idea?

"Mom's as subtle as Samara's cleavage," I whisper.

Laila lets herself grin.

I've now got a smile that makes my cheeks ache as I turn to Samara. "I think it's 'fumigated,' Lalla Sam."

"Really?" She and Laila cock their heads the exact same way. "Well," Samara then says, "regardless, it's a temporary situation. So whenever your family wants to shoo us out the door and move back in, just let us know, Henry."

Guilt must be chomping away at my mother like a flesh-eating virus. She's not only brought Laila here to help heal the rift between us, she's making sure Henry's family can return home easily, without having to worry about tenants whose lease they couldn't break.

I guess her lying to me about Zak my entire life trumps anything I've done lately.

"Tomorrow's your last night here, Henry?" Samara asks.

Still looking like a deer caught in the headlights, he nods. "But if you need to move in tonight, I can go—"

"Nonsense. The fumes don't start gating for a few days." She sweeps her hand over the luggage, pausing to smile at our two pink poufs. "We just wanted to drop off a few things."

One of those things poking out the side of a leopard-print suitcase just happens to be Mr. Gemp, the gold genie lantern with the long spout and curved handle that Yasmin originally found and that's made the rounds to each of my Zar sisters on their sixteenth birthdays, including me. I was the last one to have it. I deposited it on Laila's doorstep after she turned sixteen. It's a good sign she didn't toss it in the trash; it's an even better sign that it's among the first things to be brought to her new home.

Samara leans against the doorway to the kitchen, eyeing each of us and tapping her foot. Suddenly, excitement flashes through her eyes. "Azra, your mother and I are having a ladies' night out on the town tomorrow." She raises an eyebrow. "So if anyone wanted to throw a certain someone a going-away something, and invite anyone's cousins, who haven't all been together in quite a while, there would be no eyes a-prying."

Subtle as a Jinn's love of sweets.

Yasmin plops down on the pouf next to Laila. The sadness in her eyes somehow adds to her beauty. It softens her.

"Just don't set anything on fire," Samara adds.

Unlike my mother, whose after-prom party was so smokin' Samara had to learn to conjure water. If I invite Yasmin, Laila, and the rest of our "cousins," my party will be smokin' in an entirely different way.

Laila plays with the fringe on her pouf. "It *would* be nice to meet *people* before school starts . . ."

"People" clearly means Zak. Still, the flutter in my chest returns. "You'll come?"

She nods, and so that's it.

I'm throwing a party.

13

I'VE NEVER THROWN A PARTY.

But I know someone who has.

While Laila moving in takes some of the sting out of both Henry and Zak leaving, I'm still not exactly in the mood for blowing up balloons. But that wouldn't be fair to Henry. He deserves a good-bye party. Something I should have thought of myself.

I leave Henry with Samara, who's asking instructions on how to use the gas stove (which, with her history, she shouldn't touch—ever), and dial as I walk across the street.

Mina answers on the first ring.

"I'm thinking upscale campfire," she says, "in honor of Henry's new home state."

"How did you—"

"Oh, babycakes, Laila texted me ages ago."

Ages?

"So Evites, obviously," she continues, her voice full of her signature bubbliness. "I already texted Farrah." Of course. The two of them are as close as canned sardines. "And she's getting a list of names from her albino beach boy."

"He's not albino. He's just pale."

"I thought so too. But we were just at your little beach and that boy's as transparent as he was at the start of the summer. Mr. Cellophane's got some hot friends though." Mina's innocent baby face hides the truth of her very guilty party-girl self.

"I don't want this to get too big," I say, regretting making this call.

Silence.

"One-fifty?" Mina says.

"Are you crazy? Henry doesn't know a hundred and fifty people."

"You mean *you* don't know a hundred and fifty people."

Snarky? Really? Well then ... "Ten."

Clunk!

I pull my phone away from my ear, unsure if Mina hung up on me or dropped her phone.

Muffled sounds precede Mina's *"Ten?"*

Dropped, it seems.

"But we're seven with all of us and your cute boy!"

Nate? Oh, she must mean Henry. Nate and Henry. Together again. And don't forget Chelsea. Hey, at least I can return her earring.

I do not want to be picturing what I'm currently picturing.

Instead I picture my five magnetic, quirky, hypnotizingly beautiful Zar sisters mingling with half the incoming—*human*—juniors and seniors of my high school. What could go wrong?

By the time I make it back to my room, we've settled on forty of Henry's nearest and dearest, I've negotiated her K-pop band inside and minimalist techno band outside down to Farrah playing iPod DJ, and left Mina to decide what booze needs conjuring.

Though she needs a good editor, Mina sure is saving my Jinn butt. After what happened with Laila, I wasn't sure how my Zar sisters might treat me. I know Laila told Hana that I stole her locket. Maybe Mina's being so helpful because she and Farrah don't know?

"Hey, Mina, can I ask you something?"

"Hmm . . . hold on, I'm almost . . . Wait . . . Okay . . . okay . . . there we go."

Sounds of sniffing. Then swallowing. Then spitting.

"Everything okay?" I ask.

"*Ack* . . . paint thinner. Whatever I just conjured tastes like lemon-flavored paint thinner."

"What were you trying for?"

"Limoncello."

"I'm assuming that's not a type of string instrument?"

"Azra, we have to get you out more." Another swallow, another *ack*. "Maybe Yasmin can do better. She drank enough of it on the Amalfi."

"Amalfi? As in coast? As in Italy?"

Silence. Again. "Some of us might have spent the past couple of weeks on holiday."

"Some?"

"Just me and Farrah and Hana and Yasmin and Laila."

"So all, then." My Zar sisters went on vacation together. Without me. I thought we were past this. I thought Laila was on the verge of forgiving me. *Stop, Azra. Don't start inventing problems.* That's what my mother always tells me. I was bound by the circulus curse. I couldn't have gone even if they'd asked. *But they could have waited . . .*

"It wasn't a twenty-four/seven party or anything," Mina says slowly. "We were trying to help Yasmin. Not that she'd let us. Sun, Chianti, Italian men, baby-butt-smooth leather purses . . . Did I mention Italian men? And we barely got her onto the balcony. I mean, it's not like I expect her to forget or not be sad, but she's just so . . . angry."

As I would be. Yasmin and I have more in common than either of us cares to admit.

"And Laila?" I ask tentatively. "Was . . . Is she angry too?"

Mina sighs. "Listen, I'm not the black-robe-wearing, gavel-slamming type, Azra. This is between you two. But for what it's worth, a pair of front-row concert tickets and backstage passes helped smooth things over after my little indiscretion with Farrah's Italian stallion."

"Mina!"

"I said it was little." Mina laughs, and I can just see her twirling a lock of her chestnut hair. "Get it? *Ba-dum-bump.*"

"Please, don't. Besides, I don't think that's going to work with Laila."

"Then figure out what will. Find something she loves and give it to her."

Something she loves . . . I haven't been around her enough lately to know what that might be. I am the worst friend. No, I *was* the worst friend. Admitting is the first step, right?

"She's super psyched about the party," Mina says. "If that dude from the mall just happens to be there, you're golden."

If only the dude from the mall could be there.

"The party's an awesome idea," Mina continues. "Lalla Sam's a genius. Your mom too."

"So you know Laila's moving in across the street?"

"And Yasmin. Don't forget Yasmin. Maybe you'll have better luck with her than we did. She's mopey, bitter . . . you know, more like you."

"Hey!"

"Fine, the old you." The smack of her delicate pink lips hurts my eardrum. "Now you call that perky blonde who was throwing herself at your Henry all summer, and we'll be set."

Chelsea *was* throwing herself at him, wasn't she? Not that Henry minded donning a baseball mitt. Doesn't matter. I have my hunky lifeguard. *Right?*

"Azra, it's time." My mother's tall body appears slight as she stands next to Zak. The red lining her gold eyes and the wounded smile on her face match his.

And I wish Henry and his mitt were here.

Logs should be round, right? Because that's the third one I've conjured that's more of a trapezoid.

I'm supposed to be conjuring tumblers out of tree limbs to go with Mina's woodsy party theme, but I'm distracted. If you can call my eyes leaking like a tapped maple tree distracted. Saying good-bye to Zak—to my brother—has sparked the ricocheting in my veins. The wrenching of my internal organs I felt while out of range of Megan was a massage compared to this. My mother spent three years with Zak and longer with my father, and she had to let them both go. I knew she was strong, but I had no idea her shoulders could bear this much weight.

I arrange my collection of angular logs in the fireplace in my room and try to focus on the party. I was hoping the distraction I'm feeling would be in the opposite direction. That planning Henry's send-off would take my mind off of lumping Zak into the "lost and found and lost again" bin.

So much has happened so fast, most of it doesn't feel real. Dragooning, hadi, Megan's wish, Nate and me the other night, leaving the Reeses', Zak being my brother, my mother choosing me, Henry and Chelsea earlier tonight, Laila moving across the street, Zak returning to Janna . . . and one more time, Nate and me the other night, Henry and Chelsea earlier tonight.

My brain is full.

Nate wanted to video-chat, but I couldn't let him see me like this, not without being able to tell him the cause. There's so much lying in my life—from me, to me, about me. I can't always be honest with Nate, but I'm trying to limit my lies to those of omission as opposed to full-on works of fiction.

We talked for a while, and I even followed a bit of his lacrosse-practice recap by putting my phone on speaker and looking up things like "raking" and "man down defense," but he lost me when he segued into "Canadian egg roll" and "carry the pizza." Truly, that's one bizarre sport. I told him about Laila moving in, and his excitement perked me up for a while. But then a splinter rammed itself under my fingernail and my first thought was *Rahmah!* and that was it. I couldn't cover anymore.

Even without the visual, he knew something was wrong. Lately it feels like the connection with Nate from granting his wish isn't just one way.

Suddenly the sting of pins and needles prickles my spine.

What the——?

The sensation gets stronger.

I spin around like an overzealous Labradoodle. But I'm alone.

Then why does it feel like Zak just aported in? *How* can it feel like Zak just aported in? He left hours ago.

Wishing doesn't make it so, Azra.

My full brain is playing tricks on me.

I shake it off and wander across the hall, poking my head into my mother's bedroom. She's asleep as I knew she would be. Though I received a lecture about invading her privacy and practicing the advanced magic of spells without her permission, she couldn't deny my skill. Apparently, I've graduated to the supervised use of spells. Mostly, I think, so she could have me use one on her tonight to ease the pain of Zak leaving. The sleeping spell she had me do made her zonk out immediately, and she'll remain comatose well past morning.

Unfortunately, there's no way I can sleep. Maybe I'll do better with the tumblers if I start with real wood.

I'm halfway down the stairs when a flick of light goes on and then off just as fast. I freeze. This isn't a trick. At least not one being played by me. A chair scrapes against the wood floor. I hold my breath. Then come muffled voices. From the kitchen. Male voices.

I am so *not* alone.

"I've got it." From an unknown male voice.

"*Rahmah*, will you keep it down." From Zak's voice.

Zak? I charge down the stairs, not caring if I'm heard. I intend to not only be heard but to be heard loudly. Zak said he was leaving. He lied, and not by omission.

Right before he—right before *they*—app away, I catch a glimpse of my brother and the shaggy-haired dude from the high school. The one whose clothes made him look like Zak's twin. He still does. Except for the tangerine hue of his choppy hair.

Apping requires us to picture an object that resides in our intended destination. With time and skill, the name of the destination itself is enough. I wonder if the same is true of the reverse: if the name of the object will suffice.

I grind my heels into the floor, tune my breathing to the rhythm of my heart, which beats at the speed of a hummingbird, and focus on the name of one object.

Zak.

14

My blood boils and not just from the act of apporting when I materialize across from my brother.

His mouth hangs open. I stroll over to him, place my hand under his chin, and clamp his jaw shut.

"Azra! What are you doing here?" he says.

"Nuh-uh. The question is, what are you *still* doing here?" I jut my thumb toward Mr. I Don't Really Own a Dog. "And who's this?"

This is currently taking a seat on top of a rolling green carry-on bag in the middle of the woods. I swivel my head around. The woods behind Nate's house.

And *This* is smirking. Long and parted down the center, his red hair skims the top of his ear as he tilts his head to the side. He places his hand over his heart. "*Hala*. It is a pleasure to meet you finally, Azra."

A puff of orange hair sticks out from the open collar of his knee-length white tunic.

The way he strokes his scruffy beard makes him appear

nonchalant, unfazed. But his hand that twirls a slim black pen and his copper eyes that dart between me and Zak seem very, very fazed.

He shifts on top of the carry-on.

"What's in the bag?" I ask.

He hesitates for a split second. "Personal items."

Something's not right. *They'll come for her.*

In an instant, I app from my current spot and reappear directly behind *This*. I shove him off the suitcase, knock the bag to the ground, and unzip it with my powers.

On top of a pile of designer jeans, black T-shirts, and striped oxfords is a digital frame. I turn it on right before *This* snatches it out of my hand.

He clutches it to his chest. But the wrong way. The picture faces me, not his stomach. The picture of Hana.

"Oh my Janna," I say. "You're Hana's brother?"

Before Zak appeared, I thought Lalla Nadia, Hana's mother, was the only member of my mother's Zar sisterhood who had a son. Like so many things, the existence of Hana's brother was never discussed.

Zak sighs as he sweeps his hand to the side. "Azra, meet Matin." He then brings two fingers to each temple, rubbing as if attempting to drill holes. "Father is going to roast me on the pyre himself. And it's all your fault." He glares at Matin.

"My fault?" Matin says. "Forgive me, *habib*, my dear friend, but aren't you the one who forgot your mother's letter?"

"But I could have returned to the house for it alone. The same way I was supposed to travel here alone." Zak faces me. "Father arranged for me to apport from an obscure location surrounded by stone two feet thick. No one would be able to sense me leaving or arriving. But this one followed—"

Matin smirks. "You and I share similar thinking, Azra."

Zak ignores him. "He tackled me as I was going through."

"It was not simply a tackle." Matin turns to me. "It was an extraordinary tackle. I leapt from two yards away."

"One," Zak growls.

Matin shrugs. "You continue to believe that if it makes you feel better."

"Wait," I say, approaching Matin. He's actually a bit shorter than my brother, with more of a tackling-appropriate football-player build. His jaw is squared off, unlike Hana's, and his lips smirk a hell of a lot more than hers do (guess that's more nurture than nature), but the resemblance is obvious. Too obvious. Now that I'm up close, I see he's less Zak's twin and more Hana's. If she or Lalla Nadia saw him . . .

"You came to see Hana? And your mother?" I ask.

Matin's smirk dissolves into a sad smile. "That I did. But only from a distance." Bending over his suitcase, he pushes aside an argyle sweater to reveal a pair of binoculars and a digital camera with a massive lens. Huh, I would have thought Jinn in Janna had much more advanced snooping methods.

Matin rises to his feet. "Though my mother and sister could not know I was here, I would be as preposterous as a captive Jinn to pass up a chance to see them. Being able to mosey on over here is not an opportunity that surfaces often."

I reach out and wrap my hand around his forearm. His tunic may be even softer than Zak's. I resist the urge to pet him. "I'm sorry, Matin."

"Mat, call me Mat."

"She's not going to be calling you anything because we have to leave," Zak snaps. His tone then softens as he says, "I'm sorry, Azra, but this is our only window. If we don't go now, we won't be able to."

My "good" doesn't leave my lips, but Zak reads it on my face.

"We'd be missed," he says. "I'm assuming Father lumped Matin in with me when he discovered he was gone. But there's only so long he can fake our stay in tortura cavea for having illegal goods." Zak tips his head toward the suitcase. "Which all of that is. You know you can't bring any of it, Matin."

Matin drops to his knees and shoves the digital frame under a fuzzy lime-green scarf I recognize.

"That's Hana's," I say.

His head jerks back and his cheeks flush. "I am not normally a thief, Azra. I merely wanted a keepsake."

I nod in understanding. "Did you know she made it?"

He smiles a real smile, not a smirk. "No, I did not. I could see she had exquisite taste, but I did not know the same could be said of her talent as well."

And there's nature rearing its head. Both Hana and Matin appear to share a love of fashion.

I resist the urge to smack my hand against my head. "The clothes." I turn to Zak. "All those extra shirts and jeans you were conjuring that weren't in your size? They were for Mat?"

I realize Matin's neck is bare. He doesn't have a silver necklace, which means he doesn't have powers.

Matin pats a linen shirt in his carry-on. "Thanks for teaching him to conjure so well, Azra. It made my stay here quite enjoyable."

He zips up the suitcase and rolls it toward me. With a quick peck on each cheek, he says, "I'm glad we were able to meet if ever so briefly." He nudges the suitcase toward me. "Find it all a nice home, if you will?"

"Sure." I rest my hand on the extended handle, surprised at how much I want to do this for him. I don't know what I intended to find when I followed them, but it certainly wasn't Matin.

Zak and Matin move to a spot I now see is marked with an *X* by two pieces of wood.

"Our return must be from the same location as our arrival," Zak says.

I cross my arms. "And that was your only way of distinguishing it? What if a squirrel or a deer came prancing through and knocked your *X* right off its spot?"

Matin points above their heads. A silver scarf is looped around a branch more than fifteen feet above the ground. "You and your brother think alike. He made me climb this blasted thing. And now my scarf will be fodder for a bird's nest."

Using my powers, I unwind the scarf and float it down to him.

"*Shukran*, my dear Azra," he says. "Thank you. You have my gratitude. I hope we see each other again. In the meantime, perhaps you could keep an eye on my family?"

I nod solemnly.

Zak breathes deeply and is about to say something, but I shake my head at him. I can't go through another good-bye with Zak. He understands.

There's nothing I can do. He has to go back.

I watch him grasp Matin's elbow.

But that doesn't mean I can't go with him.

15

"It's so not my fault!" I say as I rub my shoulder. A bruise is already forming from my collision with Zak's granite chest.

"*Khallas!*" He throws his hands in the air. "Enough! Surely it is your fault. Father was to lower the shield today. For us to return through this very spot. The only reason we didn't go through is because you launched at us like a Jinn on a dessert buffet!"

"But that doesn't make any sense. How would the shield, how would *this spot*, know I was here?"

Zak paces back and forth in front of the X. "I—I—I do not know." His eyes are focused on his wringing hands. He grabs Matin by the end of his tunic. "Let's try it again." With more fear than anger, he says, "Please, don't, Azra."

He's spooked. Instantly, I take several steps back, and Zak nods appreciatively at me.

They both move into position. Zak puffs out his chest and closes his eyes. I watch air fill and then deflate his stomach. Again and again. But nothing happens. Neither one of them budges from the X.

"Maybe it has something to do with you, Matin," Zak says. "Let me attempt this myself. If it works, I'll check in with Father and come back for you." He tips his head toward the green carry-on. "But not that."

A dozen times, he tries. Together, separately, and together again. They can't get through. They can't apport into Janna.

"But why?" I ask.

"I . . . I . . ." Zak's eyes dart to me, to Matin, and then back to me. "I bet I have the wrong day. Yes, that must be it. In fact, I'm convinced of it."

He's trying to infuse his tone with lightness, but I can tell it's an act. It must be for Matin's benefit. But Matin's known Zak much longer than I have. If I know Zak's covering something, doesn't he?

If he does, he doesn't care. He leaves the X without hesitation, shoves his hand into the front of his suitcase, and then tosses Zak a cell phone. "So we are to remain here?"

Zak scratches his chin. "Temporarily."

"How very excellent," Matin says. What I think at first is a bit of fear or nerves flitting across his eyes is simply excitement. "Maybe I'll engage in conversation with Hana, after all. She doesn't have to know my true identity. You didn't know about Zak, Azra, is that correct?"

"But I didn't know I had a brother. She does."

He frowns. "Are you going to prevent me from speaking with her?"

Desperation oozes from his every pore.

"No," I say. Zak starts to protest, but I cut him off by facing Matin directly. "You can talk to her, but you can't do it looking like that." I conjure a pair of scissors and tap the suitcase. "Have a seat, Goldilocks."

"Goldie? But my hair is red."

"It's an expression."

"An odd one."

"Sit."

He flops down on the carry-on, digging his fingers into the soft nylon with each snip.

Unlike on my birthday when I chopped off the long hair that sprouted overnight as part of my transformation to becoming Jinn, his hair doesn't automatically grow back.

❧❧❧

We leave Matin with a box of brown contact lenses at the motel down the road from the beach where he and Zak have been staying. The protruding bones in Zak's cheek prevent the cartwheels my heart's begging to do upon having him back here. He didn't need to tell me he wants to wait until we are alone to talk about what's just happened.

But we're alone now, and he's still not talking. He is, however, pouring himself wine. I told him Mom wouldn't wake up for hours even if a tornado lifted the house off the ground. We're on the back porch. The sun has long since set, so I light the candles spread out on the table and the lanterns hanging from the hooks attached to the back of the house.

"Well, you said this would be your home again one day." I'm joking, but Zak's not laughing. He's drinking. Fast. I lean forward.

"You were covering for Matin's benefit, weren't you? This is the right day, isn't it?"

He refills his cup.

"Zak, tell me. What does this mean?" He drinks faster. "Zak!"

He slams the cup down on the teak table. Red liquid sloshes over the side. "It means Father's in trouble."

I suck in a breath.

"Or not."

I let the breath go.

"Maybe he's been found out. Maybe he was delayed. Maybe he'll try again later or tomorrow or the next day. That's the problem. I don't know, and I have no way of knowing. Do you have any idea how it feels to be left so completely in the dark?"

I refrain from the answer I'd like to give because I know he's upset.

He continues, "He thinks he's protecting me, but he's just making it worse."

More refraining.

"If I don't know, I can't help. Snippets, pieces, that's all he's told me." He chugs the wine. "Little good it does me now."

Even separated, our parents seem to share the same child-rearing philosophy.

Zak grasps the bottle by its neck, and I snatch it away before he pours more. "Hold on. If you know snippets, you know something. More than you've led me to believe. What has he told you? What aren't you telling me?"

His eyes remain fixated on the bottle.

"If you leave me in the dark, I can't help you either. No more secrets, Zak."

He holds out his hand. "First, that." After I hand over the wine (hoping Jinn do have higher tolerances like Samara said), he gestures for me to sit. I do, but he remains on his feet, traveling the wood grain in the floorboards of the decking. "Do you know why the council has placed all of these restrictions on us?"

"To punish us for the last uprising against them." I repeat what I read in my mother's diary.

"In part."

"And because they're cruel bastards. Sorry, I forgot that part."

"That's not the part I meant." Zak stops pacing. "I mean, that is not what I meant."

With a huff, I blow out the candle in the glass hurricane at the center of the table.

"What are you doing?" Zak says.

"Waiting for you to enlighten me."

"You do know that's not what that means?"

"And you do know that dawn's coming?" I've never been to the dentist, but I finally understand the meaning of "pulling teeth."

He plunks the wine bottle on the table, makes me relight the candle (he's still not great with fire), and finally sits. "The council is shrouded in secrecy, so most of what I know comes not from Father but simply from rumor and speculation."

"CYA, got it."

Zak frowns, clearly confused.

"Full disclosure," I say. Still nothing. "You're covering your . . ." I lean to the side and slap my butt.

"Aha, I see," he says, tapping his chin. "Clever."

I roll my hand, gesturing for him to get on with it.

"Yes, well, here's your CYA version." He leans back, glass in hand. Keeping secrets is so ingrained in us all, his internal struggle shows on his face. Finally, he begins, "The Afrit have always had their own ideas about how our world should function. It's why they wanted on the council in the first place. Alas, they were mistaken that the gratitude they received from Jinn initially for clamping down on the troublemakers who threatened our exposure granted them carte blanche. Memories fade, and Jinn wanted their lives to return to normal. The Afrit, while aware of the discontent, have always been conservative, and they insist their reforms have but one goal—"

"To make our lives miserable?" I slowly clap my hands. "Mission accomplished."

Zak ignores me and sips his wine. "To protect us and our magic."

"So you have been drinking the Kool-Aid."

"Kool . . ." Zak eyes his wineglass. "I thought this was a pinot noir."

"It's an expression, one that means 'that's a load of crap.'"

Nodding his head, Zak appears to be either contemplating my eloquence or reconsidering the loosening of his lips. He then says, "I doubt they are simply sadistic, but even if that is the case, they do have their supporters—Afrit and Jinn both who may not like the reforms but who accept that they are necessary to keep our world safe. Father is against the restrictions, of course, as is the majority of Janna. Most believe an uprising—a full-on fight—is the only way to prevent the implementation of additional reforms."

"Additional? What else could the council possibly do?"

"Never ask that, Sister, for we Jinn are a clever species. Surely the council has something up their tunics."

"Sleeve. It's sleeve. And for Janna's sake, if you're going to be sticking around, try to blend." *Is he really going to be sticking around?*

He shrugs. "Anyway, Father believes the side with the greater numbers on the council will prevail, knowledge he only entrusted me with right before sending me here. He's been making inroads to tip the scales in his favor, all while staving off the faction of Jinn eager to revolt, ready to risk their own lives to have a chance at overthrowing the council. But Father has asked them to be patient because he believes his diplomatic solution will work. He has been manipulating things for years to finagle himself into the position he is currently in. To push for and win a vote to return things to the way they once were. He believes if the council is a united front, any supporters of the old regime will fall in line behind its decision." Zak pauses and looks at me intently. "The council is twelve, do you know that?"

"Mom told me that much."

"Did she tell you that within the twelve, there is one leader? The Chemharouch?"

I shake my head, and he continues, "The council makes decisions by majority rule. However, if there is a tie, the Chemharouch's vote counts twice. The council is nearly split on reversing many of the mandates put in place in recent years. Including tortura cavea. The Chemharouch serves for a ten-year term. And guess what this year is?"

My heart begins to palpitate. "Year ten."

"Precisely, Sister. And who do you think is angling to be the next Chemharouch?"

Thump-thump, thump-thump. "Xavier."

"Father. If his plan works, he will be able to change everything, Azra."

"And if it doesn't?"

"He has a backup plan."

"What is it?"

"That's the trouble. I don't know."

16

IF THIS WERE AN AFTER-SCHOOL SPECIAL, ZAK AND I WOULD HAVE learned that this is what happens when secrets are kept. But this is life. Where secrets beget more secrets. Jinn lies are like a sheep's fleece, sheared off the original host and spun, round and round, before being woven into wool so tightly the original threads can no longer be found.

But wool isn't steel. One day a little moth will fly in and eat away at all the lies we Jinn tell. But not today.

Today, Zak and I have spun a tale about him apporting into Janna last night and our father sending him back here, giving him more time with us. We didn't see a reason to make our mother worry about Xavier—at least not yet.

She believed without hesitation. I guess logic and reason are no match for desire. Wanting something to be true can make it so. At least in one's own mind. Zak started the lie, but I'm the one who finished it. As I stood across from her, her need to believe was palpable.

And so my brother has moved into the room next to mine. Where we all now sit, weaving a new lie together.

My mother conjures another long-sleeved tee for Zak. "I'll come up with some excuse to keep them away while you're here, but if any of my Zar sisters drops by, you'll have to leave." She holds the shirt up to Zak and adjusts the length of the sleeve. "But remember—"

"Don't apport," he says, rolling his eyes not nearly as well as I do.

She folds the shirt and tucks it away in a dresser drawer. "It's too risky since they all know you exist, though only Samara knows your father has still been visiting."

I show Zak what an eye roll should look like. "Really? What about the bond between sisters? You harp on me, but it's okay that you've been lying to yours for years?"

"It's not the same as you ignoring yours."

"Well, there's no ignoring them now," I say. "At least Laila and Yasmin."

She winks. "Is your mother good or is your mother good? One stone and I nailed all your little birdies."

I groan. "You did not just say that."

She drapes a pair of khakis over a hanger. "What's wrong with what I said?"

"I'm not sure. But it sounds wrong."

"Very," Zak says with a shudder.

My mother stares at us, and her eyes become glossy with tears. She blinks rapidly. "This is what they took from us."

She keeps doing this. I don't blame her, but the shield, which Zak plans to check on multiple times a day, will eventually be lowered and he'll have to leave, very likely without warning. How will she cope? When I lost Jenny, my memories remained. And the memories made it hard to move on. For me, for Henry, for Henry's dad. There was a time I thought not having any memories made it harder. But that was before I remembered Zak, before I remembered my father. I'm pretty sure I was wrong. Having the memories is harder.

But given the choice, like my mother, I'd choose having them every time.

Zak gets up and hugs our mother. "I'm here now. Let's enjoy the time we have."

I pull my feet off the floor and slide back on the bed, distancing myself from my mother to say what I have to say. "And what about my sisters?" I wiggle farther away. "Because ... well ... Laila and Yasmin may or may not have already met him."

My mother pushes Zak aside. "Which is it?"

"May." I draw my knees to my chest.

"Azra!"

"It was an accident." I curl into a ball. "It was before I knew who he was."

"And who do *they* think he is?"

Zak's shoulders round. "Her cousin."

"Zak!" she cries. "Azra!"

"*He's* the one who said it, not me."

"Why didn't you correct it?" my mother says.

"I was flustered. Chelsea and Megan were there and it was the first time I saw Laila and ... and *he* wasn't supposed to be there."

Zak's bottom lip disappears. "*She* wasn't supposed to have written 'doom.'"

My mother shows us both how eye rolling is done. "Enough, both of you. Especially since I have no idea what you're even talking about."

I grin at my mother. "Maybe it's not so bad they took this from you."

"Hilarious, aren't you, kiddo?" She plants her hands on her curvy hips, the ones I lack. We are carbon copies only from the neck up. "Sorry, but I don't see any other way. Zak's going to have to hide from your Zar sisters too."

"But—" Zak says.

"Tonight's the—" I say.

"Party," we both finish.

"Seriously, you two?"

I hop off the bed. "They have to know it's not true. So I owe them an explanation anyway. What if I tell them he's . . . he's like . . . Henry's cousin?"

My mother pauses. "Why would they buy that when you already said he was yours?"

"Again, *I* didn't say it. But I don't think Laila was paying attention. And Yasmin . . . Well, since Megan was there, I could say I didn't want her to think I was meeting boys behind Nate's back or something."

Zak turns to me. "But even if they believe you, why would Henry agree to this lie? I'm not convinced your dragooning is strong enough to make someone believe he has a cousin he does not have."

My mother sighs. "You've already told Henry, haven't you?"

I squirm/shrug. Turns out, I did have to tell Henry about Zak being my brother via text. With Samara, Laila, and Yasmin showing up, I never got the chance to tell him in person. I've never seen so many exclamation points in my life. Or shocked double Os. Or Ss with eyes. I had to look that one up. I didn't even know there was an emoticon for "worried."

"Why am I not surprised," my mother says.

Zak's brow creases in confusion. "Told Henry what? About me? About *you*?"

My mother heads for the door, twiddling her red fingernails at us as she leaves. "I'll leave this to you to explain, Azra." When she reaches the hall, she turns back around. "Have fun at the party. Just don't set anything on fire."

⁂

"This?" I ask Zak, smoothing down the sides of a red dress that I'm pretty sure makes me look like a bloody steak.

"Fine." He doesn't even look up from the cantamen. He's been obsessed with our family's genie handbook since I first showed it to him. I guess there aren't any how-to manuals in Janna.

"Zak! Come on. I'm running out of options."

He rests a finger on the page. "Good. I can't take much more of this. Could you not have done this before Mother left with Samara? And besides, aren't you dating Nathan?"

My cheeks flush. *Dating.* Weird.

"Nate, and yes."

"So then why are you so worried about what you will wear to Henry's party?"

"Nate's going to be there too."

Zak pauses. "But he's already your boyfriend."

My stomach flips. *Boyfriend.* So, so weird.

Zak raises an eyebrow and looks me up and down. "Besides, I thought you were less . . . girly."

Narrowing my eyes at him, I pick up the white linen shirt he spent practically an hour conjuring and begin to wrinkle it.

"Stop that!" He jumps up, and the cantamen lands on his foot. "*Rahmah*, Azra!" He falls back onto my bed and clasps his bare toes in his hand.

"Oh, sorry, is there someone you wanted to dress to impress tonight?" I half walk, half waddle over to the full-length mirror. "The same someone who made you so desperate to attend a high school party?"

Zak's inspecting his big toenail. "The same someone you're cutting off your circulation for, I presume?"

We're both talking about Laila.

I begin to apply lipstick in the same red shade as my dress. "Well, Brother, it's time you started getting ready yourself. You've never worn contacts, right? Might take you a while to get them in."

With a grunt, Zak sets the cantamen on the bed and heads for the bathroom.

"You're sure Mat's not going to forget his contacts?" I pucker my lips, which could now pass for beef tartare.

"Impossible!" Zak grumbles from the bathroom. "The ways humans torture themselves will never cease to astound me."

I grab a tissue and wipe off the lipstick that makes me look like a vampire after a midnight snack. "You told him low profile?"

Another grunt, which I take for a yes.

I swap out my *A* necklace for the infinity one Laila gave me and attempt to sit on the bed. The fabric of my dress threatens to squeeze the life out of me, so I remain standing. It seems humans aren't the only ones willing to torture themselves.

I slide the cantamen to the end of the bed and open to the page marked by a yellow Post-it note. "Spell Analysis 101" is written across the top in swirly black calligraphy. Folded in the crease is a sheet of paper with unfamiliar words written on it.

"What's this?" I ask.

Zak flies through the doorway, one eye copper, one eye brown (and red from his poking). "Nothing."

Interesting . . . so he's not spilled all *his secrets, then?*

"They don't teach sharing in Janna, Brother?"

Paper in hand, I app across the hall to my mother's bedroom. The spell won't work without her talisman. I have her emerald signet ring out of her jewelry box and on my middle finger before Zak even crosses the threshold.

"Don't," he says, rubbing his brown eye. The contact lands on his cheek.

"Why not?" I ask.

He flicks the contact to the floor.

"No more secrets, Zak."

His only response is to stuff his hands into his pockets and so my only response is to hold the paper tight between two hands and start to read.

"*Khallas*, Azra!" He launches himself at me, trying to rip the spell from my hand.

He may be bigger, but my magic's better and faster. I app to the other side of the room.

"Brother?" I clutch the spell and waddle farther away from him. "Do we know more about this spell than we're telling little sis?"

I recite the first line. I don't make it to the second before Zak tosses his hands in the air.

"You don't make anything easy, do you?" He closes his eyes and starts to pace but can't even bring himself to do that. His face flushes, and he spins around in a circle, muttering to himself. Finally he says, "I'm not supposed to tell you this. Not yet. I'm supposed to wait until . . . until . . . For the love of Janna, let the carpet fly. I do not even know what it is I am supposed to wait for."

His eyes meet mine. "Our father wrote that spell. He made me memorize it so I could safeguard it in the unlikely event it was necessary. If his diplomatic solution does not succeed and an uprising ensues, it is his fail-safe. I only wrote it down now so I could try to decipher it."

"Decipher? So you don't know what it does?"

He sighs. "All I know is that it involves you. And me. He said it's for us. That if all else fails, you, dear Sister, are the key to the uprising. He said if things went awry I must find my way to you. That together, with this blasted spell, we have the ability to fight the Afrit."

A chill runs down my spine. *The key to the uprising. Me?* But I don't know anything about the uprising. I only found out about the uprising because I was being a snoop, reading my mother's diary. I only just found out the truth about the Afrit, about them being my family, about them hurting Jinn to keep their control over us and to keep themselves on the council. I only just discovered my ability to do magic without my bangle, an ability no other Jinn, at least no other Jinn I know of, has.

Is that the reason? Is that what our father means? But why? And how? And what could this spell possibly have to do with it? I give my bangle a push and watch it whirl around my wrist. Should I tell Zak? But what if I'm wrong? Then Zak will know a secret that could get him into trouble. And then get me into trouble. The Afrit might even *come for me*. We have the spell. We should find out what it does first. It might have nothing to do with my inhibitor injection being a fluke.

I realize I should probably look more shocked than I do when Zak says, "You're not laughing."

I cover by looking scared, which is easy since I am. "Why would I laugh?"

"Because it's ridiculous, isn't it? How could we assist the uprising?"

"I don't know, but why don't we find out?"

He shakes his head. "I'm not sure we can. Father said the spell doesn't require a talisman to work. But I recited it countless times while memorizing it and nothing ever happened."

"Then why were you so afraid of me saying it?"

"Because it's his backup plan," Zak says. "He said you were the key. I thought maybe it would work for you. Or maybe it only works when it needs to."

"And you're afraid it might need to. You really do think something's wrong."

He lowers himself onto the end of my mother's bed. "I honestly don't know."

I kinda liked it better when he was covering his fear for my benefit.

I twist the emerald around my finger. *Do I even want to know what this spell does? How I'm the key?* My brain shouts a loud *no*, but somehow I find myself saying, "Can I try? With the talisman?"

He hesitates.

"If there's any chance this helps us figure out if Xavier is in trouble, don't we have to?"

He hangs his head in surrender and lifts the sheet of paper in the air. "Be careful."

With a deep breath, I begin to repeat the words, some of which I recognize, most of which are in a language I don't know, when Zak pops to his feet and points to a phrase.

"You're pronouncing it wrong," he says.

"You speak . . . whatever this is?"

"No."

"But you know I'm saying it wrong?"

"I heard our father say it."

I shove the paper at him. "Here, then you do it."

"But you have the talisman."

"I thought it didn't require a talisman."

He growls before clutching my hand and reciting the words. He's halfway through when I lean in and add my voice to his.

"*Shaqiq shifa.*" We finish the spell together. We pause. We stare at each other. We wait. I'm wresting my hand from his when without warning my silver bangle snaps open and falls to the floor, followed half a second later by his silver necklace.

They lie on my mother's thick woolen rug, entwined. They do not move. And neither do we.

"We're the——" he says.

"Key," I say, my palms starting to sweat. "To the uprising."

"But how?" Zak kneels on the rug. He gently rolls his necklace off my bangle and lifts it as if it were a live snake. "It . . . it has a clasp now." He picks up my bangle and stands, holding it in front of me. "Yours too." Though it's almost hidden on the inside, if I look closely, I can see the hinge. Gingerly, he takes my arm. "May I?"

Knowing what he's about to do, every cell inside me screams for me to yank my arm back, to leave this place, to run far away.

My bangle is off. I am free.

I can grab Nate and Henry and disappear and never have to worry about my Afrit family finding me, finding out about me, never have to worry about granting another wish, about screwing up while granting another wish and risking hurting them or my mother or her Zar sisters or my own.

My mother and her Zar sisters and my own.

They are not free.

Raina is not free.

My father is . . . I have no idea what my father is.

And so I stick my arm out and nod. Zak sets the bangle underneath my wrist and closes it. He inhales, holding his breath. And then he opens it.

The hinge remains.

Again and again, he takes my bangle on and off. I do the same with his necklace. The Afrit have power over Jinn because they control our ability to access our magic.

That power is now in our hands.

But the power to do what exactly? Remove what gives Jinn access to their magic? To what end? Without magic, Jinn have no way to defend themselves against the Afrit, let alone fight them.

Except for me.

I doubt my father thought an army of one would win against

the Afrit. There must be more to this backup plan. And someone must know what it is.

"You know what they say if you can't beat 'em."

And I'd bet my silver bangle that that someone is Yasmin. Yasmin, who, after her mother was taken, said those words right after saying, "You can't win a fight against the Afrit." She also held my hand and, in a rare moment of vulnerability, said about my mother and Samara, "Don't let them risk it."

The only way her words make sense is if she knew Lalla Raina was taken for her involvement in the uprising that Xavier has been trying to prevent. And if Yasmin knows that, she probably knows more.

Wait . . . of course she knows more. Among my non-magical skills is a talent for eavesdropping. And it caught Samara saying to my mother, "Raina told Yasmin long ago." At the time, I had no idea what Raina may have told Yasmin. Now, I just hope whatever it is can help us with this.

Is it irony or karma that the one sister I never wanted to have to go to for help is the only one who can give it to me?

"Yasmin," I say at the same instant the doorbell rings.

"Jameel!" Zak's eyes grow wide. "Nice! You knew she was here? I have to admit, your powers are beginning to frighten me."

I shake my head. "Coincidence." But part of me is unsure. After what's just happened, I'm starting to realize I have no idea what my powers are capable of. I move across the room to the window and push the embroidered silk curtains aside. "It's Matin."

So that really *didn't* have anything to do with my powers. I'm surprised to find there's a bit more disappointment than relief in this discovery.

"Make sure your bangle is secure," Zak says, doing the same with his necklace. The fear he let show earlier seems to be fading. Or he's simply back to covering.

"What does he know?" I ask as we walk down the stairs. Well, Zak's walking. I'm shifting down sideways, unable to move my legs wide enough to take the steps normally.

"Only that our father sent me here to check up on you. He knows he's on the council, of course, and realizes this was a brazen violation of the rules, but he was so excited to come here that he doesn't care. Like I said, even most of our extended Afrit family is fed up with the way things are."

I hold back the snort I feel coming on. I'm about to open the front door when Zak says, "About the spell and the plan, let's not tell anyone until we have something in sandstone."

Sandstone? Now I do snort. "I'm not an idiot. I know enough not to tell anyone." *Except Henry.* I fold the spell and tuck it into my push-up bra. Between the two of us reciting it over and over again, I have it memorized. I'll burn it in the fire pit in Henry's backyard.

"Yasmin," Zak says, leaning against the side of the door.

"No, I told you, it's Matin."

"I know. But before that you said 'Yasmin.'"

"Right," I say. "Well, I'm not sure how you're going to feel about this . . . I'm not sure how I feel about this, but I think Yasmin might be able to help us. I think she knows the truth of why Lalla Raina was taken."

Zak nods slowly. "Which means perhaps she knows more than we do about the uprising. We'll have to feel her out."

The doorbell rings again.

"At the party," Zak adds.

"Tonight?" I say.

Henry deserves a good-bye party free of Jinn angst. I wasn't even going to bring up the whole me-being-the-key-to-the-uprising thing until tomorrow.

"Father could be in trouble," Zak says.

And there's the card that trumps everything.

"Okay," I say. "But let's try to be discreet so Henry doesn't know."

When I open the front door, a red- and teary-eyed Matin marches through waving the box of contact lenses above his head.

"Impossible!" He drops the box onto the coffee table. "*One.* I would like one reason why I should continue to assault myself with these dastardly things."

Remembering how Zak looked at Laila, I stroll—okay, I shuffle—over to Matin and pick up the box. "Girls within five years of your own age."

Matin plucks the box out of my hand. "Azra, do you by chance have a mirror I can avail myself of?"

MINA LIED. OR DOESN'T KNOW HOW TO COUNT. THERE ARE WAY
more than forty people here. I strain my neck to look over the
crowd. Not so ironically, since Zak, Matin, and I arrived—forty-
five minutes late due to their inability to touch their eyeballs—
Mina's been nowhere to be found.

Henry's more easy to spot, what with Chelsea in one hand and
a beer in the other. He's surrounded by his friends from school—
friends it was easy to forget he, unlike me, has. We spent most of
the summer together, and I only met Jake, John, and Ryan once.
Tonight, the three are collecting keys, which, at a high school party,
is the clearest display of friendship.

The stifling smell of sweat and beer leads me outside. Hana,
in a strapless black-and-white maxi dress she no doubt made by
hand, hasn't budged from the spot in the screened-in porch where
Matin cornered her when we arrived. She's leaned in, fingering the
soft fabric of the button-down Zak conjured for him.

Matin asked me to conjure him the I-still-can't-figure-out-why-
it's-not-as-soft-as-Zak's-fabric purple pocket square that's tucked

into his front pocket next to his black pen. Of course Hana had to choose tonight to wear her fiery-red hair in some complicated updo. With Matin's hair now shorn close to his head, the two look more alike than Zak's comfortable with. What I'm not quite comfortable with is her possibly thinking Matin's hitting on her. Because, *ew*.

Kinda like the *ew* of Yasmin with her flat-ironed black hair contrasting with her tight red dress (I'm convinced she saw me coming from the upstairs window and changed the color of her outfit just to toy with me) on one side of my brother in his pristine white linen shirt and Laila on the other.

Laila like I've never seen her. And I don't mean physically. Sure, her golden hair falls in waves down her back and her pale blue baby-doll dress accentuates her still-petite frame and the hints of blue in her eyes. But she's twirling her hair around her finger like she's making corkscrew pasta and crossing and recrossing her courtesy-of-Italy tanned legs like she's in need of a toilet.

And Yasmin appears ready to conjure a voodoo doll. She's been giving me a strange vibe all night. Zak's trying to be polite, but it's obvious he prefers blondes. How are we supposed to "feel her out" about the uprising if he's angling to reserve all his "feelers" for Laila?

Ew.

If sweat and beer dominate inside, outside smells of smoke and s'mores from the fire in the large pit past the in-ground pool at the edge of Henry's backyard. The pit where I finally find Mina. She and Farrah are wearing matching plaid jumpsuits—green and white for Mina and blue and white for Farrah—with V-necks to their belly buttons. Clearly magic is what's keeping things PG-13.

"Azra!" Farrah launches herself at me as I approach, almost knocking us both into the fire. Instead of her usual headband, a crown of acorns and pine needles winds through her straight, dark brown hair. She's also added sharper angles and more caramel highlights to her long bob.

"Hey, Farrah, how's it going?"

"Going?" She blows her bangs out of her eyes, which, like Mina's, are lined with a green the color of grass. They both really do commit to a bit.

"I'm trending!" Farrah squeals. Always as jittery as a rabbit, tonight she's a bunny on amphetamines.

I step back before her arm waving gives me a black eye. "Trending?"

"My mixing! Can't you hear it from here?"

The music, right. "Wait, *your* mixing? But you're out here."

"The albino." Mina curls a lock of hair around her finger. "She's got him wrapped around just like this."

"Mina," Farrah says, jutting a plaid-painted fingernail at her, "you promised. Do I need to bring up Marco?"

Mina raises an eyebrow at me and neighs like a horse. Marco must have been the Italian stallion. "Sorry," she says. "You *really* like this one, I know. And I can clearly see why. Honestly, Marco pales in comparison. If there's even a ghost of a chance, I know you and Mr. Anemic will be very happy."

"Thanks, *Meen*." A twinkle in Farrah's eye accompanies her shy grin.

Not surprisingly, every single one of Mina's gibes went right over Farrah's head.

Mina warms her hands by the fire while I send Nate another

text—my third. He went for drinks twenty minutes ago, and I haven't seen him since. The teensiest part of me thought maybe I'd find him here, magically or otherwise trapped by Mina, who all but drools at the mention of him. But she's my sister. She would do anything to . . . *Marco*. Mina's neighing echoes in my ears, and I make a mental note to toss my own set of reins around Nate.

Suddenly, the hip-hop song that had been reverberating off the clapboard siding transitions into smooth jazz, and Farrah screeches, "The list!" She hops up and down and an acorn tumbles from her hair. "I told him to stick to my list." She then races past us, up the backyard incline and around the pool, as she heads for the house.

"That was a little harsh, wasn't it?" I say, forcing myself to stop staring at Mina's perfectly-in-place cleavage.

She shrugs and not a thread of her jumpsuit shifts out of position. Definitely held by magic.

"Has Farrah been spending a lot of time with . . . with . . . What's the albino's . . . I mean, what's the boy's name, anyway?"

"Dwight."

"You're joking."

"I'm not that funny," she says, unconsciously fidgeting with her infinity necklace. When she lets go, the pendant hangs crooked.

I glance up at the pool, where Yasmin and Laila are still making a Zak sandwich. Considering the strides we seemed to be making the other night, I'm hoping Laila's abrupt greeting tonight has more to do with her interest in Zak than her lack of interest in spending time with me.

I close the gap between us to straighten Mina's pendant. "We're all wearing these tonight, did you see?"

"Even Yasmin," Mina says. "Speaking of, wouldn't you have

expected her to live with Hana?" Before I can respond, Mina cries, "Oh! And speaking of speaking of, did you see Hana's neck? She's got a figure-eight tan line front and center. More of a Farrah thing to do, isn't it?"

She traces the edge of her deep V-neck and stares at the house.

It's not just the color of Mina's jumpsuit that's turning her green. I ease my way into the Farrah door that she's just swung open. "Nice touch with the plaid. Whose idea was the matching outfits? Farrah's, right?" Mina nods, and I say, "She'd never ask anyone else, not even Dwight, to do that, you know."

She bites her bottom lip and looks at me with gratitude.

"In fact," I add, "I'm sure her obsession will fade once she milks it for all it's worth."

"You're not that funny either," Mina says.

But as we both laugh, Mina's usual bubbliness returns. Followed by Nate.

"There you are," he says, handing me a red cup in a wood-paneled cozy.

Cozy . . . add "up to" and that sums up my current feeling about Nate. Sure, the light gray ribbed henley he's wearing that was clearly purchased prior to his recent weight training doesn't hurt. But it's more than that. Ever since I granted Megan's wish, the hurt in Nate's dark eyes has been replaced by a longing, an intensity. It draws me to him.

The same way his smile draws in everyone else. Nate's warm, caring nature would make old Saint Nick reassess his people skills, but combined with the boost in confidence from my granting *his* wish, he's somehow able to make every girl feel like a bride on her wedding day and every guy feel like he's just won a Super Bowl ring.

And me? He makes me feel like an Azra who lives in the now. Not the Azra before becoming Jinn. Not the Azra after becoming Jinn. For too long after Jenny died, my life was about what I had lost, what I couldn't have, what I would never have. But there was so much I *could have* had if I only let myself. It doesn't seem right that Nate's loss, the loss of his father, somehow became my gain.

He pulls me in close and whispers in my ear, "Thanks for inviting me."

I press my hand against the ribs of his henley. "No thank-you needed. What kind of girlfriend would I be if I didn't?"

"Girlfriend." His lips graze my cheek and it's like someone's struck a match against my skin. "I am so in love with—"

Panic, panic, panic. I squeeze my wood cozy so hard a piece of bark cracks. *He's not going to say he lo—*

"With the way that sounds in your beautiful voice."

Whew. And, *huh?* The way that *sounds?* That's what he loves? *Nice, Azra, now you're a contradiction even to yourself.*

Nate smiles, but the grief he's always working to mask darkens the edges like a creeping shadow. "It'd be easy not to invite me after everything. Thank you for treating me like everyone else and for making me feel, well, normal."

Words I want to say right back to him. When I was forced to grant Nate's wish, I thought knowing his deepest desire would make things weird between us because I'd know him in a way he'd never know me. But what I didn't count on was that Nate didn't need magic to begin to know me. He slides his arm around my waist and faces Mina.

There was a time when having Nate here surrounded by all my Zar sisters would have had me itchier than rolling around naked in a bed of poison ivy. But tonight, I like showing him off to them, and them to him.

I'm embarrassed that my first thought upon realizing I could be free of my bangle was to leave my Zar, was to stop being Jinn. Because stopping being Jinn means stopping being a part of this.

Around me, a circle forms. Of Jinn. Of friends. Of the life I now have. The life I didn't know I needed until it found me. Until I let it find me.

A life I can't help but think my father's backup plan intends to change.

"Now this is where the real party is," Matin says, approaching with a wide smile and Hana at his side. He wiggles his paneled cup. "Pardon, but have you all found the good stuff?"

Hana smiles at me. "Having fun, Azra," she says, not asks. It's like she knows the answer.

She winks.

The Zar connection? Is she feeling me? If she is, why can't I feel her?

After our Zar initiation, when our magic became linked, we were supposed to be able to feel one another's emotions. Though I've been trying, I haven't felt anyone's. Hana's the only one who's felt mine and only once—as far as I know. Unless that really is what's happening now.

Hana bunches the jersey fabric of her striped dress in her hands as she moves forward to introduce herself to Nate. I'm filled with pride—both ways—as she does.

The way her hand lingers in his before she elbows me in the side means her feeling my emotions is exactly what's happening now. Hana's always been the smart one.

Nate's explaining the intricacies of lacrosse to Matin (in truth, to all of us) when Henry and Chelsea join us. Laila, Yasmin, and Zak are right behind them.

"Tell me, Henry," Laila says, clicking her nude-colored high-heeled sandals together, "where have you been hiding this one? Why have I never met your cuz before?"

She's referring to Zak.

Here, at the party at Henry's house, my sisters are my cousins and my brother is Henry's cousin, and Hana's brother is Henry's cousin's best friend.

It's confusing.

Farrah and the albin . . .

Farrah and *Dwight* round out the group. In Farrah's hand is a wine bottle.

"Ah, that's the good stuff," Matin says.

Farrah upends the bottle into his cup, but less than half a glass pours out. "Sorry, Dwight and I must have gotten carried away." She burps and Dwight giggles worse than Hana.

Yasmin narrows her eyes, studying the group—studying part of the group, specifically me and Zak—like she's about to draw a portrait. A family portrait? I link elbows with Nate and drag us away from the light of the fire.

Yasmin snags the empty bottle by its neck. "There's only one thing this is good for now."

"Recycled glass jewelry," Hana says.

"Candleholder," Farrah says.

"Vase," Chelsea says.

Mina snorts. "Apparently, there are many things that's good for."

Yasmin pushes her way into the center of the group, clears a circle with her gladiator sandal, and drops the bottle in the middle. "Who wants to take this for its first spin?"

Immediately Laila drops to the ground. Followed by Zak. He tugs on the collar of his shirt. He had to button it all the way up to hide his silver-beaded necklace. Is it possible Yasmin saw a glint of the metal tonight? Is it possible she saw more than a glint at the mall? Does she suspect something, or is this really just a friendly game of spin the bottle?

Nothing with Yasmin is just friendly.

And the odds here are not good. Not the seven females to five males, but the four out of five males I do not want to wind up kissing. I mean, Zak, *ew* times a thousand. Ditto for Matin—since he's Hana's brother, he's too close to being my brother (a qualm Zak apparently does not have about Laila). And Henry and Nate? I do not want to be kissing either of them in front of the other. Which leaves me with Dwight. Thankfully since he glows in the dark, I'll have no trouble finding his lips.

Then again, is Henry really going to move away with things so unsettled between us? He wouldn't talk about our kiss. I wouldn't let him talk about Chelsea and his bed and her chandelier earring. Would one more forced lock o' the lips help us figure out if "other stuff" is the only thing in the way of, well, other stuff with us?

Doesn't matter. One look at Nate, and my guilt surges like a river in a storm, and I know I can't find out. Especially not here. Not in front of everyone else.

"I'm in," Chelsea says, dropping to the ground, followed by all my Zar sisters.

All of them. Couldn't they bother to sense me this once? As if they even need to. Isn't the look of dread on my face enough?

If my look is anywhere close to Henry's, I can't imagine how it's not. I expect to see an SOS smoke signal puff out of his ear as Chelsea yanks him down beside her.

With a shrug, Nate takes my hand and whispers, "That bottle better be a good wingman. I can't have you kissing anyone but me." And my river of guilt overflows its banks as he lowers us onto the grass. "But, hey, I'm due for some good luck."

He is. But who needs luck when you have your very own genie? I may not be able to use my magic to apport my way out of this, but at least I can use it to ensure that bottle points anywhere but at me.

The gold eyes that dart around the circle suddenly make me wonder if all my Zar sisters have similar plans to rig this little game.

Starting with . . . Laila? Really? She volunteers—insists—on going first. But when the spin of her bottle lands on Farrah, I realize she's still the same sweet Laila she's always been.

Then again, she hasn't had her magic as long as the rest of us. Like Farrah, whose spin *magically* lands on Dwight. His, *shockingly*, aims right back at her. My Zar sisters let this run through one more time before Mina ends Farrah's magical interference.

With a rotation worthy of a newly discovered type of gravitational pull, Mina finally overpowers Farrah (who put up a surprisingly good magical fight) and lines the bottle up with Nate. My Nate.

She'll be gentle. Mina won't want to upset me. And then I remember her neighing and Farrah's Italian stallion and I suddenly think this game was a horrible idea.

I think we all do by the time Nate manages to pry himself from Mina's clutches.

I glare at her, but she keeps her eyes trained on Nate as she licks her lips and backs away. "I've been waiting for that all summer, Adonis boy."

The only one whose cheeks are more flushed than mine is Nate. A fact that changes when, after I nudge Nate's spin to land on me and we kiss like Quakers, it's my turn.

I'm so nervous that I spin the bottle too hard and the one person it wasn't supposed to land on it does: Henry.

With his green eyes and ruby-red cheeks, it's like he's decorated for Christmas. What does it mean that he's this embarrassed? And that I'm this nervous? That there's no need to delve further into the status of our relationship or that there's every need? *No need.* Because so what if our relationship colors outside the lines? He's happy. I'm happy. No need to adjust the picture for one little slip of the crayon.

Someone clears a throat.

I look around to find myself on all fours in the center of our circle. Stuck halfway between Henry and Nate. At least I'm consistent.

Scurrying forward, my plan is to let my lips graze Henry's cheek. Quick and painless.

But when I kneel in front of him and lean in, Henry grabs me by my shoulders and thrusts me back. "Don't."

His eyes look not just at me but through me.

With that one word, he lets me go.

I'm living in the now, in the moment. But the moment is not as I planned. It is quick but painful.

And not just for me. The gasps come from all around me. From my circle of Jinn sisters.

Sure, *now* they use our Zar connection and tune into me. For the first time, all six of us are feeling the same emotion.

Mine. And it sucks.

18

THE GAME SHOULD BE OVER, BUT YASMIN HAS ONE FINAL MOVE.

My head hung so low as I crawled back to my spot next to Nate that I barely noticed Henry leave the group. It also didn't register that Hana took what should have been Henry's turn. Not until the thing I realize Yasmin has been angling for since proposing the game happens. It's not what I would have thought. It's not the spin of the bottle pushing Zak and me together.

It's the spin propelling another brother and sister together. It's Hana's whirl, under Yasmin's powers, that means she has to kiss Matin.

No. This has gone on long enough. Which, thankfully, my brother agrees with. Because the bottle cracks in half and the neck now points at him.

But Yasmin's smug smile means we've just swallowed her bait. Hook, line, and smoocher.

I'm in the bathroom splashing my face with water over and over again, until I hit the limits of my waterproof mascara and my cheeks bleed black ink.

When I open the door, I step on Henry's pinky.

"Ouch!" He sticks his finger in his mouth and sucks on the tip. "I probably deserved that."

"It wasn't on purpose," I say. "But still, yes, you did."

Though I see Zak standing outside the room that used to be Jenny's, then Lisa's, motioning for me to come to him, and even though I've been gone so long Mina's likely ensnared Nate with a spell, I yank Henry by his elbow and drag him to his feet and into the bathroom.

With a flick of my powers, I lock the door.

A clear plastic liner is the only thing left cordoning off the shower. I shove it to one side and perch myself on the edge of the bathtub. The acrylic is cool against the back of my thighs.

"Park it," I say to Henry as I point to the toilet.

"Listen, Azra, about—"

"No. I'm the one doing the talking." But I don't. I don't know what to say. There was a time when it was just Henry and me. I had no one else to think about and no one else to worry about. Now this house is full of walking, breathing, scheming worries. My mother's wrong. Life isn't compromise, it's complicated.

Across from me, elbows on his bent knees, Henry kneads his hands together. "I met Zak. He seems nice."

"He is. But that's not—"

"I'm glad for you. I'm glad he's here."

"He can't stay forever."

"A recurring theme." He grins, and it's the grin of my best friend but also . . . not.

Things are changing. Have changed. Was it our kiss? Was it me living with Nate? Was it Henry having to move away? All of it, and more. Becoming Jinn brought us together, but can Henry really remain a part of this circle of Jinn I'm now in? Forever is indeed a recurring theme, in that nothing *is* forever. Apparently, as I've just discovered with Xavier's spell, not even the Afrit's control over me.

"It's just . . ." Henry moves from the toilet to the tub next to me. His eyes find mine, first searching, then connecting, then holding. "About Zak . . . is it really okay? Because this is huge, Az."

I shake my head. "You have no idea how huge."

Henry groans. "I'm not sure I want to know." He drops into the tub and leans his head against the tile.

"What?" I follow him, banging my shoulder against the faucet on my way down and landing my butt in a puddle of water. "Why not?"

Watching me use magic to dry the fabric of my dress, Henry says, "It's just . . . just a lot of responsibility to keep your secrets."

My head jerks up. "Oh." It is. I know it's hard on him. But I thought the trade-off of us being back in each other's lives was worth it. Maybe it was, but maybe it's not anymore. "Well, sorry, I guess."

I start to get up, but Henry waves for me to sit back down. "I didn't mean I don't want to know. Or to keep your secrets. It's just hard is all. Especially now."

Now that Chelsea's carved out room in his life, perhaps there's no more space for me. Maybe I'm in the Carwyn storage locker next to his Red Sox bobbleheads.

He drums his fingers against the side of the tub. "I mean, the thing is, I won't be here, Azra. I already worry about you every second of every day, but at least living across the street, I could see you all the time and make sure you were okay. When you were at Nate's and I couldn't see you, I had to—"

"Find ways to distract yourself."

"Find ways to let go." His eyes, which are and will always be Jenny's, drill into mine. "Are you telling me I shouldn't?"

I want to. Or a part of me does. But a bigger part of me wants Henry the way we were and Nate the way we are and I'm pretty sure that's not the answer Henry wants to hear.

His loafers, the ones I used my magic to shine, rest against my hip. I shift for more room. "I . . . I didn't want you to go away without us knowing where we stood."

He's no longer looking at me. "How very thoughtful," he mutters under his breath. He drags his fingers through his hair. It's long enough that it doesn't stand on end like it used to when he takes his hand away. He exhales, slowly. "Azra, we've always known. What happened was a mistake."

There. He's said it. Isn't that what I wanted to hear? Then why am I holding my breath?

"We will always be best friends," he says. "But you have your life and all its responsibilities and I have mine."

Always, but not forever. Et tu, Henry?

My bangle clinks against the tub as I sit up. From this angle, I can't see the clasp but I can feel it. It's still there.

"What if we didn't have responsibilities?" My voice is barely above a whisper. I know it's impossible; I know I can't take off my bangle and run. But I can't help wanting to know his answer. "What if we could disappear?"

He hesitates before shaking his head at my bangle. "There's no sense asking, because we can't."

"But what if we *could?*"

He sighs. "You could never leave your mom or Laila or all the rest of them any more than I could leave Lisa. Or . . ."

He stops talking, but for a split second I dive into his mind and hear his silent *Chelsea.*

"You two are really close, aren't you?" I say.

His hand slaps against the edge of the bathtub. "Dammit, Azra, I asked you not to read my mind." He flattens a palm on either side of his head. "Don't. I'm warning you."

Warning me? That's it. In I go. And it's all there, raw and . . . naked. Mattress on the floor. Sheets in a ball. Henry and Chelsea. The two entwined in the way boyfriend and girlfriend have every right to be.

I launch myself out of the tub, knocking into the faucet on the way out. Cold water shoots from the nozzle on the wall, drenching Henry.

He shrieks and grabs the black mildewed edge of the shower liner for protection.

"Sorry about the cold shower," I say, "though I'm pretty sure you needed it."

I toss him a towel on my way to the door. The moment it clicks shut behind me, Zak steps out into the hallway.

"What took you so long?" he says.

I widen my eyes. "You say that like I knew you were waiting for me. Which I didn't." He motions for me to follow him, but my mind is still trying to unsee what it's just seen and my heart is still trying to figure out what it feels about what it's just felt and

I'm not in the mood for any more Jinn games. "Besides, I just want to go home, but I need to find Nate first and—"

Zak hooks his thick arm around my waist and drags me down the hall. His momentum propels me through the door and into Lisa's room. Except it's no longer Lisa's room. It's Yasmin's. She's exploded all over it with her Wicked-Witch-of-the-West-meets-Edgar-Allan-Poe theme. Black ravens fly in a mural against the dark-gray walls. Red taper-style candles line every surface. A round bed rests inside a frame made of twisted ebony wood. And in the corner by the window, a curvy red velvet chaise . . . upon which Yasmin sits. Weighing down the pink pouf beside her is Matin.

"Perhaps you could use a leash for your sister, Mr. Nadira," Yasmin says in her usual condescending tone.

So that's it. She knows. Turns out she's been the one tossing out feelers all night.

My body may be fully here—taking a seat next to Zak on the bed, listening to Yasmin explain how she noticed his necklace, gleaming like a neon OPEN sign outside a convenience store when he paraded through the mall, and saw the pre-shorn, red-haired Matin stalking her and Hana like a drunken bison when they went for coffee—but my mind isn't.

The curtains are open, and the window has a perfect view of the backyard pool, where I can just make out Laila and Chelsea sitting side by side with their feet dangling in the water.

I'm jarred back inside by the bass from a blast of music that makes the bed shake. It's coming from next door and is quickly followed by a groan. *Or is that a moan?*

"Whatever in Janna is going on?" Matin says, jumping up from his pouf.

"It's a high school party." Yasmin lifts her chin in the air. "Filled with humans. What do you think they're doing? They're like savages."

Matin furrows his brow. It takes a moment for Yasmin's meaning to click. When it does, his eyes grow wide and his lips morph into a rare, full-on smile. "Hmm...I wonder...seeing as how I'm simply a, shall we say, 'tagalong,' my presence here does not appear to be entirely necessary."

"Pouf," Zak says, pointing.

Matin freezes. He then looks around, cautiously. "Aye, so that's not some sort of spell, *habib*?"

Yasmin taps her toe against the pink pillow seat and laughs. A short, quick, and clearly unexpected—even to her—burst.

As Matin sits back down, he scoops a framed photograph of Raina and Yasmin off the shelf beside him. "Your mother, I presume?" He peers at the picture and scratches his stubbly chin. "Aye...exquisite, certainly, but...intense."

I draw in a breath. No one speaks to Yasmin so bluntly.

She leans forward and takes the photo from his hand. "Perceptive."

And with that one word, Yasmin gives more insight into how she's truly been feeling about her mother's absence than I'm guessing she gave our Zar sisters in their entire two weeks in Italy.

Unfortunately, this does nothing to dull the daggers her eyes are sending my way. She sets the frame facedown on the floor and says with contempt, "As *grateful* as I am to your brother for finally filling me in, it should have been you, Azra. We are sisters, after all. Whether we like it or not."

My hands twitch, and I have to fight the reflex to ball them into fists. She sure doesn't make it easy to feel sorry for her. I shift my gaze back outside where I see the now-laughing Laila and Chelsea interrupted by Henry, who hops into the blue-and-yellow inflatable raft I spent half the summer in. He paddles to the side, extends a hand, and draws Chelsea into the boat.

"I mean," Yasmin says with a huff, "self-centered is one thing, but this is just cruel."

Cruel? Not telling her about Zak and Matin is cruel?

"Though what did I expect?" Her upper lip curls. "Like mother, like daughter."

"My mother has nothing to do with this," I say through gritted teeth.

"Exactly. Your mother has *never* had anything to do with this. Even when my mother asked her to." Yasmin pushes herself off the chaise. "Your mom abandoned mine. Let the Afrit sweep her away like dust under those fancy throw rugs she loves so much."

"That's not true," I say. "It's killing her that your mother was taken."

"And yet my mother's the one who's actually in danger of being killed." Yasmin stands directly in front of Zak and me. "Or maybe she's having tiny fish nibble the calluses off her feet. Unfortunately, I have no way of knowing. I have no contacts in Janna. Unlike you." She says this to me but glares at Zak.

Oh. She thinks we have news about Raina. That Zak does. That's what this is about. That's why she thinks I should have told her who Zak and Matin were right away.

"Yasmin," I say, forcing myself to stand and look her in the eye. "I didn't think—"

"No, you didn't. But hey, you've been having a happy little family reunion, that's all that matters."

Now Zak understands too. "Allow me to apologize, Yasmin. I'm the one who forced Azra to stay silent about who Matin and I really are. If I had details about your mother or the uprising, I promise I would have come to you."

"*The* uprising?" Yasmin flips her long black hair off her shoulders. "If only 'the' was the correct article. Instead of 'an.' Then maybe she'd still be here."

"The . . . an . . . some kind of uprising?" Matin nervously rubs his stubbled head. "Like a revolt? It's truly happening?"

"Not really." Yasmin raises her voice to be heard over the blaring music from next door.

"Wait," I say, confused. "But isn't her involvement in the uprising why your mother was taken?"

"*Her* involvement." Yasmin drills her eyes into mine. "And your mother's *lack* of involvement. Or do you not know that she reached out to your mom and Samara?"

So the conversations I overheard between my mother and Sam about responsibilities and risks *were* about this, which means my mother does know more than she's let on. "That's why you believe if our mother had gotten involved, your mother wouldn't have been taken?"

Yasmin shrugs and the *thump thump thump* of the music from next door fills the silence here inside.

Outside, Henry leans against the back of the raft. Chelsea nestles into his arms.

Inside, Matin reaches into his pocket. He clears his throat, but before he can speak, Yasmin says, "It's not like it matters. Hell, your mother's probably the smart one. Like I told your sister, Zak, you can't win a fight against the Afrit. Unless you know something I don't, there's no use in trying."

Though it's lightning fast, she catches the look that passes between me and Zak.

"What am I missing?" she says. "Do you have a way to help my mother?"

Neither one of us answers. I avert my eyes, looking past her and, unintentionally, directly at Henry and Chelsea.

Suddenly, Yasmin grabs my arm at the same time as Henry grabs Chelsea. Henry spins Chelsea around, lifts her small body onto his lap, and kisses her. Hard. A kiss full of passion. Full of desire. Full of everything the kiss between us lacked.

Because we are friends. That's all we are, all we should be, all we want to be.

But my heart's thudding in time to the fast beat of the music still pounding through the wall and I try to wrench my arm free of Yasmin but she squeezes even tighter and I push her away and she pulls me back and her other hand flies out, seizing me by my bangle, and I wrest myself free but a sharp pain tears through my arm and I pivot around and fall to the floor and . . . and she stands over me with my bangle in her hand.

My bangle that's not supposed to come off—ever.

"But how . . . ?" she says.

In the sixteen years I've known her, Yasmin's never shown fear. Until now.

Matin crosses to the center of the room. "Perhaps it has

something to do with this?" He holds between two fingers the spell I wedged into my push-up bra. I curse the fact that there's not enough padding, real or fake, to keep things in place.

Still holding my bangle in one hand, Yasmin gingerly takes the spell with her other. "What's this?" She begins to recite the words, but Zak uses the advantage of his height to extend his long reach and snatch the paper from her fingers.

Yasmin lets loose a string of expletives, and Matin returns to his pouf, legs crossed, watching like it's a game. But none of this is fun. Not Yasmin's nasal cursing, not Zak's attempts to calm her down, not Henry and Chelsea, whose own little game has capsized their boat.

The music, the talking over one another, the smirk on Matin's face. I can't take it anymore.

"Enough!" I cry.

I draw the curtains closed, whirl around, and set the spell Yasmin's struggling to free from Zak's hand on fire.

It's only when all the jaws in front of me hit the floor that I realize I did all of that using my magic. But my bangle's still in Yasmin's hand.

My secret is out.

19

WHEN MATIN'S MOUTH CLOSES, IT PREDICTABLY TURNS UP INTO A smirk. "That'll win a Jinn argument anytime. Excellent work, Azra."

It's like Yasmin's trying to balance on one leg. On top of a moving train. "But I—I—I don't understand. How could that . . . ? Did I do . . . ? Has it always . . . ? What does this mean?"

Reaching up and unhooking the silver necklace that gives him his powers, Zak says, "It means we have a chance against them. Thanks to this spell from Father. It frees us." He stands still, staring at a candle. He then shifts and stares at a pillow. Then the door. Then the curtains. "Why can't I use magic? Azra, how did you?"

I flop down on the chaise. Henry and Chelsea are no longer in the pool. "I don't know."

Yasmin swoops in next to me. "You must have never been injected. Maybe because your dad's such a head honcho—"

I stiffen. "Zak, you told her?"

"I had to. How else could I explain being sent here?"

Yasmin waves me off. "So you're related to the scourge of Jinn-kind. Not the point. What I was saying——"

Lifting my hair off the back of my neck, I point to my tiny round scar. "I know what you were starting to say, but you're wrong. I was injected with whatever voodoo the Afrit——"

"*Your family,*" she says.

I bite my lip literally so I can bite my tongue metaphorically. "As a baby, I received the injection of the compound that's supposed to block our magic like everyone else." I shrug. "I guess it didn't work."

"Who knows?" she asks.

"My mother," I say. "And my father. And now you three."

"That's it?" Zak asks, crossing his arms.

"I said——"

"No, I mean, that's it? There's nothing else you haven't told me? I didn't realize when you demanded that I no longer keep secrets from you that I had to make a formal request to be treated equally."

Matin clucks his tongue. "Interesting, very interesting."

"Shut up!" I say at the same time as Zak says, "*Khallas!*"

"Definitely related," Matin mutters.

My shoulders hunch and I drop my head into my hands. "Please, Zak, this has been a hard enough day, a hard enough few days. I'm still trying to wrap my head around everything."

He slowly uncrosses his arms but looks at me intently. "So this is Father's backup plan. You."

"*Her?*" Yasmin says.

Now I actually sink my front teeth into my tongue.

"When did you discover this?" Zak asks.

I rub my sore tongue along the roof of my mouth before saying,

"When I was on probation." I explain how I inadvertently apported, which I shouldn't have been able to do since I was wearing the bronze bangle that restricts the use of personal magic. I then describe how I put the pieces together and realized I've always had my magical powers. And that my mother hid this fact from me. "If I hadn't screwed up, I probably would have never known."

Yasmin narrows her eyes. "It's almost like that number change on your note card was purposeful. If you hadn't rushed into granting the wish, you wouldn't have made a mistake." She snickers. "At least that time."

While I can ignore the second part, the first is something I've always suspected. I ask Zak, "Was it? Did Xavier purposely—"

"I don't think he could have done that from Janna," Zak says. "And even if he could have, I cannot imagine him intentionally exposing you to that kind of danger."

"But considering the spell, he probably wanted me to know." I try to cover the panic this ignites inside me. "What does he expect me to do? And when?"

Matin raises his hand.

Ignoring him, Zak asks Yasmin, "Your mother never told you more about the uprising? About what she was trying to do?"

Yasmin shakes her head. "Just that she was warned that things in Janna were changing. It wasn't until I turned sixteen that she picked up this little crusade. Some birthday that was. 'Here's your magic, Yasmin, and by the way, the Afrit are worse than a swarm of locusts and you need to help, but you better keep it a secret to protect your Zar sisters.' Except you, Azra. She wanted you to know. She was determined to force your mother to tell you everything."

Force my mother? Does that mean Lalla Raina knows about my abilities? Does Samara? Or has my mother truly kept this from her Zar sisters?

Yasmin continues, "She had me working on some spells." She flicks her hand to draw our attention to the large gemstone signet ring she's wearing. It's her mother's talisman, which I first noticed on her hand on my birthday. "But just to practice. All she ever really said was that the Jinn here needed to be stronger than we are. That we needed to be ready to support the Jinn in Janna. That there may not be another way to keep us safe."

Matin shoots his hand higher in the air.

"Oh, for Janna's sake," Zak says. "What is it, Matin?"

He pouts. "Just for that, I should leave you all in the dark as your parents have done."

Zak puffs out his chest, marches toward Matin, and picks him up by his collar. "I swear, Matin, I will stuff you in a bottle and toss you in the ocean—"

I really hope that's just another one of his euphemisms.

"Fine, fine," Matin says, prying himself from Zak's large hands and adjusting his pen, which was about to tumble out of his shirt pocket. "Just don't ask me how I know what I know." Before Zak or anyone else says anything, Matin tosses his hands in the air. "*Rahmah!* Fine, I'll tell you, but no getting all judgy."

He settles himself on his pouf, faces Yasmin and me, and gestures for Zak to sit beside us.

When he does, Matin starts. "Excellent. See, it was a couple of days before we were scheduled to leave Janna."

"You were never scheduled to leave Janna," Zak says.

"Details." Matin smirks. "As it happens, I was visiting the, well, you know, house of ill repute, that's the term for a place where older female Jinn—"

Yasmin's body tenses beside me like she's . . . *jealous?*

She says brusquely, "We get it. We have the same term."

"Or we did," I say, "in 1864."

Yasmin stares at me and then . . . laughs. We're having a bonding moment. Pretty sure we're both freaked out by this more than anything that's happened so far.

"Anyway," Matin goes on, "I overheard, from a very reputable source, but don't ask me to violate code and name names."

Zak rolls his hand.

"*Shukran, habib*," Matin says. "So word is the Afrit council is set to have a vote in the coming days. A momentous one, apparently."

"The election," Zak says. "But that's not for months."

Matin wags his finger. "Is this your story or mine? I sat here patiently while you all acted like toddlers—"

Zak's lips thin, but he places his hand over his heart. "*Aasef.* I'm sorry. Continue, *habib.*"

Matin nods. "Again, thank you. As I was saying, the Afrit council is set to have a momentous vote *after* the Chemharouch election."

"A vote on what?" Yasmin asks.

"On a new mandate," Matin says.

"That will do . . . ?" Zak asks.

Matin shrugs. "How am I supposed to know? Am I an Afrit?"

Zak flares his nostrils. "You know this doesn't really help."

Matin frowns. "How about this? It would seem that the election is being moved up in order to have this momentous vote."

"Moved up?" Zak says. "But Father didn't say—"

"Maybe he didn't know," Yasmin says softly.

My bangle remains in her tight grip. I wiggle it free, slip it back on, and click it closed. I double-check the clasp. Twice.

Because what if he did know? What if this momentous vote is the culmination of all he's been trying to do? What if he sent Zak here, to me, because he knows his diplomatic solution doesn't have a chance in tortura cavea of working?

So he will need his backup plan. He will need me.

Does that scare him as much as it scares me?

From behind our sofa cushions, I spy on Henry.

He's in his bedroom across the street with Laila. Guess his bedroom will now be hers.

He's in the living room with Samara, moving a cozy love seat from one wall to the next. I didn't realize how much stronger the summer he's spent swimming's made him.

He's outside in the front yard with two duffel bags and a box next to him. He takes his glasses off and cleans them with the end of his cotton sweater. School hasn't even started yet and it's cool enough for a cotton sweater.

I peek my head out from in between the pillows. He looks right at me. Even though he's not wearing his glasses, I know he can see me. I sit up higher. He pushes his glasses back up his nose and waves.

I wave back and then clutch a sequined throw pillow to my chest.

Beepity beep beep.

Into the driveway turns Chelsea and her open-topped convertible. She's wearing a pink wool scarf and matching knit newsboy cap. She looks positively adorable. As Henry wedges his duffels in the elfish trunk and drops the box in the tiny backseat, I realize she's driving him to New Hampshire. Why not? She's the one with a car. Doesn't matter that my mode of transportation is faster, Henry would never let me apport him—though I know he'd love to feel the searing heat, to defy every law of physics we think we know, to simply imagine a place and then be there. It's magic. If only everything in life could change as easily.

Though our powers are not infinite, there is so much we can do. Seeing my magic through Henry's eyes is what helped to curb my resentment at being Jinn. Will all that change with him gone? Now that I have no one to share it with?

Zak, in a white tee and plaid pajama pants, lumbers down the stairs, yawning. Apparently he and Matin stayed at the party late last night finishing off the last of Mina's esophagus-burning limoncello.

"Coffee's in the kitchen," I say, still watching Henry. He tucks the flaps of his cardboard box inside one another and begins to circle around to the passenger side of Chelsea's car. Before he reaches the door, he pauses and looks at me. He points to the house and then tilts his head toward the fence gate. He mouths, "Sorry."

I smile. On my birthday, the day Henry and I reconnected, he brought me a "sweet sixteen" balloon and a small silver key that fit the lock his parents had just installed on the fence to their backyard. In the years since Jenny's death, Henry and I had drifted apart. But the Carwyn home was always a place where I felt safe. Every time being Jinn, every time being surrounded by

Jinn—my Zar sisters, my mother's Zar sisters, my mother—overwhelmed me, I'd escape to Henry's backyard. I'd spend a few precious moments being something, anything, other than a Jinn. And I'd find myself again.

All those years, all those times, I had no idea Henry had seen. He'd been watching over me. I never saw him, but maybe, somehow, I knew. Maybe that's why I felt so safe.

Stranger things have happened. I've made stranger things happen.

Now, with the last Carwyn leaving the house and three Jinn moving in, what's to become of my escape hatch?

I'd like to think I no longer need it.

Zak, blowing on a mug of coffee, sits beside me. "You're not going to say good-bye?"

Henry waves again, opens the passenger door, and slides inside.

I blink away the tears stinging my eyes. "We said good-bye last night."

Did we? And good-bye to what?

My heart's being forced through a meat grinder.

I think of Nate, but all I can think of Nate is how I took his pain away. Henry said it was cheating not to feel the hurt.

He was right. Because feeling the hurt is what keeps us honest. It's what shows us what's most important. What we can't live without. If only it showed us what to do when that list of what we can't live without has more than one thing at the top.

20

It's funny how quickly a new routine takes hold. Waving to Samara across the street. Fighting with Zak for the last cup of coffee. Setting the dinner table for three instead of two.

Crossing my fingers every morning and every afternoon when Zak attempts to apport into Janna. Trouble is, the more time that passes, the more unsure I become of what it is I'm crossing my fingers for. I want Zak to stay—so does he and presumably so does Laila, with whom he's been spending nearly all his time. But what if Zak staying means something's happening in Janna with our father—or maybe even *to* our father? Not to mention Raina.

Which is why in this last week before school, another part of the routine that's taken root is ransacking the house where Yasmin and Raina lived for clues about the uprising. We plan to go to Samara and my mother when we have concrete proof. This way, they won't be able to brush us off like they normally do. What started as an effort for the four of us—me, Zak, Yasmin, and Matin—has shrunk to just Yasmin and Matin.

I've never known Yasmin to take an interest in boys. Mina,

Farrah, even Hana started dating the instant their mothers gave the okay, but not Yasmin. She claimed boys weren't worth her time.

A fact that I may or may not have rubbed her pointy nose in when I caught her and Matin searching for clues in places I'm pretty sure Raina never went.

"He's a Jinn," Yasmin said, as if that should explain everything.

And I guess for her it does. Yasmin inherited her mother's intolerance for humans. She blames them for making our Jinn world the way it is. But humans aren't to blame; the Afrit are. Sure, granting wishes today is harder than it used to be. There was a time when humans believed in magic and the unknown, and we didn't have to hide the way we do now. But that was centuries ago. It's way past time to accept it. It's way past time to accept humans in our lives.

"There you are!" Nate comes up behind me, twirls me around, and lifts me off the ground by my waist—where his hands remain as he lowers me, kissing me on the way down.

Normally such PDA doesn't bother me, but we're in a hospital. And Megan's right here. Still, I don't want to be rude. But when his head begins to burrow into my neck, I shove him off.

"Vampire biz crosses the line," I say, taking his hand instead.

Megan rolls her eyes. "Yeah, that's what crosses the line." A streak of violet runs through a long lock of hair framing the right side of her face.

Goldie finally won. For weeks she'd been wanting to do something to "jazz up" Megan's look. That Megan finally agreed shows significant progress.

Megan tucks her violet hair behind her ear, loops her fingers into the straps of her backpack, and brushes past us toward the elevator.

"Someone's in a hurry," Nate says.

He doesn't add "finally" because we're all glad Megan is asking to be taken to see her mother, rather than having to be dragged.

"Ten pages, Nate." She jams her finger on the UP button. "We have ten pages left in the cyberthriller!"

The book I loaned her sticks out the top of her backpack.

"And you really didn't peek?" I tease.

She presses the button again and this time holds it down. "No, I promised. Besides, I want us to finish it together."

Nate peels her hand off the button panel. "You've been reading to Mom for two days straight. You're starting to sound like you smoke a pack a day."

Another eye roll. The elevator doors open and Megan scoots left, then right to find the stack of numbers. "Sixth, right?" She turns to me. "Did you know they're moving her, Azra? No more freaky tubes. Dad would be . . ."

"Happy," Nate says, though that shadow still lurks in the corners of his smile. "Dad would be happy she's going to be okay."

When the elevator dings, announcing the sixth floor, Megan's sneakers squeak with the speed with which she takes off. Nate and I follow, checking room numbers as we go.

He grabs my arm. "Did I tell you? Coach thinks I've got a shot at that scholarship. Maybe even UMass, but I'm kinda liking BU since"—he uses my arm to practice a lacrosse throw—"it's closer. Less than an hour from here."

"You don't say?" I playfully tap my chin. "Boston, that close?"

I'm about to laugh when it registers that he's talking about something that's a year away. He thinks we'll be together in a year. And the fact that this is what I'm thinking means what? That I don't think we'll be together in a year or don't think I'll be here in a year?

The vinyl tiles morph into glue beneath my feet. For the first time in my life, I don't know where I'll be this time next year.

Because for the first time in my life, there's a chance that what it means to be a Jinn today might not be what it means to be a Jinn tomorrow. It isn't until right now, this very moment, that the end result of all that's going on coalesces in my mind as something real, something with tangible, life-changing effects.

And it isn't until right now that I realize how much hope I have for that.

Odds are I'll be right here, well, not *here* here, hopefully not here in this hospital, but in this town, granting wishes, living the life I always knew I'd have to live. But what if my father changes things? What if Zak and I . . . what if *I* can change things? What if being Jinn a year from now is nothing like it is today? What if it's better?

I might be living the life I want to live, all the while still being Jinn.

But what is that life?

I may not be sure *what* it is, but I am sure of who I want in it.

Letting Nate enter his mother's hospital room ahead of me, I hang back, pull out my phone, and take a selfie. Which I then add to a text to Henry.

How 'bout this? Every day, no matter what, we do this so we can see each other and know we're both okay.

My finger hovers over the Send. On a scale of one to ten with one being acquaintances and ten being a couple, Henry and I are smack-dab at five—friends. Maybe seven if we're still best friends. Does sending this move us up the scale? No, it confirms we're both right where we want to be. In the middle.

Right?

"Azra, you coming?"

I jolt at Nate's voice, and my finger taps the screen, sending the text. Oh well. Life is complicated, after all.

Before I can even slide my phone back into my pocket, a selfie of Henry reading a bodice-ripping romance novel lights up my screen. I laugh, and the nurse behind the desk shushes me, which only makes me laugh harder.

What if a year from now, I no longer have to worry that Henry's in danger because of what he knows? What if a year from now, being Jinn is nothing like it is today?

Then again, what if being Jinn a year from now is nothing like it is today because it's worse?

21

My mother's racing through the house, muttering to herself.

"*New furniture. Don't want red wine spilled.* Oh, but it can be spilled here in *my* house."

"Mom?"

She flings an argyle sock—Zak's—into the pile of clothes in her arms. "And would it kill him to pick up after himself? When I see Xavier I'm going to ask just what kind of household he raised my son in if he can't even drop a sock in a laundry bin."

"Mom? Is something . . ." I was going to say "wrong," but that seems obvious. Instead I finish with, "Happening?"

"Why don't you ask your Lalla Sam?"

She tucks a motorcycle magazine under her arm and apps upstairs. I follow just in time to see her bury the glossy in between the cooking and travel magazines on her nightstand. She pitches Zak's dirty clothes into the bottom of her closet and slams the door shut. She then falls against it, clenching the knob in her hand.

"Mom?" I stand across from her, resting my hand on her

shoulder. Her body trembles beneath my fingers. "Lalla Sam wants us all to meet here?"

Tonight will be the first time since my Zar initiation that all twelve—*eleven*, we're now eleven without Raina—of us Jinn mothers and daughters will be together. A housewarming for Samara. A housewarming for Samara that's apparently moved across the street.

"It's okay, Mom." Historically it's been me, not my mother, grumbling when company's coming. "I'll help clean, I'll make sure Zak leaves and—"

"I can't do this much longer." Her head shakes so violently it's like she's possessed. "I can't keep this from them."

"This?" I take her hand in mine. It's as cold as a snowball. "You mean Zak?"

"They all know something's going on. They can feel it. Your Zar, you all haven't connected like this yet, have you?"

The Henry brush-off. When they all gasped. "Just once," I say softly.

"Really?" Her eyes shine with hope. "That's wonderful."

"Sorry, Mom, but right now you're not exactly the poster child for the joy of the Zar connection."

She stares at me, and I'm regretting my words until she says, "No? So much for being a model Jinn." She laughs—a much-needed release that doubles her over and sends her to the floor. I sit next to her, leaning against the closed closet door. She smiles at me, and I notice the faint lines around her eyes have grown deeper.

It's quiet in the house, just the two of us, like it used to be. It's nice in a way. It makes me want to tell her about Xavier and the spell. It makes me want to ask what she knows about the uprising, if I'm really . . . really the key to it. This is my mother. We don't need to confront her with proof. And if we do, aren't I now proof enough?

I spin my bangle to bring the hinge to the top. I'm on the verge of flicking it open when she turns to me, studying my face as if it's a question she's struggling for the answer to.

Suddenly, she pulls me to her chest. Her breath warms the top of my head as she says, "Keeping secrets is hard enough. But when your best friends know that you're keeping something from them, it's an impossible weight to bear."

It's almost exactly what I'm thinking—but about her and my own Zar sisters. "So why don't you tell them? Don't you trust them?"

She holds me even tighter. "That's the thing. I do trust them. With my life, with yours, with Zak's. They'd give themselves up before giving up any of us. How can I put them or your sisters in that position?"

My stomach drops. "You mean the position I put Henry in?"

She plays with my hair. "You didn't know what could happen."

I pull away. "But I know now."

"So? It's too late. He can't un-know what he knows."

"But he can. I can make him."

She jumps to her feet. "No, Azra. Absolutely not. You can't use mind control on him. You saw what happened with Mrs. Seyfreth."

"But Nate and Megan and—"

"That wasn't the same. You weren't making them forget. You were simply pushing them to feel something they already wanted to feel. They wanted to heal. They wanted to remember the good of their father, not the bad. But with Henry . . . do you really think he won't fight you tooth and nail if you tried to make him forget about you?"

She caresses the bottom of my chin with her thumb. "We will keep him safe. I promise. But not with mind control. Hadi is too dangerous."

"Don't worry, it's not like I need reminding about the whole Anne Wood mess."

"But that had nothing to do with your execution." She pauses, as if regretting having said that. She follows it up with, "Using it on humans may not drain your powers, but you can still hurt them and maybe even yourself. So don't use it."

"I won't."

She leans in.

"I won't, I promise," I say.

"Good." She checks her watch. *"Rahmah!* They'll be here soon." I grin.

"What?" she says.

"You're picking things up from Zak."

"Picking up Zak's things is more like it." She sighs, but it's totally fake. "Do me a favor and make sure he's gone before they get here?"

I nod yes, but all I can think is no. I understand my mother wanting to protect those she cares about, but that includes Xavier and Raina. It's time for all our secrets to be out. Tonight, both our Zars need to start acting like the trusted sisters we're supposed to be.

As I leave her bedroom, the shower turns on. I close the door behind me and almost bump into Yasmin. She's in the hall outside Zak's bedroom. "When did you get here?"

She holds up her long, thin finger—a match for her skinny nose—and continues the soft chanting under her breath I now hear.

The gemstones in the signet ring that covers three of her knuckles glow. She's doing a spell.

Inside, Matin stands with a megaphone. Zak, arms crossed, looks on intently.

When Yasmin finishes, she points to Matin and says, "Now."

He flicks on the megaphone and his mouth grows wide in a deafening scream.

Or what should be a deafening scream. Except I can't hear a thing save for the running water in my mother's shower.

"Whoa," I say.

Yasmin waves her hand. The gemstones no longer glow. "Soundproofing spell. I'm sure you could do it too." She raises an eyebrow. "Not now, of course, but perhaps once you've been practicing spells for nearly a year like I have."

She glides into the room like she's just accomplished world peace. "You could hear us?" she says to Matin.

"Loud and clear," he says.

We all wince and cover our ears.

Zak removes the megaphone from Matin's hand and turns it off. "Don't do that again."

He smirks. "Sorry, *habib*. But the gadgets here are truly astounding."

Unlike Zak, Matin, who's twenty, hasn't been in the human world since he was little—too young to remember much. Though with more than half the population of Janna having lived here at one time, it's not like this place is a complete mystery. It's not like Matin's a time traveler from the Middle Ages wondering what gods are responsible for airplanes and Spam (and by the way, it better not be a Jinn who's responsible for Spam).

Zak said many Jinn brought their favorite possessions with them when they transitioned into Janna. But over time, the Afrit banned all these vestiges of the human world and began to punish those found with confiscated goods.

Marked by an apparently impossible-to-forge ornate *A* (which I hope doesn't look anything like my necklace), it's easy for the Afrit to distinguish a "made in Janna" item from a human one. Since Jinn in Janna can't conjure, they are much more skilled in creating things by hand—woodworking, sewing, even glassblowing are apparently quite popular. The one thing they don't know how to do, according to Zak, is cook.

Kitchens and all cooking equipment are forbidden. The population of Janna depends on the Afrit for sustenance. Another way they control Jinn. In response, some of the most valuable and high-priced goods on the Janna black market are seeds salvaged from the human world.

Like speakeasies, clandestine chow clubs that grow, cook, and serve real food have cropped up in Janna. Jinn are eager to trade goods—both legal and illegal—to eat, but some will even trade for a whiff. The ability to smell the growing, baking, roasting, grilling, and sautéing of real food is a luxury.

Those Jinn willing to take the most risk keep their own small gardens at home. Buried beneath the stone and rigged with grow lights, these "someday victory gardens" are not just food for the stomach but food for the soul, since they are a way to rebel, albeit in a small way, against the Afrit. The name is a nod to the gardens planted by humans to show support during their own big wars—one and two.

My mother always said that some things turn out better without magic. My chocolate chip cookie debacle notwithstanding, I know she's right. Hana must too; that's why she makes clothes without using her powers. Like my mother said, it can be rewarding to make something with your hands instead of your mind. Maybe the Afrit have been shut up in Janna so long they've forgotten that.

Matin being shut up in Janna has made him relish everything about being here, but especially the smell of food. Popcorn, brownies, even fish, Matin can't get enough of breathing in every scent, perhaps to cement them into memory for when he has to return.

With a flirtatious smile, Yasmin squeezes Matin's arm. "Speaking of astounding . . . be right back." She apps away, only to return less than a minute later with a tray full of food. Roasted chicken, fluffy mashed potatoes, sweet corn, and a three-inch-high chocolate cake.

"Enjoy, boys," she says.

Zak dips a finger in the pool of melted butter atop the mashed potatoes. "You conjured all of this?"

"Of course not," Yasmin says. "Mat likes to smell it cooking."

I frown. "There's no way you cooked all this by hand."

She laughs.

No, she cackles.

"Me?" she says. "Like a human? The sun really has fried your brain, hasn't it, Azra?"

Matin speaks surprisingly clearly despite the chicken leg stuck in his mouth. "She hired a lovely lady in a white coat. Today we searched the bed—" Yasmin glares at him. "Den, I mean den, all the while breathing in the delightful smells of all this goodness."

Yasmin twiddles her fingers on her way out of the room. "Lock the door behind us."

"But we're all gathering here," I say, "not Henry's—not your—house."

"Obviously," she drawls. "Why else would I bother with the soundproofing spell?"

Matin swallows and holds the half-eaten chicken leg in his hand. "Please, Azra, let us stay. I . . . I haven't been able to be this close to my mother since I've been here. Even if all I can do is hear her, it's likely to be all I'll have before returning." He grips the leg tighter and a piece of meat falls to the floor. "We won't allow ourselves to be discovered, I assure you."

Heart and strings.

Well played, Matin. Well played.

But unnecessary. The time for games is over. My mother can't take the stress of keeping her secrets. And neither can I.

The Afrit have kept Jinn separated for far too long. The first step in changing things is coming together. And so I pull Yasmin into the soundproofed room, and the four of us—male and female Jinn—decide how to go about doing just that, tonight, starting with our Zars.

Yasmin and I are in the hall when Matin rushes to the door, slimy chicken juices from the second drumstick running down his hand. "Forgotten something, my dear?" He purses his lips.

"Please," she says, but he ignores her, taking her in his arms, burying his chicken leg in her long hair, and planting a hard kiss on her full red lips.

Wincing, I step back. She's going to wallop him. But she doesn't. Instead, she issues a high-pitched giggle. He grins and walks backward into the room. The door closes and the lock clicks.

As Yasmin wipes her greasy lips with her thumb, her smile—the most genuine one I've ever seen her wear—fades. "My mother would never approve."

Life without Raina is difficult. But so was life with Raina.

Yasmin fluffs out her full, bell-shaped skirt and shakes her head. "Doesn't matter. It's just a distraction. He'll have to go back."

"Maybe not. Maybe tonight will change things."

She laughs. "Azra, the optimist? Now that's the last thing I ever expected to see."

"Really? I thought this was."

"This? This what?"

"You and I standing here talking. Without coming to blows."

"The conversation isn't over yet."

But it is. We shudder and grab each other for support as all of our Zar sisters and their mothers descend on the house.

How did they all manage to arrive at the exact same time?

"Oh, Samara, it's adorable!" says Lalla Jada, Mina's mother. At least I think that's who it is.

"And you installed the fireplace in your bedroom, Samara? Amazes me that you and Kalyssa are able to do that. Never been able to master that myself."

Okay, the first was definitely Lalla Jada because the second is most certainly Lalla Isa, Farrah's mother. The level of magical talent, or lack thereof, runs in the family.

"They were all across the street?" I say.

"That's why I rushed over here first." Yasmin plucks the hem of my very short shorts, courtesy of Hana. "You better change. I'll hold the fort until you and your mother come down."

I'm at my bedroom door when Yasmin's "And Azra?" makes me turn around.

"If we're going to try this uniting thing, you and Laila need to truly end this . . . whatever this is you've still got going."

"We did." *Didn't we?* We've texted, we've talked.

Small talk. Short texts. But I haven't officially apologized. Not really. And she hasn't officially accepted.

"Just do what Mina said, okay?" Yasmin flicks her wrist. "Find something that Laila loves, give it to her, and end this. Janna knows why, but being in a tiff with you makes her all mopey. Funny, it always made me drip with sunshine."

"Oh really?" I back into my room and stick my hand on the edge of the door. "Then here's a big old ray for you." I slam the door shut.

I laugh, as I expect her to do, but I don't hear anything from the other side of the door. I'm about to open it again to make sure she knows I was joking when a push-up bra in an obnoxious skull print appears on my bed.

"And hurry up!" she shouts as she bounds down the stairs.

Yasmin and I are actually getting along. As I sift through the clothes hanging in my closet, I begin to wonder if my mother cast a spell to bring us together. But it's not my mother. It's the Afrit.

I told my mother this would happen. That this is why we stand a chance against them. Because the more they hurt us, the more we want to hurt them.

And we'll go to any lengths to do it. Even becoming *whatever it is I'm becoming* with Yasmin.

My hand lands on what I didn't know I was looking for. The perfect outfit.

Find what Laila loves and give it to her.

The lengths I will go to just got a whole lot longer.

And yet also skimpier.

22

Turns out I didn't need the push-up bra. One benefit of this outfit is that the top is bra and shirt all in one. I give a final pull on the knot in my gold halter, but unlike when all my Zar sisters wore a version of this ensemble on my sixteenth birthday, I'm in no danger of spilling out of it.

I fiddle with the sheer scarf draped around my neck as I walk down the stairs. I'm looking straight ahead, unable to bring myself to even peek over the railing and down into the living room for fear I'll lose my nerve.

I hit the bottom stair, pivot, and face . . . no one. There's no one here. I'm shivering in see-through harem pants, a sequined gold bra top, a tiny monkey-playing-the-cymbals hat with the strap digging into my chin, and there's no one here to see it?

Maybe this is a sign. A sign that this is a ridiculous idea. I'm about to bolt back up the stairs when Hana's voice steals my chance.

"Oh, Azra! It fits perfectly!" Her red hair bounces as she skips over to me. "Everyone has to see."

"No, Hana, really." I take in her sophisticated A-line black silk dress. "I was just joking. For Yasmin. I didn't realize you were all here so I should go——"

"Mom, Mina, Yasmin, Laila, everyone, get in here!" She claps her hands. "You have to see Azra!"

Don't you mean "every square inch of Azra"? I hoist the harem pants up higher and plaster a smile on my face.

She better come. She better laugh.

Laila rounds the corner, and her hand flies to her mouth. My mother, Samara, all of their Zar sisters, and all of mine fill in around me. Laughing, making jokes, playing with my scarf, complimenting Hana, who sewed the outfit by hand, on her skill.

Though Laila remains frozen in the doorway, her eyes dart back and forth, searching mine. I bring my hand to my throat, feeling the rapid beat of my pulse through my skin, and unwind the scarf. As it falls to the floor, I grasp the figure-eight pendant that was hidden underneath. I'm clutching it so hard I could crush it.

She better know this is for her.

With measured steps, she crosses the room. On tiptoes, she unclenches my fingers from around the pendant and holds my hand in hers.

"I was more hurt than mad," Laila says.

We're alone in the living room. Our mothers shooed everyone to the back deck, handling the protests of it being too dark and too cold by loading their arms up with lanterns, blankets, and our industrial-sized patio heater.

Laila folds her legs underneath her on the couch next to me. "I would have given it to you if you'd asked."

Though I'm still taller than she is, I'm huddled into an even tighter ball. "I know."

"Then why didn't you? Ask?"

"I . . ." My insides are tied up like a sailor's knot. This question, which follows on to why I didn't return her locket, is one I've asked myself a thousand times since she found out I stole it from her. I think I've always known the answer. But I haven't wanted to admit it to myself, let alone to her. "I think I wanted to hurt you."

My voice trembles, but I don't try to cover. When she found the locket in my nightstand, I had pretended to be strong. I didn't want her to think I was hurting, like I was a victim in all this. But that only made her think I didn't care. That I was callous and insensitive. That I didn't give a damn that I'd ripped her heart out and treated her trust like it was toilet paper.

And now, I admit I wanted to hurt her and this is her response. No tears. No shouts. No protests of why. Laila, my best friend even when I didn't treat her as such, knows me well enough to understand.

She uncurls her legs and slides closer to me. Her gold eyes seem bigger and rounder, but her lashes haven't given up their slight size. She looks even more like a doll that I should be protecting. But she doesn't need my protecting—not anymore. She probably never did, but I was too focused on myself to see her kind nature wasn't at the expense of her strength.

Because it takes someone with Laila's inner strength to forgive.

"You wanted to hurt me because I had what you wanted," she says. "Not a picture of a male Jinn, not a picture of a father neither one of us would probably ever meet. I had our Zar and you didn't."

I nod. "But it was my fault."

"No," she says, "well, yes, maybe, but we have been a bit insular. Inside jokes, talking about things you weren't a part of . . ."

I tap my chest. "My doing."

"Not entirely. We didn't always ask you to join us. *I* didn't ask. And I used to. Even when I knew you would say no. I just gave up on you for a while there, Azra."

This is all news to me. It hurts more than I would have expected. Still, I say what's true. "You tried harder than anyone else would have."

"But I'm not anyone else. I'm your best friend. And best friends don't give up." She covers the tears I see forming by flicking my tiny hat. "I do believe you are the perfect example of that today."

I dig into my halter top and pull out the tiny strand of silver tinsel Laila wrapped around my wrist when we were ten. She pretended it was the silver bangle I wouldn't receive for another six years. She wanted me to have fun, to play make-believe and grant her wish. "Extra points for this, right?"

Laila flings her hair in my face as she gets up, but she can't help smiling. "Certainly. Still, I'm not letting you out of wearing that for the rest of the night."

I groan. "Remind me not to piss you off again."

She laughs. "Oh, yeah, I'm a real force to be reckoned with."

Standing up and almost tripping on my stupid sheer scarf, I say, "You think you aren't? Is there anyone else I'd put this on for?"

"*Nate!*" Farrah and Mina cry as they barrel into the room.

"Henry," Laila whispers.

What was that about my best friend knowing me so well? Better than I know myself?

I plant my hands on my hips to steady myself and face Mina and Farrah. "Have you two been eavesdropping the entire time?"

Mina's verbal "no" is at odds with Farrah's effusive nod.

"Come on," Mina says. "We need more bodies outside."

"More?" I say. "The deck's going to break if it gets much more weight on it."

Farrah changes the color of her headband from blue to purple to pink, and I know she's taking me seriously. After I convince her I'm joking, she says, "They're all acting strange. I don't even think they've opened a bottle of wine."

"Something really is wrong, then," Laila says, laughing. "Let's go lighten things up."

I trudge behind, knowing that each step brings me closer to doing the exact opposite. I'm about to burst the Jinn bubble for all my Zar sisters. And I understand, a bit more, why my mother keeps secrets.

"Oh, thank Janna, you're back," Hana says. "I was just talking about the last wish I had to grant." Her freckles dance as she wrinkles her nose. "Someone else go. Otherwise it's too . . . quiet."

She says "quiet," but what I think she means is "tense." All our mothers are like wax replicas of themselves, and Yasmin is eyeing them like she's trying to make them melt. I guess it's not only my mother who she blames for Raina being taken. I didn't realize how much of a pacifier Matin's been for her. The sooner we set the stage and get him and Zak down here, the better.

Hana taps her foot, and suddenly I feel her desperation. Literally feel it.

Whoa.

She practically smashes her high heel through the wood decking, and *her* nerves make *my* palms sweat.

"Right," I say, nudging Yasmin farther down the bench to make room for me and Laila. "So, Hana, what was your last wish?"

"Oh, nothing too difficult." Hana aims for the open seat behind her. "What the . . . ?" She hops up, having sat right in Farrah's lap. "Nice apping job, Farrah. Now scooch over."

Laila asks again, "So . . . the wish?"

"Yes, the wish." Hana wedges herself in beside Farrah. "Boobs."

Yasmin snickers. "Figures. Shallow humans. I mean, is there a Jinn here who *hasn't* gotten boobs?"

Laila and I are the only ones who raise our hands.

"Seriously?" I say.

Farrah raises hers halfway. "Does junk count?"

The deck shakes with the force of our collective laughter, and a small part of me does wonder about its structural integrity.

"What about hardest wish?" Hana widens her eyes at us girls. Things really must have been painful out here.

Lalla Isa notices the new pink color of her daughter's headband, and the one in her own dark brown hair turns pink. She and Farrah used to wear matching ones, but this is the first time I've seen a headband in Lalla Isa's hair in a while. She juts her square chin, more angular than Farrah's, toward Hana's mother. "Why don't you tell them about yours, Nadia? I still think that's one of the hardest any of us has ever gotten."

Lalla Nadia crosses and recrosses her legs. "I don't think the girls want to hear—"

"We do," half of us say at the same time. Including me. I think of Matin upstairs, listening.

"Please, Lalla Nadia," I add.

"Okay, if you're sure," Nadia says. It may be the light, but her creamy skin looks paler than usual against her auburn hair, a shade deeper than Hana's. "It was years ago, before you were all born. I was given a scientist in Boston."

"A doctor, wasn't he?" Lalla Isa says.

"Yes, but a researcher. Just as precise as you'd expect. His wish was so strong I barely had to connect with his anima to reach it. He wanted to cure cancer."

Even Yasmin leans in at this because we all know that's not a wish Jinn can grant.

"You never told me this," Hana says. "What did you do?"

"Well, clearly I did not grant his wish, otherwise humans would no longer be suffering. From that at least."

"You went deeper, then?" I ask. "Found his true wish?"

She places her hand on her chest. "I tried. But that was it. It wasn't his wish because he'd lost a family member and what he really needed was solace. It wasn't because he was ultracompetitive and needed to win or even to be revered. It was simply his deepest desire. It's the purest wish I have ever been asked."

"Wow," Farrah says, her headband practically glowing. "What did you do?"

"I started by dipping a toe in the science."

"A toe?" Samara's chest heaves with her booming laugh. "She practically got a PhD herself."

Lalla Jada adds, "You should have seen your mother, Hana. No Jinn has ever been more dedicated."

Nadia's face flushes. "I'm sure that's not true, but thank you, Jada." Nadia looks at Yasmin. "It was your mother who eventually stopped me. She made me realize that interfering with science . . . with nature in this way is not something we can do. It must happen organically."

Next to me, Yasmin stiffens. Her eyes dart toward Nadia, but she refuses to hold her gaze. But this is good. Bringing up Raina. A natural lead-in to the conversation we need to start.

After a pause, Nadia continues, "So I let go. I found the most adorable dog named Cancer, of all things, that was suffering from some rare parasite, and through many, many convoluted steps brought doc and dog together and . . . eventually, there you go. Cured Cancer."

Laila sucks in her top lip. In a soft voice, she asks, "But isn't that cheating?"

Nadia nods her head. "Absolutely. Sometimes you don't have a choice."

My mother moves behind Nadia, wrapping her arms around her shoulders. "And sometimes, you don't know the ripple effect your actions might have. Cancer's owner happened to be a scientist in her own right. Together, she and the researcher discovered an important gene, and what else, Nadia?"

She playfully slaps my mother's hand. "Got married. But that wasn't me."

"Maybe not directly," my mother says, "but isn't that what

makes all this worthwhile? We never know what our helping may lead to."

Isa chimes in, "Even with boobs. Remember mine? My 'Miss Double D' became Miss Country or Miss Universe or Miss Planet Earth or some such thing, and now that charity of hers has planted more than a million trees."

All the heads in the circle bob up and down. Except Yasmin's. She leaps from the bench and cries, "*Khallas!*"

The recognition on my mother's face contrasts with her Zar sisters' surprise and confusion.

Unaware of what she's said, Yasmin launches into the tirade she's been holding in not just for tonight but for weeks.

"This is absurd!" She throws up her hands. "Dogs, trees, you cannot be serious? It's all a random farce. We do these inane things for humans at every expense to ourselves. Go ahead and attempt to convince yourselves otherwise, but I am not going to remain here, because the bull that's spilling from all of your lips, Lallas, reeks."

She marches toward the house but stops short and whips back around. "Maybe if one of you put an ounce of the energy you give to humans toward my mother, she'd still be here."

An even better lead-in, though far from how we planned it upstairs.

Samara stands, but Yasmin waves her off. "No, Lalla Sam. I know you tried. I want the rest of these *traitors* to say something."

But the only one who says something is me. And it's not so much a word as it is a guttural scream. What starts as claws piercing my skin ends as the jaws of life clenching my insides.

In my mind, the cause flashes so fast I think I'm imagining it.

A hallucination. It must be. Everything that's happening here's influencing my delusions. Or it's a bad mussel. After the hospital visit, Nate, Megan, and I had a late lunch at the Pearl. That's all this is. A mussel I shouldn't have drenched in butter and let slide down my throat.

Another flash—stronger—and I stumble back.

But how?

Again.

It doesn't matter how. It's not a hallucination.

Again. And again.

It's real.

I double over.

And act on instinct.

"Zak!" The decking tilts underneath me, and I'm reaching out not to fall. "Zak! Come . . . down . . . n-n-now . . ."

And he does. My brother. He holds me to his chest and grounds me.

"Th-the woods," I stammer out, oblivious to the circle of Jinn around us. Save for one.

Right before Zak apps us away, I find Yasmin in the crowd. "She's here."

23

THE GASPS OF ALL THE JINN I'VE KNOWN MY ENTIRE LIFE CLAMOR
in my ears for half a second, but it's the hope on Yasmin's face
that remains, that I still see, as Zak apps me to the woods behind
Nate's house.

She's there. Just as I knew she would be.

Raina.

Lying in a torn gray kaftan on the ground where the stick X
used to be. I rush to her side and clasp her hand in mine. The
same thin scratches that run down her palm also line her face. Her
waist-length black hair splays around her in a mess of knots and
clumps.

"Lalla Raina?" I touch her forehead, then her chest. *She's breathing.*
Thank Janna, she's breathing. I find her pulse and cling to it, letting myself recover from the pain of the vise on my internal organs. That
it's ebbing to a dull simmer of Pop Rocks and Coke lets me know
my father's responsible. I turn to Zak. "Water, a glass of water."

He conjures a small cup, and together we lift it to Raina's
mouth. She doesn't swallow, and the water spills down her chin.

Her almond-shaped gold eyes haven't blinked and remain fixed on Hana's fuzzy green scarf, which we left entwined in the branches above us.

"Let's take her back," I say. "Mom can heal her."

Zak kneels beside Raina and delicately slides his hands underneath her body. Suddenly her arm flies out and she grabs me by the end of my sheer scarf. The strength in her grip forces me to sink my hand into the mud above her shoulder so I don't tumble on top of her.

"Azra." Her voice is raspy, like she's been dining on thorns. "Your father lost. They know. They know everything."

Her words shoot a spear clean through my heart, but it's Zak who cries out. He rips his arms out from under Raina, and her scream swallows his. I hold her down by her shoulders, scanning her body for the source of her injury, but there are no obvious signs. No bleeding, no broken bones jutting through skin, not even a bruise. All I see are hairline scratches and abrasions whose redness indicates they are recent, but they couldn't be causing her this much pain, could they?

Zak has fallen back on his heels, and his breathing is rapid and shallow. I whip off my scarf and bunch it to make a pillow for Raina's head before circling around to Zak.

"Deep breaths, Zak," I say, rubbing his back, which arches at my touch. I continue my long, gentle strokes, muttering reassuring words that are always said in times like these, and yet their emptiness makes even me recoil.

Raina's strength and voice leave her at the same time, and she collapses in on herself, her body curling into a ball. I have to get her to my mother, but I'm not sure if I can lift her and hold her in my arms. If I app her like this, letting her dangle beside me, I'm afraid I'll hurt her even more.

I need Zak. And so I say the truth, the only thing we know for sure. "We can't do anything for Xavier right now. But we have a chance to help Raina."

He stares down at her as if remembering she's here. He blinks and roughly rubs his face before nodding. Together, we then roll Raina into his arms, and he rises to his feet. In the instant before he apports, Raina's head turns and her eyes meet mine.

"Tell Yasmin I'm sorry," she says.

We arrive in the backyard, but the deck is empty. Everyone's moved inside.

Still in Zak's strong arms, Lalla Raina's eyes jolt open. I can tell she's trying not to cry out from the pain of apporting.

"Take her to your room," I say quickly, grateful for the sound-proofing spell that will mask any noise Raina makes. I need to prepare them, especially Yasmin.

As I enter the kitchen, snippets of conversations greet me. Samara, hurt that my mother didn't tell her Zak was here. Hana, hurt and humiliated that Matin didn't tell her who he was. Nadia, hurt and astounded to see Matin and desperate for her children to stop fighting so she can hold her son. Mina and Farrah, hurt and confused and feeling increasingly left out as Jada and Isa explain all the things that have been kept from them.

The only ones sitting quietly are Yasmin and Laila. Laila is holding both of Yasmin's hands. Samara's inclination to support an uprising explains why she and Laila were the only ones exempt from Yasmin's anger and blame.

In the kitchen doorway, I feel Zak apport upstairs. The only other Jinn focused enough to feel the same is Yasmin.

But I can't let her go up there, not without bracing her for what she's going to see. As she stands, I push past everyone else to reach her, including Matin, whose eyes grow as round as saucers as he takes in me in my genie costume.

"Is she really here?" Yasmin asks.

Her voice comes out so faint and the rest of the voices ring so loud, I can barely hear her. But somehow, every Jinn in the room does. It's grown so silent that I can hear my own heartbeat echo in my ears.

I nod. "In Zak's room. But she's hurt. She's going to need—"

My mother, Samara, Nadia, Isa, and Jada apport upstairs before I take my next breath.

But the only part of Yasmin that moves are her eyelids, which flutter shut. I stare at the heavy layer of blue shadow, trying to remain focused on her, on Raina, trying to prevent my mind from imagining myself in Yasmin's shoes, about to look at the aftereffects of what the Afrit may very well be in the process of doing to my father.

Above our heads, a flurry of footsteps pad the ceiling. A burst of patter traveling from Zak's bedroom to my mother's to the bathroom and back again.

"What are they doing?" Mina asks.

Farrah laughs nervously. "Healing her, duh. And I'm the goofy one?"

Matin rubs his stubbled head. "Doesn't sound like it's going well."

Hana slaps his arm, and I shoot him a harsh look. He rounds his shoulders and I realize he didn't mean it the way it sounded.

"Aye, sorry, love." He then worms his way through the pileup of Zar sisters to slip an arm around Yasmin's waist. His voice trembles as he says, "Shall we go on up, then?"

"Let's all go," Hana says.

Yasmin pries Matin's hand off of her. "No, just Azra."

Just me. Because I'm the only one here who knows everything—aside from Matin. But now is not the time to introduce mother and boyfriend. I stand beside Yasmin, but she doesn't take a step, so I link my arm through hers. She doesn't fight me and simply moves her body with mine as I climb the stairs.

"But what should we do?" Mina asks.

Being Jinn has always been full of secrets and lies.

I've used them my whole life to pretend I'm something I'm not. I think of Nate and Henry. I'm using them now still.

Our mothers have used them too. To protect us and to protect one another. They've used them as a way to focus on the good and forget the bad. But the line between good and bad is being erased.

If we are to stop pretending, if we are to protect one another, if we are to save Raina and my father, if we are to help our fellow Jinn, we must stop hiding behind the lies.

Like Jenny once said, "Best friends share secrets." And these are not just my sisters, they are my best friends, or at least they should be.

"Why don't you start a pot of coffee?" I say. "This is going to be a long night."

I KNOW MY WORDS ARE TRUE THE MOMENT YASMIN AND I CROSS the threshold into Zak's bedroom and the sounds of Raina's anguish fill our ears.

Yasmin rushes to the bed and takes her mother's hand. Seething, she spins her head around and eyes all the mothers in the room, lingering longest on mine, who is poised on the other side of Raina.

"Why aren't you helping her?" Yasmin says.

My mother wets her lips. "We're trying, but—"

"Try harder," Yasmin spits out.

At the sound of her daughter's voice, Raina opens her eyes and stifles her cries. She even attempts to sit up, but the pain that comes with the motion makes her bite her own lip with such force that she draws blood. "Yasmin," she says. "You must ... be ... prepared." Each word sounds like sandpaper scraping her throat.

Yasmin squeezes Raina's hand and scowls at my mother. "Can't you do something for the pain?"

At that, Lalla Nadia enters the room with a bowl of water and a washcloth. She kneels beside the bed and dabs at Raina's forehead. "Your mother wouldn't let us, Yasmin. She needed to tell us something first."

"What could possibly be so important?" Yasmin asks, but of course, I already know.

I move next to Zak, who's using the wall in the far corner of the room for support, and let Samara take my place beside Yasmin. She gently caresses Yasmin's back before setting a chair in front of her and beginning to summarize what Raina has gathered enough strength to relay.

Though held by the Afrit, Raina was spared a cell in tortura cavea. Xavier had been protecting her. But he can't anymore. The Chemharouch election has been held, and he lost to Qasim, another Afrit on the council.

At his name, my mother bristles. She and Samara understood what this meant without Raina needing to say anything further. This particular Afrit is the most conservative on the council. Not only will Xavier be unable to reverse the restrictions, more will likely come.

Apparently Xavier had begun to fear the outcome of the election and that he was being watched. He couldn't risk lowering the shield to allow Zak to return. Now that the election has not gone his way but to Qasim, the Jinn in Janna are outraged, Raina said. As worried as Xavier is about what Qasim may do in the future, right now, he's more scared of the harm that would come to Jinn if they acted rashly and protested the election results. And so Xavier moved swiftly to try to stave off those in favor of inciting an uprising. But the meeting he held with the Jinn leading the underground rebellion in Janna was not as clandestine as he hoped, and his true allegiances were discovered.

As Samara confirms that Xavier has been outed as a traitor, my mother's shoulders remain squared, her body stiff, her eyes focused on her tightly clasped hands. What she's feared most since the day he left has happened. That she's not only standing on two feet but trying to heal Raina makes her not just a model Jinn but a model, period. I only hope I inherited half her strength.

For Zak's sake even more than my own. I reach for his hand and find it cold and trembling. I try not to imagine the worst as Samara explains how Raina escaped to warn us, but that Xavier didn't have enough time to properly lower the shield that blocks apporting. Raina's injuries—the ones yet to be healed, the ones our mothers cannot figure out how to heal—are a result of traveling through in human rather than animal form.

At this, Yasmin lashes out at my mother. "All of this is your fault." Though she's shouting, thanks to her own soundproofing spell, none of our Zar sisters downstairs can hear her. "My mother was taken because you refused to help her, and now she's . . . she's . . ." Samara tries to calm her, but Yasmin only gets louder. "No, Sam. I'm sick of the Nadiras being more important than everyone else. Why is my mother expendable? Tossed through like a piece of meat to be flambéed just so she could tell us poor Xavier might get a slap on the wrist? Why is his life worth more than hers?"

Zak drops my hand and in two long strides crosses to the bed. "It won't be a slap on the wrist." His clipped voice fuels Yasmin's anger.

I've seen these two fight before, and, especially since the tension seems to be increasing Raina's pain, I hurry to Lalla Isa and Lalla Jada and suggest they take Yasmin elsewhere. They have to forcibly remove her from the room.

Nadia, who has remained at Raina's side, once again begins muttering healing incantations.

My mother says over her, "It's time, Sam. Raina's told us enough. I'm doing the spell."

"No," Raina croaks. "Wait. Xavier had a message for you, Kalyssa."

Nadia stops speaking and helps Raina sip water from a straw. Then, with slow measured breaths in between her words, Raina says, "There is a portal, a weakness in the shield we can use to enter Janna without shape-shifting. To enter and support the uprising."

Samara's mouth falls open. She leans over Raina. "Where?"

"There was no way for me to get there and leave through it, so we agreed he wouldn't tell me in case I was intercepted. But Kalyssa knows."

We all stare at my mother, whose entire body shakes, denying it. "I—I—I don't."

Samara's lips thin. "I know you're against this, Kal, but are you really going to be so selfish as to hold out on us? Look what they did to her!"

"I swear, I don't know," my mother insists.

Raina lifts her head. "He left a clue here. He said you would be able to find it." Her eyes float over to me, and she groans. "I can't believe I was rescued by someone wearing that." Her head sinks deeper into the pillow. "Now do the damn spell and put me to sleep, for Janna's sake."

Our house is like a revolving door. One Jinn apps in, another apps out. Unable to handle the hurt, the anger, the betrayal, the fear, the frustration, Jinn leave in search of an escape hatch. No one likes to be kept in the dark, even when the best of intentions are at work.

Over the course of this very long night, secrets spill. About the Afrit, about my father, about Zak and Matin, about the uprising in Janna that Raina wanted to start here, and about Yasmin's blame, which, after learning what her mother said, has shifted entirely to mine.

As has Samara's. Well, maybe not blame, exactly, but Samara learning that my mother kept my ability to do magic without my bangle a secret from her for all these years ignited the worst of the night's fighting—the worst of my life's fighting.

"How could you keep this from me?" Samara said. "Especially after Raina was taken. You must have known this could be important for the future, for any uprising to have a chance."

My mother stormed across the living room, knocking into a lamp that no Jinn's powers were fast enough to catch. "That's precisely why I didn't tell you. You and Raina can take all the risks you want, but I'm not letting you use my daughter like she's some pawn in your fanciful fight against the Afrit. I won't let you involve her in this."

"Really? And what are you going to do to stop me, Kal? Hurt me? Erase my mind? Make me a vegetable? You're apparently an expert at that."

The smack of my mother's open palm against Samara's cheek

echoed through the house. A red outline of her fingers remained until Nadia healed her.

But Samara didn't back down. "I never knew how selfish you were. All these years you had Xavier. You were even able to see Zak. What would Nadia have given to watch Matin grow up? Of course you don't need an uprising, Kalyssa. Unfortunately, the rest of us aren't so lucky as to have shared an Afrit's bed."

This time, Samara caught my mother's hand in midair before it hit the target of her other cheek. She flung it to the side as she said, "Considering it's your union that's to blame for our families being ripped apart, the least you can do is—"

"That's not fair and you know it, Sam."

"Do I? Is it or is it not you and Xavier defying his family's edict to stay apart that led to the Afrit ordering all the males to leave? You two couldn't keep your hands off each other. You went right ahead and 'diluted the Afrit bloodline' to prove you could. And now our families live apart and our daughters will bring new Jinn into the world like lab rats."

Through gritted teeth, my mother said, "You want to know something? I'd give anything to know what clue Xavier left here. I'd hand it over quicker than a Jinn can apport and not even blink as you all marched yourselves right into the Afrit's clutches. Maybe you'll get lucky, and they'll give you neighboring jail cells in tortura cavea. You can listen to one another scream." My mother stared down into Samara's eyes. "Just know, I'll do anything to protect her. I won't let you put her in danger. She's my daughter, Sam." Her voice weakened, and she finally let her eyes fill with tears. "I . . . I need her."

"That's the problem, Kal. What if we all need her?"

After that, I swung the revolving door myself and left for Henry's backyard. I used the key he gave me to let myself in through the fence gate rather than app, not willing to risk someone sensing and then following me into my private sanctuary. I lit a fire in the pit and have been loading log on top of log. The flames now reach my waist. But I still can't get warm.

"There you are," Hana says, opening the door of the screened-in porch. She hurries across the yard and down the slight hill to the fire pit. She hands me a pair of skinny jeans and a blue cashmere sweater. As I change, she pours us mugs of hot chocolate from a tall metal thermos.

Both help with the warmth. But not as much as her understanding why I kept all these secrets from her.

"How could I be mad at you when I've been keeping secrets too?" Hana says. "I know a lot of what was exposed tonight. My mother has been telling me bits and pieces since I turned sixteen. She and Lalla Samara wanted to tell us everything the night of the Zar initiation, but things happened."

"I happened."

"Stop making *everything* about you," Hana says.

I stiffen.

"I'm kidding, Azra." She refills my mug. "You're not the one who got Yasmin drunk that night. You're also not the reason Lalla Raina was taken."

I jiggle my head in a half nod, half shrug, and Hana sets her cup down and faces me. "But you think you are, don't you? Look, we're in this together. Maybe we haven't always been, but we need to be now. You have to let us in."

"I will."

She wrinkles her freckled nose.

"I mean, I am," I say.

"Good." She smiles, but there's an uncomfortableness behind it. "I'm really sorry about your father."

Suddenly the hot chocolate's too sweet. "I don't even know him."

"Doesn't matter." She places her warm hand on my arm. "He's your dad."

I rest my mug on the ground and fight the queasiness in my stomach by changing the subject. "How's everyone else? Mina and Farrah?"

"They knew the least of all of us. They're still in shock. Plus, they heard Lalla Jada and Lalla Isa fighting about Isa's old flame Hairy Larry. Did you know he knew about us?"

I do my half nod, half shrug, realizing the only secret I've yet to tell all of them is about Henry.

"Well, Farrah was super interested to learn about her mom, that Lalla Isa had told a human—a human boyfriend—about us being Jinn. And Isa's all pro-uprising, but Jada thinks it's just because she hopes if we win, she can get back together with Larry and ditch all of us, which somehow made Mina bring up that albino—"

"Dwight."

"Oh, *white*. Is that, like, more PC?"

I shake my head. "His name is *D*-wight."

"You're joking."

"I'm not that funny."

The way we laugh makes me think of Henry and Jenny and Nate and not because I'd rather be with them, but because I wish they could be with me. With us. I wish life wasn't so damn complicated.

"There's one other thing I need to tell you," I say.

Hana's laugh ends in a yawn. It's really late.

She covers her mouth and then says, "About Henry? We all know."

"You all . . . *What?*"

"Zak told Laila, who told Yasmin, who somehow already knew, who told Mina, who told Farrah, who told me. And now I'm telling you. But you know, of course. And now you know that we know."

I'm dizzy.

"It's not really surprising," she says. "You've always been close to humans. Truthfully, most of us have probably wanted to tell a human at one time or another."

"Except Yasmin," we say at the same time.

I smile despite imagining the "conversation" I'm going to have with Zak about trust, and then I think about our father and know that Zak's getting a pass on this.

I toss another log onto the fire when the delicate flap of a butterfly's wings flutters over us, and Laila appears.

"Azra! Your mother thought I'd find you here," she says.

That's it. Good-bye, sanctuary. I have no more secrets.

Yes you do. Jenny. You still have to tell Henry about Jenny.

"Is something wrong?" I ask.

Hana leaps to her feet. "Is it Raina?"

"No, no." Laila's trembling fingers brush a curl of blond hair off her forehead. "It's Zak. He's missing."

25

"What do you mean he's missing?" I say, kicking over my hot chocolate as I spring to my feet.

"No one's seen him," Laila says. "I thought, I assumed, he was with you. Yasmin and I were upstairs with Lalla Raina. Yasmin did a spell to block out the noise from all the fighting between our mothers downstairs. When I finally came out, I couldn't find Zak anywhere."

Hana asks, "What about Mat?"

Laila shakes her head. "He's gone too."

"He didn't stay with Yasmin?" I ask, surprised.

"No, he never came upstairs." Laila's shallow breathing begins to deepen. "I didn't think of that. They must be together, then. They're fine. They're not . . ."

"Taken," I finish. I circle around the fire pit, trying to remember the last time I saw Zak. He was in my bedroom. I thought he needed a break from everything, which I couldn't blame him for. But he was sitting at my desk. He was—

The cantamen.

"I know where they are." I slip my hand into Laila's and tell Hana to put out the fire here. I've got my own less literal one to douse. "Come on, Laila. I think I'm going to need your help."

We app to the woods behind Nate's house. The pinpricks of light I can see from here come from the Reeses' second floor. I thought I was cursed when I was living there. That's irony for you.

We turn around to find Zak knee-deep in mud. Swatches of dirt cover his cheeks, making them match the darkness of his hair. It's like he's a five-year-old who thinks if he digs down far enough, he'll reach China.

"Oh, Zak," Laila cries. Her pale skin and blue dress become marred with black as she drops in front of my brother and pulls him against her body. "What are you doing here?"

I kneel beside her and swallow the lump that's swelling in my throat. "He's trying to get home."

Upon hearing my voice, Zak looks up, and tears stream down his cheeks. Intense as the volume is, it's not enough to clear a path through the caked-on mud.

"I have to . . . help him." Zak's head falls, and he covers his eyes with his filthy hands.

"I don't understand," Laila says.

I'm desperate to steel my own nerves long enough to get him home. "This is the spot where Zak first arrived," I explain to Laila. "Where we found Raina. If Xavier were able to lower the shield again or if this were the portal she was talking about—"

"I could go to him," Zak says.

Laila's hand flies to her mouth. I hear her teeth crunch on specks of dirt as she says, "No! You can't go! They'll just take you too."

"No, but Azra and I . . . we can . . . we could—"

I gently turn Zak to face me. "We're here. It's not opening. It's not the entry point."

He wipes his cheek with the back of his hand, clearing some dirt but leaving a line that makes him look like a football player with grease paint under his eyes.

"But we'll find it," I say. "I promise you."

Though Laila tenses at this, she says gently, "Let me take you home, Zakaria."

And then, sweet, petite, normally pristine Laila leans in and rests her small mouth on his. Zak cups the back of her head, turning a section of her blond hair as dark as ours before he nestles into her neck.

The two of them disappear. And all I'm left with is the light from Nate's house that's trickling through the trees. I sink deeper into the mud.

My father outed. Raina hurt. The spell. The portal. The uprising. It's all real. There's no more denying what I am. What I'm meant to be. The key to the uprising. Somehow.

There's no room in my life for anything else.

The lights in Nate's house go out.

Anyone else.

I claw my fingers into the dirt beneath the X as shudder after shudder of grief rocks my body like a tidal wave.

They say things are always better after a good night's sleep.

They're not.

I slip out of bed into air that hangs thick with humidity. It's too early to be this hot. Except it's not. The time on my phone shows it's well past lunchtime.

As I cross the room to my window, my feet stick to the tacky wood floors. I raise the glass pane higher, straining for a hint of sea, but the moisture in the air crowds out everything else.

Henry's house looks smaller from here. Or maybe it's just that my world's gotten bigger. Expanding to places I'm not entirely sure I want to go at the same time as it shrinks to those I can allow to come with me.

For the first time, I'm glad Henry moved away. He can't be a part of this. Already I've put him in too much danger. Danger I can't let extend to Nate. No matter how big a hole it leaves in my heart, I have to let Nate go.

I find my cell phone under the sheets and start a text. But what do I say? How do I explain that my entire world changed over-night? Again. Changed overnight *again*, just like at the start of the summer when I woke up and became a Jinn. Became part of a world I tried to deny. A world Nate helped me to deny.

I set my phone on my desk while I rinse off the sweat and dirt that coated me last night. I then pull on the lightest article of cloth-ing I own, a tissue-thin black romper I let Chelsea talk me into buying, and drop my phone into the side pocket. I'll text Nate. But why does it have to be today?

Having seen the sun rise, I'm not surprised I slept in. Though once I leave my room, I do question how. Because instead of sleeping, I'm pretty sure my mother's been setting off bombs in-side the house in search of Xavier's clue. Each room I pass—bedroom, bathroom, guest room—has been ransacked. All except Zak's room. Where Yasmin sits in the same spot on the mattress beside her mother. The separate bed we conjured for her remains made. Did she not sleep at all?

The trashed living room, dining room, and kitchen prove that my mother didn't.

As do her red-rimmed eyes and caffeinated speech that fires at me the second I step out onto the back deck. "Well-there-you-are-good-you're-awake-we've-been-waiting-for-you-want-coffee?"

She's still wearing the cobalt-blue linen dress from last night. Now creased with wrinkles, its full length and long sleeves seem too dressy—and hot—for daytime. Samara, seated at the table across from her in a fresh outfit, greets me with a strained smile.

Tension hangs between them like a spiderweb.

At first I didn't realize the golden hair sticking out the back of the pink baseball cap belonged to Samara. The Red Sox hat, which Chelsea gave Laila, is a bizarre contrast to Samara's short white kaftan, embroidered with a spiral pattern in shiny gold thread on either side of the deep V neckline.

My mother pours me coffee from a thermos and levitates it toward me. Speaking so quickly it takes my brain time to process, she spits out, "Zak said you have something to show us."

Xavier's spell. With all that happened, we never got the chance to demonstrate the spell. I know we have to. So then why are my palms sweating?

I shrug at the steam swirling above the floating mug. "Uh, maybe iced?"

"Sure, kiddo," my mother says, drawing the mug back over the table.

But Samara hops up and grabs it. She conjures a speckled glass, loads it with conjured ice, and dumps the steaming hot coffee right on top. The glass cracks, and coffee floods the deck.

"Oh, for Janna's sake!" she cries, flopping back into her chair at the table. "This is why I should have listened to my mother and spent more time practicing the art of conjuring food."

"I'll get it, Mom," Laila calls from the backyard. Her bright yellow halter dress swishes as she hurries up the steps to the deck. Close behind her is Zak, who must have spent the night across the street since he's sporting what looks to be a newly conjured T-shirt and jeans.

Both of them are free of dirt. Well, mostly.

"Morning," I say, wiping a streak of leftover mud off the back of Zak's right ear. "Sleep okay?"

A quick look passes between Zak and Laila.

"Well enough, considering," Zak says.

His cheeks flush, and Laila drops to the ground with a conjured rag.

Laila and Zak? Really? And in Henry's old bedroom? What, is that room under some sort of love spell or something?

My mother magically sweeps up a shard of glass. "Your Lalla Sam won't admit it, but her magic's all wonky."

"It is not." Samara uses her powers to scoop a spoonful of sugar into her coffee mug. She misses and coats her lap with a dusting of white. "Fine. I'm not as strong as you."

"We both know that's not true." A softness surrounds the edge in my mother's voice.

Samara stops brushing sugar off her thighs. Her eyes are heavy with apology. "But Raina *and* Xavier . . . I don't know how you're not under the covers, Kalyssa."

My mother looks to Zak and then to me. "Yes, you do."

The outer ring of their web begins to unravel.

But the mention of my father makes my knees shake. I pull out the chair next to Samara and welcome the weight of her arm that she lays across my shoulders. I inhale her apricot scent, begging the comfort her embraces used to provide to come. It does, at least a little.

When I ask where everyone else is, my mother explains that Nadia and Hana are looking for Matin, who no one has seen since last night, while Isa and Jada have taken Farrah and Mina with them on a quest to discover alternative methods of healing from other Zars.

"Certainly we must do everything we can to heal Raina," Samara says in response. "But we also need to start gathering supporters. If the Jinn in Janna are going to rise against the council, we need to help them."

The way my pulse starts racing, it's like my heart's running a marathon. I breathe in the apricot now on my skin and ask, "But don't we need the portal?"

My mother plunks a magazine onto the table. "This is why your Lalla Sam has agreed to never lecture me about not living up to my duties again."

<hr/>

"Stunning, isn't it?" Samara says for the third time. She looks around the patio table at me, my mother, Zak, and Laila. "Simply stunning."

When my mother was searching the last room in the house—

her bedroom—she flung the stack of magazines she keeps on her nightstand to the floor. As she sorted through, a shock knocked her into the bedpost. Apparently, inducing pain is my father's signature.

The source of that zap, a glossy travel magazine, now trembles in Samara's hand. The marked page reveals the location of the weakness in the shield—the spot through which the Jinn here can apport into Janna undetected.

This makes it real. This makes it possible. Which is why Samara's hand quivers like a leaf on the last day of autumn. Somehow, her nerves are more comforting than a staunch bravado would be.

I gently take the magazine from her hand and lower it to the table to get a better, less shaky look at the archaeological wonder called "Najah." More than thirty feet high with a pair of rounded columns flanking a narrow opening, the short article accompanying the photo says the temple of Najah was carved into the desert mountains thousands of years ago and yet somehow still stands today, much like the lost city of Petra in the country of Jordan. However, the fact that Najah has but this one ruin means it pales in comparison to the size and scale of Petra. As a result, the article suggests adventurous travelers seeking a place devoid of tourism may want to visit this isolated "hidden gem" of Najah.

As majestic as it is foreboding, this temple, the color of sand with hints of burnt sienna, is what Samara's calling the linchpin of the uprising's plan. Of my father's plan. For it gives Jinn the element of surprise.

"With the shield that blocks apporting in position," she says, "the Afrit would never have reason to believe that Jinn here could infiltrate Janna. But with this, we'll be able to cross over and—"

"And what?" my mother says, the sharpness in her tone returning. "Fight them? You're not strong enough."

"You're," not "we're." And also not "they're." "They" as in the members of the uprising.

"So there isn't really an uprising here?" I ask. "No real plan?"

A told-you-so look accompanies my mother's nod, but Samara—politely—ignores her. "Azra, there is no organized rebellion here. Raina had been trying to create one, telling us that the Jinn in Janna were doing the same on their side. She wanted us to be prepared for the time when we could no longer abide by the council's rules." Samara's eyes flicker to my mother. "Most Jinn have been unwilling to believe such a time would come."

"But it has," I say. "Because of Qasim. Because of what Raina told us."

Samara's hand still shakes as she adds sugar—manually this time—to her coffee. "Yes, I'm afraid so. Qasim has always been devious. Wouldn't surprise me if he cheated to win the election. Or if the first thing he does is push for a vote on new restrictions or worse."

A vote. A *momentous* vote, like Matin said.

"Worse how?" I ask, pretty sure I don't actually want to know.

Samara looks to my mother for approval before speaking. "Raina said one of Qasim's greatest desires is to end our need to serve humans."

Laila's eyes widen. "But how could he possibly do that?"

With a sad smile, Samara says, "By making them subservient to us. Through mind control, through threats, through whatever means necessary. He's harbored fantasies of Jinn being out in the open and not having to fear humans but of making humans fear us."

"But there's too many humans," I say.

"I agree," Samara says. "As do most Jinn, which is why they've been just fantasies. But now that he's Chemharouch, who knows what he might attempt or when."

We all turn silent, letting what Samara has said sink in.

She bites her bottom lip and shakes her head. "I should have listened to Raina sooner. It should have never come to this. Why, it's been almost a full year since that Afrit came through to warn her."

I sit up straighter, as does Zak. The night of Henry's party, Yasmin said her mother had been warned, but she didn't say it was by an Afrit. Did she know? And is it possible . . . ? Was "that Afrit" our father? But why would he go to Raina and not my mother? Or did he, and she refused to listen?

My mother's tight lips answer both of those questions.

Samara places her trembling hands under her thighs. "Your father hoped he'd win over the council, and so did we. But after Raina was taken, he came through to tell your mother and me that it was time to prepare, to start by telling you girls everything, just in case."

The night Nate's father died, the night I saw my father in his shape-shifted form, the night he said, "It's time, Kal. If not now, when? How much longer does she have, really? They'll come for her, you know they will," he was already scared this might happen. Is that what prompted his backup plan? Prompted the spell? Prompted me?

My mother crosses her arms in front of her chest. "It's too risky. Azra's not getting involved. Neither is Zak."

"But we must." Zak jumps up from the table. "We should be going in right now. Father might be hurt."

"Zakaria." My mother stands and reaches for his arm. "I know you're upset. I know you're scared. But this is bigger than just your father." Her voice cracks and her eyes lower to the ground. "He was . . . he is . . . my one great love. We've both risked much to be together over the years. And I'd do it again." She looks at Zak, at Samara, at me, and her strength returns. "But that's our risk—mine and his. I cannot let you or your sister or any Jinn rush into Janna and risk their own life for his. He always knew the danger of what he was doing."

"That's true, Kal," Samara says, "but he also knew things couldn't continue like this." She rests her hand flat against the table. "And this isn't just for him. We all have loved ones there whose lives are in danger."

Laila clutches the gold locket around her neck. The one with her father's photograph inside.

A wistful look fills Samara's eyes. Though she's dated human men, clearly Laila's father remains in her heart.

Zak runs his hand through his hair, sending his careful part askew. "I'm sorry, Mom, but Samara's right."

Hopping up and grabbing the picture of Najah, Laila counters with, "But Lalla Kalyssa is also right. This may be a way in, but what then? The element of surprise won't be enough. You said the council is only twelve but that there are at least three times that number of full-blooded Afrit who'd fight with them. And they're just as powerful."

Samara nods. "Which is why there hasn't been a true uprising in years. But if the Jinn in Janna believe now is the time, we can't let them act alone." She trails her finger around the rim of her coffee mug. "Of course, we'll need to strategize. We'll need a plan . . . we'll need spells . . . At least Raina was already working on ones to subdue them, to camouflage our magic—"

"Camouflage?" Laila clutches the back of her chair. "Why?"

Zak drifts behind her and squeezes her shoulder. "The Afrit are able to monitor the use of magic in Janna through our bangles and necklaces."

"Another reason why the Jinn there need our help," Samara says. "They'd never be able to write and practice the spells necessary to accomplish such a feat without us."

"Plus," Zak adds, "most supporters in Janna don't have magic."

My mother's jaw tenses. "Xavier never wanted this. He never wanted Jinn to fight one another. You know that, Sam."

Samara sighs. "Neither did I. But we may not have a choice."

Laila strokes her locket. "Doesn't sound like who we are."

"It's not," Samara says. "But it's who they've made us become."

"Maybe not," I say, looking at Zak. When he nods, I push myself back from the table. "Maybe Xavier had a way around it. He sent Zak here with a backup plan."

Samara's cleavage hits the table as she leans in. "And you two know what that is?"

"Not exactly. But maybe together we can figure it out." I circle around the table to stand beside Zak. Hands entwined, we recite Xavier's spell.

Plop go three bangles.

The spell really doesn't need a talisman to work. It only needs us.

26

MY MOTHER STARES IN DISBELIEF AT THE HINGE ON HER GOLD bangle. Laila paces back and forth across the small deck. She keeps asking for us to undo what we've done. But we can't. Not even my mother understands the spell enough to do that.

As Samara calls Nadia to tell her and Hana to return to the house, I pull my phone out of my pocket. Things are moving much faster than I expected. The portal's already been found. With my father's diplomatic plan failing, the backup plan is now the only plan. And if I'm the key to it, I can't wait. I have to text Nate. Today.

My pulse races as I tap the screen.

I need to . . .

Go through a portal? No. *Save my father from being tortured?* No. *Help start an uprising?* Probably not. *Make sure you stay out of it all?* Yes.

But you're not going to like how. I don't.

I flutter my eyelashes to beat back the prickle of tears as I finish:

. . . see you. Today.

The smiley faces that accompany his Working, swing by are the only ones around the table. Is it any wonder I haven't wanted to let go of Nate before now? Is it any wonder that I still don't? Denial is a lovely river to float on.

But I can't let it sink Nate. Though it's something I've done my entire life, this time the act of pushing someone away—of pushing Nate away—isn't to protect myself, it's to protect them. It should make it hurt less.

It doesn't.

Instead, it's like my heart's a grenade and someone's just pulled out the pin. The shattered bits swirl around my chest, making it hard to breathe, let alone think. I concentrate on the former because I'm so sick of the latter.

I play with the hinge on my bangle until Hana and Nadia arrive—without Matin. Once they're ready, we confirm what Zak and I already know. That Xavier's spell only works when we say it together. Separately? Nothing. Together with another Jinn? Nothing. Two other Jinn besides us? Nothing. The spell only hurls Hana's bangle to the ground and Nadia's into her coffee mug when Zak and I say it together.

Hana paces in time with Laila. "I'm not sure you should have done that," she says.

It seems Hana's on Laila's side, the side wary of the uprising. Not that I'm unwary. But this is about Raina and the Jinn in Janna and . . . my father. This is about my father. Do I really need any other reason?

Nadia sits with her hip-length beige cardigan draped around

her shoulders. She's halfway between my mother and Samara, geographically on the deck and mentally in terms of the uprising.

"This breaks our tie to the Afrit," Samara says yet again. She keeps repeating this, trying to work out what else it might mean. "If we remove our bangles, they won't be able to track us."

"We'll be safe," Laila says. She's said this before too.

"But we won't be able to do magic," Hana says. "We've all tried with our bangles off and only Azra can."

"Yes, yes, I know." Samara drums her fingers against the teak table before addressing Zak. "You're sure he said this was to assist his backup plan?"

Zak stands off to the side, watching Laila pace. "He was going to tell me more. Once I returned. Before the election."

Samara nods. We know the election was moved up. We know he ran out of time.

"If only we were all like Azra, we'd truly have the element of surprise," Samara says, stopping the *tat tat tat* of her red nails. "Why, we could cross into Janna and *let* the Afrit remove our bangles. They'd believe they'd won, and yet we could strike out against them, use spells to subdue them at the most opportune moments."

Nadia pushes a lock of her auburn hair behind her ear. She then begins to bob her head. "What if we *could* be like Azra?"

Everyone looks at me. What, are they going to open up a vein and drink my blood?

"What do you mean?" Samara says.

"Let's see what we know about Xavier's spell," Nadia begins. "Azra, hon, you said Yasmin knocked your bangle off by accident, yes?"

I don't know if I'd call wrenching my wrist an "accident," but I nod.

Nadia's eyes dart back and forth. "Then we must assume the Afrit can also still remove them—magically or manually." It's like I can see the wheels turning in her sharp mind as she tries to piece this together. "In essence then, what Xavier's spell does is allow us to protect ourselves. The moment we slip off our bangles, the Afrit become unable to track us. If we can't be found, we can't be punished. But the spell does not give us back our magic." She sighs. "That would have been too much to hope for." She clicks open the hinge on her bangle. "And yet it returns some control to us. What if we could take that a step further? What if we could return complete control back to us?"

"What are you thinking, Nadia?" Samara asks.

"We use the Afrit's methods against them. We prevent the bangles from being removed by anyone but the wearer. We block the ability to be tracked. We break our tie to the Afrit. Completely." She snaps her bangle closed.

A knowing smile begins to curl the edges of Samara's lips. "If we could do that, we'd no longer be at their mercy. And they would no longer be able to monitor the use of high-level magic like they can now."

"Like the circulus?" Hana asks.

"Yes," Samara says, "but more importantly for the uprising, spells of the highest order, the type we need to fight the Afrit. In the past, practicing such advanced magic was how Jinn who wanted to rebel have been caught."

There's a bounce in Zak's step as he moves around the deck.

"We'd have no need to camouflage our use of magic in Janna." His eyebrows rise to his hairline. "We'd have a chance . . . we'd actually have a chance."

Laila frowns at him before throwing one hand in the air. "Great theory. But isn't it just that? What makes you think you can do any of this?"

"Kalyssa," Nadia and Samara say at the same time.

My mother shakes her head. "A spell? You think I can write such a spell—probably multiple spells—all by myself?"

Nadia lets her sweater fall as she rises to stand next to my mother. "Yes, I do. But you don't have to." She sweeps her hand around the deck. "You have all of us. And most importantly, you have Xavier's spell to work from. We've never had something that advanced before. If you study it, I'm sure you'll be able to find out exactly what it does and take it further—as far as we need to. That must be what he intended, Kalyssa. He believes in you. As much as we all always have."

Still shaking her head, my mother leans back against the railing. "Even if I could—and that's a big if—going into Janna will still be risky. Jinn will likely get . . . hurt."

I think we all know "hurt" wasn't her first word choice.

With a deep sigh, Nadia links her arm through my mother's. "You're right. But we have to do this, Kalyssa." My mother hesitates, and Nadia continues, "And not just for Xavier or any of our children's fathers. Janna knows I want them to be safe, but this is for all Jinn. Seeing Matin after all these years . . . I mean, what were we thinking? Especially you and I? How could we not have done something sooner? We accepted this life out of fear, grateful for what they allowed us to have even though it wasn't nearly enough. It's not a life I want for Hana. I'm sure it's not a life you want for Azra."

My mother blinks rapidly and her tear-dampened eyelashes smear her day-old mascara. "We'll have to find a way to test the spells."

It's a suicide mission otherwise.

My head spins around. Who said that? What was that?

"And we won't get Jada on our side," my mother says.

And no matter what, I'm not letting Azra go in.

My mother's thoughts. In my head. I read a Jinn's mind. Just like the Afrit.

"That's okay," Samara says. "With Raina . . . without Raina, our Zar can't draw on its strength anyway."

But I'm going in. For Laila. For Laila's father. For you, Kalyssa, for your Xavier.

A shiver runs down my spine and yet at the same time a bead of sweat forms on my forehead. I'm actually reading their minds.

Laila bounds down the steps to the backyard. She wants no part of it. She doesn't want *any* of us to be a part of it.

How can they do this? How can they risk themselves? How can Zak want to risk himself? Aren't we . . . something?

But *how* am I reading their minds? And why now?

Zak follows Laila, drawing her away from the rest of us. He caresses her cheek, and her small face is dwarfed by his hand.

I'm sorry, Laila. But it's my father.

I feel faint. But not from the *act* of reading their minds. From knowing what they're feeling. From *feeling* what they're feeling.

Zak's voice is strong but tender as he says, "You don't have to be a part of this, Laila, but I hope you can still support us. Support me." Her face scrunches in fear and frustration and the two apport away together.

Everyone else retakes their seats around the patio table. My mother pushes up her sleeves and raises the umbrella. She's far from convinced that she can do this—that she should do this—but she's willing to discuss it. Hana, pale, sits by her mother's side, listening, clearly against her better judgment.

Once they have the spell, they think the biggest obstacles are how to test that the Afrit can no longer remove our bangles and how they'll convince the other Zars here to believe them, to join the cause, to stop Qasim before he's able to start anything.

I think something else. No matter what Samara's saying about it being just like Xavier to require both Zak and me to do the spell, to ensure no single Jinn has that much power, am I really to believe that repeating a few words is what makes me the key to the uprising? My father must know I can do magic without my bangle. Does that truly have nothing to do with all this?

I know my father didn't intend for things to play out this way. He didn't intend to lose the election, have his true goals uncovered, and be unable to participate as planned in any revolt against the Afrit. Still, I would have thought he'd leave us more clues than this.

All those years apart, all that time he spent preparing, and this is what it's come to? Supposition and guesswork? Doesn't there have to be more?

I slide back into my chair and open the travel magazine. I stare at the ornate carvings on the Najah temple. All across the top, under the arched roof of the building, is a line of people holding hands. I squint to see them better. Their height, their dress . . . they could be Jinn. Was this temple built by our ancestors? Will their spirits protect the Jinn who cross through into Janna? Since, despite what my mother thinks, I intend to be one of them, I sure hope so.

I'm about to close the magazine when I realize something that none of us saw before. The article we thought was short actually continues onto the next page. It quotes a scholar talking about the origins of Najah. Built as long ago as 400 BC. Thought to be a shrine to the god of home and hearth. A travesty that it's not under any historical protections. The need to preserve because . . . *What?*

The scholar's direct quote: "Because we think these things will be around always. But nothing is forever."

Always. But not forever.

Really? Can it be? I'm done believing in coincidences. This is another clue from Xavier. I scan backward to find the scholar's name. F. P. Daher, a retired historian who lives in Cambridge. Cambridge, across the river from Boston, only an hour away.

There's most definitely more. And I need to be the one to find out what it is. Because the way they're currently talking about keeping "us girls" out of this, I know if I tell my mother and Samara, they'll go without me. And they might not even tell me what the historian says. What else my father needs me to do. So I'm going to Cambridge.

My phone buzzes.

Coming soon? Miss you.

I swallow hard. I just have to break up with my boyfriend first.

27

THE TALL GRASS ON EITHER SIDE OF THE ARCHED WOODEN PATH over the dunes crackles as the wind hits it. Once a vibrant green and climbing toward the sky, the stalks are turning yellow and brittle. Soon they'll be brown and, not long after, buried by snow.

The air at home was heavy with humidity. I thought it'd be lighter here at the beach, but as I reach the last plank before the sand, my lungs still fight to take my next breath.

I kick off my sandals. It's high tide. The beach has shrunk to a narrow strip, packed, noisy, and chaotic. This is my least favorite time of day in my most favorite place.

I wind my way through the blankets, pop-up tent shelters, and umbrellas. Sweaty beachgoers desperate for this last bit of summer are clumped together like fried calamari.

The tanned clique of beautiful bods—the lifeguards—are spread out on their lofty white perches. A few call out a "Hey," "Hi, Azra," and "Long time no see" as I pass. The rules of the beach have changed since the start of the summer. Thanks to Chelsea and to Nate. A fact that even now still takes me by surprise.

I look for Chelsea in her two-piece bathing suit emblazoned with GUARD across the chest in capital letters, but don't see her. She'll be trading in the red sporty bikini for her orange-and-black cheerleading uniform. The one with the tiger paw plastered across the front. The one Laila told me last night, before everything happened, that she hoped to soon be wearing too.

I wonder if she'll get the chance. As I stumble over a plastic shovel—and almost into the two-foot hole it created—I wonder what this next year will bring. These past few days have made school the furthest thing from my mind. What I'll wear on my first day, if Nate will ask me to homecoming, if all the kids who used to ignore me in the halls, in class, and in gym will suddenly want to be my best friends because of Nate and Chelsea . . . none of it matters. The first day, homecoming, walking the halls, class, and gym will go on, but I'm starting to think they'll go on without me.

The options before me leave little chance that I'll return to the life I once lived—actually, the life I never got the chance to live. A life with friends, a boyfriend, a Zar sisterhood, a life of being Jinn.

Not that I intend to go all kamikaze if I storm the portal into Janna. But I'm pretty sure I won't be sliding into a seat in physics class afterward either. (Perk though that may be.)

My heart stretches like saltwater taffy as I contemplate the two choices I have. But, really, is there even a second choice? How can I not join the group that will be entering Janna? After all this time of wishing to have my father in my life, am I really going to stay behind?

My mother wants me to. She even wants Zak to. But he's nineteen, and I'm sixteen—an adult in the Jinn world. We hardly need her permission.

There's much to lose if we go, much that we'll leave behind. But I can't deny how much there is to gain—helping to save our father, helping to stop Qasim, helping to change what it means to be Jinn.

Then again, since my mother's Zar has already begun to recruit supporters here, that's likely to happen with or without us. Samara's willing to risk everything. For me, for my mother, just like my mother thought. Feared. If that triggers my guilt, what must it be doing to my mother? What will Laila think when she learns that Samara is willing to risk everything and my mother isn't? Wouldn't she rather be in my shoes? Am I crazy that a part of me wants to be in hers?

I walk in the ocean, letting the cool water surround my feet. It's better than traipsing around the graveyard of plastic toys left at the edge of the incoming tide.

A sailboat in the distance tacks to change direction. I never have gotten out on the ocean with Nate and Megan. There's no longer time. Because even if I do stay behind, I can't be Nate's girl-friend. Even if I wanted to be. Which I do. And I don't. It's complicated. Because of "other stuff." So much other stuff. Henry, sure, maybe, I don't know. But being Jinn, being Afrit, being the key to the uprising means other stuff will always be in our way. Same as it's in the way with Henry. With everyone. I was a fool to think anything else.

Part of me still wants to be that fool. Silly tasseled hat with bells on the end and all.

Because fools aren't asked to climb horses and join the cavalry into battle.

Fools also aren't asked to stay and protect those left behind.

Like Zak and I are being asked to do. If the uprising fails, if my mother can't master the spells it needs, the protection of Jinn in the human world falls to us. Not only will we have to recite the spell to make sure the Jinn here can't be found, but I'll be the only Jinn left in this world with the magic to protect them if they are. That's a hard choice *not* to make.

Some role Zak and I have. Once we recite the spell that frees Jinn of the ability to be tracked down by the Afrit, we also free them of their ability to use magic.

But a life with no magic beats magic with no life.

Of course that's true. Even though my life didn't truly begin until magic crossed over the welcome mat.

The sailboat completes its turn, now heading the same way as I am, to the marshy area at the far end of the beach. Though I increase my pace, I can't keep up with the boat's graceful glide across the water.

Suddenly, I'm seized from behind. Panic flashes through me like lightning striking a tree. Though I know it can't be, that they'd never do it so publicly, my first thought is that this is the Afrit *coming for me*. That I'm too terrified to blink means my mother, as usual, is right. I have no place in a battle against the Afrit.

"I've missed you," Nate says, his breath tickling my earlobe.

Relief and desire make my cheeks flush. I spin around and let him kiss me. The push-pull of the choices before me evaporates from my mind like a drop of water on hot pavement. My palms flatten against Nate's smooth chest. The supersonic beat of his heart entices my already rapid pulse to quicken to match. Our feet sink under the sand. Each ebb and flow of the tide buries them deeper, until, when we finally part, the suction is as strong as a magnet.

"Mmm, worth the wait," he says. "When you didn't answer my second text, I was afraid you weren't coming."

Second text? I draw my phone out of my pocket and press the button to wake it. It's dead. With all that's been going on, it didn't occur to me to charge it.

Henry.

With all that's been going on, it also didn't occur to me to text Henry my daily selfie yesterday. But it's not like he's actually sitting there waiting for one, is he? I'll do it as soon as I get home.

Home. Uprising central. Push-pull, pull-push, go to Janna, stay here, neither of those decisions affects this one. *Focus, Azra.* I can't put Nate in danger any more than I can risk being the cause of additional pain if something happens to me. He's been through enough. I lay my hand on Nate's chest and put distance between us.

"What's wrong?" Nate asks.

So much.

But I say, "Nothing, really."

"How was your big dinner?" he asks. "How are things with Laila?"

The dinner? That seems like ages ago. Time seems to have moved both in slow motion and at the speed of light since I've last seen Nate.

"Fine," I say. "Good."

My tone makes Nate reach for my hand, and instantly a sense of calm fills me. I'm now convinced that the connection from granting a human's wish goes deeper than most Jinn realize. We don't normally know our wish candidates. We don't usually stay in contact with them the way I've done with Nate. So we wouldn't know that the piece of them that stays with us has the ability to affect us long after the wish is granted. I suspect I'm feeling calm from Nate because of who he is. If he were an angry, mean, or jealous person, I'd probably feel those parts of myself amplified when I was around him. Thankfully Nate's who he is. Trouble is, the more I'm around Nate, the more I want to be around Nate.

Which is why I have to do this. Now.

"I know you used to have Henry for this kind of stuff," Nate says, guiding us down the beach. "But you can talk to me. If you want. It's cool if you don't. But you can. I just wanted you to know that."

My chest tightens. I lift his hand to my lips and kiss the back. It tastes like the sea. For once, I don't mind the salt. "I know. But thank you for saying it."

I've always been desperate to off-load everything to Henry right after it happens—while it's happening—but that's never been the case with Nate. Keeping him separate from my life as a Jinn has always been more important.

Never more so than right now.

I steel my resolve but keep walking because all I can tell him are half-truths, and I don't want to look him in the eye as I lie (even half) to him. "It's . . . my dad." Nate's grip around my hand slackens. "I didn't want to tell you because—"

·"Of mine," he says softly. "Azra, let me be here for you. Please."

He tightens his hold on my hand, and I so want to do what he asks.

We stop in front of a favorite spot of mine, the big black rock that juts out higher and wider than all the rest in this area of the beach.

I give in for this one moment. "I know I don't talk about him much. It's kind of a sore spot. For my mom, especially. But things are . . . not good. I'm going to have to go to him."

Nate nods solemnly but doesn't pry. That's not who he is.

"I'm not sure when I'll be back," I say, leading us onto the path neither of us wants to travel down. "Probably not for a while."

Nate erases the space between us and his lips brush my forehead. He pushes back my hair and trails a hand down each side of my face, holding my head between his strong hands and caressing my cheek with his thumb. "I'm really sorry. Is there anything I can do?"

You're doing it. Like always.

I clear my throat. "Give Megan a hug for me. I'll have Hana bring her all my books. Tell her I'll miss her. George and Goldie too. And your mom, I hope she comes home soon."

His face brightens. "She is. Well, sort of. We just found out this morning that she's moving to a rehab place. If it goes well, she'll be home in a couple of weeks."

"I'm so glad, Nate."

He shuffles his feet in the sand. "Yeah, me too. Maybe you'll be back around the same time?" It's a statement with the tone of a question. Because this connection between us goes both ways. He knows I'm lying. He knows what this is. Even if he can't let himself believe it.

I shake my head. "I don't think so." I bite my bottom lip and the pain forces me to not lose focus of what I need to do. "Which is why I need you to not wait for me."

It's like a piano has fallen on his head. He crumples before my eyes. And I do right along with him. But I keep it inside.

"What?" He stumbles back and rubs the nape of his neck with his hand. "What do you . . . ? Azra, what are you . . . ?"

"Nate, my family . . . my life is complicated." And this is the compromise. "I need to . . . We need to . . ."

He stops rubbing and his neck vanishes as he hangs his head. "It's okay, Azra. I'll . . . I'll do whatever you need."

He brings his clenched fists to his sides, bumping them against his legs. It's taken all his strength, all his respect for me not to scream the *Please, no* I'm desperately trying not to read in his mind.

Suddenly, his eyes lock on my own. "But first, there's something I need to do."

"What?" I can't look at him. I focus on the waves instead.

"This." He wraps one muscled arm around my waist and slides the other up the length of my back, resting his hand on my head. His fingers spread, and the crunch of my hair against my scalp makes me draw in a breath. My eyes close involuntarily and my neck arches in response to his gentle tug. His lips find my collarbone and glide down in a slow, smooth arc, floating over my skin, barely touching, until he reaches the center of my throat, where he lingers.

"I will always miss your *A* necklace," he says.

I've been wearing the infinity one since the night I put it on at the party for Laila.

My chest is so tight that my lungs struggle for air and my voice comes out raspy. Unintentionally sexy. "I'm sorry, Nate."

He releases his hold around my waist and brings his hand to my hip. He sets it there for a moment, grounding me. He then trails his fingers up the side of my torso, skirting my breast, tickling my neck, caressing my chin, ending by cupping my flushed cheek.

He leans in, and his breath warms my lips as he says, "The trouble is, I love you, Azra. But you already know that." The confidence I made sure he has floods through him—and me—as he says, "When you feel the same I'll be here. Waiting."

The world goes silent and all I hear is my heart beating against my chest. And then my feet leave the ground and I balance on tiptoes and my mouth is on his and my hands have a mind of their own and we're clawing for oxygen, each stealing the other's breath and all I want is *this this this*, to be so entwined that I don't know what's mine and what's his and—

No, no, no! My knees buckle, and my heart drops to my heels.

I can't do this. I can't feel this. I can't say *I love you* back. Not because I don't want to. Because I do. Or I could. I want to. I definitely want to. But I can't, because he's a human and I'm a Jinn. Because I'm an Afrit. Because I'm the key to the uprising. Because I have to leave, and I may not come back.

I press my palms against his chest. "I—"

Maybe he knows the response isn't what he wants to hear or hopes to hear or needs to hear because he doesn't wait for me to finish. He lays a finger on each of my eyelids, gently closing them. He startles me by pressing a soft kiss on each. It's warm and strange and . . . nice. Intimate. He then lets his lips graze mine. Just once. His cheeks sweep against mine and his nose greets me in a playful Eskimo kiss.

My eyes are still closed when a chill takes over, making me tremble. I open my eyes to see Nate backing away, his finger to his lips, his eyes clouded with sadness.

Nate's changed my world. He's changed me. For the better, so much for the better. And yet it still nags at me, the idea that I'm the reason his father died. That the Afrit caused the accident to punish me. I wonder if I'll be able to find out if that's true. I wonder if I'll be able to live with the answer. If it'll be another secret, another burden, I'll have to keep.

Is this it? Am I really letting Nate go like this?

My first tear is followed by a second and a third.

I have to leave. I may not come back.

And Nate will never know why. Hiding who I am—hiding who my family is—from Nate has always been between us. In the beginning, it was part of the attraction. Being with Nate meant I didn't have to be a Jinn. At least for a little while. But now . . . I can't separate being Jinn from being me even if I wanted to. Which I don't. It's who I am. It's who I will always be. And being with Nate would mean asking him to live a lie. I couldn't do that to him. It's not a life I'd want to live.

But what if I do come back? And what if when I do, everything's changed? What if being Jinn is no longer filled with the fear and restrictions it is now? What if somehow, Nate wouldn't have to live a lie? What if I didn't have to do that to him? Is it a life I'd want to live?

Nate's face is tight with hurt, confusion, and concern. I can't let things end like this. I can't let him tell me he loves me and say nothing. Not when I feel everything.

Thank you, Nate. For everything.

His feet dig into the sand.

Did he hear me? Did he feel me?

Whichever it is, whatever he thinks is happening, it makes the rejection in his eyes a little less.

Should I tell him more? Should I go ahead and tell him that a part of me does love him and always will? Because I do. How can I not?

My first love. And maybe my last. But not my only one.

❧❦❧

The tide's gone out. The next time I look up, there's a wide expanse of beach before me. I turn to face the big black rock. It rises even higher now that the water's retreated. No longer an island, it's more like a cliff. One I feel like my heart's just been pitched from.

Scattered around me are rocks of less height and girth that were previously hidden, submerged under the ocean. I weave my way through to get to the cliff. But as I climb up, I notice a set of toes popping above the surface of the water.

Toes attached to a foot, that's attached to a leg, that's attached to a torso that's exposed above water, leaning against the rock, sporting a head that's lolled back and resting in a crevice on the side of the massive black rock.

Matin.

Oh my Janna, is he . . .

"Mat!" I cry, hopping down into the water. My foot lands next to an empty bottle of gin.

The good stuff, I'm betting.

At least the source of his unconsciousness is his own doing.

I squat in front of him and roughly shake him by his shoulders. He groans. I scoop up a handful of water and splash his face. He groans louder, exhaling a breath that reeks of stale alcohol. I place my hand over my nose.

"Matin!" I shout louder. Nothing. And so I do what must be done. I slap his scruffy-bearded cheek. Hard. Harder than I intended, but I can't deny that right now the release feels good.

His hand flies to his face, and his head jerks forward and then back, cracking against the rock. "What the——?"

"Matin," I say. "What are you doing here? Did you sleep here?"

He opens his eyes and instinctually raises a hand to shield the sun. "Azra? What are you doing in my motel room? And why is my motel room underwater?"

"Let's get you up." I yank him by both arms. "Gross. You're all wrinkly." I manage to slide him partway up the rock. "How did you get here?"

He crawls the rest of the way up, looks around, and falls back, spreading himself flat against the rock. "Aye, I'm going to go with 'walked.' I'm not much of a swimmer. And I do believe the motel faces the street, not the ocean, a ways back thataway." He flings his hand over his head, pointing right, then left, then right again.

"Why didn't you stay at the house? With Yasmin?"

At her name, he winces. "Is she . . . ? How is her mother?"

A deluge of emotions hits me. Breaking up with Nate's opened a door to all I've been trying to keep bottled up inside. I choke out, "The same."

"Aye, well, that's something, I suppose." He pats the rock around him. "Azra, dear, I seem to be missing the good stuff."

Uh-huh. That flings open another door. The door to the room where I think Matin's a coward for running away just when Yasmin, when Hana, when his mother need him. "No, you're not. It's all in here." I press on his stomach.

He jerks up, makes a slight retching sound, and swallows.

"Sorry," I say. But at least now he's upright. "Have you been here the whole time?"

His brow furrows. "I do not believe so, but I also do not believe I am the most reliable source of information at the moment."

"So you don't know about the uprising and the plan to—"

"That's enough of that unless you're in the mood to conjure some beverages." He cocks his head. "Are you?" When I roll my eyes, he continues, "Shame. What I could do if only I had powers."

"*Matin.*"

"Right. Well, your dear brother informed me of what was occurring, and I had a choice to make. So my good buddy gin and I had a chat." He laughs, retches, and swallows again. "Gin, get it?"

"A choice? *You* have a choice to make? But you can't think of going back into Janna without magic. That doesn't make any sense."

"Aye, so many choices make so little sense to outside eyes."

With a clunk, he drops back down against the rock. He's still drunk. I'll have to get him out of here. I can't believe with all that's going on I have to deal with this.

I stand on top of the rock, surveying the beach. Low tide and the increase in sandy real estate has turned the beach into a parade. Which means, there's too many people around for us to apport from right here.

I spend a few minutes trying to coax Matin into the woods that line the swath of beach behind us. I spend a single minute trying to drag him. No use. If only my phone weren't dead I could call Laila or Hana to help.

Then again, maybe I don't need my phone to call them for help. The first time Hana felt my emotions, it was because I was upset and desperate. She apped straight to me to find out what was wrong.

I'm nothing if not upset and desperate now. Leaving Matin on the rock, I cross the narrow strip of sand behind it and enter the woods. My desire for help simmers right beneath my skin, so instead I focus on Laila and Hana, pleading with them to find me.

They do. One after the other.

"What was that?" Laila faces me. "That was you?"

I can't help the beginnings of a smile that tugs at my lips.

Hana loops an arm around my shoulder and then Laila's. "So so cool."

"Actually kinda creepy," Laila says, echoing my exact thoughts the first time this happened.

"Agreed," I say. "But useful." I want to tell Laila—both of them—about Nate, but there's no time. So instead, I begin to lead them onto the beach.

The moment I poke my head out, I come face-to-face with a silver-haired woman in a leopard-print bikini. The top's straps are shoved down around her shoulders. For some reason, the sixty-plus set are obsessed with tan lines, avoiding them at all costs, even if that means their boobs droop to their knees.

"When you gotta go, you gotta go, am I right?" the woman says. She laughs with three of her fellow droopsies as they continue the beach parade.

Once they pass, I hop out and gesture for Hana and Laila to follow me onto the beach and to Matin.

"Pee-yew!" Laila swoops a chunk of hair in front of her nose. "Is that coming from him?"

"Unfortunately," I say. "He's still pretty wasted."

Hana leans against the rock and lifts her brother's head. "Oh, Mat."

His eyes shoot open. "Sister, you're all right?"

"Yes, I'm fine."

"And Mother?"

"She's fine too. She's with Raina and Yasmin."

"Splendid. That's it, then, it is."

Hana squints at him and then at me.

I point to the empty gin bottle. "I think he drank that whole thing. I needed your help to get him to the woods so we can app him home."

"Thanks for finding him, Azra," Hana says, frowning at her brother. "He keeps doing this. Going off on his own. For someone who says he came here to get to know his family, he's not spending much time doing that." She sighs as she pulls the hair tie off her wrist and gathers her red strands together. She pats Matin on the top of his stubbly head. "Come on, up we go."

"That's not going to work," I say. I raise my hand as if to whack him.

Instantly he sits up. "Right, then."

Between the three of us and a little levitation, shielded expertly by Laila, we get him to the woods. We're about to app him home when he suddenly pats his pants pocket.

"My pen!" he cries. "It's missing!"

Hana says curtly, "We'll get you another."

"No! It has to be that one. I need that one." He fights against our grasp. "It was a gift."

Hana's frustration is palpable, but still she asks me, "Azra, would you mind . . ."

It's for Hana, not Matin, that Laila and I return to the beach and start searching.

Laila spreads the sand behind the rock with her foot. "He must really like Yasmin to be this torn up about Raina."

I mutter agreement but add, "Though you'd think that'd mean he wouldn't leave Yasmin's side. That's what I'd do."

"You mean, that's what you *did*. With Nate."

I swallow hard as I kneel and dig in the sand next to the rock. "I had to," I manage to eke out.

"But you also wanted to."

I pause, about to admit something I'm not proud of. "Not at first. I was scared. I wanted to leave. But then I knew, despite being scared, there was nowhere else I wanted to be."

"The definition of love." Laila's eyes flicker to the sand the instant I look at her.

Laila and Zak? In love? My brother and my best friend?

It's weird. And not.

I grab her hand and pull her onto the sand next to me. "You really care about him? Zak?"

She winds a curl around her finger, still unable to look at me. "I think . . . I know . . . I'm falling . . . I mean, I have . . ."

"Laila, it's okay. It's me. Best friends share secrets."

Thank you, Jenny, for teaching me how to be a best friend.

She draws in a deep breath and meets my gaze. "I love him, Azra." She sucks in her bottom lip.

I stifle my gasp before it escapes my lips. *Don't react. Well, react. Just don't react badly.* My heart thuds against my ribs. *Say something, Azra.* "But it's been . . . I mean, it hasn't been . . ." *Janna, why is this so hard?* "Already? How do you know?"

She smiles warmly. "When it's right, you don't have to ask that question. It just is. There's no other way it could be."

I nod as if this makes perfect sense. Which it does. Except when it doesn't. Except when you don't know if what feels right feels right because of a connection from granting a wish or from the mutual mourning of someone long gone or from the bonding over someone recently gone or from the sharing of forbidden se-crets or from a hope and a fear and a yearning for what might be and what could be and—

"Azra?" Laila's voice trembles. "Should I not have told you?"

I shake away everything. "No, I'm glad you did. I'm happy for you. For both of you."

"But what if it doesn't work out? What if he has to leave?"

I pick up the gin bottle, and the pen rises to the surface. "Then you enjoy it for whatever time you have."

I grab the pen, and we start for the woods. Out of the corner of my eye, I see a figure running down the beach. His glasses slip down his nose. I hand the pen to Laila.

"You guys go," I say. "Turns out, someone has been waiting for me."

28

"I know, I know," I say once Henry is in range. "I'm sorry. I forgot, and then my phone was dead, and then——"

Henry crashes into me with the force of a Mack truck. I stumble as his momentum propels us both backward. Somehow I manage to catch myself and plant my feet, holding him, grounding us. He smells of sweat and vinyl and fast food and fear.

"One," he says, his voice muffled by my hair. "You get one pass." He squeezes me like a corset. "Do it again, and the Afrit will be the least of your worries."

His arms relax and his torso begins to separate from mine, but I'm not ready to let go. I know I should. As much as I know he shouldn't be here. That he shouldn't——can't——become a part of this. But now that he *is* here, now that I've let Nate go, I also know I don't have the strength to do the same with Henry. My selfishness pushes me forward and closes the gap.

His rapid breaths slow while mine speed up. I open my mouth to speak, to apologize, to tell him everything, to lighten this burden that's so heavy it's contracting my spine, but all that comes out is a squeak.

Azra, I'm here. I'm always here.

I know. The trouble is, will I be?

Well, this isn't awkward *at all.*

I scoot further to the edge of the big black rock, ironically now needing to distance myself from Henry, as Nate sprints by on his afternoon beach run. Gentleman that he is, Nate waves politely. I suck in a breath as a sharpness tightens my chest. Henry's sandy-brown-haired head tilts to the side.

Having just spent the past hour telling him about Raina, my father's backup plan, and F. P. Daher, I haven't broached the subject of my newly single status.

Henry returns to his smartphone and finishes the search for Daher's home address.

"Got it," he says. "But you can't go to Cambridge alone."

I pick at a shell attached to the side of the rock, once the cozy home for some tiny sea creature. I was hoping he'd say that. But I can't actually let him come with me.

We're so close to the end of the beach that Nate's already turned around and about to pass us on his return trip. He's faster this time. Focused. He doesn't look our way.

Henry sees me watching Nate and leans forward. "You're not going with him, are you?" He places his elbows on his knees. "You haven't *told* him, have you?"

The shell cracks in my hand. "No! Of course not. I'd never put him in that kind of danger."

Henry looks over his glasses at me. "Gee, thanks."

"I mean, it's too dangerous to lay all this on him. Make him keep all these secrets."

"Again, thanks."

I bump my shoulder against Henry's. "You know what I mean."

"All too well, I'm afraid."

"Stop it. It's not the same, and you know it."

"Boy, do I ever know it."

"Henry! You're impossible!" A smile creeps up on me. Henry always seems to be able to make me smile, even when I'm at my lowest. Funny how often that seems to be the case.

Henry sniffs the neckline of his yellow T-shirt. "You know what's impossible? That I still smell like fries. That was the guy on the first bus. Or maybe it was the second. The third bus was definitely the one where I'm convinced the exhaust fumes were venting inside not outside. Did I mention the lack of air conditioning?"

I find another empty shell and start tugging. "I can't believe you took three buses just to get here."

"You're just lucky it wasn't four. Four was my limit. Four, and I'd let the Afrit swoop in and never think twice."

"You're a jerk."

"Maybe, but I'm still your best friend," he says, before his mind follows with *And best friends do more than share secrets.*

Then his phone rings.

And then, somehow, we're no longer side by side on the black rock but just as close, if not closer, in Chelsea's convertible. Henry blackmailed me into coming—threatening to call my mother if I didn't let him—but he refused to let me apport us.

We met Chelsea in the parking lot, and she handed over her keys.

With the top down on the small two-lane road that leads out from the beach, the tall trees shield the sun and I'm almost able to forget where we're going, what I'm about to do, and what I've just done.

But once we merge onto the highway with the trucks whose ginormous tires kick pebbles in our faces, all that changes. Hemmed in by semis, SUVs, and minivans, the claustrophobia and the whipping wind make me close my eyes. And that's it. I think about everything all at once—where we're going, what I'm about to do, what I've just done, and more.

I think about what's happening to my father right now. I think about how Raina's doing, how Yasmin's feeling. I think about the pressure my mother must be under to write the spells that Nadia and Samara are convinced she can.

And being here, in Chelsea's car, with Henry, I also think about the two of them in his room, which, considering the news about Laila and Zak, really could be under some sort of love spell. I then think about Laila and Zak and how they could possibly know it's right so soon. And of course, I think about Nate, knowing I did the right thing but also wanting to take it back. And I think about wanting to talk to Henry and not wanting to talk to Henry about all of this.

Yeah, so that's our fifty-minute ride to Cambridge.

"That sign can't be right," Henry says. "Twenty-five dollars to park? Are they crazy?" He's circled Harvard Square four times looking for a metered parking spot. The pay lot, despite its extravagant rate, is nearly full.

I lean over the tiny center console. "This is a sign."

"No, it's not. We'll find something."

"Come on, just drop me off. Wait for me somewhere. Like Urban Outfitters."

Henry snorts. "Right, because I'm so the tie-dye hoodie type."

"You never know if you don't try. Besides, I'm betting Chelsea would love it."

His hands clench around the wheel.

"What?" I say. "You two having a fight? Can't be that big if she gave you her car."

"Let me *borrow* her car. And no, we aren't fighting."

On this, our fifth trip down the same street, a spot opens just as we turn the corner. Henry takes it, parallel parking in front of a wood-fired pizza place whose mouthwatering aroma is like a siren call. My stomach growls, begging to go inside.

Henry stuffs his hands in his jeans pockets, searching for change. I step out of the car and notice there's no meter for this spot. I look up and groan.

"What?" he asks.

I point above our heads. "Loading zone. For another hour."

Henry steps back to check the sign. "Can't you . . . you know, change it?"

Change it? Change the sign? I look around. It is just one number. One little number that needs to tick down. No one's watching. No one's staring at the NO PARKING sign.

When I'm done, I back up to inspect my work and slam right into a woman in a sweat-soaked blue oxford and manly black shorts holding a computerized ticket machine.

No one's staring at the NO PARKING sign but her. The meter maid. Is that even what they're called anymore?

She wipes her brow with the back of her hand. "But that said . . . That should say . . . It did say—"

No, it didn't.

As easily and naturally as breathing, I make her think she didn't see a thing: *The number didn't just change before your eyes. Those have always been the loading zone hours.*

She pauses, bends to yank up her white tube socks, and says, "You kids have a nice day," before continuing down the street.

Adrenaline rushes through me, and there's a bounce in my step as I stroll beside Henry. This is *some* incredible power.

We pass a coffee shop, a dairy-free ice cream store (the horror), another coffee shop, an old-school Italian tailor, and a fancy watch store. At the end of the street, outside a too-hip clothing store that's—unfortunately for everyone—trying to bring back leg warmers, I stop.

This is some incredible *power*. One I have to be much more careful with. Yes, because I could hurt someone—maybe even myself. Though right now I don't feel any worse for having used it. I feel better. Invigorated. Which is the real reason I have to be careful.

This feeling, this high, this much *power* deserves its warning label because it could easily become addicting. It's the ultimate forbidden fruit. Each bite tempts another and another until all that's left is a rotting core. My mother said too many uses on Jinn drains an Afrit's power. How many Afrit did that happen to in order to instill restraint in the rest?

I'm betting a lot. I'm betting this power was used many times, injuring, maybe even killing both Jinn and Afrit in order to realize that this—this ability to get anyone to do anything—is too much power to have.

Even if I could use it perfectly every time, like my father seems to be able to do, I wouldn't want to. How can I take away someone's free will? Isn't that exactly what the Afrit have been doing to us?

"Azra?" Henry says. "Are you okay? If you've changed your mind, you know you don't have to do this."

Taking away free will. Exactly what Qasim wants to do to humans.

I twirl my windswept hair into a bun and use a strand to keep it in place. "Let's go. This way, I think."

The humidity makes it feel like we're walking through pea soup.

Henry's yellow T-shirt sticks to his back and sweat even drips down the nape of my neck as we stand in front of a small, single-story house half a mile outside the bustle of Harvard Square.

Squat with sky-blue shingles and black shutters flanking the double-hung windows, the house is quintessential New England. This area of Cambridge, with the Charles River a hop, skip, and a jump (across a busy road) away, has the greatest density of single-family houses in the city. And the most expensive—especially the main street we just turned off of, which is nicknamed "Tory Row" for its abundance of homes dating back to the American Revolution. Down this narrow side street, this unassuming abode was probably once a carriage house or servants' quarters.

Despite its small size, it'd probably sell for more than a million dollars. F. P. Daher must be some scholar to be able to afford to live here.

My sudden and long puff of air makes me realize I've been holding my breath.

"You have a plan, right?" Henry says.

I shrug.

"Beyond reading his mind?" He stares at me. "Why are you here? Shouldn't you at least have a cover story?"

I should. But I was too busy thinking of "other stuff." So much other stuff.

"I'll wing it," I say.

"Because you're so good off the cuff? Since when?"

I wipe the sweat off my neck. "I may surprise you, Carwyn."

"You always surprise me, Nadira."

Silence and awkward.

Henry clears his throat. "How do you even know he's home?"

"I don't." I raise my hand to knock, but my knuckles simply hang there in midair. I give myself an order: *You can do this, Azra. No, actually, you* have *to do this, Azra.* I thrust my shoulders back and rap on the door.

"Ouch!" I jump back.

"What? What's wrong?" Henry asks.

"Nothing," I grumble. "Just a shock." *Really, Xavier? This is your trail of bread crumbs? You couldn't make it the tickle of a feather?*

I rub my hand while we wait. No response. I'm about to knock again when the door flies open.

An old man stands before us. Hunched over with one wrinkly, sun-spotted hand resting on the rounded top of a black cane, he's wearing a cloak or a cape—*maybe a shawl?*—and a tweed cap with a short brim.

He flashes a yellow-toothed smile. "Azra, Henry, welcome."

I stumble back and slam into Henry's chest. "But how did you . . . ?"

"Let's go, Azra." Henry seizes my wrist. "*Now.*"

He yanks me out of the doorway but pulls too hard and my bangle cracks open and clatters against the brick front walk.

"Excellent," the man says. His voice is thin and raspy. He adjusts his eyeglasses, whose lenses are tinted a dark blue. "We won't have to go over that at least." He turns and ambles back inside the house, his cane tapping against the wood floors. "Come now, don't let all the air conditioning out. Glorious invention. I'd kiss the Jinn who helped with that, wouldn't you?"

Henry's sucked in his bottom lip, shaking his head. He widens his eyes and thunks a finger against his temple.

Oh, now *he wants me to read his mind?*

Except I don't have to. I'm pretty sure he's thinking what I'm thinking.

It could be a trap. He could be . . . He probably is *an Afrit.*

Yup, Henry's thinking exactly what I'm thinking. But it's too late for such thoughts.

"It's okay," I say to Henry, slipping through the doorway. "You can wait outside."

"No way in hell," he says, following me and shutting the door behind us.

F. P. Daher, if that's even his name, laughs a strong, hearty, full-bellied laugh. His formerly weak voice projects like he's an actor on a stage. "There happens to be no trait I value more than loyalty."

He faces us and grins. His teeth sparkle a brilliant white. He tosses the cane on the wooden bench in the entryway. He flings off his cloak and arches his back, standing straight as a rod, erasing any hint of a hunch. Without using his hands—his smooth, golden-skinned hands—he pops his tweed cap off his head, and long, shiny black locks fall in a center part to the bottom of each ear. He gently removes his tinted eyeglasses and tucks them into the pocket of his long white tunic.

His gold eyes dance as Henry and I lose the ability to breathe, let alone speak.

A Jinn.

"Actually," he says with a wink, "your confidant's original guess was correct."

An Afrit.

"Indeed, but I promise you, this is not a trap. At least not yet. Whether we arrive at one, my dear Azra, will be entirely up to you."

29

"WHERE ARE MY MANNERS?" THE MAN—THE AFRIT—SAYS. "I
do apologize. It's been quite some time since I've had guests." He
glides through the living room and with a wave of his hand, shuts
and stacks the open books scattered about on every surface, folds
and stashes what looks like a dozen newspapers, and lights a fire
in the fireplace, surrounded from floor to ceiling with distressed
red brick that must be original to the home.

"Nothing more soothing than a fire," he says. "The only perk
of these blasted New England winters." He tips his head toward
the central air vent, certainly not original to the home. "Thank
Janna for that, we can cozy up even on a day like today."

With another sweep of his hand, two armchairs bound forward, closer to the fire and the curve-backed crimson sofa that
lines the far wall. "Sit, please. What can I offer you to drink? Coffee? Tea? Port? Brandy?"

"Brandy," Henry says.

I cock my head at him, and he holds out his trembling hand. I clasp it with my own and lead him to the sofa. "I'm good, thanks," I say.

With a brisk nod, the Afrit busies himself at the tall hutch stocked with bottles of liquor.

"What's going on?" Henry whispers.

I shush him and then say, "He can read your mind. Try not to think of anything."

"Try not to . . . How exactly am I supposed to do that?"

"*Shh!*"

With a click of his heels, Daher spins around. "Let's dispense with pretenses, shall we?" He sets an iced coffee in front of me and a footed brandy snifter in front of Henry. "I can read both of your minds. I can even . . ."

Under his breath, he mutters words I cannot make out. But when he's finished, suddenly my hand lurches forward and snatches the coffee at the same time as Henry scoops up his brandy.

"Employ hadi on you both, if I so desire." Daher holds his hands in the air and makes a tent with his fingers. "But I won't." We release our glasses. His powers suspend the drinks in front of us. "So long as we can be honest with one another. How does that sound?"

Paralyzed with shock and fear, Henry and I remain still. Daher isn't just an Afrit, he's on the council, or at least he was. Zak said an incantation known only to council members is required to use mind control on Jinn. I guess my half-Afrit status isn't enough to prevent it from working on me. But somehow my half-Afrit status *is* strong enough to allow me to mind-read my fellow Jinn. How is that possible?

"Come now, drink up," he says. A brandy snifter twice as big as Henry's appears in Daher's hand. "How about a toast?"

With a deep inhale, I command my hand to move before Daher uses hadi again to make me. I seize my iced coffee and hold it high in the air, kicking Henry to get him to do the same.

The coffee smells strong. My bangle still off, held in Henry's hand, I debate using my powers to conjure sugar. But just because this Afrit knows about the spell to remove our bangles doesn't mean he knows anything else. No reason to tip my hand just yet.

Instead I manually catch Henry's drink and lower it into his hand.

"What are we toasting to?" I say, overcoming my internal panic to project a blasé air. At least I hope I do.

Daher tilts his glass toward us. "To a new day in Janna."

A new day? Because Qasim is Chemharouch? Am I really going to drink to that? Trying not to show any emotion, I simply tip my coffee toward him and sip. The bitter unsweetened liquid trails down my throat and I wince, forcing myself to swallow.

"Oh, do you require sweetener, Azra?" Daher asks. "I think I'm fresh out. Shame, conjuring foodstuffs has never been my forte."

"It's fine." I make myself swallow another mouthful, and my stomach heaves in response.

"I do wish there was something we could do . . ." There's a teasing tone to his voice.

It's like he's . . . he's . . . *trying* to get me to do magic without my bangle. But why? Is this the Afrit *coming for me?*

"Tsk, tsk." Daher wags his finger at me. "I thought we had an understanding, Azra. You're going to make me do something I do not want to have to do."

Henry bolts upright. "Listen, Daher, or whatever your name is. We're not here to play games. Either you tell us who you are right now or we're leaving." Henry pulls my elbow, and I have no choice but to lift myself up and stand beside him.

Daher raises both eyebrows. "I'm impressed, boy. Humans rarely surprise me anymore." He tents his hands again, tapping his index fingers against each other. "I, however, am also full of surprises."

Before I can take my next breath, a thick, three-stranded rope coils itself around Henry from foot to shoulder blade.

"Oh, and please, call me Farouk."

I bite my tongue to prevent the cry of "Henry!" that was about to spring from my lips. Every molecule inside my body is fighting to use magic, to unwind Henry, who stands like a giant pig in a blanket. But for some reason winning this battle of wills with Daher—*Farouk*—seems too important.

I grit my teeth and begin prying open the clump of a knot at Henry's left shoulder. Instantly, I break a fingernail.

"Stubborn," Farouk says. "Just like your father."

I try not to flinch.

"Perhaps this will give you some encouragement," he says.

And then, the length of extra rope beyond Henry's feet begins to smolder. Smoke rises, sparks flare, and the fibers ignite. Flames shoot out, snaking their way up the rope and toward Henry's flip-flop-exposed toes.

"Azra . . ." Henry hops away from the flames, but the puff of air only fuels the fire. "Azra, a little help, please."

Steeling my nerves, I reach my hand through the twisted rope to reclaim my bangle from Henry's clenched fist. Farouk gets to it first, nabbing it with his powers.

He waves my bangle above his head and taunts me. "Looking for this?"

"Azra!" Henry pushes himself into me.

I look back and forth between Farouk and the fire. Finally, I stomp my foot and cry, "Fine!"

I conjure a wave of water that douses the flames. I concentrate on the rope, and it unwinds, smacking me in the arms and legs as it whips itself free. I gather the wet, smoky twine and send it soaring at Farouk, smiling as it punches him in the stomach on the way down.

A dripping wet Henry turns to me. His mind cries out: *Was that entirely necessary? But . . . thank you.*

The grimace on Farouk's face as he rubs his torso morphs into an amused smile. "There, was that so hard?"

"Was that—?" Seething with anger, I fly toward Farouk, knocking into the coffee table and sending ice and coffee and brandy and glass scattering. "Were you really going to let him burn to prove a point?"

"Were you?" Farouk says. "I daresay I was unsure for a moment there."

"If you knew I could do magic without the bangle, you could have just said so."

"But what fun would that have been?"

"Fun?"

"Sure, why not? I think I deserve some, considering how long I've been waiting for this day. Your mother has proven to be quite the formidable opponent."

I draw in a sharp breath. "My mother?"

"Determined she is." Farouk smirks. "In fact, if it weren't for my little trick with the note card, Janna knows if you'd have ever discovered your abilities."

"That was you?" I step back, and my foot lands on an ice cube. It skitters across the floor toward the hearth. "You changed the number on Anne Wood's candidate card? You made me rush into granting her wish? You're the reason I was on probation?"

"Hmm . . . I'll concede the first two, but the last, that was all you, my dear."

"I could have hurt her." My jaw aches from how hard I'm clenching it. "*I* could have gotten hurt."

Farouk sighs. "Yes, your father was not pleased with me."

"My father? You know my father?"

"Most certainly, my dear. Who do you think was behind the notion of wanting you to discover your abilities?"

My knees wobble, and I fall back toward the coffee table. Henry grabs my arm before I jam a shard of glass in my behind.

"Her father wouldn't have risked her getting hurt," Henry says.

Farouk drifts toward the hutch. "And how would you know that, my boy?"

Henry tightens his grip and draws me closer. "I just know."

With a clink clink, Farouk drops two ice cubes into a glass. "Well, you are correct. He would have preferred something more subtle, but alas, I have always liked a bit of drama." He drowns the ice cubes with an amber liquid. "It wasn't yet urgent that you discover, Azra. Unlike now. All we wanted was to prompt you to go to your mother and present evidence she could not deny. But you like to keep secrets, don't you?"

The way Farouk glances at Henry ignites panic in my soul. *Jenny.* He knows. I hope he's still reading my mind. I stare at him, pleading that he do so. Because I don't want him to be the one to tell Henry about Jenny. Not here. Not like this.

Farouk tilts his head to the side and nods at me. He then continues, "It appears you have more Afrit in you than you like to believe, Azra. You crave control every bit as much as we do."

My heart pounds. He's not going to say anything. He's doing me a favor. But why?

With Henry still latched onto me, I sit back down on the hard couch. "You wanted me to find you. Well, now I have. Are you going to tell me why?"

Farouk cradles his glass in his hand. The ice rattles as he returns to the armchair. "I assume since you are here, you have found what Xavier left behind? The article describing the weakness in the shield? Through which one may enter Janna without the need to contort oneself into a wretched creature?"

He means a dog or some other animal, not an Afrit. Though his words describe both.

I simply nod, trying not to mentally volunteer any additional information.

Farouk bends to retrieve my bangle, which fell to the floor when the rope pummeled him in the stomach, and his dark hair covers his eye like a pirate's patch. He flicks his hair to the side as he sets the bracelet on the table. "You and Zakaria have done the spell too. Shall I also assume you know what it means?"

Blank, blank, blank. My mind must be *blank, blank, blank.*

"Come now, Azra, don't you trust me?"

"Why should she?" Henry says. "You're an Afrit."

"So is she. Part anyway."

"It's not the same," Henry says.

"Thankfully for us all." Farouk sets his glass on the flat wooden arm of his chair. "Tell me, have I hurt you? Either of you?"

Henry tugs at his wet shirt.

Farouk points at me. "That was her, not me."

A laugh bubbles up and out, surprising even me. Henry's fingernails dig into my forearm in response.

With a smug smile, Farouk says, "Proof, then? That I'm on your father's side and as such am most definitely on yours?"

He doesn't wait for a response. The armchair creaks as he pushes himself out of it. He floats over to the hutch and plucks a frame off the wall beside it. Before he sets it down on the coffee table in front of us, he sweeps the broken glass into a pile and wipes up the spilled liquid with a freshly conjured towel.

"I do hope this is enough to convince you of my intentions," he says.

Without touching the frame, I hunch over the table to look.

Dearest A. N.,

Sparing you this fate has been my life's goal. I am sorry I have failed. However, you will not. I have made sure of that. I have always known we would reunite. I am honored that it will be by your hand. Trust in me. Trust in yourself. And this will be for now, but not forever.

Love always,
X. A.

"Azra," Henry whispers. "My fingers."

I snap out of my trance. Henry's fingers are blue from the way I'm squeezing his hand.

"S-s-sorry," I eke out, letting go. It's like a boa constrictor has wrapped itself around my chest. Over and over again, I read the note, written in my father's hand. The date in the top corner is from the day Raina arrived. The day he lost the election. The day I officially became the key to the uprising.

I blink rapidly to clear the film of tears that's obscuring my vision. With a shift to the edge of the stiff cushion, I fix my gaze on Farouk. "What do I do?"

I still don't know what I'm supposed to do.

Despite Henry's arms-crossed, teeth-grinding disapproval, I described Samara and Nadia's plan to Farouk. It wasn't only my father's note that convinced me to do so, it was the fact that Farouk could have easily read my mind and discovered that much and more if he wanted to. Maybe he already has. But I like to think that, this way, I'm the one in control of the information being relayed.

Control. Way to be an Afrit, Azra.

Farouk's brow furrows as he considers what I've said. "Tell me this, Azra, do you believe your abilities truly have nothing to do with your father's plan?"

No, I don't. But you know that already, don't you?

The white of his teeth flashes for an instant before he stifles his grin. "Aside from reciting his spell, of course. Removing bangles, protecting Jinn from being found, that's certainly important." He ups the air conditioning before adding another log to the fire. "But the question to ask yourself is why it is important for *you*. Why do *you* need to be the one to do it? Why did your father design it specifically for *you*?"

My nostrils flare. "I don't know, but since it's clear that you do, why don't we *drop the pretenses*, and you just tell me?"

Farouk laughs. "Patience has never been an Afrit trait."

"She's a Nadira," Henry spits out.

"That she is, my boy. A Nadira and an Afrit. Two bloodlines coming together."

I roll my eyes. "Which dilutes the Afrit, I know. It's not my mother's fault that all this happened."

"Did I say it was?" Farouk asks, placing his hand on his chest.

"No, but I figured you were going to."

"Azra, dear, your mother and father are to be thanked." He sits on the coffee table directly across from me. "Their love changed everything. It created you." The affection in his voice, in his eyes, can't be missed.

He quickly stands and returns to his armchair. "Now, if there is any Jinn who can create the necessary spells, it is your mother. Her Zar sisters are on the right track. Gaining the upper hand, showing the Afrit they are not in control, that's certainly what your father aims to do. But your father has always been a fan of Greek mythology. Do you know the story of the Trojan horse?"

"Sure," I say.

Henry slaps his hand against the couch. "A wooden horse? You want her to ride into Janna hidden inside a hollow statue? Maybe we should bank on your mother instead, Azra."

Farouk reclaims his glass of amber liquid. The ice has long since melted. "She doesn't have to hide herself, my boy. The Trojan horse in this case is already concealed inside her."

269

"Is that like a riddle?" Henry huffs. "Because I suck at riddles."

Farouk laughs again. "A lot to take in for a human. Perhaps another brandy will help?" One appears on the table.

"A lot to take in for anyone," I say.

Farouk nods slowly. He sips his drink and winces.

I conjure ice cubes, making them appear in his glass.

"*Shukran*, dear." He swirls the liquid to cool it. "Now, let me assure you, I am not speaking in riddles. In fact, this needs to be stated explicitly. Much too much is riding on it. And so, you see, the simple truth is that Azra's Trojan horse is her magic. Her magic that even the Afrit council could not take away."

"Because I was never injected, right?"

"Ah, no, you were. I stuck the needle in myself."

"You?" I leap to my feet.

Farouk waves his hand. "Sit, child, I am not proud of it. Hard to believe I ever was. It was simply the way things were done. I've come to feel differently, of course, but I no longer wield the power I once did. The council does not respond kindly to those of us who suggest change. Your father saw what happened to me. If it weren't for him, I'd be in a cell in tortura cavea instead of exiled here."

"That's why he's been working so slowly to win council members over," I say.

"Unlike us, he does have patience." He takes a swig. "Ah, much better. Mmm . . . now where was I?"

"My injection."

"Oh, yes. You were indeed injected with the same compound as all other Jinn, but from the moment I depressed the plunger, your body resisted. It went in and spurted right out, like it hit a wall. That was the day I realized your father was right. You see, Azra, your father has always believed that by keeping the bloodline pure, the Afrit were actually eliciting the opposite of their intended effect. The strength we thought we were maintaining all these years was being lost. Generation upon generation, the weaker traits were coming out. The mixing of pure Afrit blood and that of your mother, who happens to come from an impressive line of her own, ensured the best of both sides rose to the surface. In you."

I'm hearing all of this, hearing the reason why my magic is so advanced, but all I can think is *I'm an experiment. My father didn't actually love my mother.*

Farouk leans forward, shaking his head. "Absolutely not. Do not think that for a moment. I've never seen a couple who loved each other more. Your father did not defy everything his family ordered him to do to prove a point." Farouk nervously pushes his hair behind his ears. "Azra, please trust me on this."

I sit back with my arms crossed and glance at Henry. Less emotionally invested, he asks the question I should have thought to ask.

"But why Azra and not her brother? Why did he not resist the injection? Why doesn't he have the same abilities that Azra does?"

Farouk grins. "How I love the smart ones!" He rises from his chair and searches the stacks of books that are piled in every corner of the room. He glides from one to the next until, finally, he cries, "Here she is!" He withdraws a small, thin book and sails it across the room to me.

With dulled gold writing and a crackled, worn brown leather cover, the book looks nearly as old as Najah. The title is written in an ornate script along the spine and again in small letters in the bottom right corner: *A History of Aisha Qandisha.*

"What's this?" I ask.

"This, at least, I believe," Farouk says, "is the reason why you and not your brother were able to resist the inhibitor. Why you can mind-read and mind-control humans but he cannot."

Of course Farouk knows this without me telling him.

He continues, "This is why your powers are stronger than his. Don't let the fact that two-thirds of the council are male fool you. Female Jinn have always been the true strength of our species. That's why they grant the wishes. Their magic has always been more robust. And that," Farouk says, pointing to the book, "is why."

As I flip it open, dust and corroded glue break free and fall in my lap. I blow the mess aside before scanning the foreword. I then begin to read aloud:

"It is believed that the foundation of all magic lies in the power of pure thought. The ability to embody and access this pureness of thought has always been more profound in the female of the Jinn species, allowing them to employ the greatest feats of magic. One female, Aisha Qandisha, is thought to be the most powerful Jinn there ever was.

Both a hunter and a healer, Aisha Qandisha can lay claim to the eradication of diseases that would have ravaged the human species before it even began, ending the nomadic way of life for early humans, and countless other benevolent deeds. Sacrificing a home and hearth of her own, she lived her life to preserve these for man and Jinn.

Despite her life of service, what should merely be a footnote is often relayed as the entirety of Aisha's legacy. Some say to accomplish all she did over such great distances, she seduced human men in order to possess their bodies. Legend has it that she used these bodies to perform sinister acts, thereby negating the ability of these endeavors to be associated with her name. When finished, she'd return the body to its rightful owner, but a piece of her was thought to have remained inside."

A piece remained. My breath shortens as all I can think about is Nate. Is that what happened when I used mind control on him? Did I "possess" him?

Farouk tents his fingers. "The sinister part is just lore, I assure you. But it is believed that the ability to control both humans and Jinn stems from Aisha. And is particularly strong in her descendants." He looks at me. "Which you are."

Of course I am.

I close the book and pass it to Henry. I don't want to read more. "But there have to be, there have to have *been,* other descendants."

"Yes, yes," Farouk says. "But the passing of time means powers fade with each generation. Unless you have a way to pump it up, so to speak."

"Afrit blood," I say. "Aisha comes from my mother's side?"

"Precisely." Farouk smirks. "Then again, there's also a chance this is all hogwash and the injection not working on you was a fluke."

"You're not funny," I say.

Henry clutches the book against his chest. "Hold on. You're not suggesting that being descended from this Aisha person means Azra can—"

"Jinn," Farouk says. "Aisha was a Jinn."

"Whatever." Henry's foot taps against the wood floor. "It doesn't matter who she's related to, you can't really mean for Azra to stroll into Janna all by herself and defeat the Afrit. She's strong, but she's not that strong." Henry glances at me. "No offense, Az."

"None taken. I agree entirely."

Farouk picks up his drink. "No, that is not what anyone intends. However, being descended from Aisha is why she is strong enough to implement the rest of her father's plan."

"Her father's plan . . ." Henry runs his hand through his hair, which has dried in ragged clumps. "Before you said the ability to control humans *and* Jinn. But Azra can't control Jinn. She certainly can't control the Afrit."

"And you're sure of that?"

"You're not?" Henry says. "What makes you think she can—"

"Because, my boy, controlling Afrit and Jinn is precisely what her father's spell is for."

We've been here so long it's a good thing we didn't have to worry about feeding any parking meters.

As Henry helps me stand, guiding me and my unsteady legs to the front door, Farouk lifts the note from my father off the table. He gives the frame a rough shake and hangs it back on the wall.

"A magical Etch A Sketch," Henry says.

I touch the frame, sad that my father's handwriting has disappeared. "How does it work?"

"Why, it's magic, dear Azra." He smiles warmly. "A simple linking spell, really. With the enchanted pen on his side, your father can write a note that appears here. And I can do the same." He nods toward a black pen on his desk.

"That's how you've been communicating?" I ask.

He clasps his hands in front of his waist. "And the occasional visit."

The occasional visit. My father visited my mother *and* Farouk. And still, not me. I get it; the council can't read Farouk's mind. But that doesn't stop it from feeling like a bee's repeatedly jabbing me with its barbed stinger. I cover by asking, "Do you go to Janna?"

"No, not anymore. Not since the day Qasim took my place on the council."

"You know Qasim?"

"Very well. At least I did. I helped raise him. Though not properly, it turns out. He's my son."

Henry and I aren't going anywhere just yet.

"We were quite close," Farouk says. "We believed in the same things for a long time. We wanted what your father wants. At least we did."

"What changed?" Henry asks.

Farouk's confident voice wavers as he says, "His mother died. As a member of the family, she never granted wishes. In her later years, she began to venture out into the human world." A bittersweet smile plays on his lips. "She had this whole group of ladies she played cards with down in Florida. They thought she lived in the community. She was there often enough. Then, one day, one of their grandchildren became ill. She couldn't stand to see the family suffer. She tried to heal the poor girl."

"But we can't heal humans," I say, wondering if there's an exception for Afrit. If I could have healed Nate's dad if I only got there sooner. If I could have healed Jenny.

He pats my shoulder sympathetically and I know he's just read my mind. "No, Azra, we can't. Not even us. But she had to try. It

275

didn't end well. Not for her and not for the little girl." Farouk lays a hand on the doorknob. "Qasim was never the same."

He slowly opens the door. Silently, Henry and I walk through. By the time we turn around, Farouk is once again the old hunched man who greeted us. He pushes his tinted eyeglasses up his nose. "When all this is done, I hope you return. As I said, I don't get many visitors these days."

He lingers, his eyes commanding mine to remain on his. He lays a finger on his wrist and touches his temple. He wants me to try to read his mind, which should be impossible because he is a full-blooded Afrit. But he wants to prove to me that what he's just told us is true. That this really is my father's plan. That . . . that I can do this. That I have the ability to change everything.

My heart slows, my body stills, my eyes stay on his. The only thing that moves is my mind. To Laila. To Hana. To Lalla Nadia and Lalla Samara. To my mother.

And then . . .

Good luck, Azra. I have every faith in you, my dear. You are the key to all of this. And yet . . . just in case, do what you must to protect the ones you love.

And with that, Farouk closes the door.

30

Thank Janna for Henry.

He fills the car ride home with a description of his new life in New Hampshire. His grandparents' wide, wraparound deck with pansies planted in baskets that hang over the railing every three feet, the leaves already turning colors in the forest behind the turn-of-the-century house, the room he's currently sharing with his sister, Lisa, while his grandfather, with a speed that would exasperate a snail, packs up the record collection that occupies the spare room that is to be Henry's, the flying squirrel that soared out from behind the refrigerator and the game of hockey they played with brooms and a snow shovel to force it through the sliding glass door and onto the deck. A "country moment," he calls it.

He talks without pausing, without looking for a response from me, all the way down Massachusetts Avenue, which somehow turns into Mount Auburn Street and then back to "Mass Ave" as we circle and circle, getting lost on our way out of town.

He doesn't stop until we find the on ramp to Route 93 and the wind whipping through my hair and the roar of the trucks fill my ears instead. This time, I'm grateful for the noise and the wind that make it hard to talk. I don't want to talk. I don't want to think either, but that I can't help.

I read Farouk's mind. An Afrit's mind. Something not even they can do. I can't deny that, and still it's hard to believe that what Farouk said about the spell my father wrote is true. It makes no sense and yet it makes complete sense.

Yes, it does what we know it does: It allows our bangles and necklaces to be removed. Taken off so the Afrit can't track us.

But that's not all the spell does.

The reason my father wanted me to recite it, the reason it requires the energy of both me and my brother for it to work, the reason we are the key to the uprising is that it links our magic to that of every Jinn we use it on.

We free them from their ties to the Afrit but tie them to us.

We can tap into the magic of these Jinn and enhance our own. It's like accessing the strength of every Zar that exists in the human world.

We will be able to save our father.

We will be able to fight the council.

We will be able to change everything.

So long as it doesn't kill us in the process.

Farouk insists it won't. That Aisha Qandisha's blood means it won't. The spell does the rest. The more Jinn we use it on, the more power we'll acquire. Especially me. While Zak will be stronger than most Jinn, stronger still when I am by his side, me being the female descendant of Aisha has given me alone the "gift" of mind reading and mind control.

That's why I've always been able to use them on humans. Since the spell enhances the powers we already have, that's why I was able to read my mother's and Samara's and Laila's and Zak's minds—Jinn minds—earlier today. I had just recited the spell. I had just tied more Jinn magic to my own. And drawing on that power now is how I was able to read Farouk's—an Afrit's—mind, though he was making it easy for me.

I won't be so lucky with other Afrit. I'll need more magic for that.

And more still to employ hadi. Will I really be able to use mind control on Jinn? Without the need for an incantation? Like the one Farouk had to utter before nudging my hand toward my iced coffee? The one that drains an Afrit's powers? The one that means they have to use it sparingly?

But I won't have to.

And the Afrit? There's nothing that allows them to use mind control on each other.

But I'll be able to? Seriously? If this is all true, if this all works, we won't just have the upper hand, we'll have the only hand that matters.

It's the crux of my father's plan: showing the Afrit how powerful Zak and I are, how much more powerful we will become with each bangle or necklace we unlock. He believes a demonstration of my powers, backed by a full cadre of Jinn who are on our side, will be enough to make the council back down and to bring its supporters, most of whom are only that out of fear, to our side. A war averted, just like he always wanted.

Farouk believes in this plan so much that he gave me his family's cantamen. With it and the notes he scribbled on the last page, he said my mother will be able to write all the spells Nadia and

Samara discussed; he's in favor of anything that can support the plan—support Zak and me.

I'm freaked out. Henry's terrified. On our slow walk back to Harvard Square, we both tried to fake it, to pretend it was just the jungle-like humidity that was making it hard to breathe. But it wasn't.

It isn't.

Because all of this means that Zak and I won't just have to be a part of the group crossing into Janna, we'll have to lead it. What Samara or my mother or Henry want—what Zak or I want—is irrelevant. The decision has already been made. By my father.

I should feel good, even proud, that my father believes in me and my skill so much. He literally designed it so that I have the power to help the uprising succeed. But, see, that's the thing. He designed it so I have the power to help the uprising succeed—or fail. So that I have the power to save him—or fail him. Talk about pressure. My father's the ultimate stage parent.

But he's not tossing me out to sing "the sun will come out tomorrow." He's tossing me out into a pit of snakes. Or lions. Or whatever form the Afrit like to shape-shift into. He's asking me to risk my life. He's *willing* to let me risk my life. Am I supposed to feel good and proud about that?

Henry sure doesn't. But it's the story of Qasim's mother, who reached beyond her natural abilities, that really has him spooked. He thinks Farouk was trying to warn me. That trying to access too much power may destroy me.

I'm not really worried about that.

Liar.

I'm not scared to apport into Janna.

Liar liar.

The only thing weighing on me is how to go about doing what I read in Farouk's mind: protecting the ones I love.

And now your pants are on fire.

Okay, I give. Yes, I'm afraid for those I love, I'm scared to apport into Janna, and I *am* worried that trying to access too much power will destroy me. But I'm more worried about what will happen if it doesn't. Access to power is what made the Afrit into who they are today. I'm part Afrit. I'm also a descendant of Aisha Qandisha. My lineage doesn't have a particularly good track record when it comes to self-control.

So far, neither do I. And that's what has me breaking out into a cold sweat. What will happen to me when I tap into that much magical power?

There are many ways for someone to be destroyed.

Something feels off the moment we pull up to my house.

It's more than Chelsea leaning against the side of Nate's car right out front, waiting for us to return her convertible. It's more than seeing Nate again so soon after breaking up with him. It's more than the kindness tinged with awkwardness of Nate offering for Henry to spend the night at his place rather than starting his three-bus ride home.

It's Raina, which I realize the instant Laila opens the front door of my house. Her red eyes suggest it, but Laila's mind confirms it. I read her mind like I'm reading my own.

Nothing's working. None of the spells from the other Zars are working. She's getting worse.

Dressed in white linen pants and a sapphire-blue crocheted sweater, Laila meets me halfway between the car and the house. Her blond hair spills from the tortoiseshell clip she's used to pull it back. The curls frame her weary face.

"Raina's getting worse," Laila says.

"I know." I take her hand and whisper, "Nothing's working. None of the spells from the other Zars are working."

Laila staggers back, freeing her hand. "How did you know?"

"I'll tell you, but first . . ." I gesture toward the group of humans behind us. Henry and Nate standing at the end of my front walk, side by side. Nate, whose close-cropped black hair and broad shoulders, barely contained in his midnight-blue polo, make him the yin to Henry's yang. Henry's sandy-brown gelled hair dried in spikes and his yellow tee in wrinkled folds. His hands are crammed into his jeans pockets while Nate's hang loose at his sides.

Is there anything I wouldn't do to protect the ones I love?

"What is it, Azra?" Nate asks, stepping forward.

Henry's right behind him. "It's your . . . aunt? She's still . . . sick?"

I face them and nod. "You should all go home and—"

"Home? I'm not going to leave you," Nate says.

"Me neither," Henry says.

Did I expect anything else? Wouldn't I have been hurt by anything else?

Laila smiles weakly at them both. "That's really sweet, but it's pretty much a full house at the moment."

If Henry could grow roots right now, he would. But he knows Nate and Chelsea can't be here for this. And so he does what a best friend should do: makes things easier for me.

He runs his hand through his clumpy hair. "You know, Nate, I'm just going to crash across the street." He looks at Laila. "If that's okay with you and your mom?"

"Sure, Henry," Laila says.

"I'll grab the first bus in the morning," Henry says, nonchalantly handing me Farouk's cantamen.

Chelsea bites her bottom lip. "I thought I could take you home."

A strange look comes over Henry's face before he gives her a soft smile, not one deep enough to bring out his dimples. "Let me walk you to your car."

Nate shuffles from one foot to the other, torn between the role he has here and the role he wants to have here. He begins to pull me into his arms but stops, instead resting a hand on my shoulder. "You were there for me. Let me be here for you."

"It's not the same thing," I say.

He draws his finger along my jawline. "Family's family."

I look at him and then behind him, at Henry. "Yes, it is."

❧❧❧

Jinn thoughts hit me like balls from a tennis ball machine as I enter the house.

Hana in the kitchen, mixing by hand the sugary cinnamon crumbs to top the cake batter patiently waiting in a square glass dish, wondering why Matin has yet to sit vigil with Yasmin.

Lalla Jada and Lalla Isa in the living room, each still wearing the long maroon cloaks with gold embroidery lining the edges that they like to apport in as they pore over all six of our families' cantamens, willing a healing incantation that will work to appear. I add Farouk's to their pile.

Lalla Nadia in the window seat in Zak's bedroom, an emerald-green shawl that contrasts beautifully with her deep red hair draped around her shoulders, eyes closed, hands clenched, begging for this not to happen.

Lalla Samara at the foot of Raina's bed, her blond hair secured in a low braid, rolling the hem of her crimson tunic in between two fingers, silently promising Raina that she will make sure the Afrit pay.

And on either side of Raina, my mother and Yasmin. Yasmin's greasy black hair is as desperate for a washing as her gaunt cheeks are for a meal. She glares at my mother. I don't need to read Yasmin's mind to know she's still blaming my mother even though my mother has been doing all she can to try to heal Raina.

As for my mother, I do a double take as I approach her. Though they may be daily attire for many women, the black yoga pants she's wearing are entirely out of character. She yanks the drapey white tee hanging off one shoulder back up and manages a smile as I near.

I'm glad you're here.

Her simple thought uncorks the bottle I stuffed all my fears and worries and disbelief and denial into. I rush toward her and clear everyone's thoughts from my head. I want to feel her arms around me, to have her hold me, to have her make everything all right like when I was little, but she's the one in need of support. If I let go, she won't have the strength to stand by herself.

It's worse than I thought. I never imagined my mother would truly be unable to find a way to save Raina. That the strength of her Zar wouldn't be enough. Gold bangles heal Jinn of everything but old age. A Jinn's life is longer than a human's, but we too meet our end when the time comes. This time shouldn't be here for Raina yet. But it is.

And, worse still, she knows it.

31

As Zak enters the bedroom holding Laila's hand, I tilt my head, signaling for him to take my place, holding our mother. He does, and I fill the room with chairs. Soft ones. Deep ones. To try to ease what's about to come.

I then sit on the mattress beside Raina. The scratches on her face and hands that she arrived with remain. They haven't healed. If anything, they're worse. I lift her thin, cold hand and place it in mine. Her thoughts are open to me. She knows her body is failing her.

Dark purple bags drip from Yasmin's gold eyes. "They broke the spell so she could talk, but she was in too much pain. They gave her something for it, but she's still not talking." Yasmin shakes her head. "But she has to. She has to tell us how to fix her."

"Yasmin," my mother says from across the room. "You know we tried everything."

Yasmin hisses back, "Did you? Did you really? Maybe you should have tried helping her before, so the Afrit wouldn't have done this to her!"

Please, Yasmin, stop.

Raina's mind pleads with her daughter to stop blaming my mother, to stop blaming everyone. *It was my choice. I chose to go.*

My body jerks. *You chose . . . What?* I close my eyes and concentrate, believing I read her mind wrong. *You chose to go?*

Instantly, Raina's mind flashes back: *Azra? Is that you?*

Oh my Janna. My thoughts are inside Raina's mind.

But not as a precursor to controlling her, like I did with Anne Wood. And it's more than what happened with Nate at the beach.

Me: *Lalla Raina, I'm here.*

Raina: *Yasmin.*

Me: *She's right beside you.*

Raina: *I know. I need to talk to her. I need to tell her why I did this.*

Me: *I'll tell her for you.*

Raina: *No! I have to . . . I want to be the one who tells her.*

Raina and I are having a conversation. We're communicating telepathically. This must be how my father showed my mother images of Zak. I really hope the ability to loop someone else in is a benefit of the amped-up magic Xavier's spell gives me.

Still holding Raina's hand, I reach for Yasmin's with my other. She flinches, and I say, "Trust me."

And she does. I feel it through our Zar connection. I also feel Laila, bolstering the trust between us. Though my back is to the door, I know Hana's just entered the room, and she's doing the same.

I feed off our collective strength, and then, as I did when standing in front of Farouk, I tune myself into all the Jinn with freed bangles in the room: Laila, Hana, Samara, my mother, and Nadia, who's moved from the window seat to stand beside Hana.

Lalla Raina's mind speaks to Yasmin through me: *Yasmin, please don't be angry with me.*

Yasmin's fear ripples through me a second before her body physically pulls back, trying to free her hand from mine. I tighten my grip, forcing her to stay with us.

"Talk to her," I say out loud. "With your mind, or your voice. She can hear you. Do whatever feels right."

My mother gasps. "Azra, what are you—?"

I shake my head, and the murmurs in the room fall silent.

"Mom?" Yasmin says. "Can you hear me?"

Yes, Raina says.

"Then you're all right! You're going to be all right." Yasmin pushes herself closer to her mother. "What can we do? How can we heal you?"

I can't be healed, Yasmin. You must come to terms with that. And you must stop blaming your Lalla Kalyssa. It's not her fault. It's not anyone's.

"But—"

But nothing, Yasmin. This wasn't supposed to happen. It was not the plan, but even the best of plans hit snags.

"Snags? This is more than a snag, Mother!"

Ah, there's the daughter I know and love. I was hoping I'd see her once more before . . . well, before. Weepy doesn't suit you, darling. I hope you don't spend time moping. There's much too much for you to do.

"Do?" Yasmin says, about to toss her hands in the air and break our connection. I clench my fingers around hers until I feel her relax again. "You're . . . you're . . . hurt, and this is what you want to talk about? What I have to *do*?"

Time is short, Yasmin. Which is why you must promise to stop lashing out at everyone. You will need them as much as they will need you.

Before I can stop myself, my thought seeps out: *You mean because of the uprising or because you're going to . . .*

Both, Raina replies.

Now I'm the one struggling not to break our connection.

Raina continues, *You must know that this is no one's fault. The choice to enter and to exit Janna was mine and mine alone.*

"You weren't taken?" I ask.

I was, but purposely so. I volunteered. If ever a time came when information needed to pass between Janna and here and Xavier was unable to be the one to do so, we had arranged for me to be brought through. His position afforded him the ability to protect me.

Until it didn't, I think.

Raina's thoughts are steeped in sorrow but not regret. *You also need to understand that I crossed back here even though I knew Xavier was unable to fully open the shield that blocks apporting. I knew the danger. I knew what could happen if I went through. But you had to know Xavier's plan had failed. I didn't have a choice.*

"But why?" Yasmin says, her lower lip trembling.

Because of you. This uprising wasn't my idea, but it became all I lived for once you came of age.

Yasmin's too choked up to speak. In her mind, she says: *Why not live for me?*

Raina: *I have been. You see, Yasmin, Qasim has plans for you. You and Azra both.*

Me: *Why us? Farouk didn't say anything about—*

Raina: *Farouk? What does he . . . ? Wait, have you found the portal? Do you know what your father's backup plan is? I knew he had one, but for my own safety, he refused to tell me the details. Which seems rather ironic now.*

I smile weakly. *Yes, Lalla Raina, I know about his plan. He has given Zak and me access to great power. He thinks we can make the council back down.*

Raina: *I suspected it was something of that sort, considering your abilities, Azra.*

Me: *You knew?*

Raina: *Your father needed an ally, someone to help Kalyssa see what she refused to. He and I have always been close.*

Close? Yasmin and I think the same thing at the same time as our eyes meet.

Raina: *As friends, nothing more. He and Kalyssa . . . they were always meant for each other.* She pauses and I wonder if she's relayed more than she intended. *Now, Azra, you must know that Yasmin is strong too. Not as strong as you, but she'll hold her own, especially if she uses the Zar connection to access your strength.*

"What are you two talking about?" Yasmin blurts out.

I ignore her. I need to know what Raina means. *Yasmin? But why?*

Raina: *She's half Afrit.*

Me: *She's what?*

Yasmin: *I'm what?*

Raina: *My Zar sisters do not know. I didn't want them to know. I was young and stupid and . . . jealous. I was jealous of your mother, Azra. I let our sisters harbor sole blame toward her for the mixing of bloodlines when I was equally as responsible, maybe more so. Please, tell her I'm sorry.*

Me: *You'll tell her yourself.*

Raina: *No, Azra, I won't. Promise me . . .*

I nod and silently promise her.

"Mom!" Yasmin cries, crushing my hand in hers. "What are you talking about?"

Raina: *Yasmin, I thought I'd have time. I wanted to prepare you, but there is no more time. Your father is an Afrit. You and Azra are alike. You are both exceptionally strong because of your mix of Afrit and Jinn blood. But you need*

to know, this strength makes you a target as well. I became involved in the uprising to save you both from what Qasim has planned.

Me: *Which is?*

Raina: *To use your strength to achieve his end goal. And if he can't, to make
sure you can't use your strength against him. He's always wanted to change our
world. I used to think for the better. I may not be the humans' biggest fan, but
whatever he hopes to institute will surely do them harm. And more than that, I
know it would be terribly dangerous for us all. I wasn't about to let him place my
daughter in the center of it. That was quite sobering. That changed everything for
me. If he could do that to his own daughter—*

Yasmin: *Daughter?*

Raina: *Yes, Yasmin. Qasim is your father.*

Yasmin drops her mother's hand and springs from the bed.

"Yasmin!" I cry, releasing my grasp on Raina, but she tugs me
back.

Wait, Azra. I need to make sure you understand that you mustn't delay.

Confusion, fear, anger, desperation all swell in my chest. But
it's not mine. It's Yasmin's. Hana and Laila fly out the bedroom
door to go to her. I defy every instinct to do the same to remain
with Raina.

"I understand, Lalla Raina," I say.

Raina: *Do you? Because if the Jinn in Janna act without you, there's no telling how many will be hurt. And the longer you wait, the more chance there is that
Qasim will come for you. If it weren't for your father, he would have come when he
first discovered how powerful Yasmin is. He doesn't yet know the full extent of your
abilities. I expect whatever your father has done means they will surpass us all.*

Her thoughts slip away from me, though I'm pretty sure she
muttered something about my mother being the model Jinn. She
pops back loud and clear.

You must be prepared to end the Afrit's reign by whatever means necessary. A demonstration of your abilities may very well be enough. But if it's not, you must do whatever you have to do. Lives are at stake.

Me: *Like my father's . . . Is he . . . ? Will he be hurt?*

Raina: *I'm not the sugarcoating type, Azra, so the truth is simply, yes. Maybe not right away. Qasim still hopes he can convince your father to believe in his vision. But in time . . . Your father deserves better, Azra. You have no idea the number of Jinn he's saved over the years. Including me.*

My hand trembles in hers, and she gives it a squeeze.

Raina: *You must be strong. Do what you have to do without hesitation. And let's start with getting your mother over here so I can tell her what to do next. These pain-reducing spells of hers are barely newbie-Jinn quality.* With strained effort, she manages to wink. *She'll love that. And get my daughter back here too.*

Me: *Same old Raina until the end.* I gasp. "I'm sorry, Lalla Raina, I didn't mean—"

Raina: *Yes, you did. And I wouldn't have it any other way.*

I need air.

I bound down the stairs.

We tried. We really tried. With so much to tell my mother and Zak and everyone else, I started with the one thing that mattered most in the moment: the true purpose of Xavier's spell. My mother, her Zar sisters, and I all thought the same thing. That between my increased abilities and the healing powers that come with their gold bangles, we'd be able to save Raina's life. The room buzzed with excitement. We all believed it. Even Raina.

We were wrong.

I fling open the front door and bend over, placing my hands on my knees and gulping down air. *How could we be wrong?*

After, Raina asked to be alone with her Zar and Yasmin. She insisted on not being knocked out by a spell or pain medication. She wants to feel like herself for as long as she can still feel.

She's stronger than I am. I'd give anything not to feel like myself because I'm feeling way too much. From Raina, yes, but also from having just telepathically replayed all that happened today for Zak. This really is some incredible power. One I can't let Qasim get his hands on. Because if I can employ hadi on Jinn and Afrit without my magic being drained, there's no telling what he'll want me to do—or who he'll hurt to make me do it.

I long for an escape hatch, but they're gone—all of them. I suck down another breath. Air will have to do.

A sudden warmth on my bare shoulder makes me stiffen. I look up and swallow the sob that rises to the surface. One of my escapes has come to me.

Nate. He waited here all this time.

When he asks how Raina is, I can't answer, and he doesn't make me. He simply draws me into his arms and I let him. I let his calm surround me. I let him caress my back in wide, slow circles. I want this. I want to forget everything. Like I used to.

But I can't.

He feels me tense and releases me.

"Things are still . . . complicated?" he asks.

"Even more so." It's the truth. I don't want to say anything else. Because anything else will be a lie. And I don't want what could be our last moment together to be a lie. I don't want that to be his last memory of me. Or mine of him.

So I give us another one. A better one. One where I ease his heartache. Just a little. Nothing like what I did when I made him feel less of the hurt of losing his father. But I enter his mind and gently fast-forward him past the worst of the breakup pain. I make sure he feels as I do: lucky to have had the time we've had. But also, for his own safety, ready to move on, to not keep coming around. Which sounds totally conceited. He's a teenage boy. He'll move on.

But Nate's not your average teenage boy. And neither is Henry.

As Nate slides into the driver's seat of his car, I bury the sadness in my voice. "Score lots of baskets."

He cocks his head.

"Goals? . . . Points?"

When he laughs, he sounds and looks like the Nate from the start of the summer. Before he had to shoulder so much weight. "Thanks, Azra." He pauses and adds, almost to his own surprise, "For everything."

I smile. Maybe a bit of mind-control déjà vu isn't the worst thing.

32

It's still strange to walk through the door of the Carwyns' home to find a gold-tiled octagonal coffee table, royal-blue low-to-the-floor couches, and lush orange curtains that hang from the ceiling in a circle around the room. I never thought I'd miss the Carwyns' worn brown microfiber sectional, but I do.

Farrah, in jeans and a cropped green sweater that shows her belly button, sits cross-legged on the fluffy white rug in front of Mina, who absentmindedly strokes the back of Farrah's hair.

"Where have you been?" Farrah asks, chewing on her bottom lip.

Right across the street. Right on my front porch. Saying a final good-bye to the life that drove away with Nate. Replaying for myself all that Farouk said, all that Raina said, preparing for this new life. The one a part of me knows I should have been saying hello to all along.

Farrah's knees bounce up and down. "Zak told us all what you showed him. What you are ... what you can do ... have to do ... I mean, damn, Azra, just *damn.*"

Mina ruffles Farrah's hair as she looks at me. "Is there anything we can do?" Her delicate features have always given her a baby face, but tonight, she looks more mature. Tonight seems to be making us all more mature.

I shake my head. "Not yet, but there might be. Zak upstairs?"

Mina nods and pulls a thick white blanket with silver sequins over her lap, draping the bottom half over Farrah's shoulders.

I'm halfway up the stairs when I light a fire in the fireplace in front of them.

Their thanks and rumbles of appreciation follow me into what used to be Henry's room and is now Laila's. They're both here with Zak.

"Check it out, Azra," Henry says, swiveling around in the desk chair. In front of him is an open laptop and beside him is my brother.

Laila's on the floor in front of her dresser surrounded by socks. She frowns as she pairs a pink paisley knee-high with its mate and folds the socks in thirds.

"We're updating the other Jinn who've been recruited," Zak says.

"Updating?" I move closer to the computer. "What, are you like Facebook friends?"

"Facebook?" Henry snickers. "That's ludicrous. I've got them on Witchbook."

"What?"

"Witchbook." Henry points to the screen. "Just a forum, so it was really easy to set up. And I protected it, don't worry. I just had to put a secure doohickey here and a backdoor blah-blah-blah there and generate passwords of whozewhatzit strength and then distribute them and explain it all to your more Luddite Jinn, but now everyone's in."

He didn't actually say "doohickey" and "blah-blah-blah" and "whozewhatzit." He did say "Luddite," though, whatever that is.

"You're linking the uprising supporters online? Under the guise of witches?"

"I was equally as skeptical," Zak says. "But you should see how many of these there are for witches. Astounding. Perfect cover."

"Yup," Henry says. "Humans don't bat an eye at crazies who think they're witches. It's cool to be in a coven." His eyes flicker to mine in a nod toward what he thought when he first witnessed me using my powers. "But tell them you're a Jinn and you'll get a straitjacket."

I let myself smile weakly as what they are saying sinks in. It's hard to get used to being able to talk about Jinn stuff with Henry in front of everyone else—like he's one of us. But I guess he is. He's in nearly as deep as we are.

"This is how we're going to fill everyone in on the plans for the uprising?" I ask.

"It's surprisingly efficient," Zak says. "Already we've spread the word better and faster than apporting. Hana did that with two Jinn, and when they logged in here, they thought you and I would be stealing their bangles."

"Worse than the telephone game," Henry says. "But this way, within minutes we'll get all forty up to speed."

Ignoring the "we'll," I say, "Forty? Samara's managed to get forty Jinn already?"

"With the help of Jada and Isa," Zak says.

After I left this morning, Samara called her Zar sisters back and explained what we had learned. While they continued their visits to other Zars in search of a cure for Raina, they also began to recruit supporters from those they trusted most. And now the flock of Jinn willing to risk everything to return our world to the way it once was has grown to more than forty.

That's a lot of Jinn to free from their bangles. That's a lot of Jinn whose power I'll have.

"We'll have to go in soon," I say, thinking not just about my father and the potential uprising in Janna but also about maintaining our element of surprise. Forty is a lot of Jinn to keep all this a secret.

Zak adjusts his perch on the edge of the desk. "Can't be soon enough for me." He ignores the huff that comes from Laila and adds, "But Samara's guessing three days."

Three days.

"Mother's nervous about writing the spells in that amount of time."

"Farouk's cantamen should help," I say. "But if she's nervous now, just wait until she learns the rest of Xavier's plan."

Henry nods in agreement. "She's going to roast your dad on the pyre herself."

As if what he's just said isn't enough, his serious face on top of it makes Zak and me laugh, laugh like we have no right to do considering everything that's going on. Or maybe that's what gives us every right.

Laila remains tight-lipped. My heart aches for her. I feel how terrified she is of all this. Not that I'm not, but my father, my great-something-or-other-times-a-thousand Aisha, and fate and luck and chance don't care about my fear.

I notice Mr. Gemp perched on her nightstand and make him tap-dance from one side to the other, but Laila's lips don't budge from their straight line. I set Mr. Gemp back down and kneel beside her.

"How are you?" I ask as I reach for a green-and-red-striped Christmas sock.

Laila shrugs as she digs the sock's twin out of the pile. Instead of answering me, she holds her sock up to mine and says, "Look, a perfect match. I wonder... what would one be without the other?"

She stares at me, her lips parted, waiting for an answer to what I assumed was a rhetorical question.

"Lonely?" I suggest.

"Exactly. One might even say *without a purpose.*"

Zak sighs. "Not again, Lai." He looks at me. "She wants us both to stay here. Like we haven't been over this a million times."

Laila flings a pair of black tights at him. "How about we do it once more?"

Catching the tights in one hand, Zak loses his usually even temper. "What part aren't you getting? That Qasim wants to harm the humans?" Zak places his hand on Henry's shoulder for effect. "Or maybe that the Jinn who will defy Qasim—of which there will be many, I assure you—will be hurt without our help? Oh, I know, it must be that my father's very life is in jeopardy."

Laila rises to her feet and stomps through the socks. "And the only way to stop all of that is for the two people I love most in this world to risk their lives?"

The muscles in his neck bulging, Zak was ready to go on the offensive, but this stops him. His face softens and he pulls Laila between his legs, holding each of her upper arms and staring at the tiny specks of blue in her gold eyes. "You *love* me?"

Laila bites her bottom lip. "I—I—I was talking about Azra and my mom."

At that, Zak starts to let her go.

Oh, no. I'm not letting Laila make a mess of this. I'm not going to let her act like me.

"Come off it, Laila," I say, gathering the strewn socks and dumping them in a drawer. "You meant Zak. Now's not the time to play games. You don't want regrets." I steal a glance at Henry. *Three days.* "None of us do."

It was right here, in this room, at the start of the summer, where Henry spilled a box of Jenny's most favorite things and asked me to let him in. It was right here where I made the decision to share my world, my life, with Henry. It was right here where we became best friends who share secrets. And it is right here, right now, where my biggest regret will be over telling him the truth I've been keeping about his sister, the best friend I miss even now. But the trouble is, I don't know what I'll regret more: telling him, or not telling him.

Coward. And I'm supposed to be able to stand up to the Afrit? My father doesn't know me at all.

As Zak and Laila nuzzle into each other, Henry extracts his third-wheel self. He grabs the laptop before Laila sits on it, pushes himself back from the desk, and rolls his chair next to the bed.

"Thank you for helping us, Henry," I say as I sit on the edge of Laila's soft mattress. "I know it's—"

"The absolute last thing I want to do? Help send you off to the bowels of hell? It's not easy being your best friend, Azra."

"Is that what you are?"

"Is that what you want me to be?"

"Always," I say.

"But not forever?" His dimples drill a hole in his cheeks and my heart. "I know you well enough to know there's nothing I can do or say to stop you . . ." He pauses, his eyes darting between mine. When I don't respond, he says, "Uh-huh, what I thought. So I might as well help you get the backup you need. The more Jinn that go in with you, the more chances we have of it not being you who gets hurt."

Me not getting hurt at the expense of other Jinn. The uprising's more than forty here. Who knows how many in Janna. That's a lot of Jinn willing to risk their lives on the word of an exiled Afrit, on the plans of a failed candidate-for-Chemharouch Afrit, and on the talents of a hybrid. The untested talents of a half Afrit, half Jinn.

Talents we need to test. Which, apparently, is another thing Henry and Zak have been working on.

Mina's and Farrah's bangles presumably clank as they hit the wood floors. But since Zak and I aren't there to hear them, we can't know for sure. We've just recited Xavier's spell via smartphone. Once live, for Mina, and once on video playback, for Farrah.

Both work. This is how we'll be able to free all the Jinn here. We don't have to waste time or risk alerting the Afrit by making the rounds and apporting to them all, and when the time comes—if, I mean, *if* the time comes—that the rest of the Jinn in the human world need to be protected, need to be made aware of the (presumably) failed uprising and thus have their ties to the Afrit broken, the video can be played for them in Zak's and my absence.

An "absence" no one wants to give any name other than that.

It was Henry's idea, figuring at least every Jinn daughter has a smartphone. Turns out these devices we always thought would be the downfall of us Jinn may actually be our salvation. Whichever Jinn helped create them deserves her own holiday. My mother's right (*again*): We never know what our helping may lead to.

Henry sent a message to all the Jinn on the forum. In the morning, after we fill in the missing pieces for Yasmin and my mother's Zar, who are all staying across the street with Raina, Zak and I will do the spell for as many supporters as we can. Then I'll start practicing my Jinn mind control. Maybe even pay a visit to Farouk to see if we've unlocked enough power for me to use it on Afrit. The less surprises in Janna the better.

How am I thinking about this so matter-of-factly? I don't know. All I know is that I have to. Otherwise I *can't* think about it.

We're nearly ready to challenge Qasim. Play our hand. And hope we've been dealt a good enough one that he folds. If not, Jinn will likely lose their lives. Like all the uprisings that have come before.

I know I didn't want to become a Jinn and live the life my mother lived, but this isn't exactly the alternative I had in mind.

Which is why I can't sleep. Even though it's the middle of the night, my brain refuses to cycle down. I climb out of Yasmin's round bed, and the crisp breeze still fighting the humidity gives me a chill. In her closet, I find a long black sweater. I slip it on over the lightweight romper I've been wearing for more hours than I want to count.

I pass through the living room, where Mina and Farrah are zonked out on the couches, tiptoe through the screened-in porch past Hana, who's conjured herself a fluffy, couture sleeping bag, and smile when I reach the bottom of the stairs and see the back of Henry's head.

He's sitting at the edge of the pool with his feet in the water. I plop down beside him, and he jumps.

"Sorry," I say with a shrug.

"You should be sleeping," he says.

"So should you." I heat the water to hot-tub levels before dropping my own toes in. There are definitely benefits to my whole Zar knowing about Henry.

"I'm really glad you came today," I say.

Today? Is it really possible I was at the beach earlier today? Breaking up with Nate and finding Matin at my big black rock were just today? Speaking of, where is Matin?

Henry raises an eyebrow. "Glad I came, huh? Should I take that to mean you deliberately forgot to text me your selfie?"

"I'm not that manipulative."

"No, not on purpose. Then again, ensnaring men *is* in your Jinn line."

I use my powers to splash water in his face.

He rolls his eyes and groans. He then takes off his glasses and lifts his yellow tee to dry the spots. Which is how I notice his abs. He has, like, a six-pack. When did that happen? I look closer. Maybe it's more like a three-pack, but still . . .

He sees me staring and yanks down his shirt. "I'm not a piece of meat, Azra."

When was the last time I saw Henry in his swim trunks, shirtless? Before everything happened with Nate's dad . . . before the circulus curse, which wasn't all that long ago. Surely he couldn't have gotten that ripped since then?

"Please tell me you didn't," I say.

He squirms. "Didn't what?"

"This isn't a what. It's a who."

He inches farther away from me.

"Who?" I repeat, placing my hands on my hips.

"Very good owl, Azra. What else can you do?"

I grab the end of his shirt, but he launches himself into the pool. The fabric rips in two. He surfaces, and the bottom of his torn shirt floats to the top of the water.

"Take off your shirt," I say.

Henry crosses his arms in front of his chest. "I'm not that kind of boy."

"You forget, I know that you are."

Silence.

I was joking, but his reaction gives me an opportunity: the element of surprise. If it's good enough for the Afrit, it's more than good enough for Henry. I propel myself off the deck and into the pool. Henry takes off underwater, swimming into the deep end with the speed of a shark.

With my extra powers, I'm just as fast. Faster. I'm already at the end of the pool, hanging on to the diving board, when he pops up completely out of breath. He reaches both arms over his head and grasps the other side of the board. He's totally exposed. In one smooth motion, I shred his shirt from neckline to hem.

If it weren't for the lights in the pool, I wouldn't be able to see his cheeks turn pink. If it weren't for the lights in the pool, I wouldn't be able to see his toned stomach.

"Henry!" I swat his torso.

He sways but manages to hold on to the diving board. "I didn't ask her to, I swear! When you were with Raina, she was all upset, and I gave her a hug, and she, well, she insisted on thanking me, and it was the only thing I could think of, because I'm pretty sure what she had in mind no one would have liked, except maybe me . . . but only for a minute, and then I'd have to deal with you and everything so, yes, I let her." He finally takes a breath and looks down to admire his abs. "Not bad, though, right? She's pretty talented."

"*Mina.*" Couldn't be anyone else. "She should be. She's well versed in the male anatomy."

"Damn, then maybe I should have taken her up on her first offer."

My jaw clenches.

"Kidding, just kidding." Henry tears the remains of his shirt free and tosses the dripping fabric onto the deck. We stay there, dangling in the hot water, until Henry says, "I'd have taken four buses, you know."

My pulse thumps stronger. Must be the heat.

"I know," I say.

"Conceited."

"I know." I can't help the grin that takes over my face.

Under the water, he nudges my foot with his. "It's good to see you smile. Sometimes it feels like we haven't smiled since the whole Anne Wood incident."

I kick him back. "Really? You bring up the screwed-up wish granting that put me on probation *now*? Shouldn't you be reminding me of my successes, not my failures?"

"But it was a success," Henry says. "You read her mind. You used mind control on her. You apped her all the way to Hawaii. Easily. You had no idea what you were capable of then. I was so impressed. So proud of you."

"Before my mom and Sam arrived, that is."

"They scared me sober."

"Right, the beers. You drank Anne Wood's beers and had me conjure new ones."

"And we danced."

"Not we. You. And not well. I hope you're a better slow dancer, Henry, otherwise I fear for your prom date."

Henry flips back his head to clear the clump of hair that's blocking his vision. He looks me directly in the eye. "I was hoping that'd be you."

Me? Not Chelsea? He must be joking.

I tease him right back. "Aw, Henry. Are you asking me to prom?" My arms have turned to jelly from hanging for so long. I drop down into the water and use my powers to float the yellow-and-blue inflatable raft to us. I heave myself into it, and Henry follows.

"I would have if I thought you wanted me to," he says.

What? He's serious? And he's really choosing now *to go down this road?*

I stare at the bottom of the raft. Of course he's choosing now. Henry knows time is not on our side. But what should my response be? Saying I would have wanted him to isn't fair unless I mean it. And if I mean it, it's not fair to Nate and what we have and it's not fair to Henry because there's nothing we can have. I can't leave him with hope, false or otherwise. "Henry, I—"

"Forget it," he says. He plucks the rope that runs along the top of the raft like it's a guitar string. Maybe in New Hampshire he'll finally learn to play the instrument that was just decoration in his bedroom here. He strums the rope again. "I just wish you didn't have to deal with all this. I wish there was something I could do."

"If only we knew a genie who could grant wishes . . ." His tense smile doesn't draw out his dimples. Time *isn't* on our side. The only thing my response needs to be is honest. "You've already done so much. More than enough. I'm not sure I'd be helping you if the roles were reversed."

"Believe me, I wouldn't be helping if I thought there was any chance of stopping you." He tugs at his hair. "Aw, hell, that's not true. I'd do whatever you asked me to. I'd do anything for you, Azra, you know that."

I say again, "I know." And I do. But then, *what about Chelsea?* What about our swing-set kiss that was a mistake?

"Are you really okay to talk about this now?" Henry asks.

Crap. I projected. Probably because subconsciously I want to talk about this as much as consciously I don't want to talk about this. But if we don't have this conversation now, we may not get another chance, so I nod.

His chest rises as he takes a deep breath. "Things between us have always been complicated." He rolls the rope between his fingers. "In a way, I suspect me being with Chelsea is like you being with Nate. It's attractive in part because it's *less* complicated."

That's not true. That's not why I'm with—that's not why I *was* with Nate.

My lips part, and I start to shake my head.

He lets go of the rope. "That's not necessarily a bad thing. It doesn't make our feelings any less real. And I care about Chelsea. A lot. I'm just explaining why . . . trying to explain why . . . Oh, forget it."

He slumps down into the raft, and I jerk upright.

"No way," I say. "You can't start this and not end it."

His forehead creases. "That's it, actually."

"'It' what?"

"What I was afraid of." His eyes flick to mine for a second before he takes his glasses off so he can no longer see me clearly. "Starting something you wouldn't want to end. Even though you should." He stops and fiddles with the rope again. "It's just . . . it makes me the conceited one. Too presumptuous, but . . . well . . . I didn't want anything to happen between us because I always knew you were destined for more and I didn't want to hold you back."

"Hold me back? From what?"

He goes to tuck the arm of his glasses into his shirt, forgetting he's not wearing one. "Anything. Everything." He drops his glasses into his lap. "Being with a stud like Nate, granting wishes around the world, whatever. I didn't want you to not live the life you were supposed to live because of me."

"*Because* of you?" The life I was supposed to live . . . *Is that how I've made him feel?* The thought that I have—even unintentionally—twists my stomach into knots.

I scoot forward, and the end of the raft lifts out of the water, but I don't care if we capsize. "Don't you see?" I grab his hands.

Because I do. I see. I've always seen it. I've just been too scared of it being taken away to let myself admit it. "You're the reason I have anything. You're the reason I have *everything*. The life I'm supposed to live is any life that includes you."

I always thought of his green eyes as Jenny's eyes. But as they look at me now, brimming with tears, they are no longer Jenny's.

They are his.

I tuck my legs behind me, kneeling in front of him. And this is when I realize what he actually means. He doesn't just mean *he'd* be holding me back. He means *my feelings for him* would make me hold myself back. Back from living the life I'm supposed to live. Back from being a Jinn. Henry knowing about me makes our relationship as complicated as mine with Nate, just in a different way.

And I have been holding myself back, but back from everything. From being Jinn, from Nate, from Henry. Trying to have a little of everything but all of nothing. I never gave myself over to anything, not completely. Though now's not the time to start with Henry, I can't help gently squeezing his hands and pulling him toward me until we almost bump noses.

"Azra, no," he says, hanging his head. "If you do, there's no way I'm letting you go. To Janna, to Cambridge . . . hell, to the bathroom without me."

He then slips his hands from mine and stares into his lap. "There's something I need you to know. Something I need to apologize for." He clears his throat. "The whole Chelsea . . . thing . . . I never meant to hurt you. But that night, Zak told me how important you were to the uprising. When he did, every fiber of my being screamed for me to muzzle you, strap you on my back, and run away to . . . to . . . to Maine, Alaska, Canada . . . but how could I be that selfish?" He pauses, trying to stop the quiver in his voice. "It wasn't planned or anything. But when you started to read my mind and you saw that and got so mad, I figured . . . well, you'd have to move on. So I didn't correct you."

Correct me?

He wipes his eyes with the back of his hand but still refuses to look at me. "But we . . . we didn't."

They didn't?

"If you'd hung around even another few seconds, you'd have seen. We got close. Real close. But we . . . I couldn't."

He didn't.

"I really like Chelsea, but it wouldn't have been fair to her. Same way it wasn't fair to stay with her anymore. Earlier, before she left, I . . . I broke up with her."

My pulse is racing and my mind is swirling, and though my heart still aches from letting Nate go, it swells as I hear this and I don't know what he expects me to say or what I want to say, so I simply bend my head and rest my forehead against his.

"I always knew I'd have to give you up," he says. "Maybe not right away, but one day. You have so many more important things to do than be with me."

Now my heart sinks because as wrong as he is, as wrong as I want him to be, he's not. He's right. I've always known it. Which is why I could never give myself over to him or to Nate. Not the way they have.

I press my forehead deeper into his. I wasn't supposed to grow attached to humans. But I did. And just to prove that it's me who's the selfish one, I'm glad I did. But I can't let my selfishness be at Henry's expense. I'll make sure it's not. Just not tonight.

"I ended things with Nate too," I say.

Though hope flashes in his eyes, he wouldn't be Henry if he didn't say he was sorry, if he didn't ask if I was okay. But he thinks something different.

Impeccable timing. We're both free of "other things," but "other things" have been replaced by "other other things."

"I'm sorry," I say weakly. "I wish things were different. I wish I could stay. But I have to do whatever I can to keep everyone safe. I have to do whatever I can to protect the ones I love."

At my "love," the tears he's been unsuccessfully fighting fall to the bottom of the raft, where they mix with mine.

As his breaths slow, I swallow past the lump in my throat and tug his hand. "So, seriously? Maine, Alaska, Canada? You wouldn't kidnap me and take me somewhere warm?"

He tugs back. "I'd keep you warm."

I pull my forehead away from his. I press my thumb under his chin so that I can look into his eyes. The eyes of my best friend. Always.

And it is at that moment that my heart is torn from my chest. Followed by Laila's, Hana's, Mina's, and Farrah's. We all feel what Yasmin is feeling. And what Yasmin is feeling is the worst thing I can imagine.

"Raina's dead," I whisper.

33

LAILA, HANA, MINA, AND FARRAH APPORT TO THE BACKYARD, AND
their collective signatures knock me flat against the back of the
raft. Since tapping into the magic of other Jinn, all my senses are
heightened.

"Azra?" Henry reaches his hand across the raft. "Are you okay?"

No. No, no, no, no, no.

"Yes," I say. I sit up, and the world spins. Immediately, I tumble back.

"Azra!" Henry crawls in front of me.

I wave my hand. "I'm just a little dizzy." My body starts to
shake.

"And cold," he says.

My clothes are still wet, and the air's cooler than the pool, but
it's Yasmin's shudders that I'm feeling.

The magic of one of my Zar sisters pulls the raft to the stairs
in the shallow end. Henry helps me climb out. All in pajamas,
Laila, Hana, Mina, and Farrah kneel on the ground, surrounding

me. They're all upset. They're all feeling Yasmin. But I'm feeling her the most. Must be our Afrit blood.

Laila wraps an arm around my shoulder.

"We need to go to her," I say.

Hana dries my clothes. "All of us? That might be too much for Yasmin."

Laila and Mina nod in agreement.

We look at one another, all wanting to be the one to go as much as we don't want to be the one to go. Surprisingly, it's Farrah who says, "Let me." She conjures a black headband that she uses to pull her long bangs out of her eyes.

Before we can stop her, she disappears, but the sensation of the soft flick of a bunny's tail hits us less than a minute later when she returns. Her headband flashes like a strobe light as it changes color after color. "I—I—I saw Lalla Raina...She...I just didn't expect..."

Mina rises to her feet. "It's okay." She links arms with Farrah, and despite the fear in her eyes, says, "Come, we'll go together."

The instant they leave, Zak flies out the door of the screened-in porch.

"Laila, where did you go?" he calls, his hair flattened in the back in traditional bedhead style. He comes to a halt when he sees us huddled on the ground.

Laila answers, "It's Raina."

Zak's eyes find mine. It doesn't matter that he didn't know Raina well; his heart aches for her, for Yasmin, for both my Zar and my mother's, and for the reality that this could happen to any one of us.

I conjure Henry a shirt that he slips over his head, but otherwise, we stay as we are. We're all dazed, unsure what to do. We still haven't moved when a loud clank makes us all jump. We turn our heads toward the front of the yard, where the fence gate has just slammed shut.

"Matin!" Zak says. "Where have you been?"

Looking disheveled and distracted as he walks toward us, Matin simply shrugs. A leaf clings to the back of his long white tunic.

Zak pries another from his hair. "And why are you wearing that?"

Matin shrugs again. "It's comfortable?"

Hana pops up and grabs her brother by his elbows. "Have you been drinking? How could you, with all that's going on?"

"All that's going on is why I should have been drinking, but alas, I was not."

She's furious. "What's wrong with you? Did it ever occur to you that Yasmin might need you? Or me?"

"Aye, Sister, it did. It does." Matin strokes his scruffy beard. "That's why this is so hard."

"Hard?" Hana slaps his arm. "This is hard for you? What's wrong with you?"

"Me?" He massages his forearm. "What's wrong with *you*?"

Zak pulls him away from Hana. "Do you not know?"

"More Jinn secrets," Matin grumbles. "Secrets are poison, *habib.*"

"Enough!" I launch myself at Matin. "How can you be this selfish? Yasmin's mother is dead. Dead, Matin." I poke his chest. "Raina's dead. Your *girlfriend's* mother." I poke him again. "Do you care? Did you ever care about Yasmin?" I give one final jab that causes the pen clipped to the V of his neckline—his favorite, special pen—to fall to the decking.

It spins in a circle, landing at Henry's feet.

"Dead?" Matin wobbles and then claps one hand on top of his head. "She can't be. This . . . this wasn't supposed to happen. It wasn't supposed to be like this." He begins rubbing so hard, his scalp turns redder than the short stubble of his hair. "They lied." He kneads his skin. "They lied . . . *they lied.*"

Now I feel like a jerk. Of course he didn't know. Still, he hasn't exactly been top-shelf boyfriend—or brother—material since all this started.

Henry tugs on my arm. "Hey, Azra." He's holding the pen between two fingers like it's covered in rat droppings.

I'm staring at it and him when suddenly Matin cries, "No!" and crashes into me to grab the pen himself.

He then sprints across the yard toward the fire pit.

"What was that all about?" Laila asks.

Henry's tense face means he knows. "Azra. The pen. It's like . . . it's the same as—"

"Farouk's," I say. The pen is the same as Farouk's. Farouk's enchanted pen that lets him communicate with my father. *In Janna.* What would Matin be doing with something like that? And why would he keep it a secret?

I plant my hands on my hips and shake my head. That's when I notice the two leaves on the ground that were stuck to Matin when he arrived. Leaves like the ones in the woods where Raina appeared and where Matin and Zak first arrived—from Janna. That's where Matin's been. He was waiting for someone to take him back to Janna . . . or waiting to bring someone from Janna here.

No, this is Matin. Hana's brother. Zak's best friend. He wouldn't have done something to put us all in danger.

I crunch the leaves under my feet.

But he did.

"Inside!" I grab Henry by his belt loop and shove him into Hana. "Take him away. Now!" I spin around to Laila. "Get your mother!"

"Azra, what's——" Laila starts.

"Just do it," Henry says.

I look him straight in the eye and project my thoughts into his head. *You're a genius. I love you, Henry.*

His eyes widen right before Hana whisks him away.

I don't wait for the others to go. I latch onto Zak and app us both to the fire pit. Matin's hunched over, squatting, furiously writing on a wrinkled piece of paper with his pen. His magical pen. Because when I snatch the thick parchment from his hand, it's blank. The message doesn't appear here. It appears in Janna. The question is, in front of who?

"Give it back," Matin pleads.

My entire body seethes with anger. "You can't be serious."

"Azra, please, you do not understand," he says.

"I understand plenty." I pass the paper to Zak. "Perhaps a little late, but then, you are an excellent liar, Matin. Do they have theater in Janna? You're a natural."

Zak flips the paper over and over. "What is this?"

With the speed of a cheetah, Matin leaps at Zak, attempting to yank the paper from his hand.

"Don't give it to him!" I shout.

Zak obeys but grits his teeth. "What's going on, Azra?"

I answer my brother while staring at his best friend. "He's communicating with someone in Janna. Farouk used the same method. Seems like pretty high-level magic. Not something every Jinn would have. But every Afrit . . ."

Matin slumps to the ground. "But you don't understand. I had to."

I knew this confession was coming. But still, hearing him say it is like squeezing a lemon over an open wound. For me.

For Zak, it's like losing a limb. He has the same look on his face that Laila had. The look of someone who's just been betrayed by their best friend.

Zak marches forward, drawing his arm back as he goes, ready to land his clenched fist on his best friend's face, but I stand in his way. The fear I've just heard in Matin's voice makes me stand in Zak's way.

Because traitors shouldn't be this afraid, should they?

Maybe, if he was afraid of us—of Zak's huge fist. But I don't think that's the full source of Matin's fear.

"Please," Matin begs. "I can fix this. Let me fix this."

"Fix . . . fix what?" Zak stammers out. "Matin, what have you done?"

He claws at his skull. "I—I . . . They made me. The Afrit."

Of course. It's the only explanation that makes sense. It doesn't mean I don't feel that gaping wound in my back, but right now, I need to know what he's told them.

I kneel in front of him, but he's wracked with sobs. There's no way he can speak. I gently lay my hand on his head, stopping him from tearing the skin free. I steady my breathing and let myself into his mind.

Tell me, Matin, I project.

His body flinches, but then his eyes meet mine, and his thoughts spill like water from an open hydrant. I quickly reach for Zak's hand to include him.

They threatened everyone. They already have my father in a cell. They threatened to do the same to my mother and Hana. What choice did I have? They knew Xavier was sending Zak through, and they wanted me to go too. It was only information they wanted. Information! What could be the harm in that? And I'd finally lay eyes upon my mother and sister . . . but then the shield wasn't down. That was not supposed to happen. As soon as Raina appeared and told us about Qasim, I contacted them again. Seeing her . . . I was through. But they . . .

They what? I say in my head.

You must understand, they promised to come here and heal Raina.

My heart seizes, and I release Zak's hand. "In exchange for what? What did you tell them, Matin?"

His lower lip quivers, and his voice, full of sadness, manages to eke out, "They didn't come. I waited, but they didn't come."

I grab Matin by his upper arms. *"What did you tell them?"* My fingers press through the fabric of his sleeve, pinching his skin. "Do they know about Najah? Do they know what we intend to do?"

He sniffs back the mucus clogging his nose and throat. "They know you are powerful, important to your father's plans. And they know a portal exists, but they do not know where it is. I refused to tell them that."

"You mean you were saving it as a bargaining chip," Zak huffs.

I make Matin stay focused on me. "What else? Did you tell them the true purpose of Xavier's spell?"

"The true purpose?" His eyes look tired.

That's right, he doesn't know. That's good. That's very good.

"I told them what I knew," he says. "That it frees Jinn from their spelled jewelry. If there is more, I am very glad I did not know it." He swallows and looks at Zak. "Please forgive me, *habib.*"

The two lock eyes, and I'm waiting for Zak to say something when a strangled cry pierces the air like a bolt of lightning, and . . . and I'm in *agony.*

Searing pain shoots through the side of my neck and my vision clouds. Zak and Matin reach for me, but I shake my head. "No, it's not me." It takes every ounce of energy I have to rise to two feet.

Laila. It's Laila.

That's all it takes, and I'm gone, racing toward the house with Zak and Matin so close on my heels that when my feet abruptly stop moving after bounding up the incline to the pool, they collide into me, knocking me to the ground.

Where I'm eye level with Laila. She's crumpled on the deck like a used napkin.

"Laila!" Zak screams.

She doesn't move. She's unconscious. Unconscious or . . . *Oh my Janna, please only be unconscious.*

Zak hurdles over me. He drops to the ground beside Laila and cradles her head in his lap. "Laila, no, no, no, please, no."

Is she breathing? Is she breathing? Is she breathing? I blink and blink and blink, but the tears come and come and come. *Please let her be breathing.* Panic courses through me, paralyzing me. *Please let her be breathing. Please let her—*

Wait . . . I felt her pain. I should be able to feel her breathing. I should be able to feel if she's . . . if she's not. I sink my hands into the grass and take deep breath after deep breath to calm myself enough to link with Laila.

She's breathing. *She's breathing.* But her mind is blank.

Two males in long white tunics stride toward Zak. Two Jinn. No, not Jinn. I feel it in my gut: two Afrit. Suddenly, Matin seizes me by both ankles. I start to kick and fight, but his pleading "Trust me" silences me. I let him drag my body back down the small hill, out of sight.

He crouches beside me and brings his finger to his lips.

We peek over the incline. Both figures are as tall and muscular as my brother.

"Zak?" the one with a black goatee says in surprise. "I thought you were in tortura cavea."

The other one simply turns his thick neck and grunts.

No necklaces. Definitely Afrit and not Jinn.

"Austan, Gamal, what have you done?" Zak says.

Thick Neck holds out his hand. "Us? She bit me. Who'd have thought? Pretty little thing like that."

Way to go, Laila.

The goateed Afrit, at least a year or two older than Zak, frowns at Thick Neck. "All we wanted was to read her mind and gather some information. After she saw us, we couldn't let her apport and announce our presence. But that . . ." He points to Laila. "That was not my idea."

"What's the matter?" Thick Neck rubs the webbing between his thumb and index finger. "She's merely a Jinn."

Zak growls, "She's not merely anything."

The tone of his voice sends chills down my spine. I'm about to push myself up to stop him from doing something he shouldn't when Matin's foot plants itself on my back. His thought flies into my head. *Azra, go. I'll distract them. They're here for you.*

I hesitate, and Matin presses harder, so I flatten back down. He then stands and begins to walk toward Goatee and Thick Neck, shifting his hurried gait into a nonchalant stroll once they see him.

"Gamal, Austan, welcome." Matin throws his hands out wide and laughs. "I'm not entirely sure that is the best way to endear yourselves to this world, however."

Thick Neck—*maybe Gamal?*—snickers. "That's not what we're here for."

"And what are you here for?" Zak says. "Aside from hurting innocent Jinn."

Matin tilts his head toward Zak as he places a hand on Thick Neck's shoulder. "Gamal, you must excuse my *habib*—"

"I'm not your friend," Zak snaps.

I'm unsure if he's playing a part, as Matin seems to be doing, or if his anger is real. A little of both, I'm betting.

Gamal shrugs off Matin's hand.

Not a good sign.

"We're here for your sister, Zak," the goateed Afrit—Austan—says, his voice gentler than I would have expected.

"Sidi Qasim's orders," Gamal says, his voice every bit as harsh as I would have expected. "It seems his interest has been piqued." Gamal winks at Matin. "And he wants her."

"The council wants to *talk* with her," Austan says.

Gamal, who acts less senior to Austan than he looks, simply grunts again.

Matin's head rotates slowly, taking in all of them. Does he see what I can see from my low position? Does he see Zak lifting Laila's body in his arms? Does he see him using her slight frame as cover? Does he see the knife Zak's just conjured beneath her?

Apparently my brother's gotten better at conjuring metals.

I can't let him fight. I can't let him get hurt. Not for me.

I set my palms flat on the ground and raise my head. Light filling a window on the second floor of Henry's house catches my eye. I lift my head farther back, and my heart nearly cracks my ribs with the jolt I get from seeing Henry's silhouette.

What is he doing? I try to project into his head. *Go. Go. Go. Go. Go.*

But he doesn't move. *Am I too far from him? What was Hana thinking not apping him as far away as she could?*

Henry raises his hand. He's holding something. His smartphone. Beside him, Hana appears. He taps her bangle with his finger, then touches his temple—the same way Farouk did.

And I'm flooded with confidence. Hana's, then Mina's and Farrah's. I can just make out their shapes behind Hana and Henry.

And then, warmth and love and trust and fear and desperation and anger and belief and . . . and hope . . . unreserved, abounding hope rattles my bones, simmers my blood, infuses my heart.

Yasmin stands beside Henry. She takes off her bangle and raps it against the glass windowpane. I nod. I understand. And so I rise to my feet.

At the same time as Zak does.

34

Moonlight glints off the knife.

Zak's heading for Gamal, who doesn't carry a weapon. At least an external one.

With a last glance at Laila, I spring from the grass. "Stop!" I shout.

All eyes are on me.

Together, Gamal and Austan recite a spell. I catch enough words that also form the core of Xavier's spell to understand that they're trying to remove my bangle.

So I let them. Actually, I help them.

I use my powers of magic to fling my bangle to the ground. I use my powers of pretending, honed from a lifetime of living among humans, to feign shock.

"Azra!" Zak cries. He then covers his mouth with his hand, realizing he shouldn't have said my name.

Gamal's brief surprise at Zak being able to conjure turns to nervous, then conceited, laughter as he makes the knife in Zak's hand disappear into thin air. "Don't worry, Zakaria. You two are like twins. We'd have recognized her anyway." He nudges Austan with his elbow. "And Qasim wasn't sure we could pull off that removal spell. He thought this would be difficult."

Austan's lips turn down at Gamal's comment. "Sidi Qasim thought that for a reason."

While Gamal has been posturing, Matin has inched backward. He protectively positions himself in front of Laila, and despite him being the one to have caused all this, gratitude fills me.

I then slip beside Zak and interlace my fingers with his. Somehow, neither Gamal nor Austan seems to realize that Zak's necklace never fell to the ground. I stopped them before they completed the spell. Which gives us both the power we need and the element of surprise.

I draw on the magic of the Jinn whose bangles have been freed, just like I did earlier with Raina. Except, this time, the amount of power almost overwhelms me. It's magnified. I was right. Henry must have played our spell for all the members of the uprising.

In case Zak doesn't realize this and what it means, I flood his mind with my plan. I tell him to trust in Xavier. That this will work. He agrees. Except he doesn't trust in Xavier. He trusts in me.

He then conjures the rope.

That I send into Austan's hands.

He bolsters my magic with his own mix of Jinn and Afrit blood.

And I absorb it. Then, just like I did with Chelsea, I tune myself to the minds of Austan and Gamal. I picture them picturing what I'm picturing. Austan looping the rope around Gamal's feet. Gamal standing frozen still while Austan winds the rope around his body. An Afrit pig in a blanket. I have Farouk to thank for the idea.

I picture Austan lifting Gamal off his feet and laying him down on the lounger closest to him. I picture Austan backing away and sitting on the ground next to the stairs to the pool, cross-legged and silent.

And it all happens. One after the other. We move in sync.

I lead Zak to stand in front of Austan, while I position myself above Gamal. The moment I ease myself out of Gamal's mind, releasing him from my command, I recite the spell that I used on my mother to put her to sleep.

He has just enough time to register his astonishment at my ability to use magic without my bangle before his eyes close. Before he begins to snore.

I then turn my attention to Austan. We need him conscious if we are to find out how to help Laila. But conscious equals dangerous. I stretch myself to full height and tower over him as I exit his mind. Before I can say anything, he holds up his hands.

"*Min fadlik,*" he says to me. "Please, no more. I won't try anything. That was . . ." He presses a finger to each temple. "I won't try anything."

Matin has already lifted Laila off the ground and placed her on a lounge chair. Kneeling beside her, he checks her pulse and closes his eyes in relief.

I nod to Zak, and he rushes to her side. He conjures a blanket that he delicately tucks around her body. I'm sure it's extra soft.

He then glares at Austan. "How could you be a part of this?"

Austan rounds his shoulders in deference. "I had no interest in coming, Cousin, but you know how little our interest means."

"Cousin?" I say.

Zak waves his hand. "Second or third. All the Afrit are related in some way."

I tip my head to the snoring giant. "Even Gamal?"

"Even Gamal," Zak says.

I swallow the bile this causes my stomach to toss up my throat as I crouch in front of Austan. I'm ready to bluff. To sound more confident and in control than I feel. But I don't need to. Because after what I've just done, I'm brimming with more confidence and control than I know what to do with. And so I say curtly, "Undo it. Whatever you did to Laila—"

"It wasn't me," Austan says. "It was Gamal."

"Semantics, really?" I grit my teeth. "Just undo it."

Austan shakes his head. "I can't."

"Can't or won't?" Zak says brusquely.

"Can't, Cousin." Austan reaches into the pocket of the black leather vest he's wearing over his tunic, and I magically swat his hand away.

"Nuh-uh," I say.

He raises his hands in the air. "Go ahead. I told you I wouldn't try anything."

"Azra, let me," Zak says, getting up.

"No. Stay with her." I then use my powers to open Austan's vest. Tucked inside the left-hand pocket are three vials and one syringe. I levitate all three, including the one that's empty, toward Zak, setting them down on the side patio table beside him.

"Do you know what these are?" I ask.

Zak picks up a full one and studies it. It has no label. "No. Father never mentioned anything about weapons such as this."

Austan sighs. "Xavier doesn't know. One of Qasim's pet projects. He's become fond of taking human diseases and having them manipulated so they can actually affect Jinn."

I didn't hear that right, did I? "'Affect'? What do you mean by 'affect'?"

I begin to enter Austan's mind. I have to know if he's telling us the truth.

"*Min fadlik,*" he says, covering his head with both hands. "Please don't infiltrate my head again. I'll tell you whatever you want to know." He unfolds himself and says matter-of-factly, "If I return without you, Qasim's likely to inject me with one of those himself. I'm stuck with you all whether I like it or not." He looks to Zak. "Which I do, Cousin, no matter what you think."

"Prove it," Zak says. "Fix Laila."

"I can't." Austan sighs with defeat. "Qasim's mixing a little of this and a little of that. Some things are merely intensified versions of the humans' common cold, which knock Jinn flat out for a few days, sometimes weeks."

"And this one?" Zak asks, holding up the vial.

"That one does a bit more. That one knocks Jinn out for more than a day."

"More than a day?" Zak's half laugh has an undercurrent of fear. "Why bother with a disease? A hefty spell could do that."

He's right. Even the sleeping spell I just did on Gamal will last at least twelve hours. But the pain I felt from Laila when they injected that vial into her was way too intense to be merely inducing sleep.

Matin backs away to allow me to sit on the chaise beside Laila.

"Whatever was in that vial does more than knock a Jinn out, doesn't it?" I say.

Austan's chin, pointy under the goatee, juts out. "It's eating away at her insides." His tone is full of disgust. "Like some perverted version of a flesh-eating virus. No Jinn's healing powers can stop it. And it acts fast."

"How fast?" I say, my voice tight.

"If she doesn't get the antidote, it'll be over in twenty-four hours."

"Over?" Zak asks, his eyes blinking rapidly and his lower lip trembling.

It's like my heart's being devoured by a pack of wolves. I already know what "over" means. I couldn't stop myself. I slipped into Austan's mind to read his thoughts.

"Dead," Austan says out loud. "She'll be dead in twenty-four hours if she doesn't get the antidote."

My lungs strain for air. "And where is this antidote?"

"Janna," he says, just like I knew he would.

Laila. Poor Laila. I inhale, deeper and deeper, as I realize what this means. Of course it means we have to enter Janna now, not in three days. But that doesn't mean the uprising is over before it began. With one more breath I finally suck down enough oxygen to fill my lungs, to expand my chest. I hold it in, relishing it. All this means is that the uprising has hit warp speed—and been downsized.

Because the uprising doesn't need forty Jinn. All it needs is two: me and Zak. We are my father's backup plan. We are not the key to the uprising. We *are* the uprising. I've just accessed enough strength to employ hadi on the Afrit. Something not even they can do.

I exhale in one long, slow breath.

Though Matin telling the council about the portal means we've lost some of our element of surprise, they don't know the where and they don't know the when. Zak knows his way around Janna. If we go in now, we can free Xavier, get him to help us find the antidote for Laila, and then, after she's safe, we can show the council what we can do—what I can do.

Xavier always intended for us to stave off an uprising, not start one. If Zak and I go in alone, no other Jinn need risk her life.

We do everything he wanted and more.

I breathe in and out again as the color continues to drain from Laila's round cheeks. I lift her hand to my lips and give the smooth skin a soft kiss. I rest it against her side and stand, pausing to brush a blond curl off her forehead.

"We should get ready, Brother," I say.

35

I TEAR THROUGH THE CLOTHES IN MY CLOSET. I COULDN'T EVEN conjure pants.

How am I supposed to save Laila if I can't even conjure pants?

Fifteen minutes. Zak and I said fifteen minutes to do everything we needed to do before leaving. For me, that everything is Henry.

I peel off the sweater I borrowed from Yasmin and toss it on the floor. I knock hanger after hanger aside, searching for the cargo pants I know are in here somewhere.

I fling a pair of jeans too hard, and its wooden hanger flies off the rod, clattering against the floor.

Khallas!

I need to be more careful. If my mother finds out that Zak and I are going in alone, now, she'll try to stop us. Or insist on coming with us. Neither one is an option. I want to protect her, but I also can't afford to be slowed down by *having* to protect her or anyone else once we enter Janna.

Calm down, Azra. Calm down.

The next hanger has my cargo pants. *Good.* That's a start. Off goes the romper. *Very good.* Now put those pants on, one leg at a time. *Excellent.* Now, a shirt.

Deep breaths. My chest puffs in and out as I stand in front of the mirror and braid my long hair. I sweep the finished braid off my shoulder and take one final look at my Jinn—at my Afrit—self. I hope it's enough.

I slip the silver tinsel from Laila in my pocket and turn to leave. The last thing I see before I flick off the light and everything goes dark is the photograph on my nightstand of me, Jenny, and Laila from when we were little.

I have to be enough. Because, like my mother, I've lost too much. I'm not losing anything else.

"Azra?" Yasmin calls from inside Zak's bedroom, where, I assume, Raina still is.

Damn that hanger.

Because I'm down to ten. Ten minutes to do everything I need to do.

Though it twists my stomach, I'm about to app away without answering her when she appears in the doorway, her gold eyes red.

I swallow hard as I murmur condolences. She waves her hand, saying it's okay, saying she knows I need to go, that what she needs will only take a minute. But she does need me.

And so I follow her into the bedroom, even though a part of me would rather face the Afrit in Janna than Raina here, like this.

The air in the room is, as I knew it would be, heavy with sorrow, but also, to my surprise, with lavender and cloves and streaks of light. Candles flicker from every surface. The room and everything in it glow a beautiful gold, the color of Jinn.

I stand next to Yasmin at the foot of the bed and force my eyes to look upon Raina. Her hip-length black hair has been woven into three long, thick braids that rest together along one side of her body, which is shrouded in a crisp white linen sheet. Left free of the cloth, her bare hands and feet are no longer covered in scrapes and scratches but in burnt umber henna tattoos, painstakingly drawn by hand by my mother's Zar. A simple winding vine outlines Raina's beautiful face, peaceful in death in a way I never remember it being in life.

The secret she kept about Yasmin and Qasim weighed on her in ways she probably never even realized. It made her overprotective of Yasmin. But for Raina, overprotective translated to demanding and hard to please. It made Yasmin hard, strong enough to not just accept but to stand up to her Afrit heritage. But it also made her hard in other ways, like in opening herself up to those around her, to humans, to Jinn, to her Zar. Our sisters broke through her front. Just as they did for me. Yasmin and I always have been more alike than we wanted to admit. Now we know why.

Our Afrit blood connects us. Our Afrit blood endangers us.

I thought my father was bad for forcing me into saving the Jinn world. Yasmin's father wants to force her—us—to destroy it.

"I should go with you," Yasmin says.

"You can't," I whisper. *Is this what she needs me for?* I don't have the time to talk about this *now*. Not to mention how disrespectful it feels to talk about this *here*.

I can't look at Raina's face any longer, so I stare at a lilac drawn along her ankle, most likely by my mother. My foot taps against the floor. "You're better with spells. Between you and my mother . . ." When Yasmin doesn't flinch at the mention of her, I continue, "You'll be able to protect the Jinn left here. To prepare the Jinn who will follow me and Zak if we can't . . ." *Tap, tap, tap.* "If we aren't able to . . ." *Tap, tap, tap.*

She folds her arms across her chest. "Fine, I get it. But with Matin's betrayal, there's no telling what's waiting for you. You need to . . . What I mean is, just be safe, Azra."

This is as close as Yasmin and I have ever been to showing each other affection.

And right now, Yasmin needs affection. Lately, the one she's been most willing to accept it from hasn't been one of our Zar sisters. She needs to forgive Matin. I check the clock. Eight minutes. There's no time for a long, drawn-out plea, so I simply say, "He was wrong, I know that. But it's not like he meant for this to happen. He was just trying to protect his family."

"By hurting ours," Yasmin says curtly.

"But he didn't know that. What would you have done?"

"I'd have fought."

"We're not all as strong as you."

Yasmin turns to me. "You're stronger. At least you better be."

Her eyes, whose distance apart has always made her look edge toward the exotic, betray her controlled exterior. The grief in them takes a slice out of my heart.

"Because . . ." Her nails dig into the flesh of her upper arms. "Because you can't let this happen to Laila."

Another slice, gone. "I won't."

Her nails leave red indents on her skin. "Now there's one thing you need to do before—"

"I know," I say, cutting her off to move this along. "Henry—"

"I didn't mean that." She tilts her head toward her mother. "I don't want her tied to them."

She then surprises me by taking my hand. Her grip is firm. Her intentions more so.

Though Zak isn't here to help, I draw on Yasmin's strength, on all the Jinn strength I now have, as I recite Xavier's spell. The two halves of Raina's bangle pop open like a clam. The gold shines even brighter against the backdrop of the white sheet. Yasmin walks to her mother's side and gently snaps the bangle back together, securing it around her wrist.

"You're free now, Mother," Yasmin says. "Your magic belongs to you."

Raina spent her life raising Yasmin to be strong. And not just magically. She has the strength to withstand the worst. Just like my mother. Raina would be proud. I'm proud.

But I'm also sad. I'm so damn sad. For Yasmin, for my mother, for me, for Raina. For Laila.

I can't let this happen to Laila.

I force myself to look at Raina's face again.

She's so . . . still. I didn't approach Nate's father's casket during his funeral. And I didn't even go to Jenny's. That was more my mother's decision than mine, but I've always been grateful. I wouldn't want that to be my last memory, my final image, of Jenny.

But Raina . . . I'm kind of glad this is my final image of her. Beautiful, tranquil, and . . . and home. Cared for and loved by her

Zar sisters. This image of her, right here, reminds me why I'm doing this.

Suddenly, Yasmin says quietly, "I have no more family here."

Family? How could I forget? Did it even fully register before now?

"Yes, you do," I say.

"Our Zar sisters, I know. I didn't mean to disrespect—"

"No, no. I mean, I know. But you do have family here. Your grandfather."

"Grandfather?"

"On the Afrit side. But still . . ."

"Grandfather?" she says again. "As in white-haired and frail?"

"Depends on his mood, I think. And how much he wants to toy with you."

For the first time in days, she smiles. Her traditional condescending smile.

I've missed it.

"Sounds like we're going to get along," she says.

Henry. I need to find Henry.

I rush out of the room and am already starting to apport when I catch a glimpse of my mother in her bed, lying flat, just like Raina.

My heart seizes in my chest. *She's sleeping. My mother's just sleeping.* But I can't leave with this image—this resemblance to Raina's current position—in my head.

And so I tiptoe into her room and make sure her chest is

indeed rising and falling in a calming rhythm she surely wouldn't feel if she were awake. Her hair, the same espresso color as mine, is bundled atop her head. Pieces are splayed out on her pillow and around her face. The soft lines around her eyes and full lips speak to her strength, making her even more beautiful.

Hana's going to tell Samara and my mother about Laila after Zak and I are gone. She's going to give us a head start. This will be the last rest my mother has for who knows how long.

Up, down. Her chest moves, and my own breathing begins to match her tempo.

I want to wake her. I want to tell her everything. I want her to tell me not to go as much as I want her to tell me I have to go.

I want to wake her to say good-bye. But I can't be that selfish.

Instead, I move to her dresser and quietly open her jewelry box. I slip her emerald talisman on my finger. The more power in Janna, the better.

Before I go, I untuck the blanket that's crumpled under my mother's bare feet and rest it over her body. As I do, I notice the red leather of her diary peeking out from under her arm. All the entries are hidden by a spell, except for the last one. The one she was in the middle of writing. I catch "Azra" and "terrified" and "Xavier" and "love" and "miss" and "how can this be happening?" before I shut it. I don't want to invade her privacy.

But that's only part of it. The truth is, if I read this, if I read how scared my mother is, how worried she is, how devastated she'd be if something happened to me, I might not be able to do what I need to do.

She'll understand, won't she? When she finds out Zak and I have gone?

I crack open the diary and flip to the page after my mother's latest entry. I find her pen on the rug and kneel beside her bed. There's so much to tell her. There's so much to say. So much to explain and to thank her for.

I press the pen to the page but can't bring myself to move it. The black ink spreads in a widening dot as I struggle with what letters to write, with what words to form, with what message to leave behind. I then forget about how much there is to say and write the one thing that matters above all else. The one thing that will convey the rest.

Thank you for helping me to become a Jinn.

HENRY'S WAITING FOR ME ON THE FRONT STEPS OF THE HOUSE THAT used to belong to his family. I told him I needed to see him. He thinks he knows why. He thinks it's to say good-bye. And it is. But to so much more than he thinks.

"Hey," Henry says.

"Hey," I say back, tucking my hands into the deep pockets of my khaki cargo pants.

Henry's changed too. From their high-end look, his jeans and long-sleeved light green tee, whose color matches his eyes, were most likely conjured by Hana.

He runs his hand through his messy sandy-brown hair. "Remember when your biggest worry was whether to tell your mom I caught you in the act of granting a wish?"

"And your biggest was me doing magic in front of you and getting in trouble." I shake my head. "Now look at all you've seen."

His smile is anxious. Does he suspect?

"Seeing magic is one thing," I say, "but feeling it . . ." I move closer and hook my arm around his waist. The jeans are as soft as butter. Maybe they're actually Zak's handiwork. "We should really get you home."

He tries to pull away. "What are you doing?"

I raise an eyebrow. "Hold on to your glasses, Henry."

"Azra, I don't know if—"

"It's easy. You don't even need to click your heels."

His body tenses against mine as I picture all he told me about his grandparents' house: the expansive wraparound deck, the hanging flowers, the forest of trees. It's enough. I tighten my grip and app Henry home.

The heat, usually like walking through a raging fire, is barely that of a hair dryer. On low. I hope the same is true for Henry.

I realize it's not the moment our feet hit dirt, and he lunges away from me.

"Don't. Do. That. Ever. Again." He throws his arms out to each side, shaking them, as he wheels around in circles. Around and around he goes, trying to acclimate himself to what he's just felt. Finally, his walk slows and his head is the only thing moving. This is when he recognizes where he is. "My grandparents'? You apped me home? But why?"

"I need to make sure you're safe."

"Safe?" He tugs on his hair. "Wouldn't the *safest* place be in a house of Jinn with magical powers?"

"Not necessarily."

"Not necessarily?" Now he's the owl, repeating me. "Give me one example."

"Not if the Afrit came. *More* Afrit. Not if they read your mind and discovered you know more about the Jinn world than some Jinn."

It's almost like I can see his legs being kicked out from under him, and it rattles me to the marrow of my bones, but I stiffen my body, hoping that will help stiffen my resolve. I have to do this. No matter what he says.

"But . . . but . . ." He starts circling again. "The bangle spell. If you need it done for more Jinn—"

"My Zar sisters can handle it. Thanks to what you've set up. I can't thank you enough for—"

"No! What about the rest of them? You're not going to do this to Nate and Megan and Chelsea and—"

"I don't have to. They don't know the truth. But you . . . you know, and there's nothing to stop them."

"You'll stop them."

"But I won't be here."

"Then your mom or Yasmin or—"

"Henry." My voice cracks. "Don't make this harder than it already is. I need to make sure you're safe."

"But I—I—I don't want to forget. Please don't make me forget. Please don't make me forget *you*." He stands in front of me and sets both hands on my hips. He looks at me through the eyes of my lifelong best friend. First Jenny, then him. "I have to remember you. I'm afraid of what will happen if I don't. Because, the thing is, I'm . . . I'm not me without you."

And then he kisses me. His lips on mine. Soft, then hard, like the beating of my heart. Now and forever.

He pushes himself back from me, his eyes glistening. In them I see the life I have, the life I could have, the life he wants, the life he deserves. The life I have to take from him.

I feel like I'm suspended in the eye of a tornado, watching

as my world and everything in it is uprooted and sent spinning around me.

"Henry, I have to protect the ones I love. That means I have to protect you."

"But this way? Why does it have to be this way?"

"It's the only way I know. At least right now. It's the only way I can do what I have to do. Because I can't go otherwise, Henry. I won't leave you here alone. They'll use you against me like they do with all Jinn. I won't let you be a pawn like they wanted to make me."

"Then don't go. Or take me with you."

Now the funnel cloud sweeps me up too. *"Henry..."* I struggle for solid ground. Usually it's Henry or Zak setting me down, grounding me, making me feel like my world is whole and not shattering into shards so small I'll never stand a chance of putting them all back together. But I can't rely on Henry or Zak. Not now. All I have is me.

I steady my rapid breaths. There's one final card I can play. I steady my thumping pulse. I don't want to, but I'm running out of time, and I know this will end the discussion. I steady the quiver my voice wants to be. "I'm not asking your permission. I'll do it either way. Whether you agree or not. But we both know it'll be harder if you don't. I might hurt you, and I might... I might even hurt me."

His shoulders fall. "That's not fair." The way his lips turn down and his eyes darken lets me know I've won.

A game I don't even want to be playing.

I cup his cheek with my hand, turning his face toward me. He pushes against my palm, pressing his skin firmly into mine. "You know they'd come for me. You know I'd end up there one way or another. It's better if it's like this. On my terms."

Henry straightens his head. "Always with the control."

"I am an Afrit."

"No. You're a Jinn." He smiles, and his dimples fill me with the lightness and the darkness of what it means to be a Jinn. "It'll be okay."

Will it? Or will he know something's off, like my mother? Will he constantly be searching for something he can't find? Or will it be less than that, like the lingering I felt for memories I couldn't quite grasp of Zak and my father? Or will there be nothing? Like there seems to be with Nate and his family. But that's not the same as this. The Reese family's intense pain over losing Mr. Reese was erased, but not Mr. Reese himself. They're still left with the memory of him.

Which—actually—is closer to this than I realized. I need to take away Henry's knowledge of the Jinn world. I need to erase his memories of me being a Jinn. But I can't completely erase me. Too many people know us both. That would leave too much confusion that might drive him insane. But I can ease his pain. Like with Nate. I can make sure he's not defined by my absence the way we both were by Jenny's.

I do think I'm right: that the memories of someone lost make it harder to move on. Which isn't inherently a bad thing. It *should be* hard to move on. The holes punched into our lives should feel wide and empty and raw and gaping. For a time. But the holes need to be able to close. The loved ones still here should be allowed to help those holes get smaller and smaller until they're visible but no longer functional, like a long-neglected ear piercing.

I want that for Henry. I want those left here to help him move on. Yes, even if that means Chelsea. I'm okay with that. Well, not *okay*, but . . . okay. I don't have the luxury of being selfish. Which means there's something else I have to do for Henry. I need to make sure he doesn't blame himself for Jenny's death anymore.

That I've let him blame himself for this long is inexcusable. He thinks it's his fault she fell off the swings in my backyard. He was supposed to be with her, watching her, but he was in his room finishing his model airplane. He was in his room being a ten-year-old boy. It wasn't his responsibility.

It was mine. Jenny should have been safe. She was with me. Not only could my magic not protect her then, my lack of control of my magic was what caused her to fall. My selfishness, of wanting to swing higher and higher until we touched the sky, was what caused her to die.

And that's why I've never told him the truth. It would change everything he thinks and feels about me and I'd lose him. A risk I refused to take. So what now? I unload my conscience by telling him? To what end? I'll have to take it away. I'll gut him like a fish, rip out his entrails, and then stuff them back inside. Will that make me feel better?

No, it won't. Being the cause of Jenny's death is something I have to live with. It's my secret. It's my burden. Mine alone.

And so I won't tell Henry about Jenny. Not now, and not ever. Humans are taught that honesty is the best policy. Jinn are taught the opposite. The truth lies in the gray area somewhere in between.

Magic can't do everything. It can't take away the mistakes I've made. And it couldn't save Jenny. But it can save Henry. I can save Henry. I have to do now what my mother couldn't do then. Save a Carwyn I love.

I stand before Henry, my best friend, the boy who taught me

how to be human and how to be a Jinn, the boy I love in the most pure way I didn't even know was possible, the boy I'll do anything to protect. Even if that means what I have to do is lose him, give him to someone else. To protect what I love most, I must lose what I love most. I must let him have the life he deserves. Free of all the guilt over his sister, free of all the angst over keeping these Jinn secrets. Free of all this me.

"Do it," Henry says, latching onto each of my hands.

For too much of my life, I thought being Jinn was holding me back from friends, from love, from family. But it wasn't being Jinn. Henry showed me that. Henry gave it all back to me: friends, family, love. And now I need to do the same for him. But I'm scared.

"I don't want to hurt you," I say, my voice a hair above a whisper.

"You won't."

"How do you know?"

"Because you're the strongest Jinn I know. You're the strongest anyone I know."

"You know this is tearing a hole in my heart, don't you?"

His dimples carve into his cheeks again. "Then I'm glad. Because if that's true, then you've finally granted my wish."

He leans in, his mouth barely brushing mine, before he says, "Now do it. Make me forget you." He presses his lips on the corner of my mouth, leaving a coolness on my skin. "But don't you ever forget me."

Never, I say in my head and project into his.

And then I'm gone.

From his mind. From his heart. From his life.

But he's not gone from mine.

My secret. And my burden.

37

THE SKY IS ON FIRE. I OPEN MY EYES TO BRILLIANT HUES OF ORANGE and red and yellow. A scene as beautiful as it is haunting. Does the sun rise in Janna?

Does it set? Is there a moon? Or even a sky? There's so much I don't know. So much I thought I'd have more time to learn.

At the window in Henry's old bedroom, I blink again and again until the fiery sky is no longer coated with a film of tears. I then turn to face the only other Jinn in the room, the one I sensed before I finished apporting.

Laila. In the big bed, surrounded by plush blankets and soft pillows, she looks smaller, more like the Laila I grew up with than the Jinn I was just getting to know. As I approach the bed, I reach into my pocket and pull out the silver tinsel I tucked in earlier. It's instantly slick from my sweaty palm.

I gently lift her wrist, the one without the bangle, and wind around this strand of silver that she made our pretend bangles out of when we were young, before we were Jinn. Her wrist is so small that it still fits all the way around. I'm even able to tie it into a bow.

After I stole her locket, after my actions threatened to destroy our friendship, I vowed to never let my happiness be at the expense of hers again. Which is why if it's a choice between Zak returning with the antidote or me, I'll make sure it's Zak.

Find something she loves and give it to her.

That's exactly what I intend to do.

I bend to kiss Laila's forehead, and the apricot scent I've always associated with Samara envelops me. When did Laila start using Samara's shampoo? Like mother, like daughter, generation upon generation.

I breathe in the aroma that has soothed me my entire life, imprint the curve of Laila's butterscotch waves of hair in my mind, and remember the delicate sound of her voice.

As I move away from the bed, I smile softly at Mr. Gemp, who's standing guard over her from the nightstand. I flick open the lid and reach in to pull out the rolled-up photograph that I found inside on my birthday. When Hana passed Mr. Gemp to me, there was a single picture of the six of us tween Jinn standing in a line with Laila in front, her arms stretched wide to encompass us all. That photo's still here, along with more added by Laila. One of us from my birthday, all of them dressed in genie costumes and me in my white pants and purple tunic; one of us from our last gathering, all of them dressed in normal clothes and me in my gold bra top and harem pants; and one of us from the night of our Zar initiation, when the six of us became one.

I have to make sure the six of us remain one.

My own heartbeat echoes in my ears as Zak silently moves into the room. He's wearing the same brownish-beige leather waistcoat, white tunic, and baggy pants he arrived in. The only thing new is a satchel hanging across his chest. Surely filled with illegal goods.

I step back and give him my place at Laila's side. His shoulders round as he hunches over to caress her cheek. His lips softly graze hers before he whispers something I can't make out. He then stands next to me and entwines his fingers with mine.

And it is this, this gesture full of warmth and sympathy and knowing, knowing what it feels like to have one's heart shredded, that begins to unearth the resentment at being Jinn I've worked so hard to bury these past few months.

I can't let it. If there is one way to honor Laila, who always saw the good in being Jinn, it is this.

A shy Matin, mumbling apologies for interrupting, appears in the doorway. In his arms is a length of lush cloth in a rich, deep eggplant purple so dark it's almost black.

"It belonged to Raina," Matin says, unfolding the long, hooded garment, similar to those our mothers like to apport in. "I recalled seeing it when Yasmin and I . . ." He clears his throat. "When we were searching their old house. Hana was kind enough to apport me to retrieve it."

He drapes the cloak around my shoulders and helps me slip my arms through.

The sleeves billow out, and the collar stands straight up, squared in each corner an inch below chin level. The cloak's slit from its fitted top to its delicate bell-shaped bottom. Though the only adornment is a gold toggle closure in the center right under the bustline, it's the most stunning thing I've ever seen.

"It's a jellaba," Matin says, "so you'll blend in."

And then, into the room come Hana, Mina, and Farrah. Each

in a matching jellaba. Though theirs are fully black. Mourning cloaks. And while I feel their sorrow, I also feel their hope. And their belief. In me. I couldn't ask for anything better to take with me into Janna.

I kiss Matin's cheek and thank him. Because the time for resentment has long since passed.

It is now a time for change.

As Zak comes to my side, Matin stops him, clapping a hand on his shoulder. "Good luck, *habib*."

Zak nods but doesn't say good-bye.

Sometimes change requires baby steps.

38

THIS CHANGE STARTS WITH ONE. ONE STEP TOWARD THE ARCHAEO-
logical wonder called Najah.

Zak and I stand in awe of the temple carved into the desert
mountain before us, a true hidden gem, deserted in this predawn
hour. Thousands of years old, the rounded columns surrounding
the narrow entryway tower over us. The size and scale dwarf us
but somehow empower our cause.

Here, in a place of such grandeur built by human hands, magic
seems to pale in comparison. We are doing this for Laila, for our
father, for our fellow Jinn, but ultimately, this is why we are doing
this. Because we have a responsibility to the humans. Nature made
a deal with us to help them, not hurt them. We must uphold our
end of the bargain not just so that we keep our magic and our legacy, but because it's the right thing to do.

I will the tremble in my knees not to travel to my voice as I
say, "Well, Brother, are you ready?"

"N-n-not yet," he says. Apparently my will is a touch stronger
than his. He broadens his shoulders and firms his stance. He then

pushes up the sleeve of his tunic to reveal his "Always. But not forever" tattoo. "I think you need one of these."

He's serious, being all poignant and profound, and all I can think is: *On my arm? But what will that look like when I'm in my bikini?* A bikini? Really? That's what I'm thinking about now?

I smile. I may be a Jinn, but a part of me will always belong to the human world, to Nate, to Henry, to the beach I so love.

Before Zak's furrowed brow becomes permanent, I swish Raina's long cloak aside and uncover my ankle. Zak bows in front and a warmth tickles my skin.

He's drawn an identical tattoo of curled lines and shapes that conceal the phrase "Always. But not forever." But something's missing.

Inside the design, I add two sets of initials: *HJC* and *NAR*. Henry Jeffrey Carwyn and Nathan Adam Reese. I then do the same with Zak's tattoo. Except for him, I slip in just one set: *LM*. Laila Malak.

As I do, I'm hit with a wave of emotion that I can only identify as love. Laila's love for Zak. And for me. She's still with us. And we need to make sure she stays that way.

Side by side, Zak and I squeeze into the slit in the mountain. In two short steps, we're blocked. It's too tight for us to penetrate further.

A stream of sunlight filters through the crevice, highlighting the wall directly opposite us. As we turn to retreat, we have to shield our eyes. And that's when I see it before us: a line of Jinn carved into the sandstone, linked arm in arm.

I loop my arm through Zak's. We each place our free hand on the Jinn. And we disappear.

My vision blurs and I stumble back against the cool, smooth rock of the cramped nook into which the portal releases us. My lungs fill with the smell of dirt and chalk and sea and grass and roses and cinnamon and sun. It's some mix of the scents of everything I've ever known, amounting not to a muddled mess but to a soothing pleasantness.

Zak's grip pulls me taut. *"Rahmah!* It worked!"

It worked. I can barely hear him over the jackhammering of my heart. We . . . *thump thump thump* . . . are . . . *thump thump thump* . . . in . . . *thump thump thump* . . . Janna.

Janna.

I step forward, out of the shadow cast by the wall of pale-salmon slab encircling us.

We are underground? *This* is all underground?

A stone landscape of muted pinks, corals, reds, creams, tans, and browns spreads out under a sky of iridescent aqua the color of island oceans. Across from us, a flat, raised platform surrounded by a low stone wall acts as a central hub, from which long, winding paths fan out like spokes on a wheel. Down each passageway are tall two- and three-story rectangular dwellings with carved arched entryways, squat structures with fat, rounded footprints, and rows of slender columns, one after the other, topped with what looks like aqueducts from the history books, all made of the same striated, rosy-tan-hued stone.

Monochromatic. Speaking of a time and place of the past. And beautiful. Heart-achingly beautiful.

My mind tries to reconcile what my eyes are seeing with the facts I know. A place this beautiful should not house so much pain. Or cause it.

"Excellent," Zak says, pulling me back though no other Jinn are in sight. "A perfect entry point."

He must recognize our location.

Like clearing cobwebs, I sweep all other thoughts aside and concentrate not on the fact that I *am* here but on the *reason* why I'm here. Laila. And concentrating on Laila means finding Xavier.

"Do we need to app?" We debated whether we should apport, and risk possible detection, once we arrived.

"If I'm right about where we are, there's no need." Zak lifts my hood and fastens it tight around my face before doing the same with his. "Now follow close."

He then darts diagonally across the open area in front of the stone platform. I match his pace, trying not to marvel at how soft the pink sand is underfoot or how the fine grains refrain from being displaced and kicked up by our heavy tread.

I shadow Zak as he travels through a wide, squared-off passageway that takes us down an increasingly constricted alley. The stone darkens and begins to radiate not cool but cold. Icy cold.

We reach a fork, and Zak hesitates.

He inches to the right, rotates, and then moves to the left. I follow, first right, then—*ping!*—left. All of a sudden, that mix of Pop Rocks and Coke that exploded in my veins upon first touching Zak jolts through me.

I tread another foot.

Ping! Ping! Ping!

"Definitely left," I whisper, to which Zak nods and rubs his forearms.

We slink down the dimly lit corridor built of gray rock covered in dirt and grime. The farther we go, the harder it is to take in oxygen and the less my eyes can make out what comes ahead. A blackness permeates everything.

Just as we're about to reach the end, Zak pauses. "An Afrit guard," he whispers.

This is my cue. This is why I'm here. This is why I came just with Zak, without waiting for any other Jinn. Because I can do this. *I can do this.* Just like with Austan and Gamal.

I breathe in the rotten sulfur smell emanating from what lies ahead and draw on the female Jinn power we've released. My thoughts turn to Raina and what she gave up for all of us, and instinctually, I reach for my brother's hand. His confidence ignites mine.

Before the guard's eyes land on us, I'm inside his mind. We approach, right under his nose, but I convince him he doesn't see a thing. Under my command, he opens the gate, the first thing made of metal I've seen here. He uses a spell only a few Afrit know—now including me. He closes the gate, turns, and resumes his post, none the wiser.

Zak and I are in tortura cavea. My skin crawls from the knowledge of what this place is, of what it represents, and my heart aches from the misery I feel from the Jinn trapped behind the thick walls.

I can't believe I once thought this was just a tale my mother told me to ensure I behaved. My wish, more than anything, is for that to have been true.

Trying to warm my insides as much as my outsides, I lean closer to Zak. "Just the one guard?"

Zak shrugs. "One guard and one spell no one could possibly know? Maybe."

Maybe. I don't like "maybes."

I keep hold of Zak's hand as we travel side by side through the dark entryway that leads to a fully enclosed tunnel. My eyes struggle to adjust to the lack of light. But the farther we go, the more the path widens and the rays of light trickling in from the end grow longer and brighter until they finally reach us. We spill out into a half-moon opening lit with torches, whose unnaturally bright flames that refuse to flicker must be made by magic.

Before us lie six arrow-straight halls lined not with stone but steel. Each guarded by a hooded figure in a long black cloak. This time, they see us just as we see them.

They drop their hoods. All twelve eyes fixate on me and Zak. Without even glancing one another's way, they begin to chant.

Though Zak and I have lost the element of surprise, we have another advantage. I know my enemy better than my enemy knows me.

As the spell nears completion, I project into Zak's mind: *Act surprised.* And needing all the confidence I can get, I squeeze his hand and add, *But don't let go.*

Gathering strength and volume with each syllable, the six Afrit finish with a resounding *"Eftah"* that echoes off the walls.

My body stiffens, and I feign shock as I use my powers to release my silver bangle and Zak's beaded necklace to the ground.

The fear radiating from me I don't have to fake.

An Afrit with the girth of a body builder and the face of a ferret draws closer. "Desperate for a room?" He acts as though finding two Jinn on this side of the cells in tortura cavea is an everyday occurrence, but his gold eyes that dart behind his furiously blinking lids give away his nerves. "I believe we have a vacancy."

He stops directly in front of us and magically throws back our hoods. For the first time it must register that I'm a female. A female of wish-granting age. A female who shouldn't be here in Janna, let alone here in tortura cavea. And his eyes widen as they settle on Zak.

"Zakaria? But aren't you . . ." He swivels his too-skinny neck toward the hallways behind him. "Shouldn't you be . . ."

The Afrit milling behind him are confused. Distracted. This is my chance. And mine alone. Because without his necklace, Zak has no magic. I have to rely solely on my own to overpower them and to protect us both. But there are too many. Confidence is one thing, but am I really arrogant enough to believe I can employ hadi on all six of these Afrit at once?

I'm not strong enough. The thought fills my mind and Zak's.

You are. But you have the spell. Use Mother's spell.

Of course. Her spell. The only one she'd completed before Laila's attack. Zak gave it to me to memorize after Henry showed me the forum. It links Jinn. This will be the first test to see if it does what she hopes and also links Afrit.

I recite her carefully crafted spell and ignore the ferret-faced Afrit grabbing my arm and the mangy-haired one circling behind me and the too-cute-to-be-evil black-haired one picking up my bangle and Zak's necklace. I focus on their mind—singular—and command that it makes the bodies linked to it come to a halt.

It does. They do.

I don't risk anything more elaborate than the same sleeping spell I used on my mother and Gamal, and sure enough, six Afrit collapse around our feet.

And then I breathe. And then I command my own pulse not

to puncture an artery. And then I snap my bangle around my wrist and secure Zak's necklace around his neck.

"Told you," Zak says. "And remind me not to get on your bad side."

A brief smile, full of pride, precedes a gnawing in my gut. Because it's not pride I'm feeling. It's hubris, which is dangerous. Arrogance is definitely a prerequisite to using this much power. This is why the Afrit are the way they are—why Qasim is the way he is. I understand it. But I don't like it. I hope my mother's blood means I never will.

We step over the sleeping bodies of the ferret and the cute Afrit and approach the steel-lined passageways. We circle in front of each until . . .

Ping.

The corridor chooses us as much as we choose it.

I try not to think about what else may lie ahead and that my arrogance doesn't care what lies ahead, and simply allow the pings to guide us through the darkness. They battle the cold that infiltrates from the dank stone. But the pings win out. They keep on coming, faster and faster.

We follow past cell after cell shrouded by heavy metal doors. We can't see or hear anything. Or anyone. But the force with which the pings bounce in our blood means we must be close. Hope fills Zak's eyes as he takes my hand. We turn the corner.

Ping, ping, ping, ping, ping!

Zak's grip verges on crushing my bones. I wince and shake him off. He opens his cloak, swings his satchel to the front, and draws out a flashlight.

The light illuminates the door of the cell before us. Etched into the steel are the letters *XA*. His initials. We've found him.

I repeat the words the guard at the front recited. A rush of hot air blasts my face, and the metal door vanishes without a sound. Like a room in a dollhouse, the cell lies open before us, missing its fourth wall.

He stands in the middle of the chamber with his back to us. I inch closer, and Zak shines the light around the cell. A cot lines one side of the room and a stone washbasin and primitive toilet occupy the other. The light dances around, finally landing on the far wall, on what he's seeing. On what he's feeling. On what's torturing him.

Headstones. Three of them. Each with a name carved into the rounded white tablet: *Kalyssa*, *Zakaria*, and *Azra*.

This is my father's worst fear.

Does he truly believe it's come true? He doesn't move. It's like he's in a trance. Does he even know Zak and I are here? If he does, does he think we're real? Does he think we're apparitions? An extension of the torture he's been living with?

"Xavier," I say softly as if the volume would make him disappear.

His head of black hair peppered with silver streaks turns, and my breath locks in my throat as I see his face. Older than the face of the boy in the tux, arm wrapped around my mother in her prom dress, more weathered than the face of the man whose cheek my mother's lips were attached to in the photo with the "K+X" written on the back. But it's him.

Xavier.

His brow creases, and his hands, hanging loose against the sides of his dirty gray kaftan, rise to shield his eyes from the light infiltrating the cell.

Recognition dawns on him like the first shimmering rays of light from the rising sun. He must feel the pings, for he strokes his arm from wrist to elbow. He remains still, but slowly an invisible eraser wipes the fear and confusion from his face. A weak smile forms and grows wider and stronger as hope and pride and joy draw new, more flattering lines across his forehead and around his eyes and mouth.

I nudge Zak's arm to lower the flashlight that's shining too brightly on Xavier's features. Features my eyes scan and my brain tries to place.

My olive skin, my dark hair, my slightly turned-up nose all come from my mother. I thought maybe my chin or my lips or the width of my brow, something would come from him. But none of them do.

Then I see his eyes. The shape, the distance apart, the intensity. I see all of those in my own.

His lanky frame, his squared-off shoulders, the defiance in his stance. I see all of them in me.

My wish has come true. Next to me is my brother and before me is my father. We may not be normal, but we are a family.

A warmth fills my heart, but just as quickly it seeps out and I grow as cold inside as the stone is making me outside. Because what if he's hurt or his brain is damaged or he's simply furious that we're here, risking our lives for his? What if he's given up and has no will to fight or, worse, no way to fight, no way to help us win against the council, no way to prevent the uprising from start-ing, no way to save Jinn lives?

What if . . . what if he's not what I imagined?

What if the wish, the hope I've placed upon his name before I even knew it, for all these years, the one thing I thought would make me whole doesn't?

The answer is bittersweet. Because I know in my thudding heart that it'll be okay. That *I'll* be okay. Because this is my family, yes. But there are all sorts of ways to have a family. And the one wait-ing for me back home will always be enough. More than enough.

I swallow hard. "Hello, Xavier."

He pauses and scratches the full, dark beard I didn't expect. His deep voice wavers almost imperceptibly as he says, "The least you could do is call me Dad."

My knees wobble, not so imperceptibly.

"Hi . . ." My hands, my legs, my voice tremble. ". . . Dad."

He smiles, and in him, beneath the furry coat around his lips, I also see Zak.

"Now that's more like it," he says.

Pings rocket through me as he nears. He tentatively reaches for me, laying his hand gently upon my wrist. He spins the bangle to get a glimpse of the hinge.

Is that all he wanted? To check out my magical talents? Is that all I am to him? A bundle of magical energy?

I recoil despite the pings still battering my insides.

But he doesn't.

My father pulls me to him. "You're really here," he whispers.

And that's it. Words and thoughts vanish. All I have is

feeling—the feeling of my father's arms around me. For this one moment, I let myself become the girl I didn't get the chance to be with him. *My father is real.* His embrace calms the pings, soothes my fears, empowers my magic.

"*We're* really here," I say.

"Together. Finally." His voice grows stronger. "I've wished for this every day of my life. My little Jinni." Words I now remember him saying many times before.

They took this from us. They took so much more from so many other Jinn. They can't take anything more.

He kisses my cheek and his beard scrapes my skin. A new feeling, a new memory formed.

I won't let them take anything more.

"Mom's going to make you shave," I say.

His gold eyes sparkle as he grins. "You're probably right." He holds me at arm's length. "Azra, my little Jinni no more. I am so proud of you. What you've discovered with your brother, what you've done with your Zar, your wish candidates—"

"You know about my candidates? About Megan and Nate?"

"Most certainly, I gave them to you."

"You? On purpose? Why?"

"To make it easier on you, love. The council was watching. I didn't want to give them more reason to. I didn't want them to discover all that I knew about you. It helped, did it not? Being invested in the human makes granting the wish less difficult, yes?"

And this is how I know my father never granted a wish. Because then he'd know all about my mother's "invested" theory. But he was trying to help in the only way he could from here. He was watching out for me, trying his best to protect me. A skill I hope I inherited.

For Laila's sake. I'm about to turn to Zak to begin our plans when the guilt that's been living inside me and the need to know exactly what I'm up against makes me ask something else.

"Xav—I mean, Dad?"

"Yes, Azra?"

"The car accident. Nate's parents. Did the Afrit cause it?" *Did I cause it?*

He sighs and the crow's-feet around his eyes deepen. "No, my *ibna*. My sweet girl. Sometimes accidents are just that."

This fills me with relief as much as it does fear.

My father then claps a hand on Zak's shoulder and pulls him in with his other arm. The pings ebb and what flows instead is a feeling of peace and warmth and love that defies this frigid place. But time is not on our side. So we break apart.

In a stream-of-consciousness whirlwind, we tell him about Laila and Matin and Austan and Gamal and the sleeping Afrit guards and my successful use of hadi. The power he ensured I would have.

When we are finished, I expect my father to grab me with one hand and Zak with the other and storm out of tortura cavea in search of Laila's cure. But he doesn't. Instead, he lowers his eyes to the dirt floor. "This should have never come to pass. I naively thought the rumors of Qasim experimenting with new punishments was simply another of his intimidation tactics. I should have paid more attention . . . I should have known what Qasim was capable of . . . but my focus was elsewhere."

Me? Was his focus on me?

My father should be two feet tall by now with the amount of

weight that he's set on his shoulders. And though my own shoulders droop as I share in his burden, Laila's hourglass is losing sand with each moment we remain here. The focus can't be on anyone but her.

"So what do we do?" I ask.

My father calmly clears his throat but can't dislodge his guilt. "With what's happened to Laila, we know the rumors were correct. And Gamal's involvement is not surprising for he has been serving as Qasim's *althani.*"

Bouncing from one foot to the other, Zak exhibits the impatience I feel. He quickly says to me, "Like his apprentice or houseboy."

I shift closer to the missing fourth wall and the way out of this awful place. "So he's had access to Qasim's home?"

An eagerness fuels Zak's nodding as he follows me. "The antidote. That's where it must be. Maybe . . . maybe Gamal was even acting without Qasim's knowledge? To gain favor? Maybe he's actually the one who sent Matin?"

I feel my body begin to match Zak's rhythm, but Xavier stands still, save for the stroking of his beard. I know he's been tortured, quite literally, but with every second we wait, more of Laila is being destroyed. I clutch Zak's hand and reach for my father's. "Let's get go—"

"Perhaps it was Gamal," my father says, interrupting me. "This attack does sound too rash for Qasim."

My body goes rigid. He's right. I don't even know Qasim, and I know he's right. But then . . . there's another option. A more likely one. I not only think it, but I read it in my father's mind.

Unless it's a trap.

Laila, hurt for me. Because of me.

"It doesn't matter," my pride makes me say. "I'm strong enough."
My arrogance chimes in, "Even if it is a trap."

The hope that had filled Zak's eyes only seconds ago evaporates. "Azra, no," he says.

I stand up straighter. "We don't have a choice. Laila's running
out of time."

Laila. My best friend. My brother's love. Samara's daughter.

My father's eyes show he understands the urgency, but his years
of patience and planning make him pause. He won't act impul-
sively. "I never intended for you to confront Qasim on your own.
I wanted the council behind us. I wanted the Jinn here to see what
you were capable of first. I wanted them to stop accepting this life
out of fear. I wanted them to know we had the power to fight
him—all of us."

And I want, more than anything, to put Laila first.

But wanting doesn't make it so.

"I understand."

Laila may be all of those very important things, but in the end,
she is just one Jinn. What we're doing is bigger than just one Jinn.
That's what my father is saying.

I strangle the shrieking of my heart. "Do you think we have
the time to implement your original plan? To assemble your supporters before Qasim learns we are here?"

Zak gasps, knowing what this would mean for Laila. My
father then tents his fingers, and I think he's going to object but
he doesn't. He's not the same parent as my mother. He's been in
Janna. He understands sacrifice.

"If Qasim truly is behind poor Laila's attack?" He sighs and shakes his head. "It is unlikely we will have the freedom of movement we require."

Unlikely. Thank Janna. We don't have to choose.

But . . . *we don't have to choose.* That means confronting Qasim. Now. *Just the three of us.*

"This is your decision, Azra," my father says. "I will be behind whatever you decide. But I cannot help you. I no longer possess my powers."

He turns and points to a ragged, seeping blister on the back of his neck. *Just the two of us, then.* He was injected with the inhibitor to block his powers.

This has to stop. "I trust you."

He puts up his hand. "It is not me in whom you must put your trust."

No, it's not. It's Laila and Yasmin and Hana and my mother and Samara and all the other Jinn whose powers have been given to me. It's trust in the strength given to me by my ancestors, by Aisha Qandisha. It's trust in my will being stronger than Qasim's. Fortunately, stubbornness is a skill I've been honing since birth.

Defiance in my eyes, my stance, my heart. I nod. "Qasim may be expecting us, but he doesn't yet know what I can do. We'll still have the upper hand."

Despite what he said, I'm surprised—*disappointed?*—when my father doesn't fight me on this.

"Well then," he says, "let's pay a visit to your uncle."

"Uncle?" Zak says.

"Yes, Son. And it was under his orders that I and every Jinn old enough to know the truth never spoke of it. Apparently, my brother is ashamed of me."

"Your brother?" I say. "Wait, are you saying that ... that *Qasim* is your brother?"

My father grimaces. "In name only. Blood doesn't make one family, Azra."

And with that, I know my father is everything I imagined.

"Now," my father says, "about Qasim—"

"Qasim ... my uncle. Which means ..." My head falls, and my father probably thinks I'm afraid. But then I laugh, softly.

"Qasim is Yasmin's father," Zak says.

"Which means we're related," I say. "Yasmin and I are cousins."

And Farouk is my grandfather. Which he knew and neglected to tell me.

I'm the one who wished for family. What was that about wishes not coming with tricks?

When genies are involved, there's always a trick.

39

Make that a trap.

Two dozen Afrit in black cloaks form a circle around us as we exit the passageway. Before Zak or I can lay a hand on our father to apport us somewhere, anywhere, but here, Afrit wedge themselves between us. They push us forward like a crowd at a rave.

With apporting blocked in tortura cavea, this is the spot we'd be most vulnerable. And my uncle knew it.

He's standing in the center of the platform we passed on our way in. If it weren't for the jet-black hair that sweeps his broad shoulders, his gold cloak that ends at his ankles would make him blend into the tan stone.

Options swirl in my mind. Overpower as many Afrit as I can and hope I reach my father and Zak before Qasim can act. Apport straight to Qasim and knock him flat onto the hard ground before any of these Afrit can hurt one of us. App away myself, alone, and see if he follows.

But then I read my father's mind.

Don't give yourself away.

And so I let the crowd take me to Qasim.

"My invitation to the family reunion must have gotten lost," he says, in a voice that's so much my father's and a tone that's so much Yasmin's it makes the idea of hurting him almost impossible to imagine.

"My dear niece, that long face." His deep-set eyes, sunk far apart on either side of his hooked nose, are more yellow than gold. He looks like a bird. "Is something eating away at you? Or someone you love?"

Make that a vulture. Now I can very much imagine hurting him.

Behind me, Zak growls, and it's all I can do to remain calm myself. Because he's playing with me. My uncle is toying with me. That quip can only mean he did send Austan and Gamal after Laila as a way of bringing me here. He knows I have abilities beyond that of most Jinn. Maybe he's already discovered what my father and Raina were trying to conceal: that I may be useful to him.

Giving myself away—ensuring he knows what I'm capable of—is exactly what I need to do. I climb the three short steps to stand directly across from his beady eyes and his sharp beak. Everything hinges on this one moment. If I waste it, we'll never get the antidote for Laila in time.

I face the Afrit below me. I may as well demonstrate my powers to Qasim by making this a more fair fight. And so into my father's and Zak's heads I project one word: *Duck*.

The instant their dark-haired heads disappear from the crowd, I recite my mother's spell and link the closest eight Afrit. I tighten my jaw as I enter and command this one united mind. The linked Afrit do an about-face and begin pummeling their "colleagues." A full-on fistfight.

Qasim's thick eyebrows dip low over his eyes. "This is what my brother was hiding." He bunches up the shiny sides of his gold cloak as he steps forward to get a better look. His shock turns to delight, and a wide smile soon consumes his face. "Astonishing."

He watches in fascination, not paying any attention to me. This is my chance. I must find the antidote for Laila. And then I can knock him out. Then we don't need him anymore.

I summon all the energy I can and dive into his mind. I'm drawing on the power of all the female Jinn whose bangles have been freed, and still the effort to read Qasim's mind, let alone gain control over it, is making me see spots in front of my eyes.

Am I not strong enough?

I'm doing what I've done before with the other Afrit, but this time, it's like trying to run a marathon through quicksand.

Is Qasim's resistance . . . Is Qasim too strong for me?

I'm in his mind, but I'm stuck. I can't move, and I can't make him move.

The edges of Qasim's lips turn down. He feels something. He feels me. He feels what I'm capable of. And he doesn't know that this is as far as I can go. At least not yet.

It's a good thing being Jinn has made me an excellent liar.

"The antidote," I spit out. My voice is strained and hurried from exertion, but I think—I hope—it sounds more like disdain. "Where is it?"

I'm searching and searching, but my heart's drumming in my ears, and I'm not sure how long I can keep up the charade.

"Whatever do you mean?" Qasim says, but his voice is weak.

Clawing for one last burst of energy, I flood his mind, and the image of a vial of liquid tucked into his inside pocket flies at me.

But then that's it. The effort saps my strength, and it's all I can do not to collapse against the stone, welcoming the coolness on my burning forehead.

"Open your cloak and give it to me," I say briskly.

In the midst of rubbing his temples, Qasim stops.

Open. Why did I say "open"? Why didn't I just reach out and do it, magically or manually?

Qasim raises an eyebrow and all I see is Yasmin. He steps back. "Why don't you?"

The smack of flesh against flesh from the Afrit fighting below us begins to dwindle in conjunction with my waning energy. I force a snicker. "Figured I'd spare you the humiliation of me undressing you in public. Now hand over the vial."

Qasim fastens the braided rope of his gold cloak tighter around his waist. Calm, smooth, and efficient. Not a gesture, not a flit of an eye, not an extra breath is wasted.

"No," he says.

"No?" He's purposeful and deliberate. And that's what scares me the most.

"Does that word not mean the same thing in your beloved human world, Niece?" He then leans in so close his hot breath puffs on my cheek as he says, "Make me."

The Afrit stand still. My father is staring. My brother is watching. Laila is waiting. And I can't.

Laila will pay for my arrogance. All the Jinn will pay for my conceit. I did this, I chose to confront Qasim. I should have followed the plan my father wanted me to—gathered his supporters and bolstered our strength—at the very least, made sure I could do this. And if not, made sure we had a backup plan.

A backup plan.

Like the one forming in my mind.

Qasim has a glimpse into what I can do. I don't need to read his thoughts to know he's salivating over it. He wants me on his side. He may very well believe he needs me on his side. Which shifts the balance of power.

"I can't," I say. "But you already know that."

The smug look on his face is like the one I grew up seeing on Yasmin's. The one I always wanted to slap away. The one I'd give anything to ensure Qasim doesn't get the chance to see on her.

"You also know how strong I am." I toss my hand at the bruised-eyed and bloody-nosed Afrit. "But you don't know the half of it." I have enough energy to flick off my bangle. It clanks against the stone and topples down the steps, landing in a cushion of sand. "This is a lot of power. But I can get more."

Qasim's yellow eyes dance. "How?"

"First, the antidote. And you let my brother and father go."

He snorts. "You overestimate your importance."

"And you underestimate me." I think of Raina and Laila and grasp enough magic to flip my hood up and down. It's a simple demonstration of my ability to do magic without my bangle. Simple but effective.

Qasim's eyes widen and he looks at me with greed and awe. But not surrender. Not yet. He opens his cloak. "You can have it, if you can take it."

He's daring me. Challenging me. I dig for the strength to retrieve the vial but come up empty. I lift my chin and act as if it's beneath me. "I want you to give it to Zak."

"Trust issues?" Qasim says.

"I wonder why?" I grumble. I can't let Qasim know I'm bluffing. For now, he's confused. He doesn't know what's real and what's fake.

I think again of Raina. Of her sacrifice. The one she made when she crossed back into the human world knowing the shield would destroy her. She sacrificed herself for all the Jinn, for me, but ultimately for Yasmin.

I know what I need to do. It's the only play I have left. *You know what they say if you can't beat 'em.* I do, Yasmin, I do.

"You could use someone like me on your side, right?" I say. My father begins to speak, but I shake my head and turn away from him. I don't want him to stop this.

A grimace on his pointy face, Qasim closes his cloak. "Whatever game you are playing, you should be very careful."

"This isn't a game. That was a simple yes-or-no question."

"What exactly are you proposing?"

"A trade. You hand over the antidote, and my brother and father leave here. Banished. Like your father—my grandfather. And whatever happens, my family, my mother, my Zar sisters, and hers are unharmed. And I'll stay here with you."

"All of them for one of you?"

"You're right. I'm getting a lousy deal."

He tosses his head back and a conceited laugh bubbles out, chilling me to the bone. "Ooh, we're going to get along well, Niece." Qasim opens his cloak, and the glass cylinder floats in the air toward my brother.

"Is that a yes?" I say.

"No!" Zak cries, but he does what he needs to do and pushes the Afrit holding his arm aside to catch the vial. "Azra, you can't."

"I have to." With as much force as I can muster, I say, "Take it to her, Zak." I then face my father, pleading with him to understand. To let me do this for him—for all of them. "Go, Dad. Laila doesn't have much time left."

I'm sorry I wasn't strong enough.

With the barest tilt of his head, my father shrugs off the Afrit holding his elbow and wraps his arm around Zak's shoulder.

"Come, Son," he says. "I learned long ago there's no reasoning with my brother. And I see that same quality in your sister."

I will come back for you, he adds, just for me to hear.

My father has no magic. The portal he and my brother are walking to is the only way in and out of Janna. Qasim will surely find a way to seal it once they go through. And yet I believe in my heart that what my father says is true. At least in his own mind.

I'm quite familiar with the concept of lying to oneself.

Zak can't even look me in the eye as he clutches the vial in one hand and my father's waist with the other. I stare instead into my father's defiant eyes until they vanish and I'm left with simply the pale salmon slab of stone.

"Well, look at that," Qasim says. "I didn't quite believe that Matin, but it does indeed seem we have some security repairs to do."

They're gone. My heart clenches like a fist. *My family is gone.*

I look at Qasim.

Not all of it. I've still got the black sheep.

I laugh. I can't help it. I laugh because otherwise I will cry. Otherwise I will cry and not be able to stop.

Beneath Qasim's quizzical look is an undercurrent of fear. Good. Let him think I'm crazy.

He sits back on the short stone wall surrounding the platform. "Do you know what this place is, Azra?"

"Hell."

His lips thin. "Ah, so you take after your mother, then?"

Don't talk about my mother. Don't talk at all.

He taps the platform with the toe of his tan boot. "I mean this. This exact spot."

I cross my arms in front of my chest and put my back to the portal. I'm afraid I might give in to the screaming urge inside me that says to flee, to app to the portal, to get home to my family. My true family.

Qasim tents his fingers and continues, "Long ago it served as our *haqq*, our place of judgment. Jinn who defied our rules could plead their case here. If they could not persuade the council that they were worthy of redemption, they would be punished. Unless they were lucky enough to have a loved one willing to offer him- or herself up instead."

I haven't wanted to listen, let alone speak, to my uncle, but the vibration that rumbles through me as he says this makes me ask, "What do you mean?"

"A sacrifice. If another Jinn was willing to accept the wrong-doer's punishment, that Jinn would be given a second chance. Do you know how many parents, lovers, children, even, gave themselves up? How many suffered for the sins of others? My father was right to separate Jinn from one another. To lessen the ties. Attachments are a weakness we cannot tolerate if we Jinn are to continue."

Pulses shoot through me like electric shocks. With every word, with every mention of the Jinn who gave themselves up to save the ones they loved, my powers increase, inflating inside me so intensely that it's like I've swallowed a water balloon with a hose still attached.

Qasim adjusts his cloak to prevent it from puddling on the ground. "That's what I was trying to get Raina to understand. But she repaid me by keeping the knowledge of my daughter from me. Tell me, Azra, is Yasmin as strong as you?"

The water balloon billows. "We have a deal. My Zar sisters are left out of this."

"But she's my daughter. Your cousin. That takes precedence over her being your Zar sister."

"This is why I have trust issues." I drive my feet into the ground and pop the water balloon. I zero in on his mind.

He stands and tries to block me, physically and mentally, but all the strength of this place courses through me, and I knock him back against the stone wall.

Sacrifice. That's why the portal, the weakness in the shield, was created here. Sacrifice. That's what fuels my strength. That's why, here, my mind, my powers, have continually turned to Raina.

I move closer to Qasim, who's crouched on the ground, fighting me. As I attempt to control his thoughts, the taut pull of muck creeps up my feet, sucks me down to my ankles, and I'm afraid, that's it, the quicksand is dragging me down, and I won't be able to overpower him, I won't be able to erase his mind like I hoped, I won't be able to put an end to all this.

I have to put an end to all this.

I trip on my way to him, uncovering a rock of Granny Smith green, the color of nothing else in this monochromatic tan place. But it's a color I know. It's a color I love. It's the green of Jenny's eyes. The green of Henry's eyes.

And that's when it hits me. What I did to Henry—what I want to do to Qasim—erasing his mind, erasing his heart, may end this. But there's a better way. Henry showed me that. Nate too. Megan, Chelsea, my Zar sisters. All of them have shown me that letting someone in is the way to change. That's the way to a power that doesn't destroy. That's the way to a power that builds.

Not knowing if it'll even work or if I'll be cursed or if I'll waste this surge of energy, I recite the circulus incantation my mother helped me to memorize. I stare at Qasim's yellow eyes and connect with his anima the way my mother taught me to do.

I hurl myself in, invested in every way, and dive down through layer upon layer: the thirst for power; the need to be better than his brother; the cravings for his father's affections; the betrayal by Raina when he realized she kept Yasmin's existence from him; the inferiority that rocked him to his core when he learned he was Raina's second choice: that she actually loved my father.

But there's one more thing. There's the event that turned Qasim into the Afrit he is: the moment he learned his mother died trying to save a human. Humans who commit atrocious crimes against loved ones and strangers alike; humans who start wars against one another, century after century, decade after decade; humans who concoct weapons to destroy one another, weapons with the power to destroy all that inhabit their world; humans who, if they ultimately succeed in what seems to be a battle to eradicate their kind from this earth, will take the Jinn right along with them.

We'll cease to exist. Because of humans.

I can't let that happen is the last thought in Qasim's mind. His deepest desire rises to the surface. His truest wish is to protect the Jinn species. To ensure our survival.

His heart is in the exact right place. It's just his mind that's got it wrong.

How can I make him see that?

Our connection begins to falter; the sludge reaches my waist as Qasim struggles against me. He doesn't want to see it. He is afraid of what will happen when he does. What he'll regret. What he's done that he'll have to live with.

Just when I think the quicksand will drown me comes the vibration of a stereo, the tickle of a feather, the soft flick of a bunny's tail, the trail of pins and needles down my spine, the sting of a wasp, the feel of a breeze rustling a pile of fallen leaves—Hana, Samara, Farrah, Zak, Yasmin, and my mother. Their apporting signatures followed by those of all the other members of my mother's Zar and then the signatures of half a dozen, a dozen, two dozen, and more Jinn I've never met.

Through the portal comes a monsoon of Jinn willing to sacrifice themselves to change the Jinn world.

I told you I'd come back for you. My father's thought fills my head. I turn to see him latched onto my mother, whose gold eyes are full of the warmth she directs solely at those she loves.

It is with their strength and their willingness to sacrifice themselves for me that I project that love into Qasim. That I show him what he's been missing. That I show him what he could have if only he'd open himself to it. And trust. Trust the humans. Trust the Jinn. Trust what he cannot see but what he can only feel.

The yellow of his eyes flickers a deep gold as I feel Yasmin behind me. She bends down next to me, facing her father. She doesn't mean to. I know she doesn't understand. But it is the hatred that she unleashes on Qasim that closes him off from all I've tried to open him to.

Right before our eyes, his ears sharpen to points, his cloak turns to fur, his nails grow into claws, and he shape-shifts into a wolf. A stunning gray-and-white wolf that lifts its snout to my father, turns its sad eyes on Yasmin, and lowers its tail to me. A wolf that doesn't need the portal to transition out of Janna.

He leaps over the stone wall.

And then he's gone.

SILENCE. NEVER IN THE SPAN OF HISTORY HAVE SO MANY JINN BEEN in one place and it been this quiet, of that I am sure.

"We must hurry." My father's insistent but strained voice breaks the silence. "The council chamber. Kalyssa, Samara, Azra, we must get to them before Qasim does."

Beside me, at the sound of her father's name, Yasmin's body caves in on itself. Her chin burrows into her chest, her back rounds, and her bent knees drive into the stone underneath us. "He killed her. He killed my mother." She lifts her head and her wide-set gold eyes, a match for her father's, plead with me. "He can't get away, Azra."

No, he can't. Because then all this will have been for nothing. And I can't have that.

"He won't." I curl a hand under each of her elbows and bring her to her feet. "You'll come with me?"

She doesn't ask where. Or why. She just will. The Zar connection has never been as strong as it is here in this place that should be our home—that we will make into our home.

Hand in hand, we walk down the stone steps. I know where Qasim is. In his mind, one image that would not leave lets me know where he is. We just have to move fast, because I don't know how long he'll stay.

I let one more beat pass before I tell everyone, because in that beat, my family surrounds me. My whole family. My mother rushes forward and crashes into me, squeezing with a strength I've always known she possessed. Behind me, my father closes in, stroking my long braid. And next to me, Zak, my brother.

Laila, I project into his head.

Mina is with her.

The antidote? I ask.

Zak hangs his head and closes his eyes. He didn't stay long enough to find out if it's working. He came here, to me. As did Hana and Farrah and Samara and Isa and even Jada, who never wanted any of this, as did all these other Jinn I've never even met. And more. My mother releases me, and I step back to see more Jinn flow through the open portal. Including . . . is that . . . *Tayma?*

Her long sapphire-blue cloak, her ash-brown hair gathered into a perfect bun, her scarf, expertly draped around her neck in the way only Parisians can do. Yes, it's her. I turn to Yasmin and tip my head toward Tayma, the Jinn we both met long ago on an unauthorized excursion. Of course she's here. Her Zar was broken too. I didn't know what that meant then. I didn't know how it felt—and I hope the antidote for Laila means I won't ever know.

Tayma winks at me and her whiskerlike eyelashes flutter. How many of these Jinn belong to broken Zars? How many have sisters, brothers, parents, children in tortura cavea? They're here so that their families can be whole too.

"I know where he is," I say to my mother and father. "You go to the council. I'll return as soon as I can, but—"

"Qasim must come first," my father finishes.

I break the circle around me to reach for Yasmin.

"Azra, wait," my mother says, grabbing my wrist and encircling it with her hand the same way my bangle used to do.

I try to shake her off. "Mom, don't. I have to go. I'm the only one who has a chance to stop him. I was so close. This time, I know what to do." I pull away, but she doesn't let go. "Please, Mom. I have to do this."

She tugs even harder and draws me to her. "I know, kiddo." She pries open my clenched fist and presses something into my hand, and in that moment my mind flashes back to Laila on the day after my sixteenth birthday, pushing the piece of silver tinsel into my palm for luck at my very first wish granting.

But this isn't tinsel. And I'm betting it's not for luck.

"This," my mother says, "will help you. If you can tie it around his wrist, it will block his powers." She holds a folded slip of paper between two fingers. "With this spell, he will be bound to you. I expect with his strength, neither will last indefinitely, but it should be long enough for you to bring him to us."

I open my hand to reveal a thin black leather cord, as unlike our large, gaudy bangles as can be. But a shackle nonetheless. Simple but, I hope, effective. Guess that theory, like so much else, is something I learned from her.

"Farouk's cantamen?" I ask.

My mother nods, but Samara cuts in. "And *her* talent." She hooks her arm through my mother's and gives me a tight smile. I don't need to read her mind to see right through it to the scream she's holding back because of what's happened to Laila. But she's here for her Zar sisters. The connection is strong.

I reach for Yasmin. Mine better be just as strong. Stronger.

A curt nod to my family is all I allow myself. Any more and I won't go. And so, with that, I app Yasmin to the portal and then . . . home.

My home.

Yasmin swivels her head, taking in my backyard. "Here? He's here?"

"I think so." I quell my thumping heart, I tune my ears to the blue jay that lives in the trees above us, I inhale the scent of the sea and lilacs, and I focus. "I know so."

"But why?"

"I think you know."

She tilts her head back to look up at the second floor of the house where I grew up. At the room where her mother lies in the peace we gave her. "Because of her? He wants to see my . . . my mother?"

I take her hand in mine. "He still loves her, Yasmin."

Denial flashes through her eyes. Her thin nostrils flare, and quick as that, she moves into anger. "He can't. He doesn't deserve to."

"He's bad," I say. "I won't lie to you. But he's not all bad. I saw it in him. I also saw that, in his own way, he loves you too. Even when he was angry with your mother, he never stopped loving either of you. That's why he's here. He knew from Matin that Raina would be here." I suck in a deep breath and force myself to say the next part. "We can use that to our advantage."

I am an Afrit. And sometimes, I have to act like one. No matter how smarmy it feels.

I dangle the black cord in front of her. "He won't let me get close enough."

Does she feel it too? The taint of our Afrit blood? Maybe. But we are the next generation. Change will come from us. Right after we trick her father.

He's kneeling at Raina's bedside when we appear in the doorway. In his brief moment of surprise, Yasmin rushes into the room. Her sable-black hair that's a match for his flies out behind her.

She stops at the end of the bed where her mother still lies, and her grief courses through me. But she pushes through it.

"Father?" she says. "Is it really true?"

Qasim's gold cloak spills around him. If our eyes dripped tears to match their gold color, it'd look exactly like the pool of fabric he's sitting in. Not that he's actually crying. But the way his hooked nose twitches, it's as close as I imagine he's been in years. Maybe since his mother—our grandmother—died.

"Yasmin?" His stringy black hair sweeps across his eyes as he stands. He wants to go to her. I can tell. And yet, still, he's an Afrit. He's maybe *the* Afrit. An ability to trust is not in his nature. His right ear lengthens into a point and a tuft of hair curls down the edge. He's about to shape-shift and flee.

"Don't let her take me!" Yasmin cries in an ad lib.

With a swish of her hand, she sends one of the soft chairs I conjured earlier into my stomach. Another ad lib, one completely and totally in character.

I gasp and double over in very real pain. Better to sell it, I suppose.

She inches back, away from me and closer to her father. She's butting up against him, directly even with her mother's wrist. With the bangle we freed her from. And that's when Yasmin does the thing that will sell it completely. She lifts her mother's wrist and snaps the bangle shut around it.

Her eyes pool with tears as she looks up at her father. "She was wrong to keep you from me."

She means this to her core. It's written in her stance, the way she thrusts her shoulders back; it's written in her lips, the way she tightens them into the whisper of a line; it's written in her eyes, the way she trains them on the long braids that lie alongside her mother. Which is perhaps why Qasim lets down his guard and allows Yasmin to take his hand.

They stand there as a family. Until Yasmin pulls the black cord out of her pocket. It's already tied into a loop. All she has to do is slip her hand from her father's and slide the leather strap up his wrist.

"I'm sorry," she says, and she means this to her core too. And yet it doesn't prevent her from magically tightening this noose around her father's wrist.

I recite the spell my mother gave me before Qasim realizes what's happening. The emerald in my mother's talisman glows a golden yellow. As I finish, a stream of light shoots from the gemstone and winds its way around the black string. The yellow snakes around and through the black, consuming it in a flash of brilliant color. Qasim jerks back, away from Yasmin, crashing into the nightstand beside the bed.

When the yellow light burns out and the cord fades again to the darkest of blacks, Qasim raises his other hand and tugs on the leather. It doesn't break. The knot refuses to budge. He takes a step toward Yasmin, and I mentally command him not to. And he doesn't. He can't.

He's bound to me.

A circumstance I'm positive neither one of us wants to go on for a second longer than necessary.

But it means something. It means that even though being Jinn in a world of humans may always require it to be filled with secrets and lies, it's time to add one more thing.

Hope.

Oh, and bangles. Lots and lots of new and pre-owned bangles. The next generation of Jinn will have no use for them. Perhaps they can seed Hana's very first fashion line: Circles of Jinn.

EPILOGUE
One Year Later

THIS STREET IS INTERMINABLE. I MEAN, SERIOUSLY, WHEN DOES A street become a highway? Because I've been trudging down this one much longer than is permissible for something called a "street."

Or maybe I'm just extraordinarily spoiled. Apping everywhere for a year will do that to you.

I can't believe it's been a full year. A full year since I've seen him. What will he think? Will he be happy to see me?

The worry that he won't, the fear that he's moved so far on he won't even remember me, makes me want to app away right here right now in front of this four-story brick building. This entire town is brick buildings. There must have been quite a sale on brick when this place was founded.

With my next step, my blister bursts. One of my blisters. All these humans, running, walking, chatting, laughing, buried in their smartphones, I'm sure they wouldn't notice one little apping Jinn. But it doesn't matter. I can't app. I've tried. Even though I haven't been to his dorm room, the name of the place should be enough.

It's not.

And I don't know why.

But at least the name of the place being enough worked for the past year. Because, and let this be known, the Afrit are slippery little suckers. And fast.

When my father and Zak first crossed through the portal, they went straight to Laila. Everyone was there, including all the supporters that had been linked through Witchbook. My Zar sisters were trying to do as they'd promised: give us a head start. It's a good thing they were failing. Even before my father and Zak appeared and told them about the deal I had made with Qasim, the Jinn were ready to use the portal to cross into Janna. To rescue me.

Though my father suspected that I'd get a boost from the Jinn being present in Janna, he had no idea that part of that bump would come from their selflessness or from *haqq*, from the place of sacrifice in Janna.

Zak, gut-wrenching as it must have been, left the antidote in Mina's hands so that he could return to me. Another sacrifice. More power for me to draw from.

While Yasmin and I were with Qasim, my father's loyalists forced a meeting of the full council of twelve—sorry, make that eleven without their Chemharouch.

After I brought my bounty in the form of Qasim back to Janna, I joined the rest of the Jinn and we confronted the council.

I was able to overpower almost half. After a demonstration of my abilities, three of the others were eager to rejoin my father's side—though they didn't display quite enough after-the-fact groveling for my taste—but that still left three other Afrit who were able to flee.

And flee they did. Again and again. Here, there, and everywhere. I've spent the past year tracking them down. Not by myself. Sometimes Zak was with me. Sometimes Yasmin. Occasionally, even Farouk. But mostly, it was me and my dad. Not quite the normal mode of "quality time," but normal's overrated. Mom was there too sometimes, when she wasn't worried about watching over everyone else. And especially when she needed an "Xavier fix."

Ew.

We've found all but Gamal, who managed to escape while Mina was alone here with Laila. My mother believes he may stay hidden forever. Zak hopes he does. My father suspects he won't. He had quite the mentor in Qasim.

Now that the school year has started, watching over a certain someone else fell to Farouk. Between my grandfather's real-world connections and his magical talents, he was able to whip up a scholarship, a full scholarship, to Harvard of all places.

I hope he likes it. I hope he's okay walking every day to what must be the absolute farthest dorm on campus.

When my father wasn't with me, and even when he was, he spent the past year creating a new order in Janna—and creating a new Janna. It's no longer underground. It's risen, occupying its rightful place in the plane between earth and what lies beyond. I like to think nature's happy about this.

We don't have a formal hotline or anything. Though it was an exceptionally warm winter this past year. That's got to mean something, right?

In some ways, everything has changed since I've last been here, tromping through the streets of Cambridge. And in others, nothing has. Zak and Laila are sickeningly googly-eyed. Matin and Yasmin are the Yasmin equivalent. Farrah's still with Dwight. Mina's still peeved about it and rebelling by dating the lead singers and guitarists of every band Farrah likes, and Hana's a sought-after, though reclusive, designer to the stars. She works under an alias, and the world thinks she's forty-two and a hermit living in Dubai.

My mother's Zar is more on the changed side. Some are back with their daughters' fathers (Samara; Jada), some lost their daughter's father (Nadia), and some have rekindled old flames (Isa and her human beau, Hairy Larry). Of course, Raina is still gone.

That's the same.

As is Qasim's imprisonment. And Yasmin's refusal to visit him. My father's working on her. Farouk too. Because, after all, family is family.

Meanwhile, I've traveled all over the world, just like my mother before me. Except I wasn't granting wishes. I was searching for the Afrit. I've also taken a self-guided tour through every crevice and every magically concealed hideout in Janna. And so far, my use of hadi hasn't injured me and I haven't succumbed to any manic grabs of power either. I haven't become an Afrit. I'm still a Jinn. At least until we work on some rebranding.

But through it all, one face stayed in my mind. The face I'm about to see now. Though I've imagined this moment more times than I can count in the past year, I still have no idea what I'll say when he answers the door.

We'll have to start over. But that's okay. I've learned from helping to re-create the Jinn world that starting over can be a good thing. Sometimes it's better to start fresh.

Tell that to my aching feet. I stop in front of an indistinguishable brick building in this campus of clones. This one is his.

"Oh, sorry," a boy in a backward blue Red Sox hat says as he reaches for the door to the dorm that's about to swing closed. "Coming in?"

"Yes," I say, though my feet remain still.

"Now?" he says, balancing a pizza box and bike helmet in one hand and a brown paper bag of . . . *so not soda* . . . in the other.

I command my feet to move. I've gotten used to giving orders.

The Red Sox boy gives me directions and even points the way—after I agree to stop by to "hang" when I'm through visiting whatever "dude" lives in room 12, that is.

Guess it's not a close-knit dorm if he doesn't know what dude lives in room 12.

Do I know what dude lives in room 12? Has he changed? Have I? Am I ready to find out?

Ready or not, here I am: room 12. The numbers shimmer in gold. Right before my eyes.

I toss back my loose hair, longer now. It almost hits my waist. It's a hassle to wash, though I do love the apricot shampoo I wrested away from Samara. The scent's with me all the time now.

My heart thuds against my chest, making me light-headed. Must be the walk. *Right, Azra.*

I smooth out the sides of the emerald silk kaftan I borrowed from my mother and straighten my infinity necklace. With my wrist free of my silver bangle, I shortened my *A* necklace into a bracelet. I raise my hand in the air to knock, and the letter dangles back and forth in midair.

"Azra?" a voice I know every timbre of calls from behind me.

I fall against the door as I turn to face Henry.

His hand tightens around the strap of the backpack slung over one shoulder. His green eyes narrow as I shift from one foot to the other. He doesn't remember me. The real me. The Jinn me.

I inch forward and slowly, carefully, enter his mind. I bring it all back. All the lies. All the Jinn. All the me.

Henry drops the backpack to the floor. Everything I've shown him has remained in my mind, and still, reliving it all at once has my hands shaking and my breathing shallow and my knees knocking against each other underneath this silk dress. What must this be doing to him?

So much, so many emotions run through his eyes, his face, his mind, and then, finally, he grins. "Took you long enough."

And there they are, the dimples that kept me going for an entire year.

Suddenly, behind me, the door opens. I spin around to see Nate in a full-on lip-lock with . . . Chelsea.

Genies aren't the only ones fond of tricks.

The reason I couldn't app here isn't because the name of the dorm room wasn't enough, it's because the name was incomplete.

Well, isn't this cozy, I hear run through Henry's mind.

Life may be compromise, but being Jinn doesn't have to be. Not anymore.

Facing Nate and Chelsea, I grab hold of the hand of my best friend. Always.

But maybe not forever. Because maybe forever holds something more.

ACKNOWLEDGMENTS

Many authors will tell you that they've wanted to write since they were old enough to pick up a pen—some since they could wrap their fingers around a crayon.

I am not one of those authors, though I've always lived in the world of words: English was my favorite subject in school; I was a journalism major and editor in chief of my college newspaper; and I worked as a nonfiction writer and copyeditor. I was also a voracious reader. Books have always been my escape.

They still are, but now, not just as a reader but as a writer too. I've lived, breathed, and dreamt the world of the Jinn for more than three years. This speck of an idea about a genie has changed my life, professionally and personally, and apported a sisterhood (and brohood) of people into my life who support me, inspire me, and will have me forever in Azra's debt.

My agent, Lucy Carson, has been my partner on this journey. You once said you'd always have an opinion—and you do! Fortunately your opinions are always the best ones. Thank you for your unwavering support, honesty, and encouragement. The Friedrich Agency is my happy place.

Jean Feiwel, my publisher; Liz Szabla, my editor; and Anna Roberto, my associate editor, welcomed Azra and me into Feiwel and Friends and ensured we'd both come out smarter and more polished than we were before. Thank you for making all of this real.

Thank you to my publicist Brittany Pearlman for not just listening to, but also supporting my every crazy idea. Thank you to the entire team at Macmillan for helping to bring these books to life.

If it weren't for all of you above, I wouldn't have all of you below. And my life would not be nearly as full as it is.

First, a ginormous thank-you to all the readers and book bloggers who have embraced Azra. Your support means more than you know.

Thank you to my critique partners and beta readers, who have blurred that professional and personal line, becoming some of my closest friends: Chelsea Bobulski, N. K. Traver, Jen Malone, and Jen Brooks. Thanks for your insights and for always including a smiley face—for my writing and for me!

Thank you to the YA community, which brought such friends into my life as Laurie Elizabeth Flynn, Nikki Kelly, and Anna Banks. A huge thank-you and shout-out to the Fearless Fifteeners and the Freshman Fifteens. The highlight of 2015 has been seeing the books of these talented writers and supportive friends in bookstores.

Special thanks to my good friends and tour buddies Jen Brooks, Lee Kelly, Trisha Leaver, and Jen Malone. It is a pleasure to be able to finish your sentences. Thank you to my confidants Kim Savage, Charlotte Huang, and Jenn Marie Thorne. Thank you to Chandler Baker for teaching me to write pitches and to roll with the story that comes, to Virginia Boecker for late-night gossiping and hand-holding, and to Kim Liggett for well, everything.

When you write about genies, you are inevitably asked what your own wish would be. For me, that wish is to have those I love always be with me. Thank you to Martha and Steve Goldstein, who have supported me for more years than either of us wants to count; my brother-in-law, Adam, and new sister-in-law, Lana, whose adventures keep them far but who are always in my heart; my sister, Jen, brother-in-law, Charalambos, and nephews, Andreas and Stavros, whose determination, positivity—especially when life sucker punches you—and energy (specific to the boys) inspire me; and my parents, Denise and Frank Montemurro, who gave their own wishes up for me to have mine.

Of course, that list is not complete without my husband, Marc. I started writing because he told me I could. Little did he know how that suggestion would fill his days with reading revision after revision, his nights with plotting disaster after disaster, and his weekends with a wife who says "just one more e-mail" but really means "ten more." These books would not exist without you. Thank you being my first reader and my last, and more than that, for being my best friend—always and forever. And yes, if a second wish comes, I'll definitely use it on the beach house.

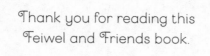